THE STANDARD BOOK OF ANYTHING

ANDREA H ROME

This is a work of fiction. Names, characters, places, and incidents are the product of the author's imagination and/or are used fictitiously. Any resemblance to actual persons, places, or incidences is entirely coincidental.

ISBN 979-8-9898225-0-8 [paperback]

ISBN 979-8-9898225-1-5 [ebook]

Library of Congress Control Number: 2023924591

Printed in the United States of America.

10 9 8 7 6 5 4 3 2 1

Cover design and artwork by Michael Perry

❀ Created with Vellum

For Jay. May you have one thousand dreams.

PRUTIAN TRIBAL LANDS
(DISPUTED TERRITORY)

NORTHERN
COLONIES

ESNANIA

THE HIGH
PLAINS

FRIDERA

ZANIT

ANTILLEI MOUNTAINS

FARROW

BROOKERBY

EPERILA

DRECOVIA

EXETON

KAROKI

EVEDERELL

ARRENMORE

THE SUN
CORRIDOR

ABINGDON

GILLAMOR

BRILDONIA

FRIENDSHIP
SEA

TO AGLEN

CHAPTER 1

A lazy wind drifted over the walls of the Golden Lark Palace to the tendrils of ebony hair that escaped the braided crown of the new empress. The breeze carried a lingering hint of grain, and as it toyed with her locks, she felt a flash of insight. This moment was the beginning of the end for the Age of Magic.

IT IS GENERALLY ACKNOWLEDGED that broken must be fixed. The leaky roof must be patched. The cart rewheeled. The scythe blade sharpened. The competent repair person stands between order and chaos, screwdriver in hand.

Em Strider wanted to be that person. She longed to examine an electrical circuit and repair one of the lights powered by wind. She wanted to peek under the hood of the carriages that moved without being pulled. She wanted to repair the unfixable magical junk that littered the countryside.

But Em was still learning the ordinary jobs. Smoking fireplaces, leaky roofs, and crumbling stone wells were plentiful in Brookerby, Em's village. She felt a thrill every time she was summoned for a repair. The prestige she gained began to stack up in her satchel alongside her tool collection, and soon, she would have a shop of her own— once enough of the townsfolk saw her as a woman of industry, and not the raggedy orphan she had once been.

This morning, she eyed a mammoth wooden printing press spewing tiny metal letters from its maw. Possibly magic, but not broken. Very expensive—if not impossible—to replace. Repairing it would take finesse. It was exactly the kind of challenge that, if conquered, would get her neighbors talking.

"It was like this when I came in. It's exploded two trays of letters already," said her companion, Ilna, the *Brookerby Leaflet* editor, a mountain of a woman with dusty blond hair and an easy smile. Today, her round face was splattered with ink and drawn in worry. "I was going to call Gram. I need to get the *Leaflet* out today."

Em turned from the fussing behemoth to Ilna. "Don't call Gram. I can fix it. But you should get one of those new linotype machines to speed your lettersetting."

Ilna rolled her eyes. She was like family to Em, and thus she frequently fielded the younger woman's gripes about technology. "If I inherit the empress's crown jewels, that will be my first purchase. Besides, I'm not going to buy expensive equipment for you to take apart and tinker with."

Em flashed a grin. That had been Ilna's response the last seven times Em brought up the subject. She turned back to the task at hand. The press was still in motion. Magical items, once broken, were inert and never moved again.

"I think it's angry, not broken." She brushed a strand of honey-brown hair off her face, and then put her hand out, tentatively touching the side of the press. It tingled under her fingers. That same tingle she always felt on a difficult repair. Like the object was opening itself up to her.

She leaned in, held her touch steady, and focused on the wobbling machinery. A letter *W* flung up and smacked her cheek, stinging. She dodged a *T*, then an *F*. Then the press stopped spitting. Quickly, Em slid out the galley of inky words and set the tray aside.

"Well done!" Ilna praised.

"I'm going in. Shout if it starts moving again." Em ducked under the heavy wooden frame and began to examine the moving parts. They needed oil. She grabbed her oilcan.

Ilna started collecting the metal letters scattered around the otherwise orderly print shop. "You visit that new bookseller yet?"

Em bumped the back of her head as she tried to oil the galley track. She rubbed it ruefully. "No. Why?"

"Handsome. Single. You should introduce yourself at the mercantile tonight."

Em tried to ignore her surge of irritation. Why was Ilna bringing this up now? During the most exciting repair Em had encountered in months, no less.

"It couldn't hurt to be sociable, dear. Who knows? Sparks might fly."

Em cringed. Since she came of age, Ilna had been trying to shove her in front of every unattached man who entered the province. It was humiliating. It undermined her credibility.

The bookseller. Em paused—she did like books. "Maybe," she muttered. If nothing else, the shop he had purchased was falling down around him. She had done a little work on the building already, but she could introduce herself with additional repairs in mind.

She finished oiling and shifted to inspect the lever mechanism.

Ilna was refitting the rogue letters in the tray. "Let me know if you want me to put in a good word for you," she said over her shoulder.

"No need." Em had dismissed the topic in her brain and refocused on the printing press. The lever seemed functional. Everything was moving as it should. She extricated herself from the machinery and gave it an experimental pull. Smooth as Gram's pudding.

Em turned back to Ilna. "I didn't see anything wrong with it, but I oiled everything, and it seems calmer. Should we try again?" She slid the tray of letters back into place and set the paper.

Ilna gingerly pulled the handle to start up the press. It rolled smoothly across the removable type, revealing a perfectly printed sheet when Ilna peeled up the paper. "Perfect!" she exclaimed. "Em, you're a wonder."

Em glowed as she wiped at her inky hands with an oily rag. "It wasn't a big thing. Keep it oiled, or it'll get angry again."

The ink wasn't coming off. She scrubbed at it harder.

Ilna glanced over and laughed at Em's efforts. "Occupational hazard, love. That'll take days to wash off with soap. I should've warned you to wear gloves."

Em dropped her hands with a sigh and pocketed her oily rag. "Well, glad I got you up and running, anyway. Come find me if it starts hurling letters again."

"Should I pay you?"

"Let people know I fixed it. That's payment enough." Em started for the door. "Are you going tonight?"

"Sure am. See you there? Grab a *Leaflet*, at least. Stack of last week's pages by the door."

Em located the stack and grabbed a copy. "Haven't seen this one yet. It's longer than usual," she commented on the pages.

"With the unrest throughout the country, we're not hurting for news. I saw five more notices this morning on the ticker."

"Crumb, that's a lot," Em remarked, shoving the pages in her bag and pulling open the door. Glancing back, she asked, "Any message for Mendel? I'm headed over there now."

"Yes. Tell him there's a big storm coming."

"You should probably just print that," Em tossed out.

But Ilna had already turned her attention back to the printing press, using her handwritten copy of the latest news to reset the type. Em shrugged and pulled Ilna's bright yellow door closed behind her.

Outside, the afternoon sun blazed down mercilessly. Em could almost feel her numerous freckles multiplying. She donned her wide-brimmed hat, slung her tool bag over her shoulder, and started for the next potential job. Not many were out, but she waved to a few familiar faces belong to people strolling toward the mercantile.

Along the way, she mentally scanned her checklist for the day.

Butcher's leaky sink, check. Printing press, repaired. Tailor's shelving, not yet. Mendel didn't even know she was coming.

Em hiked up the hill of the main road toward the tailor shop. The cobblestones were dry and dusty. She kept her head down, stepping over countless wheel ruts and divots pockmarking the surface. She made a mental note to repair the largest holes in her spare time.

"Miss Strider! Wait!"

Em jerked her head up and saw Earl McBean jogging toward her. He hired her for the first time last autumn to build a harvesting device. Em had impressed him with her ingenuity and skillful construction. The device worked beautifully. She gained a customer for life, and now he spoke to her like she was an equal. It was a huge victory.

But now, Em had never seen the old farmer move so fast. And he wasn't smiling. She stopped in the road to wait for him.

"Some of the kids were building a treehouse near the river," he wheezed. "They started nailing boards to the sycamore, and they made a huge crack in the tree. We moved the kids away, but the tree might topple."

Em understood Earl's urgency. "Show me," she ordered.

They jogged back down the road and arrived at the small wooded area in the center of town. An old footbridge spanned an active creek, bubbling over jagged rocks below. In the grassy clearing sat the sycamore. Em had scaled to its very top as a child, but it had grown so rapidly, she didn't think that was possible anymore. Its branches spread wider than Em's cottage, providing shade to the whole clearing. She once tied a rope on a protruding limb and swung into the creek, until Gram had told her not to. This tree was her second girlhood home.

Em rushed to the trunk. Two boys stood at the base, one guiltily holding a hammer. Alfred, the butcher, looked on worriedly.

"We didn't mean to, Em!" the bigger boy protested.

"It's all right, Grady," Em said, squatting to face the child. "Where is it?"

The boy pointed. Em's eyes followed the tip of his finger to a huge fissure in the white-gray inner bark. It was the height of a door and as wide as her fist. She whistled. "You did that with a hammer and nail?"

Grady nodded, on the verge of tears.

"You must have a big, strong arm!" Grady's eyes widened, then he let out a tiny smile. Em continued, "I think you should find a different tree for your treehouse. Maybe the walnut near the blacksmith?"

The boys trotted off, chattering. Em turned to Earl and Alfred, raising her eyebrows.

Earl shook his head. "We heard an earsplitting crack. We would've stopped them sooner if we'd known, this being a gift from the empress and all."

Em glanced over at the stone marker near the base of the tree. A bronze placard, green and illegible with age, was attached to the flat top of the stone. The townsfolk understood the significance of a gift from their sovereign, but the little ones would not have known.

"We were most worried about it falling. Crushing a kid."

"No, you did right. If it broke that easily, something is definitely wrong." Em ducked under a branch to examine the crack.

Up close, Em thought she heard groaning from the massive tree and felt the familiar vibration in her fingers when she placed her hand on the bark. This was something very broken. A challenge. She felt it beckon her more strongly than anything she had felt before. She lifted her hand from the tree.

"There might be a hollow cavity in the trunk," she considered. Glancing back at the other men, she realized they were waiting for her to tell them what to do. She felt a surge of pride, which she shoved down as she gave the closest branch an experimental shake, considering solutions. "It seems stable for now. Let's put up a warning sign, and I'll put it on the top of my list for tomorrow."

EM TRUDGED BACK up the street. Her brain was occupied trying to remember everything she knew about tree repair, and she passed the new bookshop without a second glance.

Ahead, a wooden sign displaying a needle and thread hung above the cheerful chartreuse door of the tailor's storefront. In the window, a dress form held a flouncy lilac gown with a low neckline. Em snorted, momentarily distracted by the ridiculous garment. Who would buy such a gown here in Brookerby?

Her eyes flew from the dress to her own middling figure reflected in the glass. She was clad in a plain green blouse and brown trousers splattered with ink. Her blue-gray eyes passed their reflection and landed on a smudge of ink—shaped like a W—on her cheek. Em winced. Mendel would not be pleased with her appearance, and his displeasure usually led to some very heavy-handed suggestions for improvements. He saw it as his duty to keep her looking tidy.

Steeling herself, Em took a deep breath, and pushed open the door. The bell tinkled to announce her arrival.

"It's me," she shouted toward the back room. She heard Mendel reply with something unintelligible, and Em cast about for the unfortunate shelves she was to fix.

As always, the store was immaculate. Notions organized by type, size, and color. Ongoing projects folded into perfect squares and placed in a queue on Mendel's workbench. His sewing machine looked like it was scrubbed daily. The tailor's neatness appealed to Em's own sense of order, but she thought he took it a bit far.

Spotting the offending shelf, askew and empty, was a quick exercise of observation. Em set down her tool bag and prodded the shelf experimentally. No vibration. This would be an easy repair.

Mendel bustled into the room. The tailor was an elegant gentleman with cocoa-colored skin, wire-frame spectacles, and a knowing, self-possessed arch to his eyebrows. Em kept herself turned toward the shelf, hiding her ink stains.

"Oh, Emaline! That shelf—ah, you found it—it's been driving me crazy. It's a little crooked, as you can see. And creaking in the middle. I don't believe it will hold anything heavier than a pincushion. You're repairing it?"

"Gram mentioned you needed the help."

"Yes, please. I tremble each time I set a bolt of fabric there. I had a beautiful shipment of printed calico arrive two days ago, and I simply had nowhere to put it but the floor. Oh, how I wish you'd let me make you a more fashionable shirt out of that calico."

Em smirked. It hadn't taken long for the fussy tailor to try to style her. "How could I fix your shelves in a fancy shirt? Besides, I hear your fabric sits on the floor for days."

Mendel groaned in frustration. "Please don't tell anyone. I wouldn't do it unless circumstances were dire."

Em tried not to giggle. Mendel never quite picked up on teasing. "I promise this shelf will hold all the fabric you wish, my dear tailor," she said in mock seriousness. She wiggled the shelf out. Mendel was right about it being wobbly. Whoever installed it did a poor job of keeping the brackets even.

"I don't suppose," Mendel ventured, "that you've seen Ilna today? I've been expecting a message from her."

"Matter of fact, I just came from there. The printing press had some trouble. Oh! Ilna said to tell you there's a big storm coming." Em examined the brackets, wondering if she could reuse them.

Mendel was silent. Which was unusual. Em turned and saw his face morph from worry to dismay.

"My dear, your clothes!" he shrieked. "That will never come out!"

Em sighed. She embraced the lived-in look—it was a walking advertisement for her fledgling business. But Mendel was horrified.

"Emaline, you know I owe it to your parents to look out for you. I wish you wouldn't wander the streets in rags. I have offered many times to make you clothes appropriate for a young lady."

Em bit her tongue in frustration. This was her ritual with Mendel. He treated her like a child to be scolded and dressed, and it was getting old. She pushed back, trying for logic and calm.

"I appreciate your offer, and you have done a fine job looking out for me. But it's very hard to mend leaky roofs and rickety shelves in the lovely dresses you make."

"Please let me send you home with a new dress. For the social tonight? It's the least I can do."

Em started to protest again, but Mendel had already flitted to the

8

back room. She rolled her eyes. Whatever outfit Mendel sent home with her would be sneakily donated to one of her former schoolmates, so it didn't really matter. She returned to the shelf. Working quickly, she removed and reattached the supports, taking care to make them perfectly even. Mendel would surely notice if the shelf was slightly askew.

CHAPTER 2

he empress assumed the throne from her father, Henrich, who had neglected Esnania and allowed all manner of thievery and villainy to run rampant throughout the empire. The wealthy and elite could pay for protection from mages, but the small towns had no defense from the degeneracy that ravaged the country.

EM LEFT the shop an hour later with two new shirts, a skirt, and a gnawing hunger in her stomach. The repair took ten minutes, and Mendel had barely acknowledged her work. The fittings and fussing took much longer. She turned her feet toward home. Clouds had moved in, and the setting sun flashed saffron among the darkening gray.

Gram and Em's cottage sat isolated at the base of a steep hill. It was a ten-minute walk from town. Em could make it in five if she picked up her feet. Her tool bag bounced on her hip as she trotted, which stung, but getting home to food was more important than avoiding a bruise. Smoke rose from the chimney of the cottage, curling lazily. Em's temples dripped with sweat, and she impatiently swiped it away, knocking off her hat in the process.

"Crumb it all!" she cursed, floundering with her tools and spilling some as she scooped up her hat. "Bah!" She slammed the hat back on her head and plucked up her tools, only to drop the packages Mendel had given her—the nice new clothes that she had promised to keep clean. Kicking the packages like a beanball, she waddled her way down the lane to the garden gate.

Gramalia—Gram—stood staring, eyebrows raised. She was barely taller than the wooden gate, and her bunned white hair stood in stark contrast to the browns and greens of the cottage garden.

Em blushed. She knelt, plucked up the wrinkled and torn brown paper packages, and presented them to Gram. "From Mendel. He thought I might like a new shirt or two." Gram's left eyebrow twitched, and a corner of her mouth involuntarily lifted. Em reddened. "He said they should be kicked home...to enhance the...fashion."

Gram straightened her ancient features and shook her head in reproof. Then she reached up and playfully batted Em's hat off her head.

"Hey!" Em yelped, but she couldn't suppress a grin.

Gram had watched over Em since she was orphaned as a small child. Now that Em was grown, they were something more akin to roommates. Pranks were a regular occurrence.

As she bent down to collect her hat—again—she caught a whiff of Gram's stew, the aroma a complex blend of herbs, spices, and flavorful meat that made Em's mouth water. She scooped up all her belongings and scampered down the flagstone path to the kitchen entrance.

The cottage door protested with a squeal as she pushed it open. "I'll take care of that hinge tomorrow," Em promised. She deposited her tools by the door with a clank.

Gram didn't respond. Six years ago, she'd developed a serious infection that put her in bed for weeks with fever. Her throat had been damaged beyond recovery and it was painful for her to talk. Now, unless something was important enough to endure pain to communicate, she made hand signals and jotted notes.

Em recalled that, before her illness, Gram had a commanding, brassy voice that jumped from topic to topic at high speeds. Her laugh was like a musical horn. Em remembered childhood bedtime readings of fairy stories; Gram could convincingly do all the voices, from the distressed damsel to the fire-breathing dragon. Em missed that Gram sometimes.

Distracted by her memories, Em stood with her parcels in their massive great room, until Gram poked her gently in the back of the knees with a kitchen chair, encouraging her to sit. She plopped down, sighing. The room was basic, but it was home. It held their iron cook-stove, plain wooden cabinets, and a wobbly kitchen table. Lumpy chairs surrounded a large bookcase that edged their stone fireplace. Peaked ceilings showed the wooden underbelly of a thatched roof. The only other rooms in the cottage were Gram's room at the front of the house, and Em's room in the back. The windows were flung open, and a pleasant cross-breeze cooled down the room. Gram returned to the stew with her ladle in hand.

"I've been thinking about this meal all day, Gram. I was so distracted that Ilna's printing press spurted ink all over me." Gram turned mid-scoop to glance at Em's clothes. She made a hand gesture for "mess," rolled her eyes, and turned back to the stove. Em smiled at Gram's sass.

"I know. I should've been more careful. Mendel already scolded me. Ilna is happy to have the press up and running, though. I think that press is an artifact from the Age of Magic." Gram dropped her spoon with a clatter and studied Em with pinched eyebrows.

"What is it?"

Gram looked at Em as though trying to find something written on her face. Then she made the gesture for "fix" and "magic" with a question. It took Em a minute to remember the second word, as it wasn't a frequent topic.

Em tilted her head. Then, understanding her roommate's shock, she explained. "It might have been magic, but it was only angry. Not broken." After a moment, Gram shook her head and returned to her seat. Em, ready to eat, snatched up her spoon. The meal in front of her looked and smelled amazing.

Between bites, Em asked, "I almost forgot. Do you have any books on trees? I think something might be wrong with the sycamore by the footbridge."

Gram face froze midbite, looking shocked. Em backtracked. "It's fine, Gram. It's still standing for now, and it didn't fall on anyone. There's a huge crack in it. I'm wondering if there's a way to figure out if it's hollow, or if I can fill it with something. And—Gram?"

Gram jumped to her feet and crossed to their floor-to-ceiling bookshelf next to the hearth. Em twisted in her chair to watch. "Gram? You're finding a tree book?"

Gram's eyes traced the spines of the well-loved books. Em knew them all by sight, even from across the room. *Faublica Geometry*. *Ancient Fables*. *War of Minds*. *Historical Heroics*. Gram paused, snapped her fingers, and retreated to her room. Moments later, she reentered with her hands closed around a thick book, leather bound and covered in dust. One Em had never seen before. Gram crossed the room and held it toward Em as an offering.

Em stood, reaching out to receive the book gingerly. The spine felt like dried leaves, and the cover was more dust than anything else. But there was that tingling sensation in her fingertips. Maybe it needed repairs?

"Is there a page number I should turn to?"

This was a standard question. Gram knew her books well and could usually point to the guidance Em needed. This time, the older woman shrugged. In this case, Em knew she should just start at the beginning. Em set the book on the round, weathered kitchen table, bumping her stew bowl aside. Still standing, she flipped the cover open.

The Standard Book of Anything.

Odd title, Em thought as she turned to the table of contents. A neat printed list of items and page numbers pointed to such eclectic topics as "Purposes for Bat Guano," "A Personal History of Alfred P. Johnson's Fish Sandwiches," "Lutes and Flutes," and "Galoshes and their Discontents."

No wonder she'd never read this one. The topics were as dry as the book's cover. Usually Gram was helpful, but she was allowed a rare misstep. She turned to face her guardian, who watched eagerly. "I don't think this was the book you were looking for. There's nothing about trees."

Gram's face fell. She shook her head and went to wash the supper dishes. Em could hear Gram's annoyance in the way she banged the pans around. "Okay, fine," Em relented. She sat down, flipped randomly to a page, and began skimming.

A lute is any plucked string instrument with a neck and a deep round back enclosing a hollow cavity, usually with a sound hole or opening in the body. To tune such an instrument, you must procure a lute. This is essential, as imaginary lutes are nearly always in tune already. (See "Unseen Music of the Mage.")

Em started. Imaginary lutes? Was this a satirical reference book? But why would Gram bring it out after Em asked about trees? Gram wanted her to read this nonsense, and she was usually right about everything. Em recalled the incident last month with the cart wheel schematics. Gram *was* usually right. She flushed at the memory and kept reading.

Once a lute has been purchased, you must familiarize yourself with its body, frets, and pegs. The pegs may be twisted for tuning purposes. Tightening the pegs will produce a higher-pitched sound on the corresponding string, while loosening the pegs will produce a lower-pitched sound on the corresponding string. It is essential...

Em found the mechanical advice mildly interesting, but she wasn't making the connection. Why was it important that she read this right now? She glanced at Gram, who was elbow deep in dishes. Gram always had her reasons, but Em didn't have time for this right now. Em closed the cover, pushed back from the table. She needed to get the ink off her face before the social tonight.

~

THE MERCANTILE WAS overcrowded when Em and Gram arrived. The cavernous single-room store sold most of the dry goods in town, but there was also a small café in the back corner that served as a meeting place for the locals. Tonight, the mercantile advertised "Sweet frozen cream, one night only." It was a delicacy few had ever tasted this far away from the big cities, and it seemed the whole town was there for the opportunity.

Em left her work clothes on, and she expected immediate comments from Mendel. But he didn't notice. He was over in the corner, whispering with Ilna. They were not smiling. Gram eyed them, gestured "I'll go see" to Em, and pushed her way along the wall to reach them. Em nodded to a group of farmhands, and then saw Alfred, the butcher, smiling and waving her over to an open seat at his table. Also sitting there were Gendry Houton and the schoolteacher, Fern.

"Gendry! What's your project today?" Em asked in greeting. Gendry was constantly knitting, and she had made scarves and sweaters for half the town. Last year, she gifted Em a moss-colored sweater with one giant hammer knitted into the pattern. It was very ugly, but Em wore it regularly. Em took a twisted pleasure in seeing the sweaters gifted around town—and the polite-but-secretly-horrified looks on the giftees' faces.

"Em! I'm makin' one for the new bookseller. You met 'em yet? It'll have a colorful stack of books right in the center. Tricky, but I'm gettin' better at swappin' colors."

Em ignored the question. What was it with this bookseller? She turned to Alfred. "How's the sink?"

"Works like a charm, Em. Thanks! I'm saving my best ham for you. Come by tomorrow sometime."

Gendry spoke up, "Isn't this just lovely? We all should get together more often, don't you think?"

Em tried not to snort. The annual fish fry was less than a week ago. Before that, the swap social. Before that, several barn raisings. Even on nights with no events on the calendar, a sizeable contingent of Brookerby's finest chatted at the mercantile café until the owner shooed them out. Everyone got together plenty. At least, to her mind.

"Nichols said the ice was carted down from Fridera. Couldn't have been cheap. Have you tasted frozen sweet cream before?" Alfred asked Fern.

"Once. Stars, it's been nearly three years ago. I went to visit my aunt in Gillamor, and she treated me to an iced cream." She sighed. "It was heavenly."

The mercantile owner, Miranda, swooped by and tried to address the crowd. "It will be a few more minutes. We're still churning back there." Her thin voice didn't carry over the conversations in the room, and she clasped her hands anxiously. Then she spied the butcher. "Alfred! I thought you had given up sweets." Alfred reddened and muttered something unintelligible.

Em came to the rescue. "It's a special occasion, Miranda." The woman pursed her lips and returned to behind the counter.

"Emaline, dear," Fern said, "you must promise to relax tonight. You spent last week's fish fry tending the fire pit and building that contraption for the children. I don't think you even got a dance in."

Em wanted to defend herself, but the schoolteacher had turned in her chair and was waving to someone. Apparently, Fern's criticisms didn't require a response.

"It was a happy-go-around. The kids loved it," she muttered to no one in particular. She had gotten the idea from one of Gram's physics books, and the children were lining up for hours to take turns spinning like a top. At the time, she didn't think it would be a problem, but apparently, she should've been dancing instead.

Gendry stopped knitting long enough to pat her knee. "Never mind, dearie. We're all just looking out for you."

Fern turned back, hauling forward a gangly fellow who stood a head taller than everyone else in the room. "This is the new bookseller. Cornelius. I think you've met everyone but Em, yes?" The last was directed at the man, who nodded. He wasn't bad looking. Ginger hair. Friendly eyes. But very pale. He must always stay inside with his books.

"Emaline Strider. I do a lot of the repair work in town." Em stuck out her hand. Cornelius shook it with a limp, clammy palm. *Ech.* He said something in reply, but his voice was so soft, she couldn't make it out over the noise of the crowd. Then a patchy flush grew on his wan cheeks. What had he said?

Miranda brought out trays of sweet frozen cream at that very moment, which saved Em from having to respond, and she took advantage of the distraction. She snatched up her sample, offered her chair to Cornelius, and said a hasty goodbye to the table. Then Em scanned the room for Earl McBean and the other farmers. At least they wouldn't try to play matchmaker.

Pushing through the crowd, she glanced over at the corner where Ilna, Mendel and Gram still stood. Ilna was whispering, and Em saw Gram make the hand gesture for "prepare." She filed away the word to ask Gram about later.

Suddenly, she realized she hadn't tried her sample. She stopped in the middle of the crowd and spooned up a bite of the blueberry-flavored frozen cream. It was cold, but velvety, and it tasted like summer and winter dancing. The crowd faded into the background as Em hastily finished her scoop. It was maybe the best thing she had ever eaten.

LATER THAT EVENING, back at the cottage, a steady rain started to fall. Em had ducked out of the social after making cursory rounds. Nobody had any new projects for her, Miranda wouldn't give her a second scoop, and Gram had already gone home to bed. Ilna and Mendel vanished soon after.

The tree and the book were still itching at the back of Em's brain. Gram rarely missed the mark, and she still seemed in possession of her wits. Maybe there was some tidbit about trees in the other articles. Something Em would have to look for. After all, the lute article tangent on magic was unexpected. Maybe she should have followed the cross-reference? By bedtime, she was ready to give *The Standard Book of Anything* another read. Gram was asleep, and the book rested on the table, waiting. Em sat down and carefully lifted the cover.

The Standard Book of Anything.

The table of contents was on the next page. To Em's surprise, it looked unfamiliar. She tried to find the lute article, but it was nowhere. A series of equally diverse academic titles had taken its place: "Tree Varieties in the Western Hemisphere," "The Origin of Flannel as a Textile," "Common Storm Clouds and How to Identify Them." Perplexed by what appeared to be the complete rearrangement of the tome, Em stared at the pages. Was this book magic? She swiped her hand over the letters. They seemed normal, but words did not rearrange in normal books; printed letters tended to stay put. If it was magic, this was a rare and valuable book. How did Gram get it?

Maybe if she followed the references long enough, it would lead her to advice on how to fix the tree. That could take a while. The cross-reference method was not very efficient, and Em thought it was a poor design for an informational book. Rolling her eyes, she turned to the tree article and began reading.

The largest trees are defined as having the highest wood volume in a single stem. These trees are both tall and large in diameter and, in particular, hold a large diameter high up the trunk.

Measurement is very complex, particularly if branch volume is to be included as well as the trunk volume. Measurements have only been made for a small number of trees and typically only include the trunk. Few attempts have ever been made to include root or leaf volume, except by botanist Grover Washer, who lost his sanity in the process.

The exception to the measurement rule is the warding tree of protection. These trees are located near protected townships. They grow broadly and quickly. Thus, they defy the proper measurements of large trees and should be

excluded. For more on warding trees of protection, see "Imperial Programs of
Progress from this Millenia."

Em sighed in frustration. This article gave her nothing about how
to fix trees. Maybe the sycamore was a warding tree, whatever that
was. It was extraordinarily large and growing rapidly, which fit the
description. Perhaps *The Standard Book of Anything* was just ramping
up to the "fixing" part. Em flipped to "Imperial Programs of Progress
from this Millenia."

Philanthropic imperial sovereigns have implemented community projects to
improve the lives of ordinary citizens and increase prosperity for the whole
empire. Below is a summary of these projects by date.

Em skimmed through the list of projects, searching for warding
trees. She finally found them next to a date from fifty years ago.

756 RQ. Warding Trees of Protection. Empress Regina de Silviana Augusto,
in the early years of her reign. The empress led a planting tour that estab-
lished these magical trees in small villages throughout the empire. The
venture was abandoned before completion due to unforeseen complications.
Some trees remain to this day, adding a shield of protection and goodwill
around each hamlet. Some trees have fallen. Towns with felled trees have
decayed and crumbled within weeks of the loss.

There was no cross-reference. The trail ended here. A waste of
time then. Em sat back, irritated. Why had Gram given this to her?
She needed to fix the tree. She skimmed back through the article. The
description of the warding trees was disturbing. The stone marker in
front of the Brookerby sycamore was dated fifty years ago. A gift from
the empress; it might be a warding tree. If that was true, the town
could—how did the book phrase it—"decay and crumble" if it actually
fell.

"Tell me how to fix it, then!" she scowled at the book. She closed
the cover. Opened it. Same table of contents. Closed it. Opened it.

Same. Useless. Maybe she could talk to Mrs. Witherwill tomorrow. The woman had so many lovely plants, she might know how to care for a tree.

The storm outside had intensified. Lightning lit up the room, followed by a deafening crack.

A crack that sounded—to Em's uneasy mind—like a large tree splitting into pieces.

CHAPTER 3

he empress summoned her mages and advisers to her. A young and beautiful mage of much renown, Bronwyn Featherweight, supported the idea of a protective barrier around each town and assured Her Majesty that it could be accomplished using magic and a living plant. Perhaps a tree.

EM STARED at the felled tree, cursing softly.

It was impossible to tell whether the storm brought it down, or whether it would have fallen eventually. Em supposed it didn't matter. Feeling as if one of the huge branches had fallen on her chest, Em struggled for calm. She was too late. If only she had done something yesterday.

A large portion of the top branches had split from the trunk, falling across the creek. The other side, no doubt unbalanced by the loss, had fallen in the opposite direction. All that remained of the sycamore was a partial trunk—almost Em's height—with a jagged point where the tree had broken unevenly. Her temporary sign warning people away from the unstable tree was still there.

Overwhelmed by the scene before her, and knowing this would

take days to clean up, Em shifted her focus to the footbridge. One substantial branch had split from the creek limb, smashed into the guardrail, and now blocked the path. She could at least clear the walkway. Em tested the planks of the bridge and determined they were still safe to stand on. Then she grasped the obstructing limb and tried to pry it off the platform. No luck. It was almost as thick as Em's thighs, and the other end was stuck in the mud of the creek bed. Trying again, she wedged her back underneath the largest part and pushed up from the ground with her legs. As she reached the limits of her strength, she felt the limb shift. The branch lifted a few inches off the bridge and then slid down into the creek. Gasping from the exertion, she flopped down onto the now-clear footbridge and closed her eyes.

The book had said something about the tree protecting the town. From what, she couldn't fathom. But according to *The Standard Book of Anything*, Brookerby was weeks away from total extinction. She wondered how that would even happen. Would it be a force from without— wolves or bandits—or from within? Would all her neighbors pack up and leave without warning? Was it even a warding tree at all? She hoped not.

She suddenly realized that no one else in town had come to see the wreckage, and her eyes flew open. Yesterday as she was headed home from the mercantile, she saw multiple people loitering in the clearing, just to glimpse the crack in the tree. Now, she glanced around at the empty green with a sense of dread. Had the decay already begun?

Em was due at the cobbler's shop for a shoe-rack repair. She stood and looked at the sycamore once more. Other than clearing away the wood, she couldn't do any good here until she worked out how to stop the unknown damage to come. She turned away from the broken tree, hoisted her tool bag onto her shoulder again, and headed toward the shopfronts.

~

SHE HEARD the crowd before she saw it: shouts of anger sliced through the morning air. A small crowd had assembled outside the butcher's shop, and they did not look friendly. She spotted Cornelius, the bookseller. The outraged expression he wore made his pale face unattractive. Earl was also in the crowd, his usually mild expression twisted into a mask of fury.

"Earl?" Em hollered, but her voice was drowned out by shouts of "Pig!" "Bastard!" and various other slurs that Em recognized as ugly without quite knowing their meanings. Earl was yelling along with everyone else. Time slowed, but she felt her heart speed up. She'd never seen this kind of hate on display so brazenly, and it frightened her. She knew these people, most of them. They were all together last night, laughing and eating frozen cream. What happened between then and now? Her mind flashed to the broken tree. "Really?" she wondered out loud. A fist smashed into her shoulder and she recoiled, moving deeper into the group. "Earl!" she tried again. He seemed not to hear.

As she ducked through the crowd, someone threw a rock at the butcher shop's large display window. Em cowered, shielding her eyes as shards of window shattered in all directions. She was going to get seriously injured if she didn't get out of the press of bodies around her.

The crowd's yelling continued. She looked up and saw cut glass littering the ground and protruding from the meat that hung in the window. Alfred protested weakly over the din, his balding head poking out of the bright orange door.

"Please, I beg of you! I did not cheat anyone."

A deep voice in the crowd roared, "Liar!" Other voices joined in, hurling angry insults.

He whimpered something Em couldn't hear. A glass bottle struck the doorframe near Alfred's head, quickly followed by a rotten head of lettuce. Alfred slammed the door.

The crowd pushed forward, as if with a single purpose: to break it down.

Em battled her way to the edge, nearly getting trampled in the process. She needed to get to Alfred before the mob did. Taking a deep breath, she pushed her way sideways out of the crowd, gaining several more bruises from flailing fists. Finally, she made it to the corner of the building, gasping, her body aching. From the side of her eye, she saw more rocks flying, and two men yanked a large cut of meat out of window display. It was peppered with glass, but they didn't seem to care.

There was a side entrance to the shop, down the alleyway. Peering around the corner, Em saw it was propped open. She looked back to the crowd, and determining that their focus was singularly on the storefront, she darted into the alley and jogged to the side door. With one more glance back, she stepped in and pulled the handle closed behind her.

At that moment, Alfred came to the back of the store.

"Alfred!" she hissed.

His eyes darted wildly before finding hers. "Em! Please! Don't—"

Em felt momentary confusion before she understood his fear. The mob was made of friends and neighbors. Alfred clearly thought she was part of it. She patted the air, attempting to soothe him. "I'm here to help."

Alfred continued to frantically scan the room, but he allowed her to approach without flinching. "I don't think it's a good time to repair the sink," he said.

"I did that yesterday, remember? Alfred, what happened out there? Those people are getting dangerous." As if to prove her point, the pounding on the shop door grew deafening.

"I don't know what happened," he cried. "I know most of these folks...Earl. Mrs. Cassini...But I don't understand why they're so angry."

Em seized Alfred by his shoulders, "What triggered the mob? Did something happen last night? Or this morning?"

Alfred began sobbing, "I don't know. I sell only the finest meat. They've lost their minds..."

"They're going to tear the place apart. We need to find Marshall Denget."

Alfred gaped. "The marshall?"

Em grabbed Alfred's arm and yanked him out the side entrance just as the front door burst open. Her adrenaline surging, she slammed the side door shut and dragged the butcher toward the marshall's office, away from the crowd.

MARSHALL DENGET COULD BEST BE COMPARED to an ancient hunting hound. Em had heard marvelous tales of his adventures in his youth, but nowadays, he usually lounged on a cushioned, three-legged stool just outside the jail in town. Em rarely saw him leave it.

But the marshall wasn't sitting down today. As Em and Alfred puffed up the street, she saw him speaking with what appeared to be the leader of a small squad of armored men and women. Their armor was dented and dull, but its peacock-blue-and-gold crests declared their service to the empress. They were imperial soldiers. All stood at attention, and appeared impressively fit despite their shabby equipment. Em had never seen any soldiers up close, and only once in her life had a squadron ever marched through Brookerby. She stopped, unsure how to proceed. Were they here to help? Did they already know about the riots?

Without pausing, Alfred pushed his way through frantically, still out of breath. "Marshall Denget, sir—my shop, it's being—well, they're looting, sir."

"Well, that's interesting," Denget drawled, meeting Alfred's and Em's eyes with a significant look. "These, er, fine folks say they've been sent here to keep the peace." He turned toward the captain once more. "Is this what you meant, sir? We aren't accustomed to riots in Brookerby."

Em tore her gaze from the marshall and studied the soldiers. To the person, their expressions were stone. *A pickpocket or cutthroat would be more sympathetic*, she thought severely. Marshall Denget scratched his head lazily, but his eyes were like bullets as he stared down each of the soldiers in turn.

None of them moved. The captain of the squadron, a tall man with a slender face and a long scar on his cheek, broke the silence. He glanced in the direction of the mob noise, and then addressed Alfred as though he were explaining sums to a thick-headed child. "We cannot save every shop that is set upon by unhappy customers. You will simply have to rebuild once they leave."

"What?" Em exploded. "Those people are destroying his livelihood over nothing. If you are meant to protect Brookerby, why don't you get on with it?"

The captain's eyes narrowed at Em, but he brushed her off like a fly and turned back to the marshall. "Your concern is noted, Marshall. We were sent here to collect someone. If unrest breaks out, we will protect people, not property. We expect more turmoil in the coming days, but you shall not interfere unless lives are at risk. If you step in, Brookerby will have the wrath of the empress to contend with."

The marshall looked more tired than usual, and Alfred groaned.

Em's blood boiled. "Cowards," she exhaled and turned to leave.

"Miss. For your own safety, I recommend you go home." The captain's righteous tone bounced off her back.

Em felt something snap within her. "Unlike these spineless weasels, I don't take orders from you." The soldiers shifted uncomfortably, but Em was not finished. "I intend to fix whatever I can. But if this town is destroyed, the empress will have the wrath of Brookerby to contend with." Biting back further treason, Em marched away, back down the road. She overheard the captain quietly order his soldiers to stand down, but when she glanced back, the was captain staring daggers at her. Alfred let out another whimper and sagged into the marshall's chair, his head in his hands.

Em's legs burned with exhaustion as she raced back toward the rabble. She couldn't stop a riot or looting. She knew that much. But there had to be some way to disperse the crowd. If only it would rain again. She glanced at the sunny sky, wishing in vain for another storm. She could create rain by redirecting Alfred's pump water to spray over the crowd. She had learned all about plumbing the other day, and such a rig wouldn't be too difficult to create. Yet, by the time she built the thing, the mob would have surely destroyed the shop and moved on.

Feeling helpless, she passed the *Leaflet's* yellow door and skidded to a halt. Ilna! She might know what to do. Em leapt at the entrance and pulled at the handle. Locked. Peering through the window, she saw the printing press sitting motionless. She knocked lightly, but the place was dark. At a loss, Em kicked a pebble in the street and stared down the road for signs of trouble. All seemed quiet, but the air felt heavy with dread.

Turning to look the other direction, she could just make out the clump of soldiers still standing with the marshall. Em scoffed. No doubt they were issuing more haughty orders for why Marshall Denget couldn't do his job. She did not understand. Why would they allow riots and looting? One of the men was looking her way, and she jumped back into the shadow of the awning. Best not to draw further attention. Insulting them—and the empress—was not smart, she conceded. As to her next move...well, she was stuck.

"Pssst."

Em turned to see the door open a crack and Ilna's face peeking out, looking a bit more disheveled than usual. "Ilna? Are you—"

"Shhh!" Ilna grabbed her arm and yanked her inside, shutting the door quietly behind her.

"Ow! You can let go." The printer released her surprisingly vice-like grip on Em's arm with an apologetic look. "Ilna, there's a—"

Ilna hushed her again and gestured toward her office.

Em followed her to the back room. Her friend seemed apprehensive. Had she seen the mob too? Did she think her shop was next? Ilna peeled back an ornate Brildonian rug to reveal a trap door. Opening it, she hissed down the shaft, "Em was outside," and then motioned for Em to go down the steep stairway. Ilna followed, arranging the rug so it would hide the entrance and closing the hatch behind her.

"Hello?" Em called out.

"Just me," came Mendel's voice as a match lit a lantern, revealing the tailor's face. He looked as tidy as ever in a fitted shirt with brown paisley swirls.

Em reached the bottom of the stairway and looked around at the irregular gray stone walls of what appeared to be a tunnel. It stretched out in front of her and disappeared into pitch-dark. If she spread out her arms, she could almost touch either wall. Roots sprang haphazardly from the ceiling, brushing the top of their heads. "What is this place?" she directed back to Ilna.

Mendel answered from behind her, "This tunnel connects Ilna's shop to mine. Very secret, you understand. Only for dire circumstances."

"Is that what this is? Dire circumstances?" Em's voice broke just asking the question.

"For the tailor here, yes." Ilna said gently, stepping off the stairs and patting her arm. "A big storm is coming for him."

Em turned to stare at her. "Your storm message yesterday. Did you both know the tree would fall?"

The printer and tailor exchanged a look of confusion. "What tree?" Ilna asked.

Em's mind spiraled. What were they talking about? Did they even know? "The warding tree of protection! Isn't that why you're down here?"

Mendel looked at the printer. "The tree again—"

Ilna patted his hand. "We can't—perhaps in the chaos..."

"—but for how long?"

They were speaking in fragments. Their own world. Their own language. They knew about the tree. But there was something else. And Em was running out of patience. "Will someone clue me in, please?"

"Yes, indeed," Mendel waved her farther down the tunnel. "The message you so kindly brought me yesterday about the storm meant imperial difficulties for me are imminent. I am hiding down here until I can make my escape."

Ilna jumped in. "I saw his arrest warrant published on my news updates."

This was a wrinkle Em hadn't anticipated. It was hard to imagine gentle, fastidious Mendel in trouble with the law. A warrant. "What did you do?"

"All in good time. We should visit my shop, briefly. This way." Mendel took the lantern from Ilna and suddenly held it up to Em. "Emaline, dear, that blouse looks lovely. It brings out the blue in your eyes. Thank you for wearing it."

Em glanced down, remembering that she had worn a ruffled, cream-colored blouse Mendel had gifted her yesterday. She noticed he made no comment about the dirt on the blouse from shoving the tree off the bridge. The town was in peril, but he was still trying to dress her. She muttered her thanks, letting the topic pass.

Mendel led the way down the tunnel, lighting the way. It was musty and cool, like an old cellar. After several minutes of travel, he reached a fork. Pointing left, he explained, "That way leads to Gramalia." Then he took the right fork and continued.

"Do these tunnels only connect you three?" Em asked. She peered down the fork into the darkness, trying to make out any distinguishing features.

"Gram and I dug them, seventeen years ago. It was necessary to travel without drawing attention," Mendel responded carefully.

"Gram *dug* them?"

"Emaline, I cannot explain everything at this moment. We are on the threshold of danger. Best to keep moving," Mendel said briskly.

"There was a riot outside Alfred's shop. I'd say we've crossed that threshold," Em said.

"Oh dear. Poor man," Ilna lamented. "The same thing happened before. Not to him, specifically. But the same mood. Same strangeness in town, spreading rumors, looting, rioting, and violence. People you thought you knew…as if they'd been enchanted."

"Before? Before what?" Em was lost again.

"Before the sycamore. I have no doubt it's happening again."

"Before—? The sycamore was planted fifty years ago by the empress."

"The sycamore was planted seventeen years ago. After the original tree fell," Ilna clarified.

Em put her hand out to rest on the wall. Everything suddenly felt unstable. "Seventeen years? When you dug the tunnels. You planted a new tree?"

"All in good time, Emaline," Mendel hushed.

"Did soldiers come then also?"

Ilna's eyes flashed. "Soldiers?"

Em nodded. "Yes, about a dozen. They wore the crest of the empress, but they were very content to let Alfred's shop be destroyed."

Their pace slowed, and Mendel swiveled his head around to glance at Ilna. "Soldiers did not come last time. They're here for me."

"What did you do, Mendel?"

He ignored Em's question and turned back to a dead end in the tunnel. He scanned the stone wall, as if seeking the right bolt of fabric. "Ah. Here." He pressed one of the stones that was a slightly different color from the others, and part of the wall swung forward to reveal the backside of a tapestry. Mendel pulled the heavy curtain aside, entering his cellar stockroom. A moment later, Em heard his feet tapping up the stairs, and the stockroom door closed behind him.

Em hung back in the tunnel. It was isolating to realize how many things had been kept from her. How little she actually knew about her friends. She turned and cornered the printer. "Ilna, please. What did he do?"

"That's not for me to share. But the charges are unjust. We just need to keep him safe until this blows over."

Em sighed. "What about the tree? If we don't do something, the town—"

"I know. I'll go ahead to Gram and let her know what's happening. Will you wait here for Mendel?"

"Uh, sure, I guess," Em said. Ilna was trying to keep her out of the way. It was hard not to feel resentful.

"Keep an ear out for soldiers and crowds," Ilna cautioned, patting Em on the arm. "It might take some time for Mendel to pack, but it will give that magnificent brain of yours time to think up improvements for our hidden tunnel."

Even that challenge couldn't pull Em's mind away from the fear of losing Brookerby. But she nodded all the same and offered the lantern to Ilna.

"Keep it," she said in response. "I know these tunnels. I'll see you at the cottage soon."

Ilna hustled back down the tunnel in the direction of the fork, fading into the darkness as she passed outside the reach of the lantern.

Em leaned her hand against the stone wall and listened to Ilna's fading footsteps. Then she shook out her nervously twitching limbs. The past hour had flipped everything she knew about Brookerby and her friends on its head. The broken sycamore was daunting, and her friends' secrets were compounding by the minute. But the most frightening development was the mob. What dark enchantment could turn Earl McBean into that monster she witnessed above? And what if it couldn't be fixed?

CHAPTER 4

*E*m woke with a start. How long had it been? She was leaning against the cool stone of the tunnels, and her legs were starting to cramp. She stiffly got to her feet and tried to stretch. She was sore all over. Her rumbling stomach told her it was close to midday, which meant Mendel was taking far too long to collect his things. She felt a pang of worry. Perhaps something had happened to Mendel. Or maybe he had already left without her. She needed to find out.

Leaving the lantern and her tools in the tunnel, she carefully pulled back the tapestry and entered the storeroom. Like everything else about Mendel, it was tidy and fastidiously organized: Bolts of fabric sorted by type and color, stacked on floor-to-ceiling metal shelves. Notions in identical silver tins and neatly labeled in Mendel's perfectly formed script. Patterns stacked up by type and size. Em normally loved this room, but today, she crossed to the stairs without a wayward glance.

Listening for movement upstairs, Em tiptoed up the wooden steps, testing each before she put her full weight on it to minimize creaking noise. At the top of the stairs, she carefully cracked the door and peered out. Her stomach dropped. The shop had been ransacked, fabric bolts unfurled and lying carelessly on the floor, Mendel's work-table upended, and buttons of various colors and shapes scattered across the ground.

Em felt ill looking at the mess. She hadn't heard anything. Maybe the rioters had targeted the shop after all? *Where was Mendel,* she wondered with a growing sense of panic. With her senses heightened, she stopped and listened. She heard muted angry voices outside. *The mob,* she thought, casting about for anything to use as a weapon. She snatched up a pair of pinking shears—more for her own comfort than for actual fighting utility—and tiptoed to the door. She was careful to keep herself out of view through the display window. The voices grew louder and more strained, and she was able to pick up the conversation.

"...order of the empress."

"Would you..." The next few words were muffled, then, "... accusing me of?"

A haughty voice responded, "You are hereby charged with endan-gering..." Em pressed her ear against the door and held her breath. The soldiers' voices spoke over Mendel's muted tones.

Her pounding heart seemed louder than the conversation outside, and she was missing every other word.

"...treason, and sedition. As such you will be...justice will be served by your..."

Then Mendel's voice, "These are slanderous...but a loyal citizen to her majesty."

Mendel's voice faded and the sound of many feet crunched away. Em jumped back from the door as if bitten. Mendel had been hiding in the tunnels to avoid this outcome. The soldiers had come to collect him. But what could Mendel have possibly done? Feeling angry at her own lack of action, she started to turn the door handle and saw a note on the backside of the door. It was hastily written on a small piece of ripped patterning paper and jammed into the door with a thumbtack. Em released the handle. Mendel would never tear his patterns, or scratch up his door, but the handwriting was undoubtedly his.

Em,
Please tidy up the room.
~Mendel

Em almost laughed despite herself. The man did keep a tidy shop. Perhaps he saw the soldiers coming and expected them to destroy the store… So his last act was to hastily scribble a note directing her to clean up? Maybe it was a subtle scolding to Em because she had not come to his rescue?

The sounds of the soldiers' boots had receded down the street. Em had no guarantees they wouldn't be back.

Clean up. She shook her head in amazement. This hardly seemed the time. Her eyes scanned the room, and she wondered if she could put off the chore. After all, there were more important things happening. Then, she spotted it. A button jar was placed next to toppled stacks of multicolored thread. Clearly out of place. Buttons belonged on a different shelf. But no one would know that but Mendel. And Em.

She moved closer to investigate. Inside the jar, mostly buried, was a scrap of paper. "Very clever, Mendel," she breathed as gratitude spread across her like a wave. The tailor had thought of her waiting down in the tunnel and used his last free moments to hide something in plain sight. Something she could find but the soldiers could not.

She pulled the thin paper out and unfolded it. It was a drawing of a tree, with a series of notes and runes surrounding the branches. Em studied the drawing for a few moments. The carefully swirling letters of the notes seemed to be an instruction for incantation and planting. She had never seen anything like it, and it made her fingertips tingle when she touched it. She wondered if this was the solution to the fallen tree. Replant. Like they did seventeen years ago.

She refolded and pocketed the note to look at more closely later and made a final eyeball sweep of the room for any other misplaced items. She spotted a small knapsack on the ground, partially shoved behind the upended worktable. Em grabbed that also. If they could free Mendel from the soldiers, he would need whatever he had packed.

Em set the button jar back with the other buttons, rolled up the fabric bolts, reset the worktable, and locked the door. She returned to the tunnel, careful to replace the tapestry as she retreated. Her whole body was shaking, and she fought back against the feeling of helplessness that first sprouted earlier that morning. They would sort this out. Mendel was a simple tailor, not a criminal. Em closed the hidden stone door and took two large breaths to steady herself. Picking up the lantern and her bag of tools, she labored back toward the fork Mendel had pointed out hours ago. The fork that led home.

GRAM'S END of the tunnel came out in sight of the cottage. A round plug of dirt and grass lifted behind some well-placed shrubs that hid Em's emergence from the underground walkway. A friendly bit of smoke curled from the chimney of her cottage, and Em almost sighed in relief. She half expected soldiers or rioters to be invading. Instead, her cozy home was bathed in sunshine and serenity. Em left the extinguished lantern in the tunnel and replaced the turf plug. She shouldered her tools and Mendel's satchel and trudged toward home.

The door hinge squeaked when Em pushed it open. She cringed. She was supposed to fix that today. And the cobbler must be wondering where she was. She pushed those thoughts away. Behaving as if everything was normal was a luxury she needed to forgo for now. Em dropped her tools and the satchel by the door.

Gram and Ilna were seated on the lumpy chairs with a teapot, cups, and biscuits spread out on the small table before them. Everything appeared untouched. "You took so long we were ready to send out a search party," said Ilna, her head swiveling toward Em. "Where's Mendel?"

Em felt helplessness clawing back into her. "Arrested. Just now."

Gram jumped up, alarmed.

"It had been a long time—I fell asleep," she admitted. "When I woke, I went up to the shop and he wasn't there. I heard soldiers outside dragging him away. Something about treason." Em shared the rest, everything she overheard, and about the clue on the back of the door. Her face felt hot with shame, remembering how she cowered on the other side of the door instead of intervening.

Gram walked over while Em spoke. She grasped Em's hand with both of hers, looking grim.

"It was my fault," Em burst out, "I should've—"

"What?" Ilna interjected. "You should've fought off imperial soldiers? Gotten arrested too? No, love. It can't be helped." Ilna's words were comforting, but she couldn't quite meet Em's eye. Em felt the clawing helplessness climb from her stomach to her throat. If only she could fix some of this. Letting go of Gram's hand, Em pulled Mendel's tree paper from her pocket.

"Here's what he left me." Em stepped over to the fireplace, pushed aside the teacups, and smoothed the tree paper out on the low table. Both older women leaned toward the document. Gram scanned it quickly, then sat back. Ilna studied it closely, as if trying to work something out. Em watched Gram with new eyes. The older woman had seen the paper before. How long had she held secret meetings and traversed the tunnels right under Em's nose? And Mendel, who knows what secrets he had kept.

"Well?" she interjected, focusing on Ilna again.

"Regrowing of a new tree might be possible," Ilna said.

Em raised her eyebrows. She suspected as much, looking at the paper herself. But how did Mendel come by this document?

"Maybe Mendel had a spare after last time," Ilna mused.

"So, you all know about the protective tree," Em said.

Gram nodded with a guilty expression. Ilna looked at Em, surprised. "I imagine anyone over a certain age was there at the planting. But some of the younger generations are blissfully ignorant. We had to figure it out on our own last time."

Em seized on that. "Last time. Yes. Tell me what happened." She perched on the arm of the chair and waited.

"I remember the storm. I was still married to Vanin then, and he had come home in a rage that evening, like he did sometimes when weather prevented them from fishing. A strong wind blew the warding tree, a maple, to the ground.

"I opened the *Leaflet* office the next day and the mob appeared. They smashed my windows with a brick. People I had grown up with. Scattered and tore my printed papers. Dumped out my ink. Vanin was with them, but he didn't seem to recognize me. They used their fists on me. Vanin, too, although he never had before."

Ilna closed her eyes and shuddered. Em waited a few moments, knowing that Ilna was reliving one of the worst days of her life. An image of the bookseller, transformed by his rage, flashed in her mind. Perhaps Ilna's ex-husband had been similarly affected.

"In the aftermath, Mendel, Gram, and your parents helped me clean up."

A flag raised in Em's brain at the mention of her parents. New details about them were scarce. "They were not part of the mob?" she asked hopefully.

"They were part of the solution, love. When Gram found details of the trees in one of her books, they volunteered to help."

"One of her books," Em looked quickly at Gram, who did not look back. But Em detected a slight shaking of her head. *Ilna doesn't know about* The Standard Book of Anything, Em thought with rising panic. Did Gram not trust their friend? She schooled her face and turned back to Ilna, who was still speaking.

"The book detailed how one of the trees could be obtained, which Gram shared with the three who went on the quest. Your parents and Mendel. They set off, came back, and we had a new tree."

"Where did they go?"

"I think somewhere around the capital city."

"Did you not remember what they did? Maybe it's printed in an old *Leaflet*?"

Ilna flushed. "I was…not functional when they came back."

Em's eyebrows flew up.

"To my shame," Ilna said, "the madness overtook me eventually."

"Is that what a fallen tree does? Induce madness?" Pieces slid into place.

"We think the protection of the tree—in addition to external protections—provided a mental barrier against the darkest of all human emotions. When the tree fell, the mental barrier was gone, and we weren't prepared..." Em looked to Gram, who was still watching Ilna with a pained expression. *Destruction from within*, Em thought, recalling the passage she had read. How does one defend against that?

Ilna gathered herself with a shaky breath and continued. "We had hoped Mendel could remember more about where they went and how they acquired a tree. But with him arrested and your parents gone, we are blind as we ever were."

Em's head felt a little foggy. "Why did my parents volunteer?"

"Oh, Em." Ilna *tsk*ed sympathetically. "They loved you so much, you must know that. They didn't exactly volunteer for the journey, if that eases your mind. They never would've left, except they were the few people who could reliably go. A lot of people in town weren't quite themselves at that point."

"And the fever that killed them, was that related to the journey?"

Gram and Ilna exchanged a worried look. "We—I don't know. It was sudden," Ilna answered.

Em stared at the squeaky door while trying to piece together all she had learned. Her parents fixed this last time. Her parents may have died because of their efforts with the tree. The tree had fallen. Again. Mendel had been taken by soldiers. As they sat here, everyone in town was experiencing a flood of dark feelings. Come to think of it, Em didn't feel great either.

"Em?" Ilia's voice broke through. Em turned to see Gram and Ilna watching her with concern.

"Thanks for telling me," Em said woodenly. "I'm fine. We can fix this. I just need to figure out what to do next. How do we get Mendel free?"

After a stunned pause, Ilna stood and squeezed Gram's hand in farewell. "I should probably get back to town and discover Mendel's location. I'm arranging a meeting at dusk at the *Leaflet*. For anyone who is still master of themselves. We can decide what to do there. In the meantime, see if you can find that old book," Ilna smiled wryly and exited the cottage. The door hinges squeaked to announce her departure.

Gram eyed Em with concern once more. Em pretended not to notice and moved to collect the tea things. "I...need a minute." She ferried the dishes off to the kitchen. Setting them haphazardly on the counter, she fled to her room, fighting tears.

All her life, she had been told little snippets about her parents by the older townsfolk. Her father's legendary wit, and how he won them over when he, a stranger in town, was courting her mother. Her mother's speed in footraces when she was a child. Her love of card games. How much they adored her. But Em had very few memories and very few stories of her early years with them. And now she knew why. They had tried to repair a magical tree and got themselves killed. Em didn't know for sure that the tree killed them. But she felt in her heart that somehow, the two were connected.

Em dropped onto her bed and buried her face in the blankets. She lay there for some time, trying to regain control of her emotions. She felt empty, and sad, and small. And then a new feeling surfaced. Anger. At her parents. At everyone who knew her parents, who had lied to her. Gram, Ilna, Mendel, anyone else in town for the past seventeen years surely knew. Why had they kept it from her?

Then Em remembered one important fact.

The barrier protecting her brain from all these feelings was gone.

It would be so easy to give in. To let them spiral and float around her until all her friends and neighbors were the worst of villains. But she couldn't repair the damage if she simply joined the mob.

So, she sat up and tried to think through the facts of the situation.

Another thought popped into her head: Gram didn't trust Ilna with the book. But she had trusted Em. Despite everything else, Em held on to that one tangible fact. Gram had shown her the book.

The book. Was it still lying on the table where she had left it? It must have the same answers it provided Gram last time. She heard the door hinges squeak as she got up from her bed. *I need to oil that hinge today.* Em unlatched her bedroom door and strode out to reinvestigate the book.

Someone had entered the cottage. Gram stood stiffly in the middle of the room as the troop of soldiers trotted in and formed a wall. The soldiers from this morning. The soldiers who had arrested Mendel. But Mendel was not with them now.

They leered at the items in the small cottage, at anything of value, like they were ready to ransack the place. The scar-faced captain issued orders. "You two search that side room. You search the book-cases. Jemson, check the cupboard. The rest of you, get to it."

"Stop!" Em found her feet and bolted forward, moving to stand in front of Gram. Em's eyes shot daggers at each of the soldiers in turn. Most looked past her, but many of them halted at her command. The captain stared at Em for a long moment, letting out a grunt of frustration. Noticing the men and women behind him were still, he repeated his order through gritted teeth. "Start searching!" They jumped into action and fanned out to the various nooks of the cottage. Em heard sounds of shattering glass and their possessions being thrown about.

"How dare you come in here? We have done nothing wrong, and we won't be bullied," she seethed at the captain.

"Emaline Strider, I presume," he growled back. "You have caused enough mischief this morning. Know your place, girl, unless you want to find yourself in a jail cell."

"Found something, sir," shouted a man from Gram's room. Despite his announcement, the crashing and smashing continued unabated. The captain's glare was temporarily directed away from Em, so she glanced back. Gram's lips were pressed in a thin line, and she stared straight ahead. The victorious soldier reentered the living area holding the tree drawing aloft. It fluttered as he made his way to the captain. Em's mind raced. She wasn't sure what they intended, but Mendel had gone to great lengths to prevent this band having possession of that paper. And it might be their only way to replant.

As the man approached, the captain nodded approvingly and reached out his hand. Hardly knowing what she was doing, but knowing she had to act, Em stuck up her hand and snatched the paper, just before the captain could reach it.

Chaos ensued. The soldier who carried the paper moved like molasses. The captain's eyes flashed with rage as he whirled on Em. She ducked away, but as she evaded fists and rifle butts, she was cornered near the smoldering hearth. "Stop her!" Two more soldiers vaulted the overstuffed chairs to block her. She was penned in. A man three times her size moved in on her menacingly. Behind the man, Gram watched in fear, but Em also detected a glimmer of something else. Pride?

"Hand that over, by order of the empress."

Em recoiled at the command from the captain. She had to keep Mendel's notes out of their hands.

"No," she said stubbornly, holding it behind her back. "I don't know what you think this is, but it's nothing of importance to you."

The sound of a gun cocking made Em stiffen.

"Hand over the drawing, or we will take it from you," the captain issued calmly.

"Give it." The painful rusty words came from Gram's lips.

Em met Gram's eyes with horror, then slowly handed the parchment to the man in front of her.

The man turned back to the captain, who gave him a quick nod. He spun and tossed the scrap into the hearth fire; flames licked up from the embers to consume the thin paper. She heard her own voice roar in anger as she rushed directly at the man. Then, with a thunking noise, the world went dark.

CHAPTER 5

he mages and advisers debated the nature of the protective barrier. They established that the barrier should be a prevention of ill thought and intention that could lead to crimes and malcontent. This safeguard would prevent any number of undesirable situations in the small hamlets. Thus, the warding tree of protection was conceived.

EM FELT a shooting pain in her temples. Fluttering open her eyes, she saw the living room ceiling, and that one spot in the roof that needed to be rethatched. Then the whole horrible scene came back, including the rifle butt that caused the shooting pain in her head. "Owww," she moaned, sitting up slowly.

The room was in shambles. Cushions on their wooden chairs had been torn apart. Gram's lovely books ripped and scattered throughout the room. Dishes shattered on the floor. The fireplace was cold.

The house was empty. Judging by the shadows in the room, it was midafternoon. Which meant she had been out for at least an hour or two.

The pain in her head pulsed, and she reached up a hand to find something wet in her hair. Blood. Her head was bleeding. Dizzily, she sat up and looked around. A dishtowel lay on the floor by the hearth where Em had fallen. She bunched it up and held it to her head wound. Crumb, she was dizzy.

"Gram?" she called out.

Silence greeted her.

"Gram!"

She stumbled to her feet and rushed to Gram's room. Then to her own room, searching but not finding her guardian.

They might've arrested her. Em shook with anger. Perhaps Gram was on their list, like Mendel.

Glancing down, she noticed her cream blouse was splattered with blood. *Not a very practical color,* was Em's petty thought. Then she remembered Mendel's arrest and felt instant remorse for judging his gift. Pulling the blouse over her head, she tossed it aside, and began to rinse the blood out of her light brown hair with a pitcher of water over the sink. Finally, pulling on a clean blue work shirt, she braided her wet hair and tied it off with a simple ribbon.

Feeling steadier, Em suddenly gasped. The book. Did they take that too?

She stumbled toward the table. There was a pile of books on the table and floor, all roughly tossed about. She started pawing through the pile on the table and found *The Standard Book of Anything* at the bottom. Still open, but the text now detailed the dangers of a particular garden snail. Em let out a breath. Scooping it up, she closed the cover and reopened it to a random page. The book had told Gram what to do seventeen years ago. Perhaps it would do the same for Em. It reopened to the snails article, so she began to read, looking for the odd sentence out of place.

The common garden snail is a species of land snail. It is a terrestrial pulmonate gastropod mollusk in the family Helicidae, which includes some of the most familiar land snails. The snail is relished as food in some areas, but it is also widely regarded as a pest in gardens and in agriculture, especially in regions where it has been introduced invasively and where snails are not considered a menu item.

They are numerous in Gillamor, the capital city of Esnania, along with many other pests that surround lush gardens of the city dwellers. These gardens produce rare plants that the snails find delicious and helpful to their survival. See "Tourism of Gillamor Gardens."

Em stopped reading. If she understood this book, it would point her in the right direction, but maybe not provide all the details at once. Seeds and plants in the Gillamor gardens? It reinforced Ilna's story that Mendel and her parents went to the capital city all those years ago. Em would need to go to Gillamor. She could volunteer at the meeting tonight. She flipped over to the "Tourism" article, and nearly dropped the book. There on the page was a reproduction of Ilna's *Leaflet*, dated from long ago. Eagerly, Em began to read.

In light of recent events in Brookerby, nine prominent citizens met at the Leaflet *headquarters to discuss plans for improving the town. Citizens will recall that several riots have occurred over the past few days, and many storefronts have been damaged or destroyed by marauding groups of malcontented villagers. There have also been other disastrous occurrences, listed on page three, that have brought our normally cheerful village to its breaking point.*

The meeting was attended by the tailor, Mendel, whose own shop was brutally destroyed two days prior, and Anne Strider, with her family. Anne lost her childhood home to fire last week. A few citizens were put out of the meeting when they started shouting and trying to overturn the large printing press in the Leaflet *office. As evidenced by this publication, they were unsuccessful.*

Several volunteers have left town in search of a magical solution to our town's problem. As we all know, magic has become rarer than it was even thirty years ago, so a solution may not present itself. Nevertheless, we wish them luck. This editor encourages her readers to remain kindhearted and vigilant in the face of violence and uncertainty. Brookerby will endure.

Meeting Held for Town Revival
Brookerby Leaflet, *4ᵗʰ lunar month, 789 RQ*

EM CLOSED THE BOOK, standing stunned with her hand on the cover. That article could've been tomorrow's headline. History was truly repeating itself. But strangely, Em was encouraged by Ilna's words. *Brookerby will endure.*

Em grabbed Mendel's brown leather knapsack to review its contents. He had packed some bread, cheese, apples, a waterskin, a bedroll, matches, and a substantial coin purse. Apparently, he had expected to start his journey today. Em wondered if he had been reunited with Gram in the town's holding cell. She shuddered, and then suddenly her stomach flipped. She should try and rescue them. After all, the marshall had asked her to play locksmith a few times for that holding cell. The lock was old; she could easily break them out.

And then what? she asked herself. *Be arrested yourself? Take them out into the wilderness until this blows over? Watch the town fall to ruin while the soldiers stand by and do nothing? Send Mendel and Gram off to find a new tree, to die like your parents?*

She shook her head. The last thought was irrational. A journey didn't mean death. And Mendel was probably the best person to go and find a new tree. After all, he had already done it once before. But Em couldn't shake the feeling that she needed to go herself. Maybe it was her own sense of responsibility for how things had shaken out so far. She had ignored the crack in the tree. She had fallen asleep in the tunnels. She had surrendered the tree drawing.

Ironically, a jail cell was probably the safest place in town until a new tree could be planted, she rationalized. Mendel and Gram could take care of themselves. The best thing she could do was bring back a new tree as quickly as possible. She would tell Ilna that a town meeting was unnecessary and then set out today.

Em slid *The Standard Book of Anything* into Mendel's knapsack, along with a change of clothes and a few of her tools she considered essential. She grabbed her wide-brimmed sun hat from the hook by the door. Gripping the handle, she pulled open the door and was confronted by an ugly squeak from the door hinges.

Stopping, she dropped her pack and ran to the cabinet where she kept the oil. At least she would do one thing right today. Retrieving the oilcan, she squirted a few drops on each hinge, and pulled the door back and forth to work the lubricant throughout. The squeak subsided, then disappeared.

Putting the oil away, she snatched a small piece of paper to leave a note. She scribbled:

I volunteer. Stay safe.

If Gram were freed and came home, she would understand. But if they were lucky, the soldiers would not. Lifting the knapsack to her shoulder once more, she left through the silent door.

Through the tunnel, Em took the fork to the *Leaflet* office, and emerged under the rug in Ilna's office.

"Ilna?" she shouted, pushing the carpet aside.

"Who is it?" Ilna responded, sounding very faint.

Em followed the voice, emerging into the printing shop. "It's Em. Listen, I'm going to go find a tree. You don't need to have a meeting."

She spied Ilna, who sat on the floor under her printing press. Ducking down to meet her eyes, Em could immediately tell this was not the same woman she had spoken to earlier that day.

"What's the use?" Ilna wept, half her face smeared in ink. "Why bother with meetings and trees when all it does is get your friends arrested and killed."

Em sat on the floor, feeling very uncomfortable. In all the years Ilna had been like family to Em, she had never behaved like this. She had been steady—until now.

In a real sense, Ilia's words were true, and they threatened to capsize Em as well. But Em steadied her mind by reminding herself that they both were feeling the effects of the tree. And Ilna had given in to them.

She took the printer's inky hand. "You are allowed to feel these things, but know that you don't have to let this consume you."

Ilna gripped Em's hand like it was her last tether to reality. "I feel— like I'll never be hopeful again."

"I promise you, I will make this right."

After a few moments of holding her friend's hand, Em coaxed a shivering but slightly recovered Ilna out from under the machine and guided her upstairs to the small flat where she lived. Em made a cup of tea and tucked Ilna in a comfy chair with a quilt. When she was certain her friend was safe and comfortable, Em pulled closed the door and headed back to the tunnels. She had never been more alone in her entire life.

She emerged by her cottage again, and a wave of fear swept over her. The problem was just too big. Better to wait for Gram and Mendel to come home.

She moved to the garden gate, but then hesitated, hand on the latch. The longer they waited, the more danger Brookerby faced. Em had to go. She was the only one who could. She turned away from the gate, her feet facing the western path.

But she was following the advice of an old crazy book. That didn't make any sense. She took a step toward the cottage.

Then she thought of the mob. The soldiers. Mendel. Gram. Ilna. Somebody needed to fix this mess. She could do nothing if she stayed in Brookerby, and soldiers would likely arrest her, or the cloud of madness would overwhelm her.

Brookerby will endure.

She turned her toes back away from home and—before her emotions could stop her—she began walking. She needed to bring back the only thing that would save Brookerby now—a new tree.

CHAPTER 6

he empress proclaimed that warding trees would anchor each village in Esnania. Beneath the protective shield of these trees, townspeople could flourish. Henceforth, their lives would be blessed with serenity, fortune, and refuge from the ills of the world, so long as their town tree remained standing.

THE CAPITAL CITY WAS SEVERAL DAYS' walking, south of Brookerby. The Imperial Road through town would take her that direction, but Em didn't want any more run-ins with the soldiers. Nor did she want them following her. Shrugging her shoulders to adjust her pack, Em took the walking path west away from town, past the hidden tunnel entrance behind Gram's cottage, up the hill, and across sloped fields of weeds and tiny yellow wildflowers. The path was a narrow dirt trail through the flora that Em was confident she could follow for a day or two until it connected with the Imperial Road, far away from town.

But a few minutes into the climb up the hill, Em was ready to leave the path entirely. The rain from the night before had soaked the trail, turning it into squishy mud that slowly baked in the afternoon sun.

The soldiers, if they were looking, could find Em quite easily from her deep muddy tracks. Em sighed and stepped off the path, swiping her feet in the tall weeds to clear her boots. She knew she had to head south, so she could use the sun as a guide, keeping it to her right through the afternoon. She forged into the tall grasses and continued through the hills, relieved that her slacks protected her from burrs and thorns that brushed against her legs.

At a high point, she turned to look back over the town. From her vantage, she could see the whole valley. A miniature Gram's house with stone walls, thatched roof, and the tiny garden surrounding it. The footbridge spanning the creek was visible in the large hole left by the downed sycamore tree. The shop storefronts in town, with their brightly colored doors and dangling signs, were little more than specks, a village for bugs. She saw smoke coming from somewhere on the far side of town, near the small schoolhouse where she had spent her younger years learning her sums and geography.

Not friendly smoke from a hearth, but smoke from a fire.

A flutter of panic worked through her stomach, and she was on the verge of turning back to...she didn't know...raise the alarm? Help? She saw a few people running up the main street, followed by the town alarm bell ringing. The fluttering settled into a sour pressure in her gut. With the mob this morning, and the soldiers' ransacking, she wouldn't be surprised if the fire had been intentional. She had to remind herself that she was helping her town more by leaving it behind. With difficulty, she turned south once more, and started moving her feet.

It was slow going, wading through the hip-high grasses and climbing up and down the slopes. She felt like an auger, slowly drilling her way through the difficult land in front of her. She held her pack straps with both hands to keep them above the sharp weeds and nettles. Em discovered the demon-weeds early in her walk, and she had a few paper-thin swipes of beaded blood on the backs of her hands as souvenirs.

After several hours, her stomach growled, and her feet ached. At another hill crest, she swiveled back to see if she could still glimpse home and realized that she could not. The sour knot in her stomach returned, and she realized she was farther from Brookerby than she had ever gone before.

Once before, she had ventured into the unknown. When Em was nine years old, Gram had denied her permission to climb on the roof to rig up a rather dangerous flying experiment. It was foolhardy, according to Gram. Em remembered being very angry, certain her invention would change the world.

In a fit of childish indignation, she decided to run away from home. She laughed now to remember how she stomped and shouted that she hated living with Gram and that she was going to leave and find a new family.

Gram didn't stop her. She calmly packed Em a lunch, guided her into a jacket, and waved goodbye. Em had scornfully marched down the garden path and up the hill away from home. Dark clouds matched her mood as they hung overhead.

Little Em made it to the top of the hill, ate her packed lunch, and then started walking as far as she dared. It began raining, and she took shelter under a pine tree. Feeling like a drowned kitten, Em discovered she wasn't angry anymore, and when the rain let up, she scampered home.

Gram had played it just right: equal levels of surprise and indifference that Em had decided to come back. And then a tasty dinner to seal the deal.

The memory made Em smile at first. Gram always knew exactly how to react to Em's wild schemes. But the story suddenly felt tainted. She had tried to run away then. And now she actually was leaving. Just like her parents had. To continue, she had to ignore the tether in her heart, even now, tying her back to the only home she remembered. She hoped Gram was okay. That Ilna was okay. That Mendel, and Earl, and Fern, and Gendry, and little Grady were okay. She was doing this for them.

❧

THE FIERCE GRASSES gave way to uneven pastures with livestock grazing in them. Em spotted a mansion-sized metal cube in the center of one of the fields. Whoever planted the crops had left a wide alley around it. She'd never seen anything like it before. Was it functional? She inched around the fence to get a closer look.

There were no wheels on the bottom, and the design was quite simple. It may have been a harvester or some other kind of farming equipment from the Age of Magic, left out here to rust. Em hunted around the cube for rivets or any kind of seam in the metal, but it was a single solid piece. She wouldn't know how to begin taking it apart. Em knocked on the metal, and her knuckles thudded rather than echoed. She understood why these impenetrable boxes were being replaced by ordinary gears and wheels. At least you could fix those when they broke down. Reluctantly, Em pressed on. She glanced back occasionally, using the rusty box as a landmark. But she wasn't moving very quickly.

Frustrated by the zigzagging route she was following, Em hopped a log fence, hoping for a shortcut. Halfway across the field, she heard a snort to her left.

Whipping her head around, she saw two pointy horns attached to a grumpy-looking black bull. He let out another snort, staring her down with onyx marble eyes.

Em took a step away, and the bull trotted slowly in a semicircle, turning to face her head-on.

She darted her eyes to the nearest fence. Could she outrun the creature? Before she could consider her options, the beast lowered its head, lurching forward in a charge, horns aiming for her abdomen.

With a yelp, Em sprinted to the exit, leaping over the logs just as the bull crashed into the barrier.

She lay in the grass, wheezing, until her heart slowed back to normal and the irritated bull wandered back to the middle of the field. Then Em trembled to her feet, resolving to remain outside the fences from now on.

～

THE LATE AFTERNOON sun was sweltering, even as it dipped in the sky. Em's hair, still damp and plaited, clung to the nape of her neck. She stopped under the shade of a large tree next to a field of sheep and slumped against the trunk, sloppily wiping her face with the sleeve of her shirt and taking off her wide-brimmed hat to fan herself. She took a swig of water from the cracked leather waterskin Mendel had packed. It was odd. She had been drinking from it all afternoon, but it still felt full.

Once she cooled down and her breathing slowed, she pulled out a piece of cheese and a generous hunk of bread from her pack. In all the chaos of the day, she had forgotten to eat lunch, and just now realized how famished she was. She also reached for an apple, devouring it before stopping herself. She had a long way to go before the next town, and her meager food supplies were diminishing. But her stomach still rumbled. She took another drink from the canteen and distracted herself by reopening *The Standard Book of Anything*. Perhaps it would point her to a nearby edible plant.

No such luck. The book fell open at "The Development of Arthritis in the Elderly." Gram had arthritis. Maybe the book thought she was with Gram. She rolled her eyes, but knew better than to question the seemingly random factoids the book presented to her:

> *The term arthritis literally means "joint inflammation," but it is generally used to refer to more than one hundred different conditions that affect the joints and may also affect the muscles and other tissues. Osteoarthritis, a degenerative arthritis, is the most common form, which happens due to the breakdown of the tissue inside the joints. This is more common in the elderly due to "wear and tear" over time. Often, light exercise, like walking, can be beneficial. It's also important for sufferers of arthritis not to get too cold, which is why many elderly move south. (See "Influential Cities in the South.")*

Em breathed a sigh of relief that turned into a short "hah." If she trusted this book, she could feel confident in her decision to travel south. But the book was suggesting the elderly should move south.

"Gram isn't here, Book. It's just me," she whispered to it, feeling foolish. There was, obviously, no sign that it heard her. *At least I'm going the right way*, she thought, flipping pages to arrive at the "Influential Cities in the South" article.

Gillamor is the second-largest populated city in Esnania, behind Abingdon, both of which anchor the Sun Corridor. The city is located 108 miles southeast of the Growtide province and 60 miles north of the Esnania-Aglen border. Gillamor is also the seat of the sovereign of Esnania, the empress.

The empress is traditionally housed in the Golden Lark Palace. It is named for the golden patterns and intricate carvings in the palace wall, which display local birds and flowers. (See "Local Flora of the Southern Cities.") The star-shaped fountain within her palace is magical. It is not only decoration, but the only known artifact where unbreakable oaths can be administered. Oaths are required by the empress in cases of dire importance, in official treaties with other sovereign nations, and in cases where the other party may not reliably keep their word.

The empress. The soldiers worked for her. Until this morning, the empress had seemed very far removed from her world, like a queen in a fairy story. She governed their country, but nothing she really did impacted Em's tiny world. Until today, at least. Now Em's home was being destroyed, and her closest friends in the world were being held under the woman's insignia. Em found it very hard not to resent her.

The fountain was a new piece of information. As a child, Em had heard many tales of unbreakable oaths, mostly from Gram when she had neglected her chores. They seemed like legends told to frighten children. One particularly gruesome tale involved a girl who had vowed never to take things that weren't hers. The story girl ended up losing her fingers to the power of her own oath. Em's eyes rolled involuntarily. Perhaps the empress intended to frighten her subjects. Frightened people didn't rebel. Em closed the book. It was very unlikely that she would need to know more of the Golden Lark Palace or its magical fountain that administered oaths.

The sun continued to sink toward the hills. Repacking her dwindling food and the book, Em rose and continued south.

CHAPTER 7

Her Royal Majesty embarked on a joyous processional. She planned to visit each village and bear witness as Bronwyn enchanted a sapling in the center of town. In this way, the empress signaled to her people that she was a very different ruler than her father.

EM WAS on the wrong side of nowhere by nightfall. The fields of sorghum and cattle had given way to an open, rolling plain. Em found a flat, rocky area near the top of a hill with a few trees and began to build a small fire. The day had been exceptionally warm, but the night air had a chill to it, so she was pleased Mendel had included matches in his pack.

Taking a long drink from the waterskin, she was surprised again at the weight of it. Staring down the narrow spout, she saw an impossibly high water level, almost as if it was newly filled when she wasn't looking. *Is this magical?* she wondered.

Testing the waterskin, she boldly dumped out what she estimated to be half the water. Righting the container, she peered in again to find it full. Em offered thanks to Mendel, but mischievously wished instead he had included a magical flagon of cider. Sipping from the skin once more, she spewed out the liquid in shock. It tasted like the apple cider Gram made! It was tangy and sweet and cold. Wiping her mouth with her sleeve, Em stared again at the unassuming waterskin. *Maybe it can produce any liquid*, Em thought.

Experimentally, she thought of wine. The pitcher changed to wine. She drank a small amount, and then quickly set it back down and thought of seawater. The pitcher was full of briny water. Then pear juice. Again, the waterskin filled with juice.

Where had Mendel been hiding this? Magical artifacts that still worked were rare, especially one that could produce any drink you desired. She imagined it must be worth a great deal. Shrugging her shoulders, Em wished again for cider. She continued to sip as she prodded her small campfire to life with a stick.

Once the fire blazed steadily, Em toasted some bread on a long stick and melted a bit of cheese on top. She ate slowly. When it was gone, she longed for more, but wanted to preserve what little she had left. *Darn Gram for feeding me so well over the years*, Em thought ruefully. It was much harder to tolerate mild hunger when she had never gone without before.

Em's mind turned to defense. She was alone, she needed sleep, and she couldn't stand guard while sleeping. Not that she expected any living soul to happen across her in this wilderness, but there were wild animals that might pose a threat. She had already heard the far-off cry of wild dogs. Each howl put her more on edge.

Circling her campsite, Em glanced up at the wild pines and maple trees around her. If she could scale one and sleep in it, then most predators couldn't reach her.

She grasped the first tree branch she could reach and tried to swing herself up. The thin branch snapped off in her hand, and she crashed to the ground. "Owwww," she whined.

Gingerly, she stood and brushed herself off. She searched for another low-hanging branch as she strolled among the mostly puny trees in sight of the campfire. She spotted one. Learning from her mistake, she tested the low-hanging branch by first dangling from it before trying to swing her body up. A cracking noise made her let go and continue searching.

The next three were also too thin or brittle, cracking dangerously or bending under her weight. Finally, she found a tree that seemed slightly sturdier, and the lowest branch held her weight without protest. She tested a few more branches of the tree before dropping to the ground once more.

She doused the fire using water from the waterskin. Then, snatching up her pack, she returned to the sturdy tree. Scaling it with her pack on her back was slow, but she was able to clamber up several branches to a vee in the trunk; this spot looked like it would keep her secure in the tree while she slept.

Without the campfire, she shivered, and she unpacked her blanket roll and quickly wrapped it around her. It would be a brisk night, but at least she wouldn't wake up to a wildebeest gnawing her leg off. She hung her pack on a nearby branch.

The moon was a sliver, not bright enough to scan through the book, so Em settled in, placed her hat over her face, and closed her eyes. One day of traveling, and she felt very, very capable.

EM'S FIRST repair job was unplanned. She had just finished primary school and Gram arranged for her to learn bookkeeping from Mendel, the tailor. "It's important for you to develop some skills," Gram advised. "I won't be around forever, and I want you to be self-sufficient."

Em had protested the bookkeeping. It seemed dull and soulless to her, but Gram was firm, so off to the tailor Em went one rainy morning.

She sat with Mendel for over an hour as he patiently walked Em through his accounts. She was a quick study with a head for numbers, so she found herself absorbing the new information with ease, but she dearly wished she were somewhere else.

Finally, the lesson ended, and Mendel returned to his back workroom. Moments later, he let out a loud yelp. Curious, Em padded in his wake to see rain dripping from the ceiling. The rainwater had intruded into the tailor's tidy shop.

As he rushed around trying to save his fabric from damage, Em decided to get a closer look at the leaks. She retrieved a ladder from the basement storeroom, dragged it up the stairs and out of the shop, and climbed to the roof in the rain.

It was liberating to climb to the roof. Even in the downpour, Em was surefooted, traversing the shingles and locating the hole. Em climbed back down and explained the leaks to Mendel. He scolded her for climbing the ladder in the rain, and instructed her to fetch the blacksmith for the repair.

When Em got to the blacksmith, the man was too busy to help, but handed her some oilcloth, putty, and new thatch, and explained the process of patching the holes.

Em followed his instructions and found the whole process thrilling. She climbed down from her successful patch, soaking wet, and reported back to Mendel that the roof was repaired. He was ecstatic and thanked her for fetching the blacksmith so quickly. Then the truth came out.

After that day, Em eagerly sought out broken things around town. She slowly acquired tools. And it made her happy. She felt free, and capable, and needed.

Em remembered the approval on Gram's face with pleasure. Smiling, she nestled deeper into the tree crook, wrapped her blanket tighter, and fell into a listless sleep.

Nearby, a lone wolf crept closer to the doused fire, circling the campsite and hunting for scraps.

EM AWOKE JUST BEFORE DAWN. Her back felt like it had been folded like one of Mendel's fabric bolts. She stiffly climbed down from her perch, taking her supplies with her. Bruises had bloomed on her arms and shoulders from the events of the previous day, and any pressure from the tree or her pack was unpleasant.

The sun hadn't yet breached the horizon, yet the sky lightened, and the air was still crisp. Em shivered, and on a whim, she wished for hot tea out of the waterskin, and received warm tea. "Close enough," she mumbled, sipping the hibiscus-flavored brew. Em ate an apple and the last bit of cheese for breakfast. Sending up a silent plea, she hoped for signs of civilization today, and a chance to replenish her food.

After the previous day's walk, she assumed she had put enough distance between herself and the soldiers in Brookerby. Maybe they hadn't even left town yet. Armed with the comfort of this reasoning, Em used the rising sun to navigate a southeastern path toward the Imperial Road.

Several hours of cutting across the countryside elapsed before Em spotted the gray ribbon of main road weaving its way through the fields. It was wide enough for four carts to traverse side by side and flanked with thick hedges. There was not a soul in sight. She had felt lost moving across the fields the way she had, and now she was back on track. Letting out an involuntary whoop, Em sprinted down the hill to the wide flattened-stone highway.

The pitch of the hill grew steeper, and Em tried to slow herself, but her body picked up speed, and her feet couldn't keep up. Her shoulders pitched forward, her hat flew off her head, and her heels left the ground. She tumbled down the last quarter of the hill, rolling through the weeds and dirt, her pack dropping on the hillside as she did. Finally, she lost momentum and sprawled at the base of the hill, behind the irregular hedges.

Em groaned for her poor back, still aching from the night in the tree. Then, involuntarily, she giggled to herself. *How long since I've rolled down a hill?* she wondered with a burst of laughter.

She lay a few moments more and relished the feeling of the shady ground on her cheek. Finally, rolling to her side, she glanced back at her pack, ten steps up the hill. With a sigh, she pushed herself to her feet and started climbing after her supplies.

With her back to the road, Em's ears detected footsteps. Many synchronized footsteps. Turning, she saw the very group she'd been avoiding: imperial soldiers.

It was impossible to miss the flashes of blue and gold from their uniforms, but the soldiers were still far away. Em couldn't tell if they were the same group that had terrorized her village, but they were marching from that direction. She yelped and dove for the cover of the bushes, dragging her pack behind her. With dread, she saw her hat still sitting on the hillside, in plain view of the road.

The marching grew louder. Em's heart clattered around the inside of her chest. She tried to remain perfectly still and watched the boots stomp by her hiding place from under the leafy branches of the shrubbery.

Once they had all passed and the footsteps faded, she counted to twenty and let out her breath. Relief flooded her. She had only seen boots—she didn't get a good look at the men and women—but it seemed a good policy to avoid soldiers, whether they recognized her or not. She prodded the side of her head, which was still tender from her wound the day before. *Yes, a very good idea to avoid soldiers,* she thought.

Rising, she brushed off her shirt and trousers, which were covered in dirt, and snatched up her pack. She labored back up the steep hill to retrieve her hat and slanted back down to cross the wide, dusty road.

Still a bit edgy, she decided to walk in sight of the main road, but behind the tree line on the opposite side, which would offer better cover than the fields. *I might even be able to slip by the soldiers once they make camp for the evening,* she planned, *if this tree cover continues all day.*

PICKING her way through the trees turned out to be more difficult than she thought, however. The route required significant bush-whacking for stretches at a time, and Em had to avoid thorns and burrs of all kinds as she ducked from tree to tree.

She pushed a particularly evil-looking, thorny branch out of her way only to see three more dangling in its place. Cursing, and realizing this route wasn't doing her any favors, she left the underbrush. Soldiers or no soldiers, she wasn't going to fight through thorns all the way to the capital city.

Yanking burrs from her pants, she absently stepped out of the trees, and heard a gun cock. Jerking her head up, she saw a squad of soldiers lounging in the grass on the other side of the road, eating their midday meal.

Slowly, Em released the burr she had been so absorbed in plucking off and held up her empty hands.

The soldier with the double-shot pistol looked her up and down, impassively. He called for the captain, who briskly strode up to them. She recognized the newcomer as the scar-faced captain she had met in Brookerby.

Biting back a string of curses, she tried a milder approach. "Good afternoon," she said. She avoided eye contact. Best-case scenario, he had somehow forgotten her, and would let her go on her way.

"Miss Emaline Strider, we meet once again. Drop your pack, please."

Of course he remembered her. She hadn't made a great impression.

She didn't know of any law she had broken, but that sometimes didn't stop soldiers from mistreating civilians. Ilna had printed five stories in the last month about soldiers overstepping reasonable bounds. Em focused on the barrel of the gun. Best to comply and hope they let her go. She slowly unslung the bag and lowered it to the ground. The other soldier still had his gun trained on her chest.

By now, a few others had drifted over. A brawny fellow with a surly expression was ordered to take the pack. Em recognized him as the brute who burned Mendel's tree paper.

He grabbed her pack and immediately turned it upside down to dump the contents. Em winced. Her blanket, matches, and waterskin fell into a disgusting-looking mud puddle. The final apple rolled away, bouncing into a ditch. *The Standard Book of Anything* fell into the grass with a sickening thud. The meager bunch of coins jingled and spilled out of their pouch. Her clothes and tools dropped in a heap.

Glancing stupidly at the bottom of the bag, the surly soldier flung it aside and reached for the pile. Another few soldiers wandered up. How many of them would remember her insults from yesterday?

Fright and ire mingled within her. She reminded herself to mind her manners in this encounter, as they decidedly had the upper hand. Glancing up, she met the captain's gray eyes with her blue ones as he studied her, his face unreadable. What would he do? She broke contact, studying his scar instead.

"Miss Strider, why are you traveling this road? Did we not leave you in Brookerby?"

Em bit back an ugly retort about arresting helpless old ladies, and instead answered the question. "Is traveling illegal, sir?"

"Highly irregular. These are dangerous times, and no one travels alone anymore unless they are criminals."

"I'm not a criminal!" Em blurted.

"That remains to be seen," the man responded evenly. "Jeralt, anything of interest?"

The surly man replied, "Some money, and this book, sir. But I can't figure..."

"Let's have a look, then. Finn?"

A slight man with spectacles inched forward—a man she didn't remember. He didn't look like a fighter, but he also wore armor and the blue-and-gold crest of the empress. She quickly scanned the faces of the gathering squad and recognized half of the soldiers from Brookerby. She unthinkingly reached up to rub the tender spot on her head.

Finn gently took the book from the ground. He must have been their resident scholar because he adjusted his spectacles and slowly scanned each page. A few of the other soldiers were idly collecting Em's coins back into the coin purse. She doubted they would all be returned.

Em focused back on the captain. "Miss Strider, what is your destination?" The captain's voice was mild, but his subordinate was still aiming a gun at her chest. She tried for innocence.

"Why, the capital city, sir. Isn't that where this road leads?"

"And what is your business there?"

Time to lie. "My town is not safe." Em couldn't help a pointed glare at the man. "I am traveling to my aunt, who owns a flower shop in Gillamor. I'm hoping she'll take me on as an apprentice."

Finn piped up as he continued turning pages, "There does seem to be quite a bit here about flowers and plants. Lots of herbal growing techniques. Odd that I have not heard of this text before."

Em was relieved that the book had decided to back up her story. "Oh, my Gram gave me that as a gift. I believe it was hers as a girl. Probably out of print now."

Finn nodded congenially. "Seems okay to me. A very dull read, though. You should find an updated text. I can give you the name of a bookseller in the capital city."

"Thank you, that would be very kind," Em simpered, reaching to retrieve her book. "Now, if there is nothing else, may I continue on my way?"

"Not quite yet, Emaline. It seems we have ruined your food, and your supplies are not sufficient for the journey," the captain said.

"Ah," Em hesitated. What was he playing at? "Is there a town nearby where I can restock?"

"Indeed, there is. But we would be happy to escort you all the way to the capital."

"Oh no. Not necessary at all, I assure you," Em said with a wave. That would be the worst possible outcome from this. She started toward her bag, which had been flung into the thistles. The captain's voice stopped her.

"Miss Strider."

She stiffened and turned. The gun was still trained on her. "Am I not free to go?"

"You are not. We will escort you. That was not optional. Jeralt, give the young lady her things."

Jeralt roughly snatched the book from Finn and shoved it carelessly into the pack, along with the muddy blanket roll, her tools and cloths, and the waterskin. The food he left in the dirt. He tossed her pack at her feet, and the other soldiers reluctantly dropped her coin purse in front of her. It hit the ground with a sparse clink.

The captain gestured for the gun soldier to lower his weapon, and then strode away, barking orders to the group still lounging in the meadow.

Em's mind clicked with competing logic. On one hand, this turn of events was disastrous. The empire had moved into her town quickly after the tree had fallen and seemed to be systematically rounding up anyone who knew anything about it. Since Em was in that circle, it was likely she would also eventually be arrested. Maybe that's what was happening right now, in a roundabout way. On the other hand, the soldiers who had raided her house were at least behaving (somewhat) professionally now. The squad was going to take her to the capital city and, in the meantime, keep her protected and fed. It was a fair deal. These roads weren't always safe for a lone traveler. Although, even with the soldiers, she might have to sleep with one eye open.

Scooping up her pack, Em tried to wipe the dirt off her blanket roll and ended up just smearing it all over her hand and sleeve. Grimacing, she wiped her hand on the grass, and then hurried to join the group forming up on the road.

Jeralt approached her again with a rope dangling from his hands. Em raised her eyebrows in disbelief. "What? Are you going to tie me up?"

Jeralt smirked. "A precaution. Captain Marcellus's orders."

Finn piped in, "Sorry, Miss Emaline. It's not personal. Typically, when an outsider joins a squad, they must be restrained. It's proper procedure."

Em froze. This was starting to feel less like safety and more like an arrest. She wondered if she should try and run for it. Glancing around, she saw most of the squadron watching her warily, including Captain Marcellus. Now was not the time to bolt.

She held out her wrists, pressed together, and Jeralt jerked the rope around them. It was rougher than was strictly necessary, and Em hypothesized that this fellow had a mean streak. He gave the ropes another good yank, and the rough fibers bit into her skin. Her wrists would be raw by evening. *I suppose this is payback for calling them spineless weasels*, she thought ruefully.

CHAPTER 8

In the midst of the first tree gifting festival, a cry sounded. A beloved child had been afflicted with painful boils and was wailing in agony. The villagers tried to soothe the child. The empress, while pained by the child's cries, was optimistic. Perhaps her gift would prevent future tragedies such as this.

LATER THAT AFTERNOON, Em's prospects looked grim. Her wrists cramped from her bindings, and she was being hustled along at a quick march by the soldiers. They traveled faster than she had walked on her own, and it would have been very efficient had she trained for it. Instead, her leg muscles ached, and she struggled to catch her breath. Worse, there had been no opportunities to quietly slip away, or fall back, as procedure dictated that she be placed right in the middle of the group. If she started to slow, someone from behind would shove her back to the middle. Usually Jeralt.

Finn was almost worse. He kept asking her questions about her supposed apprenticeship with her aunt, and she had to keep inventing backstory. She struggled to keep all the lies straight; it was mentally exhausting.

Captain Marcellus maintained a stoic silence, but she caught his gaze more than once during their march. His gray eyes were like stone walls, completely expressionless. Em tried to wheeze out a question about Gram and Mendel, but Marcellus quickly responded with a guttural growl and moved farther away from her.

After several hours, they abruptly left the hilly plains and entered a thick forest. Many branches had fallen across the byway, and often the squadron would have to stop to move a large log blocking their path. Roots twisted out under the road, pushing up the flat pavers; Em tripped often on the uneven ground, nearly falling, until hands caught her and shoved her back to standing.

Finally, as the sun dipped below the trees, the squadron halted, turning off the road into a large clearing. Jeralt gave Em one last shove, and she collapsed to the grass with an "oof" and a sigh of relief.

The soldiers went multiple directions: setting up camp, building a fire, and establishing a watch for the evening. Em pulled herself up to a tree stump and slid her pack down her arm to rest it on the ground. Her hands were still tied, and she was so exhausted that she could do little but wait until directed where to go.

She took in her surroundings. Her stump was near the edge of camp, farthest away from the road. Behind her was a thicket of trees and tall shrubs. She considered inching away as preparations buzzed around her. Suddenly, one of the women in the squad stood before her. She was fit and long-legged; she looked like she could give Jeralt a run for his money. "I'm Briggs," she introduced herself briskly. "Do you need to, ah, relieve yourself?"

Em nodded gratefully.

"Come on, then." Briggs gestured toward the thicket just beyond the perimeter. Em rose, awkwardly inching her pack back on her shoulder, and then had a thought. "Briggs? Would you mind untying me? Just for…this. It will be difficult without hands."

Briggs glanced back, and the problem registered. The corners of her lips ticked up in amusement. "Didn't think of that when they set the restraint regulations, did they? Yeah, we can let you use your hands. But leave your pack."

Em smiled wearily. At least Briggs was reasonable.

They tramped several minutes through the thicket until they were out of earshot, and then Briggs pointed to a nearby tree. "You can go behind there for some privacy. I advise you not to run." She caught Em's bound wrists and cut the knot quickly with a small knife, saving the rope.

Em thanked her and hobbled over to the tree, trying to memorize her surroundings without any obvious head swiveling. Briggs had good instincts; Em *was* looking for an opportunity to dash. In this thicket, Briggs would hear her immediately and easily catch her. She could try climbing a tree, but Em had flashbacks to her climbing attempts the night before and quickly crossed that off the list. Briggs's advice was solid. Em would not run. For now.

In the dusk, crickets were starting to chirp, and Em had delayed long enough. She did what was needed and rounded the tree back to Briggs. Then her eye caught on something. It was a hollow in the ground, exposing the roots of a nearby tree. She almost didn't see it but for a small shadow in the dirt, edged in green moss. The hole looked deep, and wide enough to hide a person. In the dim light, she passed some downed branches that could be used for camouflage. It would be easy to miss, especially in the dark. If she could get back out here tonight, maybe she could hide and wait out the search party. Her heart started to thump loudly.

She counted her steps, taking note of landmark rocks and trees as she walked back to camp with Briggs. At the clearing, Briggs retied her hands, and Em thanked her graciously. Briggs gave her a friendly nod and led her back to the stump where her pack sat, untouched.

Smells of stew wafted through their camp. The sky was getting darker, and the only light came from the campfire and from lanterns where the soldiers gathered. Bawdy laughter broke out in the group, and Em thought she heard a lute being tuned. She wondered if it was an imaginary lute.

Briggs made a beeline for the stew, and Em aimed to follow, her mouth watering. She hadn't eaten a proper meal in two days. She took a few steps toward the campfire where Briggs had gone, but then noticed how close she was to the thicket. And how alone she was. And how no one was watching. Regretfully, because food and music sounded better than cowering in a dark hole all night, she silently lifted her pack and took a few slow steps backward, into the thicket. Once she was several trees in, she turned and ran, recounting her steps.

She kept her ears perked for shouts of discovery, but none came yet. The woods had grown dark quickly, but she remembered the flag-stone at the halfway point, and the birch with white bark near the fallen log, which was a few paces from the burrow. She nearly tripped over rocks and stones, panic rising with each misstep and because her tied hands would not catch her. Finally, the hole was at her feet. Tossing in her pack before her, she grabbed a large fallen branch and placed it over the top. Then, she dropped blindly into the dark.

The hole was deeper than it appeared, and she fell to the bottom with a thud, landing on uneven terrain. Something in her ankle crunched, and immediate pain shot through her. She crumpled and bit the sides of her cheeks to keep from whimpering.

Nearby was a large, flat stone with a sharp-looking edge; she grabbed it, held it firmly between her knees and started sawing at her wrist bonds. Her ankle was throbbing, but she gritted her teeth against the pain. One problem at a time.

Finally, the rope snapped, and she was able to unwind it and work out her wrists, which were scraped raw, as expected. Crawling toward her pack, she grabbed the waterskin, wishing for some salve. It produced an oily substance that had a sharp woody odor to it. She gently rubbed the medicine into her wrists, then on her ankle, feeling an instant cool relief.

Unable to see much, she decided to leave examination of her ankle for the daylight. Wrapping herself in her muddy blanket, Em settled in for a miserable night. Above her, soldiers' clipped shouts began to ring through the trees.

~

EM FOUND it difficult to sleep at first. Her pursuers passed impossibly close to her foxhole several times, but never looked down.

If they had, her blanket, muddy thanks to Jeralt, was good camouflage.

The night grew colder and the shouting less frequent, and finally Em drifted into a fitful sleep. She had a vivid nightmare that Finn opened *The Standard Book of Anything* and found a detailed list of everything Em had ever done wrong. He read each one, looking more and more disappointed, while Briggs stood by menacingly with a knife. Then her Gram appeared with a giant steak on a plate, which Em tried to eat with her hands, but it was slippery and kept falling out of her fingers. As she dropped to the floor to retrieve the steak, Captain Marcellus grabbed her ankle and started squeezing it until she yelped in pain.

She woke with a start. The sky was the somber gray of predawn, and a lone bird warbled nearby. Her stomach let out a mighty growl, and she remembered with concern that she hadn't eaten anything since breakfast yesterday.

She considered staying put for another day until the soldiers were truly gone. After all, they would probably be breaking camp in another hour or two. But her hiding spot would be much easier to find in the daylight. That was the sobering thought that drove her to move.

Standing, she yelped and sank back to a sitting position. Her ankle was red and swollen to twice the size. *Not good.* It needed to be stabilized if she wanted to make her escape today.

Em reached up for a sturdy-looking stick dangling from the branch above. She gave it a hard tug and it split off and fell on top of her. "Oomf." She reached for the rope she had removed from her wrists last night.

She worked quickly, aligning the stick along her ankle and looping the rope around until it felt stable. She carefully slid the boot she'd removed for the procedure over the splint and loosely tied it. The fix was crude, but she could put some weight on it. It should last until the next town.

Now, how to get out. She stood gingerly. More birds sang, and the sky was lighter. She had to hurry before the soldiers woke up and started patrolling again. If she raised her arms, she could just reach the edge of the pit, but Em wasn't confident she could pull herself up. She studied the walls and her available tools for solutions.

Brainstorming, Em collected a few more sturdy sticks and pulled out the hammer from her bag. She pounded the sticks into the dirt wall of the pit, making footholds for herself. After each was hammered in, she gave it a tug, or partially stood on it, to make sure it would hold her. Proud of her rudimentary ladder, she dropped her hammer back in the pack, and slung the bag over her shoulder.

Using her makeshift handholds and footholds, she climbed her way out. It was painstakingly slow, as her ankle would not accept much weight. Finally, she wiggled through the small opening between the edge of the hole and the tree branch that masked her hiding spot. Flopping to the dirt, she sighed in relief.

Then, rising, Em started her slow trek, delicately stepping along the uneven forest floor. She wasn't headed strictly south, but her path wound away from the road and around the clearing full of soldiers. *Hopefully toward a medic,* she mused as she limped along in the early morning light.

SHE HAD BEEN MOVING for over an hour when she heard barking. She stopped quickly, straining her ears. It was getting closer, coming from the direction of the road. Looking around, she spotted an evergreen tree with low branches. *If a wild dog finds me, I'd rather not be on the ground,* she thought desperately.

She limped over to the promising pine. Her arms protested the climb, but fear fueled her when the barking animal burst into view, and she pulled herself higher, ducking behind thick branches of evergreen needles.

The beast stopped nearby and put its nose to the earth. *It's tracking me!* Em thought with panic as the dog started following her trail directly toward the tree she was currently in. She gripped the main trunk, silently hoping the animal didn't spot her. Perhaps the beast would lose interest.

The dog stopped at the base of the evergreen, stared up the trunk with a tilted head, and then sat, looking glum.

Then sounds of crashing came through the underbrush. Em silently cursed. The dog wasn't alone. Footsteps approached the tree, and a laughing deep voice called out, "There you are, Bob! What did you find? Did you tree a squirrel?"

The man came into view. Em could see the top of his sandy-brown hair, and she ducked back, farther into the branches. He patted the dog, presumably named Bob, on the head, and then, almost as an afterthought, looked up.

His face was young, maybe a few years older than herself, but square, as if shaped for a rock wall. His dark eyebrows shot up when he spotted her, and he squinted through the leaves until he found her face. "Hi," he said simply.

Em flushed, eyes locked onto his. "Hi."

"My dog seems to have treed you. Would you like help getting down, or shall I throw you some acorns for the winter?"

"I can manage, thanks," Em clipped back. As if to prove it, she descended, slowly. "I didn't know if he was safe," she tossed over her shoulder."

"Who, Bob? He's perfectly gentle, unless you're a squirrel."

Bob flopped down and rolled on his back, as if to prove the point. The man laughed and bent down to pat his belly. Bob's back leg kicked the air in time with the belly rub.

Em was on the lowest branch and sat down to try and ease herself to the ground without further injuring her ankle. The man, seeing her wrapped ankle peeking out of her boot, left Bob and came to offer a hand, which Em took, putting her other hand on his shoulder. It felt like pure muscle, and she tried to ignore the heat creeping into her face. She dropped down, trying not to put all her weight on this stranger. Her feet landed on solid ground, and she winced in pain, trying to steady herself.

"What happened to your ankle? Fight with a chipmunk?"

Em glared. The squirrel joke was getting old. "I fell. Tried to wrap it as best I could."

"I'm Liam, this is Bob, and I can offer you breakfast and some proper bandages if you can spare an hour."

On cue, Em's stomach let out a roar. She reddened further. "That would be kind of you." Then, remembering her manners, she held out her hand, "I'm Emaline. Em for short." He shook her hand briefly, but warmly. She saw his eyes dart to her wrists, which were healing but still red and bruised from the day before. He dropped her hand with no comment, and held out his arm for support. Gripping his solid forearm, Em hobbled beside Liam away from the pine tree and back toward the road.

They moved in silence as Em tentatively picked her way along the uneven ground. But she could feel his eyes. He was laughing at her.

"What?" She prickled.

"You look like you've had a rough time of it, squirrel," he observed with a grin.

"You're very quick. Do the imperial scholars know about you?"

He continued, unabated, "You're out in the middle of nowhere, away from the road, with no food, hardly any supplies, no companions, and a twisted ankle."

"What's your point?" she replied stiffly.

"It looks like I rescued you."

"Yeah. From Bob. I was fine before he showed up."

"I have no doubt. You would have been really fine once those soldiers found you hobbling around."

Em didn't respond.

"Actually," Liam continued, "that's what's puzzling. Shouldn't you be traveling on the road?" His mouth quirked up again. He was working something out. Em stared straight ahead, biting the inside of her cheek in annoyance.

Liam sighed in mock surrender. "Okay, that's fine. You don't have to tell me you're a fugitive from the law. I'll just run forward and ask that squadron if they know you."

Em's eyes widened, and she tightened her grip on his arm. Liam laughed and patted her hand reassuringly. "I won't. Hopefully you're not dangerous. If you are, I don't think Bob's going to protect me."

They glanced over at Bob, who was wildly digging in a patch of dirt and sniffing at nearby bugs. Em let out her breath in a huff and cracked a smile.

Liam wasn't going to turn her in. At least she didn't think so. Em decided to come clean.

"I'm not a fugitive. Well, I don't know. I might be now. But yesterday, I was detained against my will. For traveling alone, I guess."

Liam frowned. "That old protocol? I didn't realize they were still doing that."

Em nodded. "They dumped out my supplies, tied up my hands, made me travel with them." She winced, thinking about the grueling march from the day before.

Liam was studying her with a new gleam in his eye. "You escaped? I'm impressed."

Encouraged by his response, Em spilled the details of her escape, about spotting the hiding place on her outing with Briggs, and then her clumsy drop into it, where she hurt her ankle. Liam listened with rapt attention as he continued to help her through the forest. They arrived back at the road, and Em paused, hanging back at the tree line.

"Come on, squirrel," he laughed. "The soldiers are miles ahead, and the turn off to my place is just over that hill."

Em stared down the road, listening and watching for dust. Turning her eyes back to him, she saw him laughing at her once again. Em stiffened, irritated.

He prompted, while offering his arm once more, "So then you made a splint, bushwhacked through the woods, and then Bob chased you up a tree."

"That sums it up." Em nodded, leaning her hand on his forearm. "Bob does not seem nearly as intimidating now that I've gotten a better look at him."

Bob was happily chasing his tail around a skinny tree. Liam laughed. "His bark is the only thing remotely scary about him."

They started down the road and quickly found the small dirt path cutting across the main road. Liam tilted his head, guiding her to turn right.

Em asked, "Is it just you two?"

"Just us. Out here anyway. I go back and forth between my cabin and the capital."

"Do you not like the capital?"

"I like it fine. But sometimes, I just have to get out. Breathe the fresh air. Bob likes it out here a lot better too."

"What do you do out here?"

"I have some land, and a small place on it. Would like to eventually build a real home there, but for now, I camp."

They both fell silent, listening to their joint footsteps. Em studied him. He was irritating, she decided. His sharp jaw was covered in untidy stubble. A lot of him seemed to be messy, she realized, and she wondered what state his cabin would be in. After a few moments, Em's stomach noisily rumbled. The corner of his mouth quirked up, but he said nothing. The uncomfortable quiet continued, until Em broke the silence. "Are we close?"

Liam nodded, guiding her to the edge of the trees. They emerged out of the forest and off the path onto a hilltop clearing in full summer bloom with a magnificent view of the valley below. Em gasped.

The valley below was a patchwork of farms and wilderness with a small river running through it. The snow-capped mountains of Antillei stood in the distance, to the west. The mountains were faintly visible from Brookerby, and Em had caught glimpses on the road, but she had never seen such a view before. The sun was beginning to rise over the trees and cast their long shadows onto the meadow. The sky was a magnificent bird's-egg blue.

A little shack stood in the clearing, surrounded by wildflowers. "There she is." Liam pointed. It was as close to a perfect place as Em had ever seen. She wanted to spin in circles across the meadow and then lie in the sun watching butterflies float past. She glanced at Liam, who was looking at his home with unfettered delight. And that made her instantly like him.

They moved forward again, with Bob running wildly around the meadow, tongue hanging out.

When they reached the small house—more like a shed—Liam dropped his arm and retrieved a three-legged stool for Em. She gratefully sat.

The rough one-roomed hut was partially shaded from the morning sun by a large birch tree. Liam disappeared inside, and she heard him opening cabinets and tossing things around. Bob lay nearby, panting happily. Em grinned at the dog.

Liam came out again with a tray containing some simple food—bread, dried meat, cheese, and berries. To her, it was a feast. Her mouth watered in anticipation. He set the tray down on a tree stump next to her. "The bread just came out of the oven this morning. Help yourself." Throwing manners to the wind, she tore off a chunk of the bread and took the biggest bite she could manage. He dragged over another stool and began slicing pieces of cheese with his pocketknife.

"Mmm." Em could not stop the involuntary sigh of relief as she munched the still-warm bread. It was good. Reaching for more, she said, "Did you make this? It's wonderful."

"I did," Liam bragged. "The trick is a good starter and knowing how long to knead it. I've been working on the perfect loaf for years."

Em offered a closed-lipped smile and kept chewing. The bread was first-rate. Warm, chewy, and soft with a crispy, thin crust.

Liam continued, "The cheese comes from nearby Exeton. There is a woman who raises goats and makes it. She gives me a discount because I look like her son."

"That's lucky," Em commented between bites.

"I play it up. Call her 'mom.' She misses him, I guess."

Em felt a pang, remembering her own parents. She distractedly reached for a bit of cheese and her third slice of bread.

"Why are you traveling alone?" Liam's voice cut through her thoughts. The tone was conversational, but he had stopped moving around, betraying a greater level of interest.

Em answered evasively, "Because there was no one to travel with."

Liam seemed taken aback. "Really? No parents? Spouse? No siblings?"

"None of the above."

"I'm sorry."

"It's fine. Not fine, exactly, but I'm used to it," Em admitted, feeling more at ease than she normally did with men her own age.

"My parents are gone as well. I have other family, though. My brother. Aunts and uncles."

"Do they live nearby?"

"Most live in and around the capital city. I see them from time to time, and on holidays. We aren't close."

"I see. Sorry about your parents."

"It's not fine, exactly, but I'm used to it," he said with a sad smile. Then he jumped up again. "I should take a look at that ankle. Don't move!" He disappeared back into the shack.

Em swiped some berries from the breakfast tray, tossing them into her mouth. They were sweet and tart and perfectly round. She sighed contentedly. The world looked friendlier with a full belly. Bending down, she rolled up her pant leg, pulled off her boot, and unwrapped her makeshift splint, which had held up well during the hike here.

Her ankle was still red, swollen, and painful to the touch. Em winced. She wondered how she was going to get to the capital city if she could barely walk.

Liam reappeared with a small pouch. "You're in luck," he announced. "I have recently restocked my medical supplies, so I think we'll have you patched up in no time."

He dropped a knee by Em and set the medical bag next to him. "Wrists first, please," he announced. She held out her bruised and scabbed wrists for inspection, rolling up the sleeve of her blouse. He held her forearm, examining it. Finally, he said, "They don't look too great, but they appear to be healing. I can give you some aloe." Glancing up at Em's face, he asked, "May I check your ankle?"

"Sssure," Em replied, suddenly uncertain. She wasn't expecting him to play the physician to her wounds.

He stretched her leg out and began to softly prod the back of her heel and ankle with his fingers. "Does this hurt?"

Em tensed at his touch. "A little."

He felt the bones along the front of her ankle and along the sides of her foot, testing for breaks. He was gentle, working inch by inch, and she wasn't feeling the shooting pain that she felt earlier this morning. She took the opportunity to study him. He had impossibly long eyelashes and eyes the color of rye-bread crust, rich brown with some gold in their depths. He was unlike any young man she had met in Brookerby. Not the new bookseller, that's for sure. She flushed as she fought an involuntarily image of her wearing the purple dress in Mendel's window. Feeling foolish, she internally flogged herself. He had just spent the past hour teasing her. Now after a few minutes of kindness and food, she was ogling him.

She firmly turned her eyes from him to his tiny house. It needed some work. Perhaps she could repay her breakfast and doctor's bill with some odd jobs. She started drafting a list in her head.

His voice interrupted her list-making. "I don't think it's broken. Just badly sprained. I can wrap it up tightly, and you might have a limp for a few days. I can also give you something to help with the pain and then you'll be back on the road."

She felt a twinge of disappointment at this last statement and fought back with logic. Of course he didn't want her just hanging around. She shouldn't anyway. Brookerby needed her to keep moving. She turned up the corners of her mouth and tried for banter. "Are you actually a physician? Because, if so, I think you should've led with that."

He grinned and returned, "No, but I've picked up some basic first aid during my life. Glad I've done such a professional job and tricked you into thinking so."

"I'm definitely impressed," Em responded.

"Let me wrap this, and then you'll be free."

She countered, "I want to help you out here, since you've patched me up and fed me. Can I fix your shingles?"

He sat back on his heels in astonishment. "You want to climb up on the roof with this ankle? I can't possibly agree to that, squirrel."

"Fine. If you have some extra lumber, I can reframe your windows and add shutters. I can also fix your door so it latches properly, and I noticed gaps in your walls, which I can patch."

"Now it's my turn to be impressed," he said in amazement. "You can fix my door if you insist, but otherwise, you owe me nothing. Happy to help."

"I'll start with the door," Em agreed. Liam began to firmly wrap her ankle with clean white bandages. She smiled, feeling proud that she could help this man in exchange for his kindness. She was no helpless damsel in distress. She decided to brag, "Back in Brookerby, I'm the handyman—handy person—for most of the town. Everyone needs something fixed. The cobbler had terrible gaps in his walls, and they let in such a bad draft last winter that he nearly froze stitching a pair of slippers."

"All done," he announced. "Did you say Brookerby?"

"Yes, my hometown. Do you know it?"

"Yes! I visited several years ago. Brookerby had one of the finest warding trees of protection I've ever seen."

CHAPTER 9

"*W*hat did you say?"

"I was there several years ago," he began again, confused.

"No, about the tree!" Em insisted, almost giddy.

"The tree of protection?" he asked cautiously.

"Yes! How do you know about the tree of protection?"

"I've encountered a few. They're easy to pick out if you know a town has one. Em?"

Em stood, turning her back, fighting back tears and laughter at the same time. Here she was, keeping this big secret, getting hurt, traveling halfway across the country, and it turns out she didn't have to do this alone. She felt almost giddy.

She felt a tentative hand on her shoulder. "Are you okay?"

"The tree is gone," she blurted.

"What?"

"Our tree." She turned to face him, hoping her words would inspire something. "There was a huge thunderstorm. Lightning broke the sycamore. And the next morning, everything was different. There were angry mobs breaking windows, and soldiers, but they didn't want to help calm anyone down. They just wanted to burn our papers and arrest us. They took Mendel, and Gram, and I was the only one who—"

"Hold on—" Liam took her by the shoulders, staring intently into her face. "Your tree has fallen?"

She nodded mutely, hopefully.

He stepped back, as if struck. His eyes flickered as if he was working something out. She was still watching when his brown eyes finally connected with her blue ones. He looked different. Serious.

"How long ago?"

"Three nights ago. In a thunderstorm," Em repeated. She suddenly felt uneasy. Should she be telling him all this? His manner shifted so abruptly it was like he was a different person. She was still alone in this, and she shouldn't implicitly trust this man she had known for an hour.

"You'd better sit back down." He gestured to the three-legged stool, and then began to pace. "Were there any effects yet?"

"A mob. They destroyed the butcher's shop. A fire. My friend Ilna was also—" Em couldn't finish, remembering her friend sobbing under her printing press. That was too much. Too intimate.

Em eyes sought his, and she was disturbed to see them cloudy and unfocused. Like his mind was somewhere else. She probed, "Have you had personal experience with the trees?"

"I've encountered a few," was his terse reply.

Em was silent a moment. Then, feeling uncomfortable, she stood. "I need to get moving. I'll fix your door, then I should get on the road. Thank you again for your hospitality."

"Did you just leave?"

Em was rooting through her satchel for her screwdriver. At his question, she froze. "What?"

"When the tree fell. You said you fix things. Did you try to fix it? Or did you just leave?" His tone was flat.

Em felt anger surge up in her. How dare he assume she hadn't? "Yes, I tried! I'm still trying." She shot him a scathing look, snatched up her screwdriver from the bottom of her bag, and limped over to the front door. Taking a breath, she fought down the steam and focused on the askew door. She would check to see if the hinges were loose first.

Suddenly Liam was beside her, hand over the hinge she was examining. "How do you plan to fix it?"

Em dropped her arm and met his eyes, ready to retort. But he didn't look hostile. Curious, maybe. She let out a breath. Then she tried to explain like she would to little Grady. "Well, it's a magic item, isn't it? So, it can't be repaired by normal means. I know that much. I have information about a plant or seed in Gillamor that might be able to help. I've seen the paper with runes that makes the planting possible, so maybe I can find one, or have one made. If nothing else, I can track down a magic user to come back home with me."

Liam was silent but studying her with new respect.

"Can you move your hand?" Em demanded unkindly.

He did, and she began to tighten the hinges in the silence that followed. Em worked out her irritation in turning the screws.

"Do the soldiers know why you're traveling?" Liam's question came again.

"No. I'm not a fool. They burned the paper with the runes and arrested my friends. I'm not giving them another chance to ruin things for Brookerby."

Another stretch of silence. Em moved to the lower hinge.

"I'm coming. I'm helping."

Em blinked slowly and stopped rotating her wrist. She felt—she didn't know what she felt. Bafflement and defensiveness intertwined as she struggled to form words. "What—? You don't—"

"First, I'm not letting you travel alone. Not after your run-ins with those soldiers."

"But, I—"

"Second, I'm guessing I know the capital better than you. We can find help quicker with me by your side."

"You—"

"Third," he plowed through her protests, "well, third, this is personal for me. If there's a way to fix this, a way to save the protected towns, I want to know."

Em turned her head from the hinges to study him. There was fire in his gaze, anger in his clenched fists, stubbornness in the set of his jaw. And breadcrumbs decorating his clothing. Did she want this man to come with her? He was teasing and taunting one moment, then kind and solicitous the next. The mention of the warding trees seemed to trigger a sort of darkness in him. What tumult was she inviting in by saying yes?

Then she thought of the soldiers. The night in the tree, avoiding wild animals. Hunger and fear that had met her on the short journey thus far. Wouldn't it be easier with someone? It was only a few days. If he turned out to be unbearable, she could always slip away, or lose him once they reached the city. She felt her clenched stomach flutter when she looked at him. And she felt relief. "Very well, you can come."

Liam slowly untightened his fists, looking surprised. "You aren't going to argue?"

"You were making good points," Em remarked. "I don't know the city. And I need to find a new tree as soon as possible. I'll take the help."

Liam's eyes crinkled as he flashed a hesitant smile. "Thanks, Em. Really. Thank you. Okay if we leave tomorrow?"

"Sure—" Em turned back to the hinges. Pocketing her screwdriver, she experimentally closed the door. It latched perfectly. She wouldn't have to rehang it. "That gives me time to fix your windows. And the walls. And the roof—"

"Not the roof!" He laughed.

Even though the tension had dissipated from Liam, Em still felt more on guard. What had she gotten herself into? If nothing else, it could be a very strange few days.

EM FOUND a few more things to fix around the shack. After three or four additional repairs, Liam insisted she stop and take it easy on her ankle. He also diplomatically handed her a towel and a bar of soap, offering a bath and clean clothes. Em glanced down at her muddy, burr-covered trousers and chuckled. *I must look a mess,* she thought. *Not that he has any room to judge.* Liam had already begun boiling water and had found some smaller shirts and trousers of his own that might work until her current set and muddy spares were washed. She gratefully took the opportunity to get clean.

Liam pumped water into his washtub, adding the kettle he had boiled. Then he ushered Em inside, leaving her alone in his cottage.

Glancing around the cabin, she noticed that, although old and sparse, it was clean. Maybe her impression of "messy" from Liam was misguided. There was a wood-burning stove in the corner, burlap curtains on the windows, and a tidy cot in the corner with a folded blanket. There was even a small cushion near the bed. For Bob, she assumed.

Em closed the door securely, unwrapped her ankle, and speedily disrobed under a blanket. She awkwardly tossed her clothes out the window to Liam while holding the blanket firmly around her shoulders.

After he had disappeared to the river to do the laundry and to collect supper, she dropped the blanket that she had wrapped herself in and slid gratefully into the metal washtub. She washed her face, and a tiny clod of dirt scrubbed off her cheek. *Has that been there the whole time?* she wondered in embarrassment.

Em settled deeper into the warm suds. Unplaiting her braid, which was covered in dust, she tilted her head back in the washtub, swishing her hair back and forth. After scrubbing her hair and everything below with soap, Em leaned back against the tub side and spent a few minutes prying the dirt from under her fingernails. Scrubbing off the days of dust and mud was wonderful. She had to be careful of her many bruises, but they seemed to be healing. Her ankle was feeling better too. She wasn't sure if it was the warm water or the willow-bark salve Liam had provided, but it was less painful than this morning.

Once she was clean, Em dried off and dressed in the shirt and slacks Liam had left for her. She was swimming in them, but at least they weren't muddy. Rolling the cuffs and sleeves, she inhaled deeply and was hit with the scent of lavender and pine needles.

For the umpteenth time that day, she wondered at the odds that, of all people, she had been found by this man. She felt a slight twinge of trepidation about traveling with him. She wondered if his teasing would get irritating, or if his dark mood would return. Why had he wanted to help her? Before the trees were mentioned, he was ready to part ways with her. There had to be more that he wasn't saying, and that put Em on edge.

She had set her pack by the door, and now went to retrieve the book, flipping it open as she perched on Liam's cot. The book presented the following: "Star Charts of the Northern Hemisphere," "Squirrel-Hunting Regulations near Gillamor," "The History of Buttons in the Country of Zanit," and "Romantic Rituals during the Festival of Rashorbuj." Em's cheeks flushed at the last one.

She became very aware that she was wearing Liam's clothing and sitting on his bed. The man was, objectively, handsome, but any kind of romance was the last thing she needed at this moment. She relocated to the floor, recognizing the need to discourage any feelings she might form. She flipped to the article about squirrel regulations, just to be safe.

Squirrels are common fare among the wilds of Esnania, and often they make passable stews for travelers, if a bit stringy. The stringy meat comes from the activity level of squirrels, who are often on the move and have a great deal of muscle fiber. (See "Correlation of Muscle and Physical Exertion.") Travelers can often fell a squirrel with no laws broken, but seasonal professional hunters should acquire a permit from the capital city magistrate. Travelers should also be careful not to mistake other game, or people in trees, for squirrels.

Em laughed out loud. She wasn't sure what clues the book was trying to share, other than a delayed warning from this morning. She continued reading.

Squirrels are an invasive species that did not originate in this area of the world. They are often where they are not expected to be, and they may surprise you with their innovation and physical prowess.

Em wasn't getting anything. Was the book saying *she* was invasive? Peculiar. She rolled her eyes, closing the book again.

She wished *The Standard Book of Anything* was easier to decipher. For example, if she were headed into danger, like with the soldiers, the book would be much more useful if it provided warning. None of this "romantic ritual" and "invasive species" nonsense.

Em decided not to tell Liam about the book. Not yet anyway. After all, she had only known him a day. His bread was good, but he hadn't proven himself yet. She figured she could check the tome on the sly while they traveled and then invent another source for any information she gathered. The way things were going, she might not get any new information out of the book until they reached Gillamor anyway.

At the sound of whistling outside, she slid the book back into her satchel. Pushing to her feet, she limped to the door to see Liam returning with a basket of laundry and a stringer with a few fish. He whistled a happy tune, which broke off when he spotted Em. "I found dinner!" he announced. Bob bounded around him happily, trying to snap at the dangling fish. The sun was just beginning to sink in the sky, and Em, for a moment, felt her traitorous heart flutter.

BEFORE THEY ATE, Liam rewrapped Em's ankle. The swelling and redness had subsided a great deal. Then, waving away her offers of help, he hung out her clothes and the rest of the laundry to dry overnight.

Em roasted the trout over an open campfire, and Liam brought out the rest of the bread from this morning. They planned their journey to the capital between bites of fish sandwich.

"The way I see it," Liam said, "we can make it in two or three days.

Once we get to town, I would be delighted to host you in my home until we find a seed, or another tree, or something."

Em was wary. "I've intruded so much on your time already. I would feel more comfortable—"

"Nonsense," he cut in. "I've already told you, I'm in this now. I want to help in any way I can."

"You've been very kind. I wish I could—"

"What? Fix up my place in town too?" he said, brown eyes glittering.

"Well, if it needs fixing, I would feel obligated. I don't like being indebted to strangers," Em said simply. She took a bite in the silence that followed, wondering if she had said the wrong thing. Sneaking a glance, Liam was staring fixedly at the fire.

Determined to lighten the mood, she brought up the upcoming festival of Rashorbuj, a harvest festival celebrated with days of music and feasting. "In Brookerby, there would be one large dance in the street, and the whole town would come," she said fondly.

"Gillamor is much the same," Liam said, a forced cheeriness in his tone. "Only there are street vendors, and games of chance, and performances by minstrels all over the city. It's quite remarkable."

"Sounds it."

More silence. Then Liam said haltingly, "Maybe we could go. That is, if you haven't found your solution by then."

"Do you dance?" Em teased.

"Not usually," he admitted. "But you don't strike me as a dancer either," he teased back, pointing to her ankle.

He had her there. Beyond the injury, Em had mostly avoided dances, and everything that came with them. She had observed the other Brookerby girls her age get swept up in the harvest dances, canoodling with apprentices and merchants and young farmers from down the road; the next she knew, they were marrying and having children. Not that one directly led to the other, but Em had a close call with a young fisherman a few years ago and decided to steer clear. She glanced up and saw Liam watching her.

"You're right. I'm not suited for dancing." She smirked. That was probably the easiest way to sum up the tangle of thoughts bouncing around in her head.

"That's a shame," Liam said. And he sounded like he meant it.

Quickly, he shifted back to travel plans. He produced a weathered, creased map to mark their route to the capital. Spreading it between them, he pointed to Brookerby and to where they were now, to orient Em. It seemed a massive journey to her, but was barely two fingers' width on the map. He circled the largest village with his finger: Arrenmore, where they could purchase supplies. He traced the side paths, where soldiers were less likely to travel. Although Em was relying on his expertise, Liam was very careful to incorporate her thoughts and opinions on the route, she noticed. After all, he was joining *her* mission, not the other way around.

Their path would take them two and a half days. They would travel through a wooded area, and then a series of towns, including Arrenmore, before arriving in Gillamor. Liam seemed to know the route well. At the conclusion of planning, Em felt confident that everything would go smoothly. Yet, there was still a small itch at the back of her brain. She didn't like giving up any control, however insignificant, and Liam seemed inclined to take charge.

Liam insisted Em take his cot for the evening. She strongly protested, but he had already strung up a hammock in the yard for himself and dragged out Bob's cushion. "Your ankle is on the mend. A solid, stable bed is more conducive to healing," he reasoned. Bob happily flopped down on his small makeshift bed, seemingly delighted that he would get to sleep outside.

Em relented. She slept soundly that night, with no disturbing dreams.

CHAPTER 10

The empress's hope faded as the planting tour continued. Tragedy had befallen each village who had received her gift, at the very hour of each planting. Although Bronwyn remained optimistic, the empress started to believe that the plantings were the cause of the calamities.

TRAVELING with Liam was indeed an improvement on solo travel. If nothing else, he came with fresh bread, which he'd somehow baked and packed before they left the next morning. But the benefits of Liam didn't end there, and Em was adding to that list hourly. He showed her a trick to estimate remaining hours of daylight using his hand and the horizon. That one he learned from his father, who raised cattle in the high plains of Esnania and needed to know when to drive the herd home for the day.

He was a lively conversationalist, and more often than not, Em found herself drawn into a deep philosophical debate one moment, and then laughing uproariously the next. He would call for a break just before Em knew she needed one. Even Bob was a delight. He would chase small critters, or jump around Liam and Em, panting happily as Liam threw sticks for him to fetch.

By late afternoon, Em was again thanking her luck that Bob had found her, but the small itch in the back of her brain was still there. She was indebted to this man, and that fact alone made her uneasy. She warned herself not to get too attached, remembering two things: His uncomfortable mood shift the day before. And that she must quickly find a solution and return to Brookerby.

They traveled over a smooth dirt path that ran parallel to the main road. Liam had known how to find it, just a short jaunt from his cabin. The trail was flanked by rolling hills of wild grasses, cattle and sheep grazing, and large boulders that appear to have tumbled haphazardly down the hills and stopped mere paces away from the walkway. A vast wooded area loomed ahead, growing closer as the shadows grew long.

Her ankle had healed significantly from the day before. Nevertheless, hours of walking had taken its toll, and she was trying to hide a limp. But Liam noticed.

"Is your ankle flaring up again?"

Em feigned cheerfulness. "I'm okay. It's just a little sore."

Liam stopped. "Em."

Still walking, Em slowed and turned slightly. "What?"

"You've gone far enough for today. We're stopping."

"I'm fine. I can handle a little pain, if it gets me there sooner." Betraying her words, she stopped and turned to face him. The late-afternoon light cast one side of their faces in golden light, and long shadows perpendicular to the path where they faced off, several paces apart.

Liam seemed amused, which, for some reason, infuriated Em. "What?" she demanded.

He shook his head. "I'm going to have to keep an eye on you, aren't I?"

Em felt hot. "I am not a child that needs minding, sir."

"No indeed, miss. You would march all the way to Gillamor on no food, no sleep, and two broken legs," he said sarcastically.

She huffed, "I don't take orders."

"Clearly." Liam's grin was gone, replaced by a stony glint in his eye.

89

Em placed her hands on her hips. "I'm not sure why I should be taking your orders. After all, you joined me, not the other way around."

He raised his eyebrows, not expecting this line of attack. Then, shrugging, he dropped his pack on one of the large rocks by the path. "I am stopping. We've covered nearly as much ground as we intended for today. You may continue, but it will be on your own, and you might reinjure your ankle. Up to you." He left the path and began setting up a campsite.

Em recognized the logical reasons for stopping, but her pride was hurt. She was used to going where she wanted and did not like being ordered about. Especially not by some scruffy man who thought he knew everything. Even if her ankle was starting to throb, she stood motionless where she'd stopped on the road. After several minutes of indecision, she decided to sit on one of the rocks nearby. She truly was ready to rest, but she thought it would set a bad precedent if Liam thought he was the foreman in this arrangement.

Em had experienced this many times with the young men in her village who tried to take charge of her repair projects. After a few moments of inexpert observation, they would march in and explain how to properly fix a fence, or oil machinery, or whatever she was currently working on. Often, these men would attempt to pull her tools out of her hands to "show her." It never ended well. They generally ended up looking foolish and wasting her time. And she resented their behavior. Deeply.

Em sat on her rock stiffly, watching her long shadow stretch toward a tree. Liam worked in silence setting up the camp.

Feeling her ankle pulse, Em reached down to ease off her boot and began unwrapping her ankle. It was red and throbbing, but not nearly as painful as yesterday. Liam was right. A few more miles down the road would do significant damage.

She glanced up, and her eyes met his. His look was calm, but blank. Taking a steadying breath, she picked up her boot and pack, and barefooted, she adopted a dignified hobble over to the campsite.

He watched her warily.

"One thing you should know about me," she began, "is that I don't say, or do, the smartest things when I get angry. I'm sorry. I know you intended well," she finished lamely.

Liam's guarded glance was replaced again by warmth. "I really thought you were going to keep walking," he teased.

"I thought about it," she said bluntly. "Especially when I realized what a perfect idiot I'd made of myself."

"Oh, come now. Nobody's perfect."

Em rolled her eyes, accepting the jab.

"I do want to make sure you still feel in control," he said simply, prodding the campfire to life.

"Thank you. I'm grateful for everything you've done. I just don't like the feeling of...I guess not having dominion over my own quest. Or needing someone's help."

"I understand the feeling. But Em, everyone needs help. It's not a weakness."

Em watched the flames grow, not meeting his eyes. He was right, she knew. But the itch in the back of her brain remained. She tried to lighten the mood. "Do you accept help?"

Liam took the bait. "Most certainly! Whenever I can get it."

"Excellent. What can I do to help set up camp?"

He laughed, snorting. "Nice try. You can't do anything until I put salve on that ankle. Hand it over, squirrel."

She rolled her eyes and stretched out her leg in his direction.

EM HAD LET her guard down with Liam, if only until she could get to Gillamor. She studied him in the firelight later that evening as she lounged on her blanket roll. He was handsome, in a relaxed sort of way. She'd thought him too scruffy, but the longer she looked, she found herself revising that first impression. His dusty-colored hair had subtle gold flashes in the firelight. His brown eyes had flecks of warm amber. His nose had a small bump, like it had once been broken. Feeling her eyes upon him, he looked up from scratching Bob's ears with a questioning expression.

"Did you ever break your nose?" she asked.

Liam let out a surprised laugh. "Not what I expected, but yes. I did."

"Thought so. My friend Millie broke her nose in primary school when she got hit in the face with a ball. She was so embarrassed about the little bump that she tried to smooth it out with a night-splint." Em wrinkled her nose at the memory. "What a mess."

"I bet."

"She met Gleb five years ago, and he didn't mind the tiny bump, at all. They have four kids now."

"So you're saying there's hope for me yet," Liam teased, rubbing Bob's belly.

"Something like that. It's weird what I remember and what I forget. I remembered Millie's nose bump when I saw yours, but I hadn't thought of that in years. How'd you break yours?"

Liam grimaced. "A fight," he admitted.

Em sat up, startled. "Really? A fistfight?"

"Yeah." He was sheepish.

"Must've been some fight. What was it about?"

He stared into the fire for a moment, reliving a memory she could only guess at. Finally, he said simply, "I stood up to a bully."

Em pictured a young Liam standing his ground against a snarling boy twice his size. She wanted the details of that fight; she expected Liam to instantly launch into a riveting story. But he didn't. Em didn't want to step into some kind of emotional trauma, so she didn't pry. "I'm glad you did," she said simply, leaning back on her elbows.

"Me too." He continued staring into the fire, deep in thought.

THEY HAD FALLEN ASLEEP, exhausted from the day of traveling, relying on Bob to stand guard. The next morning, Em woke with a start. It took her a moment to remember where she was, and who she was with. Glancing across the cold ashes of last night's campfire, she could make out Liam's shape under his blankets, the rough woven material rising and falling softly with his breath. Bob was curled up next to him, tail thumping sporadically. *Best let them sleep,* she thought, warmness spreading across her chest unexpectedly.

She turned away quickly and reached for *The Standard Book of Anything.* It was beginning to feel more like a ritual than an actual search for information. She thumbed through the pages, selecting randomly an article about ancient tools. If nothing else, maybe she would learn something she could apply.

The sky lightened as she read a basic mechanics article about simple levers and ramps, and their uses in ancient construction. Midpage, the book suggested she seek out "Writing Implements of the Ancients" for factoids about ancient language, pens, parchment, and ink. *Riveting,* she thought ruefully as she flipped to the suggested title.

She gasped. Gram's handwriting. It looked like a letter Gram had written! Em's pulse quickened as her mind raced through possibilities. Was Gram able to track Em's journey and direct her? Was she all right? Could Em write back?

As quickly as her hopes soared, they leveled off. The letter was addressed not to her but to Mendel. The date was old. Seventeen years ago.

> *My Dear Mendel,*
>
> *I hope this letter finds you well and prosperous in your new town. Things are much the same here, with Anne and Farrigan still absent and searching. I help when I can, using my skills and resources. Little Emaline is blissfully unaware, and I am able to keep her secluded from the madness that stirs the residents in town, which does not seem to affect her. Perhaps she has the skill of her parents. The skill you and I possess. I will discretely test her to determine if she has been thus gifted.*
>
> *I truly fear that, if we do not find a new tree, we will have to leave those who have been changed to their fate. Ilna is losing that battle. The symptoms came on a week or so after you left, which means she is stronger than most. She is restless, prone to weepy outbursts and fits of temper. I have*

been keeping information from her should she prove to be irrevocably lost to us.

I hope they come back soon. Brookerby cannot last much longer. A mob burned the library last week. This morning, I heard shouting in the square and discovered old Mr. Joefer and sweet, quiet Micheal Leanot slugging it out, both bloodied. There was no logic to it. The Hopen family was killed last week by bandits, and they were left for days without proper burial. It is truly becoming the darkest place in the world.

I will continue writing, so long as I can find a way to send messages. I hope our dear friends do not fail. Our town and little Em are depending on them.

With Trepidation,

Gram

Em realized she was holding her breath, and she exhaled. A tear dripped down her cheek, unbidden. Gram's letter was written after her parents had left on their quest, but hadn't Mendel gone with them? It painted a dark picture. Em had a horrifying thought that her town might be repeating history. She had an image of bandits breaking in and hurting her friends, her neighbors. Of fistfights in the streets. Unbidden, her mind flashed back to the mob outside the butcher shop. She closed the book, hugging it to her chest to stop her hands from shaking.

Her mind kept whirring. Why was Mendel not on the quest?

She recalled Ilna weeping under her printing press, an image indelibly printed on her brain. Apparently, the treefall had affected her badly before as well. Why had it not affected Gram or Mendel—or herself for that matter? What skill did Gram think she possessed? She tried to remember if Gram had ever tested her, and she recalled numerous childhood tests Gram had applied to measure her capabilities or her schoolwork.

Em missed Gram desperately. Seeing her handwriting and her words made Em wish she had stayed by Gram's side and kept her safe, just as Gram had done for her all those years ago. She wondered if Gram was locked up somewhere, growing fainter and weaker by the day. She tried flipping to another article but ended up scanning through the book without absorbing anything new. She couldn't sit still any longer.

The sun was peeking over the horizon now. Em shoved the book back in her pack and began to lace on her boots. Her ankle looked almost normal. Her stomach rumbled, anticipating breakfast. She entertained these normal thoughts, trying to push out the despair she felt from the letter. Liam had begun to stir, and she must keep her distress from him. If Gram had protected the secret of the book—even from her friends—Em would also.

EM AND LIAM shared a quick breakfast of cold bread and dried meat. Em feigned cheeriness but was utterly distracted with worry for Gram. Liam cast side glances her way each time she said something and trailed off midsentence or forgot what they were talking about. She saw his concern and quickly assured him that she was completely fine, only she wasn't quite awake yet. They packed up camp and were on the road before the sun had cleared the trees.

"How's the ankle?" Liam inquired after a short distance.

"Just fine. It almost feels normal." Em was astonished to discover that was true, and relieved that she wouldn't have to limp down the road today.

"Good. Just let me know if you start to feel strain. Then we'll need to rest it."

Em nodded. A silence fell between them, broken only by their footfalls on the dirt and Bob's happy panting as he trotted alongside Liam. Em's mind kept going back to the letter. Why had the book shown her that? To urge her on? To make her afraid? She felt a tightness across her chest and realized she was clenching her jaw. Inhaling slowly, she commanded herself to relax. She started doing sums in her head to occupy her mind.

Some time later, Liam began to whistle, a simple tune with a lilt. She recognized it as "The Old Shanty," a song the town fiddler would play at dances. Flashing Liam a grin, she began to whistle the counter-melody. Their tune intertwined and floated ahead of them on the warm breeze. Liam began to speed up. *A race then*, Em thought, and matched his pace. Their voices danced 'round and 'round, faster and faster, until Em finally couldn't keep up with her whistling. She blew out a huge burst of air and started laughing. Liam kept going but grabbed one of her hands to twirl her around, like in the dance. Caught off guard, she squeaked and protested, "Too fast, too fast!" but then attempted the twirl anyway. She wobbled and put out her arms to catch her fall when strong hands caught her waist, holding her up. "Steady, Em." There was laughter in Liam's voice, "Maybe a little fast, huh?"

"The fiddler was slower." Em giggled, turning to him as she tried to regain her balance. His hands still firmly held her, righting her, and she could feel every point of contact and their additional warmth through her light summer blouse. His amber-brown eyes glinted with good humor, and maybe something else Em couldn't quite decipher. Her brain was throwing up a warning signal, and she realized she had been standing in his arms, looking into his eyes, saying nothing. Bob yipped.

Feeling foolish, and a little warm, she stepped away. "I'll try to keep my feet under me from now on," she said lightly.

"Uhrm," Liam cleared his throat, "I thought you said you weren't suited for dancing."

"I think I proved that statement correct." She smirked.

"Quite the contrary." His eyes twinkled. "I wouldn't mind a repeat sometime." Then she rolled her eyes and the spell was broken. Liam abruptly turned, whistling for Bob, who bounded over from the tree he was sniffing. Then he started moving his feet down the road again.

Em still felt a little dizzy. There was a red flag flashing in her brain. Warning bells. She would have no time for dancing on her quest, and she'd better remember that. Resolving to keep her head on straight, she trotted to catch up and cleared her throat. "How close are we? To the next village, I mean."

"Just up ahead," he returned. "Although, I should warn you, Arrenmore is not what it used to be."

"What do you mean?" she asked. "Did their tree fall too?"

Liam shook his head. "I don't know that they ever had a tree. But something is off there."

~

THEY ARRIVED in the small village of Arrenmore quite suddenly. The road widened, surrounded by buildings on what appeared to be the main street. Each of the buildings had an unwashed and faded appearance. Although the sun was invitingly warm, there were few people out and about. The people Em spotted kept their faces down as they scurried between the shacks. This was nothing like the friendly feel of Brookerby. At least, how Brookerby felt before the storm.

Em glanced at Liam. His forehead was wrinkled in concern. She spoke softly, as if the deserted streets had ears.

"It does feel off here."

Liam nodded his assent. "It gets a little worse every time I come through."

"We should split our efforts," Em suggested. "I'll find matches, rope, and maybe a knife. You want to find us some food?"

Liam conceded, reluctantly. "Just be careful, okay? And let's try to be quick. I don't want to stay here a moment longer than we have to."

He crossed to a sad-looking bakery. Em scanned the dusty storefronts for merchant signs, hoping for a supply shop or general mercantile. She saw a shingle halfway down the thoroughfare that looked promising and started that direction, shifting her pack to her right shoulder. Em's stomach began to clench. Something was really not right about this town. Maybe it was just the appearance, and Em reminded herself to not judge the town based on a few run-down buildings. Still, her body did not relax.

Approaching the promising sign, Em read

Mel's Mercantile and Supply.

"Good enough," she breathed out, realizing the tension in the street was causing her to hold her breath. "Relax, Em," she scolded herself, and then reached for the door.

Inside, there were wagon wheels, rope, and other farming tools hanging on the walls. A long counter ran the length of the store, and most of the merchandise appeared to be behind it, requiring a clerk to retrieve what was needed. Everything had a neglected appearance. Even the new items for sale seemed a bit tired. She picked up a gray canvas tarp from a rotting wooden shelf.

"Yeah?" A surly voice cut through the dust.

"Hello? I'm looking for some supplies."

"Look around. If you see what you need, then you found supplies." A compact man with black hair emerged from the shadows of the stockroom. His face might've been handsome except for the scowl that marred his features.

Em tried again. "I would like to purchase a few things…please." The last bit was added in the hope that politeness might get her better service, although that looked doubtful.

"Ladies' store is down the block, girl," the man grumbled, turning back to the storeroom.

"I need a knife, some rope, matches, and this tarp," Em recited, holding up the canvas. "Do you sell those things?"

"A knife?" the man mocked. "What would a little girlie like you do with a knife?"

Em was confused. Little girlie? She was wearing slacks covered in dirt. She was clearly a traveler. Context clues were not this man's strong suit. She decided to give him the benefit of the doubt and state the obvious. "I am traveling. I need those things."

The man spat, "No good having women in my store. You don't need none of this. I won't sell it to you. Don't cry, girlie. Maybe if you smiled more, I'd take you dancing."

Em gritted her jaw. This guy was the living embodiment of toenail fungus. But it might be the only place in town, so she bit her tongue and pulled out her money from her pack. Maybe he would understand cash.

But he wasn't done. Stalking around the counter, and coming

much too close, he eyed her up and down. "You ain't much, but you still look like a woman. Why don't you leave supply-gettin' to the men and buy yourself a pretty little dress?" His breath smelled like tobacco and garlic.

Em resisted the urge to simultaneously throw a punch and gag. Instead, she stepped toward the weapons, hanging on a side wall, and eyed the large hunting knife. Reaching up, she yanked it down and studied it.

"Hey, gittoutta there!" The man darted over, but then froze as Em spun to face him, holding the knife point-first in his direction.

"This looks adequate," she said sweetly. "I could gut a wild animal, if he were small." She sliced the knife across and in front her in a practiced arc, coming very near to hitting the man, who jumped back to avoid the blade. "Although it probably needs some sharpening after sitting in this disgusting shop for so long. I'll need a whetstone. I also see matches and rope up on that third shelf. Should I get them myself, or do you want to do your job?"

The man's scowl was briefly replaced by a look of surprise. Eying the knife once more, he decided not to risk further confrontation and silently went behind the counter to reach for the items Em requested.

"Wonderful." Em sheathed the knife, added the tarp to the heap, and placed a silver coin on the counter. "This pile of sad-looking junk looks to be worth about half a crown. Here it is. I would normally try to haggle for a bargain, but I honestly don't want to spend another minute in this filthy rathole. So congratulations. You've made a sale."

Em grabbed her pile and strode out, leaving the man behind the counter speechless and unable to collect the money she had dropped.

Once Em was outside, she allowed herself a victory grin. It was not her first time putting a nasty man like that back on his heels, and it always made her feel triumphant. *When someone makes you feel small, make yourself absurdly large.* Gram taught her that.

A few paces away, she knelt and stuffed her newly acquired goods in her pack. It was messy, and she vowed to reorganize once she found a place to sit. Standing and hiking up her pack again, now heavier, she crossed the street to find Liam. But he wasn't visible in the grimy bakery window. The oppressive tension began to creep into Em once more. There was definitely something wrong with this town.

Straining, she heard a faint tinkling of music coming from down the block, across the street. The first sign of hospitality. "Maybe a pint would make this place bearable," she mused, striding toward the sound of the piano, hoping to fate that Liam was within.

CHAPTER 11

The Gray Horse is an established stop on the main road of Esnania on the way to Gillamor. It was built long before the town of Arrenmore was formed around it by an enterprising spice merchant who traveled frequently between the two towns. Jathen R. Monterey (675–748 RQ), the spice merchant, wanted a spa-like retreat from the dust of the road, and the Gray Horse was born, named after his own horse of the same color. The pub initially included a full menu of food items, beverages, spa treatments, and other adult activities. The town of Arrenmore grew around the massive place as a large force of workers was required to keep the pub running. The Gray Horse has stood for nearly a century but has undergone a series of changes as the world changed around it. Initially, pub wenches were more popular than spa treatments, but as more women moved into Arrenmore, the less reputable parts of the Gray Horse were shuttered, and the spa became a central feature. Monterey's spices from his other profitable activities found their way into the food, beverages, and spa treatments. This tradition is maintained to this day, as Monterey's descendants run the establishment. The pub stands in a rural area as a monument to civilization. We recommend the spiced ale and the sage facial treatments.

"History of the Gray Horse"
The Standard Book of Anything

. . .

EM READ TO THE END, intrigued. Both of the book's suggestions sounded delightful. Reaching into her pack, she pulled out the water-skin and wished for spiced ale. The result was a cold frothy mixture that tickled her nose and made her think of falling autumn leaves.

She was currently sitting in the main lobby of the Gray Horse, occasionally checking the floor-to-ceiling windows for signs of Liam on the street outside.

It was indeed a massive establishment. And, had she been there twenty years ago, she might have been impressed by its opulence. Now, the faded gray furniture and cracks in the plaster crowded out the grandeur. Em's chosen seat near the door was a high-backed chair with a purple velvet cushion. She saw other gray chairs in eclectic styles scattered across the room. Throughout the first-floor lobby, multiple chandeliers dangled from the lofted ceiling; a few of them appeared to have broken strings of crystal and glass hanging at funny angles. The room was empty, save for the auto-player piano in the corner, plunking out a song as if a ghost pressed the keys. A rare, functioning relic from the Age of Magic. It was probably worth more than everything Em had ever owned.

Growing increasingly uncomfortable in the abandoned lobby, Em put away her waterskin and stood to make her way to the exit. She passed by an archway that led to a compact, tabled area with a bar, directly opposite the Grand Dining Hall. The bar had high shelves filled with all colors and shapes of bottles, and gray booths and tables indiscriminately placed throughout. The nameplate above the door said THE PARLOR. The room was poorly lit and empty.

Em continued to scan the foyer with her eyes. The Grand Dining Hall, illuminated by light from its high windows, had haphazard tables with water spots and scratches from decades of wear. Behind her, fog floated out of a room at the end of the hall—a steam room perhaps—with several other archways lining the corridor. Em assumed this was the spa portion of the Gray Horse. There was a glittering staircase in the lobby that meandered in an arc to the upper level. The railings looked to be gold-plated and had started to chip.

Still no persons in sight. And still, the weird feeling that something was not quite right. She turned toward the door.

"Miss." A voice close behind her made her jump. She tripped as she turned to the voice, which belonged to a heavy-lidded employee, a waiter perhaps. His voice bounced off the empty room, absorbed by the purple velvet. Em barely regained her balance before he spoke again.

"You are requested in the Atrium. Mr. Monterey would like to see you."

"Uh." Em stumbled over her words as her brain also tripped. Monterey, she had just read that... Someone named Monterey founded this place, and it was being managed by his family. Odd that the owner would want to see her.

The employee was still waiting for a response.

"Oh, sorry. There must be some mistake. I don't know Mr. Monterey."

The man looked at her blankly. She tried to explain, "I am traveling through. Waiting for my traveling companion. I'm probably not the person Mr. Monterey wants to see."

The gray-clad employee smiled indulgently. "Our owner likes to greet all his guests and provide them with a complimentary steam."

Em had never been in a steam room, but it sounded intriguing. She supposed a short visit, just to say hello, couldn't hurt. Maybe she would get that sage facial after all. "All right, where should I go?"

"The Atrium is the central steam room. You will find it at the end of this hallway." The man observed her dust-covered slacks, "You do have steam room attire, yes?"

"No. I didn't realize I'd be entering one."

"Ah." The man sighed, as if he was being unfairly overworked. "I believe we have swimming costumes and towels in the ladies' changing room. Last archway on the right." With that, he turned back toward the Grand Dining Hall and disappeared.

Em glanced around again. Her stomach clenched uncomfortably, and she began moving toward the large steam room. She was the lone patron of this place. Why?

In the ladies' changing room, the "swimming costume" turned out to be a small strip of material for her upper half and a very short pair of bloomers for her lower half. A little embarrassed, she changed quickly and then wrapped a towel around her torso. Quickly, she unbandaged her ankle, thinking the steam might speed the healing. It was still a little swollen. At least the towel covered everything, except her bare shoulders and lower legs. Her mob-induced bruises had faded considerably. Good enough. She placed her pack in a small wooden box for personal effects, along with her clothes, and stepped back into the hallway.

The steam floating out of the back archway had increased. Em padded barefoot on the tiled floor into the mysterious room. She smelled eucalyptus, and the moistened steam was quite agreeable to breathe in.

Through the fog, she could make out some greenery scattered throughout the room: varieties of palm trees and exotic, large-leaved plants. Looking up, a magnificent skylight, several stories tall and spanning the width of the room, provided an airy openness and sunlight that made her feel a bit more at ease. As she inched through the space, which seemed to go on without end, she occasionally ran into damp wooden benches. No one was here. Finally, getting frustrated, she called out.

"Hello?"

A voice echoed, "Hello."

"I was asked to meet Mr. Monterey here. Is he present?"

"Sam, please. Mr. Monterey is my father." The voice was a polished baritone, and it sounded like the owner of the voice was a younger man.

"Ah, Sam. Pleasure to meet you. Thank you for the complimentary steam." Then, peering through the fog, she asked, "Where are you?"

"Ah, but you have not told me your name."

Em thought briefly about giving a fake name, but then realized that could get complicated when Liam showed up. Better to tell the truth, but concisely. "My name is Emaline Strider," she said.

"Well, Emaline. Em. Can I call you Em?"

"Uh…yes. If you wish."

"Keep moving, follow my voice to the back of the Atrium."

Em did so, cautiously. "Mr. Monterey, why did you want to meet me?"

"Sam, please."

"Sam. I really am not sure why you wanted to see me. Is the Gray Horse still open to the public?"

"It is." The disembodied voice sounded closer.

"Then why does it sit empty? Why is the whole town empty and, if I'm speaking frankly, a bit off?"

"You have identified the heart of the matter, Em."

The voice was near, and Em could make out a figure sitting on a bench ahead. She slowed. Then the figure spoke. "Come and sit down."

Em inched closer, now realizing how foolish it was to meet a strange man in such an unfrequented place with no visibility. Alone. In a towel. Liam was probably ready and wondering where she was. She debated making a run for it, but curiosity got the best of her. She took a few more steps.

The man came fully into view. He might have been the most handsome man Em had ever seen. He was also wearing a towel, wrapped around his waist. He was lean and muscular with thick dark hair on his chest and head. Oddly, he wore several large gold and silver rings with glittering gems that he toyed with absently.

He observed Em with a curious expression on his angular face as she approached and awkwardly sat on the farthest end of the wooden bench. Em had the feeling he was checking her over, like she was an acreage he was considering for purchase. She didn't like it. She wished she had worn her normal clothes.

He spoke again. "Why are you here, Em?"

"I came in for a spiced ale. Maybe a sage facial."

He laughed, surprised by her comments. "Yes, I suppose that's why most folks come in. But you are not most folks. Are you?"

His eyes were aquamarine, and he watched Em's reaction intently.

"I'm not sure what you are implying, Mr. Monterey."

"I know who you are. I know who your family is, at least. Let's cut the games, shall we?"

"I think you have the wrong person—"

"Anne and Farrigan Strider? Your parents, I believe."

Em was immediately off-balance. "They died when I was a small child," she replied truthfully.

"Ah." Sam scooted an inch closer; his eyes bored into her. Em was sweating from the steam and suddenly felt flushed. Was he coming on to her, or threatening her?

"Why are you here?"

She didn't know. She shouldn't be here. Em stood up quickly, and nearly lost her towel. She made a frantic grab and rewrapped it around herself. "If that's all, *Sam*," she emphasized, "I believe we have nothing to discuss. My business is my own."

His hand shot out and grabbed her wrist. She winced and tried to pull away, but his grip was firm. What was happening? Em had never had an encounter like this. Was she supposed to fight? Reason with the man? Use her wiles to get away? She shuddered at the last one. He pulled her over in front of him and stood so he towered over her. "We are not done here, Em. Your parents have information I need. Surely it has been passed to you. If I have to hold you here at the Gray Horse to get it, I will."

Em tried to twist away, and Sam tightened his grip. It hurt, and she felt her eyes leak from the pain. She stopped yanking her arm and tried persuasion. "I have a friend who is expecting me."

"The boy with the dog? I wouldn't worry about it. We have told him you continued on alone."

Em scowled. *Liam wouldn't believe that.* She hoped he wouldn't believe that. She tried another tactic. "Look, I'm traveling for the adventure of it. You've sent away my traveling companion, and I have no idea what information you seek. I can give you nothing. Honestly. Please let me go."

"You are quite the actress, lovely Em, but I simply do not believe you." He tightened his grip, and she felt a ring of pain in her wrist. She bit the side of her cheek to keep from yelping. Could he break her arm? He had a malicious gleam in his eye that suggested he was capable. They were both perspiring from the steam, and Em tried very hard to ignore his sweat, which was dripping on her. How was she going to get out of this? The man didn't believe her. Wouldn't listen to her. Was hurting her.

"I'll see you for dinner this evening. Perhaps you will be more reasonable once you've had time to think over your situation." He snapped his fingers, and a large male spa attendant, dressed in gray, appeared out of the steam. Without words, he took Em firmly by the arms and led her away as Sam released his grip. Em's legs were wobbly and her hands were shaking. She should've run when she had the chance.

EM HAD BEEN USHERED to a bedroom on the second floor. The room contained a small bed with an iron bed frame shaped into graceful swirls. A gray quilt was draped over the sheets. An ornate wood-and-iron dresser and a plush, high-backed gray chair were arranged opposite the bed. A broad window was set into the far wall, providing second-story views of the gardens behind the Gray Horse. Fashionable oil lamps were placed throughout the room, giving the place a friendly glow. It would have been a very pleasant room, had she come there voluntarily.

Her pack had been delivered to the dresser top, and she was relieved to discover her clothes, waterskin, coins, and the book had not been taken. However, all her other supplies were gone. Once she was alone, she quickly slipped back into her own dusty, but modest, clothes.

Upon trying the door handle, Em discovered that the gray attendant had locked her in. She had tried unsuccessfully to pick the lock but only succeeded in breaking a hairpin and ripping off her fingernail. Next, she tried the windows. She was only on the second floor, but first-floor lofted ceilings made for a dangerous jump that would land her on the cobblestones of the garden below. She would surely break something and be right back where she was now. She thought to shout out to someone for help, but not a single soul passed beneath her window.

The worst part of her predicament was that she told the truth. Her parents had told her nothing. Had left her nothing. But she suspected Sam's query had to do with the tree somehow. Maybe her parents traveled through here on their quest for a new tree? But she didn't know enough detail to satisfy Sam Monterey. She had to get away before the dinner he mentioned.

Perhaps she could knot the bedsheets to make a rope out the window?

A knock at her door. Then a female spa attendant, middle-aged, also in gray, entered. "Mr. Monterey sends you a sage facial, with his compliments."

Em rolled her eyes. Sam was just taunting her now. "No thank you."

"He insists." The stern woman closed the door behind her and carried her supplies to the dresser, directing Em to the high-backed chair.

Em crossed her arms. "Miss...um, sorry, I didn't catch your name."

"Randler."

"Miss Randler. I would love to leave. It's a very pleasant room, but I'm being held here against my will. If you could just let me go—" As she spoke, she inched toward the door. She made a dash, yanked it open, and bounced off a human wall of a man wearing a gray uniform who was blocking the door.

"Urr," Em stuttered as she stumbled to regain her balance. The man stepped in, caught the doorknob, and pulled it closed. Em heard the click of a lock.

"Boss's orders. Sorry." To her credit, Miss Randler did look embarrassed by the situation.

"Your boss is a monster," Em spat.

"The facial is very nice, though," she offered. "I'm to stay until the service is complete. I don't get paid otherwise."

If this is the only way to get her to leave, I might as well get it over with. I can try to escape after she leaves. Sitting reluctantly, Em was propelled backward as the chair reclined. The woman began smothering all sorts of products on Em's face. They smelled wonderful, and despite her current predicament, Em felt herself start to relax. Then everything went black.

CHAPTER 12

*E*m groggily became aware that she was still sitting in the reclining chair. The attendant was gone, and the sky outside was growing dark.

She swore furiously. She must've fallen asleep during the facial. Her mouth felt dry, and she looked around for her waterskin. She felt off-balance. Foggy. Like the steam room. She stumbled to her feet, and immediately her legs gave out. What was wrong with her body? It felt like she was trying to move through a thick mud. Then her mind slogged to a dark place… Had Miss Randler drugged her?

She saw from the floor a very fashionable evening gown, with elaborate black-and-gray beading, off-the-shoulder straps, and a low V neckline, spread out on the bed. Monterey mentioned dinner. How long ago had that been? "I am expected to wear that, I suppose?" she said to the empty air. Although, parched and fuzzy as she was, it came out as "Amm esspcted tware that, susssss."

The sky was getting darker by the minute, and the room with it. Em pulled herself to kneeling and fumbled with the nearest oil lamp. Miss Randler must've turned off the lights? *What to do? Where is Liam?* Surely he had been searching for her for hours. That is, if he didn't give up and leave. She pulled herself to standing, but she felt like a colt just learning to walk. Something was wrong with her muscles. She stumbled to the door. Still locked. She could try to run for it at dinner, whenever that was. The dining room was certainly closer to the entrance than her room. But she didn't trust her feet to cooperate right then.

Perhaps she could make up a story that would satisfy Monterey and he would let her go. She suddenly remembered the bedsheets. She was going to make a rope ladder. Staggering to the bed, she flipped the dress and quilt aside and began to knot up the sheets into a rope that she could use to climb out the window. It was not going well; she kept knotting her hands in with the sheets.

Another knock. Em messily shoved her handiwork onto the floor and stood up before another gray-clad attendant entered. His face looked familiar, and then it clicked: the heavy-lidded waiter who had summoned her to the steam room.

"Mr. Monterrey will collect you for dinner in two minutes. He requests that you follow the dress code for the formal dining room by wearing appropriate attire." He nodded to the dress that had been flung on the floor.

Em, not trusting her mouth to form words, instead held up her fingers in a rude gesture.

The man sighed. "Mr. Monterey warned me you might say that. He asked me to tell you that if you are not properly attired when he arrives, he will be happy to assist you."

The attendant pulled the door shut, and Em squawked in frustration. Two minutes did not give her enough time to climb down her shoddy bedsheet ladder and get clear. And she really didn't want to know what dressing "assistance" looked like coming from a brute like Sam Monterey. There was nothing to do but attend this dinner, let whatever substance that had infiltrated her muscles wear off, and escape afterward.

She clumsily pulled off her dirty slacks, blouse, and boots, and pulled on the dress. She had to wiggle into it, because the row of tiny buttons on the back were already fastened, and her fingers weren't working properly. It was the most beautiful thing Em had ever worn, but it certainly wasn't practical. She had no idea how she was going to get out of it. She also felt quite exposed and wished for her steam-room towel to wrap around her shoulders. She tried to do something with her hair, but her fumbling fingers produced a messy lopsided hairdo, so she pulled it all back apart and just pinned up the sides, leaving the rest free. Then, the knock came once more. She shoved on the black silk slippers and padded toward the door.

When it swung open, it was not the attendant, but Sam in a sleek, fashionable suit. Em took an involuntary step back.

Sam looked her up and down and whistled. "The towel was delightful, of course, but you look simply stunning in evening wear."

Em hated this man more than she realized she could hate anyone. More than that guy at the supply store. But she hadn't been able to pull a knife on Sam yet.

"My dear, you are glowing from that facial. I should charge more for our spa," Sam self-congratulated.

"Kidnapping and drugging are bbad forr busssiness," Em slurred back.

Sam smiled indulgently and held out his arm. "Shall we?"

Em followed, wobbling, but she refused to take his arm. Sam let it fall stiffly and walked beside her. Em could sense his muscles, coiled like springs. He would pounce if she ran.

She took in her surroundings as they walked. She was being kept in a room at the back end of the upper hallway. Up and down the hall were identical doors, which, Em guessed, led to identical hotel rooms. Sconce lights illuminated the hall, and Em couldn't tell if they were some magical form of light, or a new technology with electrical current. Either way, they were probably very expensive.

They approached the guided staircase and began to descend, with Sam leading the way. Em gripped the polished wooden banister to prevent her sluggish body from taking a tumble.

On the main level, Em saw waiters and other staff, all in gray, and a few patrons entering the Grand Dining Hall. At least nothing too terrible could happen with other folks around, Em decided. But then she remembered the supply store earlier that day, and wondered if any of the townspeople would actually come to her aid.

As Em struggled down the stairs, Sam stopped suddenly and turned to face her. Em almost crashed into him. She stood a step above him, so they were eye to eye. Sam leaned in and said, his mouth to Em's ear, "Just to warn you, I have armed staff stationed around the dining room. They will shoot on my command. So I expect a very uneventful dinner." Em shivered and nodded her understanding.

The dining hall was aglow with chandeliers. It looked far more striking in the evening than the faded establishment Em encountered earlier that day had. She thought perhaps a trick of the light made it so. It was half full of patrons, mostly townsfolk from the look of them.

Heads turned as they passed, watching Sam and wondering who the lady was. Em looked at faces, hoping for a sympathetic one she could silently communicate with, but most turned away quickly. Multiple gray-clad gentlemen lined the perimeter of the room. Were they waiters or marksmen? And then suddenly, she saw a pair of familiar brown eyes and felt relief wash over her.

"Em?"

"Liammmhm!"

"Em!" Liam rose from his table and crossed to meet her, grabbing her hands in his. Her hands fumbled his grasp. He noticed, and his eyes scanned hers, agitated. Em had a moment of panic, hoping that Sam's staff wouldn't be too trigger happy, and she thought she heard the cocking of guns. "What have they done to you? When they told me you had left—" Em shushed him quickly, glancing at the guards around them.

But Sam permissively held up his hand and Em felt the guards relax. "Ah, Emaline. Is this the boy with the dog?"

Em cringed, but Liam's face was stone.

He turned to Sam. "I don't believe we've met."

"Sam Monterey. I own this establishment. Em and I have recently met, and she has kindly given me the pleasure of her company for dinner." Sam offered a thin-lipped smiled, and Em detected a crafty glint to his eye.

"Pleasure to meet you, Mr. Monterey. I don't wish to interrupt your meal, but I would like my traveling companion returned to me in one piece after dinner," Liam replied stiffly, still holding firmly to one of Em's hands.

Em's heart leapt. Liam would get her out of this.

"We'll see how cooperative she is."

Liam raised an eyebrow.

Sam continued, "Have a pleasant evening. The trout is our special tonight." He took Em's hand from Liam's and pulled her quickly away. She glanced back and mouthed "help" before stumbling over her own feet. She saw both of Liam's eyebrows shoot up.

As they sat, Em glanced back. Liam's table was empty, and he was gone.

"That was unexpected. Seems you are closer to the young gentleman than you let on. Perhaps he knows your itinerary."

"I mmmet him three daysh ago. He knowsh nnnothingg."

"As you say."

A waiter approached and Sam held up two fingers. The waiter bowed and turned on his heel.

Em leaned forward and hissed, "Wwhat kind of drrugg wasssh in that facial? I can barely wwwalkk. Or sshppeak."

Monterey leaned back, appraising her. "A simple sedative combined with a muscle relaxant. Don't worry. It seems to be wearing off."

Em felt rage course through her. She eyed the knife at her place setting, wondering how quickly she could grab and throw it. Not very quickly, in her current state. And she would likely be killed by marksmen before she could get away. Em eyed the silent guards. They might be less attentive if she was more at ease. She made an effort and found she could mostly speak now without slurring. She took control of the conversation.

"It's ddifferentt in the evening. The Gray Horsshe," Em remarked.

Sam eyed her, "What do you mean, different?"

"Well, lessh ssteam, for one."

Sam's mouth twisted in amusement.

"But Arrenmore, and this place. Today it seemed, well, rrundown. And ttonnight, it looks very grand."

"Thank you. Run-down, you say?"

"Yes, everything could use a neww ccoat of paint. And some of the merchantssh could do with some new mmannerssh."

"You must mean Mel."

"The supply store? He was an assssh."

"He's one of mine," Sam offered, steepling his hands. "It's how I knew you were in town, although it took a bit more to discover your identity."

Em said nothing. Sam continued.

"Sounded like you were a little spitfire in his shop, so the steam room gave me the chance to meet you when you were unarmed." He chuckled.

"Ddummb of me to fall for that. It won't happen again," Em said sourly.

"Pity. It was one of my more memorable meetings this week." Sam's eyes twinkled with repressed laughter. Em fought down the rage and tried a different tactic.

"The ttown is yours?"

"Yes, and no. I am simply one of many concerned business owners. There are forces at work that are beyond my ability to control."

"What forcess?"

Sam glanced around, and then leaned in. "Do you believe in magic, Em?"

"Magic?" Em felt a shiver down her spine. She kept her face neutral. "Of course. Yyou should as well. You have some artifactss from the Age of Magic."

"Yes, yes. Those are a mere shadow. Trinkets. I'm talking about real power. Forces beyond what can be explained. Influence beyond what your reason says is possible."

Em considered. "Like magic users casting mmassive enchantments? That encompass a whole town?"

Sam continued in a whisper. "This town used to have it."

"It? The town had magic?"

"Yes."

"You mean, fffifty years ago."

"No. I mean five years ago."

"What makes you say that?"

"It was a feeling. No, it was an ever-present surrounding, like a warm blanket, until it was pulled away, and we were left in the cold."

"I'm not sshure I understand, Mr. Monterey."

"You mention this place being run-down. Unfriendly. Arrenmore didn't used to be like that even a few short years ago."

Em recalled the eerie feeling she had throughout the day in the town. "What wassh it like before?"

"Folks knew and liked each other. If you met someone familiar on the street, you would stop and talk for hours. The place had a glow about it. And the Gray Horse was the central hub. We were always busy. My employees were delighted to work here. We were a desired stop for travelers. Everything we did seemed blessed.

"I took over the Gray Horse from my uncle when business was booming. And then suddenly, the warm blanket was yanked off."

"Did you ever consider that you might be the probbblem?" Em asked, unkindly.

To her surprise, Sam nodded. "Yes. I thought it was me. I thought it was me for over a year before I discovered the decay all over town. Even places I had no employees, no business with, who were previously thriving.

"So, I called a town meeting. Everyone came. Everyone felt the change. They wanted to know how to fix it. And I could do nothing."

"I'm sorry," Em interjected. And she was too. She imagined Brookerby permanently falling into decay and strangeness. The thought made her very uncomfortable, as if Arrenmore was a glimpse of the future.

"I strongly believe we had good magic guarding us, or charming us or something. Or we have been cursed now." Sam looked thoroughly distressed.

When he closed his eyes and rubbed his temples, Em snuck a glance at the gray-clad men along the wall. They were still very alert.

Her head felt a lot clearer now, but she didn't dare make a move. She turned back to Sam. He had opened his eyes and sat forward once more, looking intensely at Em. "We do have a lead. On the very day of the change, several years ago, there were only two travelers in town. Your mother and father." He leveled an accusatory glance at Em and waited, twisting his finger rings methodically.

Em's jaw dropped. "What?"

Sam nodded, watching her closely, still playing with his rings.

Em shook her head. "N-no, that's impossible. My parents died many years ago. I've been raised by a family friend my whole life."

Sam glared intensely and said nothing.

"It must be something else. That makes no sense. Maybe they looked like them? Used the same name?"

"No mistake. It was them. You look a great deal like your mother."

Em's head spun.

At that moment, their meal arrived.

THE MEAL—THE trout special—was eaten in silence. Sam, having said his piece, was ingesting his food with obvious enjoyment. Em had completely lost her appetite and was aimlessly pushing food around her plate.

There were two possibilities. Either this man had mistaken others for her parents, or he was telling the truth. But what did that mean? Had they been alive her whole life? Had they left her behind? The possibility made her shiver. *Did Gram know?* She scooped up a few potatoes absentmindedly as she tried to determine if her Gram was capable of concealing such a thing. Then she remembered the book. So carefully hidden for so many years. Gram was capable of secrets.

The only part of the story that rang familiar was the protection of the town. Em recalled the first night she had opened *The Standard Book of Anything* was the same night the thunderstorm had broken the tree of protection. She nearly gasped but bit her lip. Maybe this town had a similar tree? *But what if they did? It's not like they could get it back.*

And if she explained about the tree, she would have to explain how she knew about it. And where she was going. She glanced up and saw Sam watching her face change with great interest.

"You remembered something." It was a statement, not a question.

"Yes. Was anything destroyed that night? The night of the curse. A tree or something?"

"What?"

"You know, a tree of protection. I know very little of those things, but it would shield a town from danger. I've heard of towns falling into ruin after such things were destroyed."

Sam studied her a moment, then shook his head. "I knew you would never willingly tell me the truth, but to make up something crazy like that—" He snapped his fingers over his shoulder. "We're done for tonight. We'll try again tomorrow."

"Tomorrow?" Em growled. "I can't stay here."

"You will. And eventually you will tell me the truth."

The waitstaff slid away Em's quarter-eaten dinner, and a gray attendant pulled her to her feet. She swiveled her head, searching for Liam in the lobby, but he wasn't there. In a daze, Em was led back to her room. She had told him as much as she knew—or could surmise. Why was he so inclined to believe Em was lying? Was a tree of protection so difficult to believe? She stumbled a few times on the steps, and the gray attendant had to drag her back up by her arm. She expected some new bruises by morning.

They shoved her once again into her room at the end of the hall. It was just as she left it, except the bedsheets, the ones she had begun to knot up, had been removed. Em groaned and flopped down on the blanket-less bed.

Her mind jumped fences. She had to get out of here. Maybe she could try the lock again. Or she could knock a hole in the wall with a lamp and get out through another room.

Then a knock sounded at the door.

No one entered. Em went to the door. "Hello?" she answered cautiously.

"Em?" a careful voice responded. She knew it instantly.

"Liam!"

"Can you open the door?"

"No, they locked me in."

Em saw the handle jiggle. And then Liam said, "Looks like I'll need to find a key, or another way to get you out. I'll be back."

"Wait, do you think you could find some rope, or even bedsheets? There's a window."

"Don't you have bedsheets?"

"I did. They took them."

"Okay, give me a minute."

Em rested her forehead against the door and closed her eyes. Liam had come back. She mentally apologized for doubting him.

"I'm back." Liam's voice came through the door again. "I'm going to feed this under the door. I found some supplies in the room across the hall. Matches, tools, a knife, a tarp… Did someone just leave this stuff here? Crazy!"

It sounded like Liam had found her confiscated items. "Those are mine. They took them as well. I'm guessing you found the rope."

In response, the rope started snaking under the door. Em grabbed the end and started pulling. Tying the end to the bedpost, Em continued yanking the rest of the rope through. The other end finally came under the door, and Em tossed it out the window.

"Looks like it'll reach the ground, Liam. Can you meet me outside and around back? The window faces away from the main street."

"On my way. Be careful, Em."

Em listened to Liam move down the hallway and hurried to gather her things.

Then she realized she was still wearing the beautiful evening gown, which was impractical for climbing out of windows. Clumsily, she retrieved her old clothes and tried to shed the gown, but the row of tiny buttons impeded her progress. She yanked hard, and the gown tore. Buttons clattered to the floor and the gown slipped off. She pulled on the old trousers and blouse, feeling a little better already. She kicked off her thin slippers, hastily rewrapped her ankle, and pulled on her work boots. Then, impulsively, she grabbed the gown and slippers from the floor and shoved them into her pack. Maybe she could sell them once they reached Gillamor.

Em pulled up the rope end and lowered down her pack, the book cradled carefully inside. Then Em began her own descent.

It wasn't easy, especially with the drugs still lingering in her system. The rope cut into her soft hands, and when she'd try to ease her way down, she would slip. Halfway down, she changed her tactic and wrapped her boot around the rope. This worked better, and she was able to inch down without ripping up her hands further. At the bottom she dropped with a soft "oof."

She untied her pack and inched away from the window under cover of the bushes. After a few minutes of waiting for Liam, Em started to get nervous. *Has Liam been caught by those gray attendants?*

She heard a dog barking around the front of the building and shouts of men rushing out into the streets. Was that Bob? Where was Liam? Em hoped they hadn't discovered her missing yet, and began to worry that they wouldn't make it away in time.

Minutes later, Liam came from the opposite direction, panting and carrying his own knapsack.

"What happened?"

"They tried to stop me at the bottom of the stairs. After an unpleasant conversation, I decided to escalate the encounter."

"You fought them?" Em gasped.

"Well, I threw a punch or two. Knocked away some firearms. Then I ran, but I had to lose them before I came back here. Bob is leading them on a wild chase. I think we're safe, but we should probably get going. Can you run?"

"I think so. They drugged me, but it seems to be wearing off."

Liam started, and he faced her fully, eyes furious, "I knew something was off at dinner. I'm glad you're okay."

Impulsively, Em grabbed his hand and squeezed it. "Thank you," she said, feeling awkward.

He nodded. "Sure. I said I'd help you get a new tree. Hard to get a new tree when you're being held captive by an evil spa owner."

Em let out an unsanctioned giggle. It was a harrowing ordeal, but it sounded ridiculous when Liam said it. Then, to cover her embarrassment, she dropped his hand and pointed away from town. "Let's get out of here."

～

THE DARKNESS WAS their friend as they trotted away from Arrenmore. The sound of barking and the flicker of evening lights grew dimmer as they found the road on the far side of town. They moved in silence, both of the same mind: as much space as possible should be put between them and the Gray Horse. Bob even sensed the need for stealth and silently jogged at Liam's side. Em was still sluggish. She studied the ground in front of her, devoting her whole mind to putting one foot in front of the other.

After an eternity at a quick pace, Em began to feel a throbbing in her ankle. She slowed and glanced back. She saw no lights and heard no sounds of pursuit. Stopping, she planted hands on hips and exhaled. Liam halted, paces ahead, and looked back and nodded. Mutely, he left the road to begin scouting for a campsite. Em commenced collecting firewood.

"No fire tonight," he tossed back. "Just in case they're still looking."

Em dropped the small pile of sticks she had amassed and followed Liam into the trees, near a small clearing. She shivered as a cold wind began to blow. Sliding down next to a boulder that would block the wind, she pulled her blanket around her. Liam sat beside her, his bedroll also wrapped around him.

"You want to tell me what happened back there?"

"Well, you saved me. Again. Thank you."

"No really, Em. You were getting supplies, and then, hours later, I found you in a fancy dining room with some gangster who held you captive, drugged you, and dressed you up. Want to fill in the blanks?"

Em explained how she found her way to the Gray Horse. The steam room. The sage facial drugging. The dress. The dinner conversation. "I should've left instead of going to the steam room, but I'm not sure they would've let me," she mused.

"Do you really think he met your parents?"

Em gulped. He had struck at the heart of what was troubling her.

"I don't think—I don't know. My parents died when I was very small." Em fell silent, mind reeling with the possibilities. Maybe her parents had been alive this whole time. Or maybe Monterey was lying.

"Oh. I'm sorry."

"It was so long ago, I barely remember them." Em said flatly. "Sam must have been mistaken."

"Sam seemed quite convinced. Or he really wanted to keep you around."

Em turned to Liam. "He seemed desperate. Like I was the only person who could save his town and he was willing to kidnap me to make it right. Is it so different from what I'm trying to do?"

"You aren't hurting anyone. He was."

"But I guess I understand. In a small way. I will have some bumps from the encounter," she grumped, rubbing her wrist. "And I never want to encounter that guy again. Although, I'm not sure why the ruse of dinner when he could've just interrogated me."

He looked at her steadily, his face partially lit by moonlight. "You can wear a dress quite well. And Sam noticed."

"Ugh! No, he—that's—I—" she stammered.

Liam averted his gaze. "Not that's it any of my business, but it kind of seemed like a date."

Em shivered, not just from the cold. She forced a laugh. "With that guy? Not in a million years." Their conversation ceased, and her mind kept replaying her ordeal over and over, each time revealing nothing new except a growing sense of horror and embarrassment. If only she had run. If only—

Liam's shoulder brushed hers, his warmth taking the edge off the wind. She shifted, leaning in, their arms pressed together against the cold. Bob curled up by her feet. But her mind continued to race, giving her no hope of a restful sleep.

CHAPTER 13

he disasters continued, one upon the other. Financial tragedies. Diplomatic crises. Famine. Deaths. After one last tragic planting in Evederell, where a beloved local cobbler lost the use of his hands, and an earthquake struck Gillamor at the hour of planting, the young empress ended the experiment, and returned to the capital. Her grand plan had backfired.

IT WAS A LONG, hard march that next day. The wind from the night before continued to blow, getting dust and grit in Em's shoes, in her clothes, in her ears. Liam was quiet today. Em wondered if he'd slept poorly also. Or maybe he was eager to get home so he could be rid of her. The Gray Horse kidnapping had probably been more than he bargained for.

They walked through a few small towns, but they didn't stop, and no one seemed curious. It must have been normal for those towns to encounter travelers so close to Gillamor. None of the places seemed so warm and cheery as Brookerby, or as dark and wrong as Arrenmore. They were just…*neutral* was the only word Em could assign. Liam confirmed that none of these places, to his knowledge, had ever possessed a protective tree.

Finally, as the sky was starting to turn rosy with the setting sun, Liam and Em crested a hill, and the capital city lay below them, stretching to the horizon. The houses stepping down the hillside were every color you could think. Lamplights and magical relic lights were starting to flicker on in the dimming of sunset. Large domes and arches marked the center of town, and trees lined the long, straight boulevards that decorated the city like Mendel's finest ribbons. The smells of spiced nuts floated in the air, and faint music reached Em's ears.

Mrs. Witherwill hosted a beautiful garden party every midsummer's eve in Brookerby. Gillamor looked like that, but a thousand times larger. Em gasped in delight.

Liam stood beside her, grinning. "It's quite a sight."

"I've never seen anything so grand in my whole life."

"You've come at a fine time. The festival of Rashorbuj has started. There will be decorations and food and music for dancing all over town. It's my favorite time to be in Gillamor."

Em suddenly felt uneasy. She had brought a few coins with her, but her purse had been looted by both the soldiers and the Gray Horse attendants. Would her remaining coins be enough to purchase food and lodging in such a grand town? Perhaps Liam could direct her to the right place. "Could you point me toward an inn—safe, but not too expensive? We could meet back in the morning, if you'd still like to aid me in my search."

Liam's eyebrows raised in surprise. "Em, you don't have to go to an inn. We're in this together, you're staying with me."

Em's mind flashed back to Liam's one-room shack in the woods, and imagined trying to bed down, dress, and bathe in the same single room as him. It did not feel proper. She shook her head, "I don't want to impose. You've done so much already. It's okay. I have a few coins—"

"Em, please. Let me offer you my humble flat. At least come see it. If you are still not comfortable, I can guide you to a respectable inn nearby."

Em hesitated. "I suppose I'd like to see where you live, even if I don't stay," she said diplomatically.

"Good," he said happily. "Just a little farther now."

They jogged down the hill and started to weave through the people and carts filling the streets. Em spotted a carriage that moved on its own—with steam power or magic, she couldn't tell. She stared in awe until Liam called her name to urge her on. The closer they came to sounds of music and flickering torchlights, the busier it became.

Liam grabbed Em's hand to keep from losing her in the crowd. She felt her cheeks flush at this gesture, but she ignored the impropriety with the practical thought that there was no other way of keeping together in the crowd.

Music from a fiddle and drum came from somewhere up ahead, and vendors flanked the road now, selling fine cloth, precious gemstones, and spices. Liam and Em wound through the crowd, ducking around shoppers and dancers. Em had never seen so many people in one place, and tried to look at everything as Liam's hand tugged her along. She noticed soldiers in the crowd and quickly turned her head away. She'd just as soon avoid another run-in.

Just before they reached a giant archway celebrating some historical victory of Gillamor and marking the center of town, Liam veered down a side street lined with ornate stone buildings and doorways painted every color of the rainbow. He stopped and knocked at a door the color of jaybirds with elaborate carvings detailed in gold.

Em thought perhaps he had taken a detour to see a rich friend about her lodgings. The massive door swung open, and as Liam walked inside, he was greeted with "sir" and "master" by the multiple men and women in the vast entry hall.

Em followed, addled. What was this?

"Sir, we must get you into a warm bath."

"Master, perhaps a spot of tea for the lady?"

"How was the country lodge this time of year, Lord Hallson?"

Em hovered in the marble foyer in a state of shock. She realized she had been staring, mouth agape, and quickly closed it. It was a lavish residence. Looking up, she saw an exquisite blown-glass sculpture hanging as decoration from the high entryway. The sconces—

were they electric or magic?—lining the windows and doors had gold detailing. She glanced down at her clothes, rumpled and dirty from days of traveling, and felt as if she had landed in the wrong place.

Liam answered questions as quickly as they were flung at him. He glanced back to see Em standing just inside the door, ready to bolt, clutching her satchel nervously. Striding back, he held out a hand to guide her farther in. "Em, this is my home. You are very welcome here." Em took a step forward.

To the staff, Liam announced, "Everyone, this is my honored guest, Emaline Strider of Brookerby. She and I have traveled a long way and have joint business to attend to in Gillamor. Please prepare a room for her." Turning back, he said quietly to Em, "Unless you'd feel more comfortable at an inn. I would however consider it a personal slight if you left." His eyes twinkled, and Em couldn't help but wince. This was so vastly different from what she had pictured, and he had seen right through her.

She nodded and spoke loudly. "I'll stay. Thank you for the kind invitation." The household staff, who seemingly held their breath while she deliberated, were now in motion, whisking her off through the mansion. As she was floated out of the foyer, she turned her head and gave Liam a bewildered look. She heard him burst into laughter.

SHE WAS LED to a room with dark cherry-wood furniture, and beautiful paintings of tranquil waters hung on the walls. The room had an adjoining room for bathing, and a tub was being filled with steaming hot water and rose oil. Was that a magical tub, or indoor plumbing? Either way, Liam must be very rich indeed.

She hesitated only a moment, but then peeled off her clothes, which were caked in dust, and slid into the elaborate copper tub. A sigh of relief escaped her body. She had made it to Gillamor. In one piece. With help, she conceded. And now she was inexplicably being waited on.

One of the maids scooped up her clothes and bustled out of the room. To wash them, Em hoped. Although there was a coin flip's chance the staff would unceremoniously toss them in the rubbish heap. A soft-looking mint-green robe appeared on a clothing rack near the tub. *At least I'll have something to wear,* Em thought wryly.

As the maid bustled about, changing bed sheets and airing out the room, Em nestled deeper into the warm water, leaned her head back against the rim, and closed her eyes. *Liam has some explaining to do,* she thought lazily.

~

EM FINALLY FORCED herself out of the water when it turned lukewarm. She had scrubbed every inch of herself and was pink with the friction. She toweled herself dry, pulled on the silky robe, and padded barefoot to the bedchamber.

Her satchel had been placed on the bedside table. The maids must not have known what to make of her tools and supplies, as they were laid out in a neat row, like hairbrushes. Em let out a blast of laughter at the sight. The dress from the Gray Horse was hanging in the wardrobe, which otherwise stood bare.

The Standard Book of Anything was sitting innocently by her tools. Her fingers itched to pick it up and read cover to cover, searching for details about her parents. Sam Monterey had seemed so sure. He said Em looked like her mother. Maybe they—

A knock sounded on the door, and Em quickly spun from the book. "Yes?"

A maid entered. "If you please, Lady Emaline. The master had some business to attend to and will not be present at dinner. We have brought you a tray but would be happy to serve you in the dining room if you'd prefer?"

On cue, Em's stomach rumbled. She smiled graciously. "Thank you, a tray would be just fine." Looking down at her bathrobe, she added wryly, "I'm not sure I'm appropriately dressed for a dining room."

The maid, a frizzy-haired girl with dark, smiling eyes and skin the color of cinnamon, grinned, but then quickly schooled her face back to professionalism. "Yes, miss, we did take the liberty of sending your traveling clothes for washing. There are bedclothes in the bureau. We can send for the tailor tomorrow morning if you'd like additional garments to wear in Gillamor."

"That's very kind. I believe I might need help there; I'm not very fashionable, you see."

The girl's smile was so wide it nearly stretched off her face. She began to chatter animatedly about Gillamor fashions. Despite Mendel's tutelage over the years, Em did not understand how lace and bows added anything when all you needed was a functional shift to keep you warm and decent. She listened, trying to retain which colors were in style this season, brain spinning to keep up with the numerous rules for avoiding a fashion faux pas.

The girl's monologue was abruptly cut off when an older woman poked her head in the door and began to scold her for leaving the tray out in the hall to get cold. With apologies, the tray was set on the small breakfast table by the window, and the serving women exited quickly, closing the door with a quiet click.

Slightly relieved, Em plopped down at the breakfast table and began inhaling the feast Liam's staff had sent up. Pheasant, root vegetables, soft rolls, berries, cheeses, and a tiny cake of dusted sugar, lavender, and lemon.

She wondered again at this large house in the center of town and tried to reconcile it with the scruffy man from the woods with the dog. *Did he lie to me?* she wondered uncomfortably. Mind scanning back through their interactions, she had a general impression of a self-made man. He baked bread. He could bandage an ankle. He was happy in a tiny hut in the middle of nowhere. But he uttered no falsehoods that she could detect. Just an impression that turned out to be wrong. Then, unbidden, she recalled how he held her when they danced on the road. The warmth of his hands on her back. Her waist. How he'd mentioned Monterey's less-than-honorable intentions. How his shoulder brushed hers last night. His hand guiding her through the streets.

Where is my mind? Em scolded herself. Brookerby needed her. All she was interested in was if Liam was as committed to finding a tree as she was. Popping the last of the berries in her mouth, she decided to keep her eyes open, and her heart firmly shut. Despite, or perhaps because of, the opulent mansion around her, Em's mind relaxed slightly.

Stomach full, she flopped onto the large bed, and reached for *The Standard Book of Anything. Mystery number two, let's see what we can find about Anne and Farrigan Strider of Brookerby.* Opening to a random page, she found:

Current Fashions of Gillamor. The capital city of Esnania has some of the most ostentatious clothing in the entire Eastern Hemisphere. This is no surprise that residents wish to be as brightly colored as their buildings. Men wear audaciously colored suits, and prints in the form of scarves and neckties. Hats with significant height or detailing have become desired in recent years. Women have embraced brightly colored gowns with square necklines. Bows have fallen out of fashion, but there is a great demand for ruffles, and lace gloves are expected in polite society.

"Oh, joy," Em muttered. She skimmed the rest of the article and found no cross-references except a statement about notable tailors of the region. "Now the book is just torturing me," she groaned. Nevertheless, she flipped to the "Famous Tailors of Southern Esnania" page. And then Em was so startled, she almost fell off the bed.

There was a large portrait of Mendel in a black paisley jacket, fingers tapping his chin thoughtfully, as he often did, and under the picture, a caption read "Mendel of Drecovia, fashion icon and builder of clothing empires." She was baffled. How?

She devoured every word, learning how he had moved to the bustling northern hamlet of Drecovia seventeen years earlier and— with the guidance of an established designer—launched a fashion design studio that shook the world. His dresses were desired all over the country and were carried, at great expense, from one end of the empire to the other. He eventually established shops in every major town in Esnania and sent his designs regularly for construction onsite, altered to fit the clientele. He was the foremost authority on fashion in Gillamor, and his good opinion was considered the dream for any other clothing designer hoping to make a name for themselves.

The article concluded that Mendel of Drecovia was active still today but had retired in a sleepy little village close to the capital city. His designs were still being carried to his shops all over the country.

Em sat back, shaking her head. How? Mendel had been in Brookerby as long as she could remember. How had he run a fashion empire that nobody caught wind of? From another town, no less! Then Em remembered the letter from Gram to Mendel—she referred to his "new town." He had fled to Drecovia when the tree fell seventeen years before. But he had come back after a few months, hadn't he?

Her mind began to flash with memories of Mendel: the fastidious shop full of clothing that was far more than the town was buying from him; the purple dress in the window, wholly unsuited for Brookerby's dances in the town square; his regular use of messengers, and his lovely designs pinned to the wall of his office. Yes, she could believe he was doing far more than he let on. Em's heart ached. She longed for home. For Mendel and Ilna. For Gram.

She flipped to the cited article about the "sleepy town" he had retired to—and recognized some familiar script.

Dearest Mendel,

I hope you are well and that this letter finds its way to you. I worry for your safety. I understand your reasons for leaving, and the prosperity that follows you wherever you go is a sign of everything we know to be true. Be careful, my friend. Using your abilities, even for something as inconsequential as clothing, could attract unnecessary attention.

We are losing Ilna more and more day by day. She will sit and weep for hours and then grow irate. She has twice destroyed her own shop. I have repaired her printing press twice, but I am fearful the empire will detect my skill if I continue to aid our friend. As her dearest confidante, I believe you

are the only one who can endeavor to bring her back to herself. Will you not
come and try?

Forgive me for writing so directly, but prosperity is nothing if you cannot
face yourself in the mirror each morning. Is your empire of needles and
thread worth losing everything else?

Please Respond,
Gram

Gram said "empire of needles and thread." To Em, this seemed to be confirmation of the previous pages. But much of what she said seemed to be pulling Mendel back to Brookerby.

She knew Ilna and Mendel had a special bond of friendship. They had been the best of friends as children. Many in town assumed they would marry, but Mendel preferred romantic attachments with men. He was unlucky in that arena, and Ilna had often picked up the pieces when his relationships didn't work out. He had wholeheartedly supported Ilna's ill-fated union to Vanin Thorne, and supported her further when the marriage dissolved. This letter marked another big moment on their list of friendship. Mendel apparently had returned to pull Ilna out of a very dark place.

Em's mind flashed to Ilna on the floor of her shop. Ilna admitting that she was not in control when the tree had fallen before. She imagined Mendel sitting next to Ilna under the printing press, bringing her back to herself, and her heart ached once again.

She imagined Gram and Mendel in the town holding cell. Had their arrests been short-lived? If not, who would look after Ilna? Then Em pictured Brookerby falling into ruin, like Arrenmore. All of this stoked an urgency within Em to find a solution.

And find it soon.

THE NEXT MORNING WAS A WHIRLWIND. A seamstress arrived in her room just after her breakfast tray to provide her with some Gillamor-appropriate clothing. Em selected two plain-looking blouses and basic skirts, accepting without comment the disapproving looks and *tsks* from both the seamstress and the frizzy-haired maid, Tilly, whom Em had invited to the fitting. Em also selected a pair of cerulean trousers that were made to look like a skirt, with fabric that swished and swirled when she walked. The frowns of her companions turned to neutral looks, so she thought it fashionable enough to be a good compromise.

She also selected a new pair of shapely leather shoes, much more fashionable than her walking boots but sturdy enough that they wouldn't fall apart upon contact with the ground.

The seamstress also urged hair ribbons and clips ("traditional for the festival"), new undergarments ("absolutely necessary"), and lace gloves ("no proper lady goes outside without them").

Em began to beg off. "That's all, please. I cannot afford much more than this," she insisted, starting to pull out the few coins she had brought.

The seamstress pushed back. "Oh no, dear, you don't have to worry about that. It's all taken care of."

Em was taken aback. "What?" Then it registered. Liam. "Oh no!" she said, embarrassed. "That's not necessary. Please, I'll just—" She helplessly glanced at Tilly, but the girl's eyes were shining happily. Em could see how out of context this gesture would be taken. By afternoon, all the maids would know that Liam was purchasing her clothes and would draw some inappropriate conclusions.

"No," she said firmly. "Absolutely not. Liam—um, Lord Hallson—has been very kind, but I do not wish to be indebted to him."

"He thought you'd say that." The seamstress chuckled, handing her a folded note.

Em took the note, addressed to her. She broke the seal and began reading. The writing was unfamiliar, but she instantly knew it came from him.

Em,

If you are reading this note, then the fittings have

progressed as I imagined they would. You have selected simple clothes and have refused to let me cover the cost. I want to remind you that your quest may require you to make connections and enter exclusive places in the city. Clothes open doors in Gillamor. Do not let your pride stop you from saving Brookerby. I promised to help, so please let me. And try to have some fun.

    Your Friend,

    Liam

Em refolded the note quickly, mind racing. His logic was undeniable, curse him. Glancing up, she saw the seamstress watching with bated breath.

"Very well," Em conceded. "He may cover it, for now, but I will pay him back."

After the note's coercion, Em tried on the fancier dresses. Each one was more impractical and ruffly than the one before it. Yards and yards of flowing material, yet most still dipped dangerously low in front. Each dress she tried brought a sign of admiration from Tilly, and an eyeroll from Em. She was shocked to learn that women in Gillamor really dressed like this.

Finally, at a loss, she turned to Tilly. "What do you think?"

The girl glowed, as if Em had bestowed a great gift upon her. She clapped her hands gleefully, jumped off her perch, and quickly sorted dresses from the pile Em had tried on. "This one compliments your figure... Not that one... This looked very nice with your eyes... Ah, the green one is in the latest style, you will stand out... This is a good day dress."

Em held the dresses, bewildered, but giving in to the windstorm that was Tilly. After the selection, the seamstress took up the dresses that required altering and promised to return them within a few days. The rest of the new purchases remained with Em, scattered around the room, and Tilly chattered happily while hanging them in the closet. Em retrieved the swishing skirt-pants and a blouse, dressing for the day. Taking a quick bite of toast from her now-cold breakfast tray and a few coins, she thanked Tilly for her help, and headed toward the door. She didn't attempt to find Liam in the grand house. She just had to get out.

BREATHING IN THE LATE-MORNING AIR, Em felt slightly more at ease out of doors. The fitting had made her feel helpless, and she didn't like it. She shook out her arms quickly, trying to banish the feeling, and she quickly replaced it with a different one. Urgency. She had to find a tree. A seed. Something that would save her town before it fell to ruin. Something that would save Gram and Mendel and Ilna.

She began by crossing toward the nearest park, a tiny lot at the end of the boulevard. She examined each plant for something—anything—unique. Em even paid attention to see if touching the leaves or bark produced that telltale tingle, an internal sign of something special. She felt nothing and realized she had no idea what to search for. Perhaps a library would help?

Leaving the park, she started crisscrossing the streets. She stopped at each green space, no matter how insignificant, to examine each plant and tree. After three tiny parks, she found a public library several blocks from Liam's house. Diving into the stacks, Em spent a few hours flipping through each book in the plant section, reading each tome on magical objects cover to cover.

Finally, an ancient man approached, asking if she needed help. Looking up from the pages of her latest goose chase, she noticed the pile of books that had led nowhere scattered around her haphazardly on the table, making quite a mess.

Em blushed. "No, I'm sorry. I promise to put these away."

The librarian picked up the nearest book, reading the spine. "*Properties of Regional Flora...* Is your garden giving you difficulties, young miss?"

"No, sir," Em said respectfully. "I'm trying to find information on a type of tree. It's quite rare, I'm afraid."

The librarian's eyes twinkled. "Aha! A real quest, then! You seem to have read our whole plant section, but I can provide you with a list of other libraries in the city. There are a few with collections much more extensive than ours."

Em thanked the man as he scribbled out a list for her. She hurried out of the library, gripping the paper tightly. It contained nearly ten locations, and she didn't know the addresses. Perhaps she should acquire a map. Or a guide.

Her thoughts turned again to Liam. He would be the ideal guide, if he were available. But the itch in the back of her brain made her pause. When they were traveling, he seemed very interested in helping her. He also seemed to be a person with ample time on his hands. This impression might've been false. Apparently, Liam was a person of some importance, given his home and title. What other impressions had Em formed about him that were counterfeit?

Pulling out the note from this morning, she studied his words. He wanted to help. But why? Was he getting something out of it? Was he, like Sam Monterey, trying to glean some personal benefit from her knowledge and efforts?

Em took a calming breath. There was nothing for it. She would have to confront him and get his reasons. If he was not forthcoming, she could leave his home.

She glanced around, finding herself on a narrow wooden walkway outside the library that wove through the streets and narrow passages between buildings. Taking another deep breath, Em stepped onto the planks and turned left, following the path. She wouldn't need a guide. The next time she encountered someone, she could show them the list and ask for directions, until they were all checked off. A new tree could be found. With or without Liam. She began to whistle "The Old Shanty" as she trod the planks into the heart of the city.

CHAPTER 14

eeling a deep sense of failure, the young empress queried the damage to her realm from the well-intentioned gifts to each village. She paced the Golden Lark Palace's gilded halls, obsessing over each new report. The woman concluded that magic wielded carelessly was the culprit.

HOURS LATER, dejected and weary, Em found her way back to the first library near Liam's house. The sun dipped, the sky darkening to a tangerine shade. She had only made it to three libraries, counting the original one. The second was so small they didn't have any books on magical items, and only two books on plants. The third was closed for the festival.

Gillamor revelers had not been particularly helpful either. Some had outright ignored her, and one lanky, inebriated man tried to pull her into a dance against her wishes. He had a new welt on his shin to show for his attentions, but Em was certain he wouldn't feel any pain until he sobered up.

She plopped down on the wide steps of the library, rubbing her aching feet through her new shoes. Her ankle seemed to have mended just enough, but she was in danger of developing a blister on her heel from the footwear.

Across the street, a small band of raggedly dressed men and women shouted, attempting to shove printed slips of paper into the hands of those walking by. A flyer fell at Em's feet. Its top line called out to her: "Are you a truth seeker?"

Em smiled wryly. "Always," she said aloud.

She read further, and her heart began to quicken. The paper had the picture of a large tree, and the words "Veritas Hamadryads" and the place and time of a conclave during the festival.

A woman across the road was still speaking in a fluttery voice. "— the trees connect us, and we are connected to them. And yet, it is kept secret. We just want the truth."

Em's heart hammered. This was about the trees. And it could be a solution.

She plucked up the paper and stood, blisters forgotten. Maybe someone in this group would talk to her. But when she eyed the cluster of raggedy people antagonizing a well-dressed old gentleman, she had sudden flashbacks to the mob outside Alfred's shop. They didn't quite seem in control of their senses. Did their rags indicate they were refugees from broken tree towns? If so, perhaps they had never recovered. Or maybe they were beggars paid to hand out flyers for someone else. After another person was victimized by the group, Em backed away and turned toward Hallson Manor. Perhaps Liam would know what to make of this.

LIAM WAS HOME when Em arrived. She entered through the front door, only to be whisked to the parlor, where Liam sat reading an evening paper.

"Em!" he cheerfully intoned, setting down the paper on an oak side table. "You didn't run away after all. Come sit!"

The room was alight with candles, and a massive, ornate rug covered the floor. The furniture, several upright chairs and a sofa, were upholstered with a dark green fabric that looked like velvet. A bookcase covered one entire wall, with a large fireplace taking up another. Bob slept on a cushion at Liam's feet. The room felt like the extreme upgraded version of Liam's shack, tidy and welcoming.

Em's pants swished as she crossed the room to sit in the seat opposite Liam, remembering to sit gracefully instead of flopping into the chair. "Ah, yes. About leaving this morning. I— That is to say— Um—" Em blushed, feeling awkward. "My apologies, Lord Hallson," she finished lamely.

Liam's mouth quirked up. "You've learned the rest of my name."

"I suppose I didn't ask you enough about yourself when we were traveling. Seems like you left out a few details."

"Did I forget to mention the large house, the fortune, and the title? Blast! Knew I was leaving something out," he said in mock seriousness.

Em huffed. "A few *minor* details." She studied him: his brown-amber eyes had a subdued twinkle, but the stubble had been shaved, hair combed, and casual traveling clothes had been replaced with a well-cut suit. He looked good. Really good. She had to keep reminding herself that this was the same man she had danced with on the dusty road.

Then she realized he was studying her. What he saw, she didn't know.

"Did you find anything today?" he asked.

Em produced her one clue, the flyer. "I might've found something. A group related to the trees. Maybe they can help. Have you heard of them?"

"May I see it?"

Em handed the note over.

Liam studied it for a moment, looked at Em, and then burst out laughing.

Em felt annoyed. "So, they don't know anything," she surmised.

"Oh, Em. This is a cult. They inhale hallucinogens and pray to the great tree. I'm pretty sure they don't know anything."

"Well, it's the only lead I found today. Are you sure—"

"They'd be happy to try. They'd also take all your money and whisk you into a barking and branching ceremony." Liam chortled.

Em snatched back the paper and wadded it up. "Fine. They're a cult. Dropping it."

Liam wiped a tear from his eye, he was laughing so hard. "Oh, Great Tree!" he intoned, giggling. Bob had been riled by his laugher and now trotted around the room, panting happily. After a few moments, Liam finally settled down, let out a breath, and gave an apologetic grin to Em. "You didn't know."

Em was irritated. But she patted Bob and changed the subject. "Your note this morning," she said lightly. "How did you know?"

"Lucky guess." He shrugged, eyes smiling.

"Well, thanks. I think. I'm still not entirely sure what I've agreed to, fashion-wise. I let Tilly do a lot of the picking."

"Good idea. Tilly knows her fashion. She's studying to become a designer when she isn't working here."

Em smiled. She could well believe it.

She glanced back at him; a question kept itching the back of her brain. She had pieced together a history of Liam from the stories he shared on the road. Things about his brother. His mother's baking. Living in a small town called Evederell. Getting in fights. His father tending cattle. Nothing in this richly furnished place matched those tales.

"Liam, I want to ask you something, but I don't want it to sound rude."

"Ask me anything. I'll answer it if I can."

"How does one become a lord from tending cattle? That's what your father did, right?"

"Ah. I had a feeling this question was coming. It's a bit complicated, but I'll tell you. At dinner."

"Dinner?"

"Yes, would you care to take the evening meal with me? My staff tells me I have a very fine dining room that should be used more often. Then maybe after, if you are interested, we can see some of the festival."

"That sounds— Yes, that would be great." Em stammered dumbly. Dinner? Festival? It was only Liam, why was she suddenly nervous? Glancing down, she noticed how rumpled her blouse had become. Perhaps she should put on a dress for tonight. Standing, she said, "Let me go freshen up. Give me ten minutes."

"I'll be here." He picked up his newspaper, a small smile crossing his face.

~

EM FLOATED down the stairs a short while later wearing one of the fashionable dresses Tilly had chosen that morning—one of the few that did not need alterations. It was light blue silk with silver-and-gold flowers embroidered on the hem and bodice. A square-cut neckline showed more than Em was used to displaying.

Tilly had assured her it would be appropriate for the festival, and arranged her hair with the decorative pins. Em fought the urge to tug up the bodice of her gown, remembering Tilly's lecture about proper young ladies who do not adjust their clothing in public. And proper young ladies can wear low-cut garments, if they are wearing lace gloves. Em was skeptical, of course, but Tilly was the expert, so she donned a pair of light blue lace gloves that stopped at her wrists.

All in all, Em felt very much like someone else. Someone elegant, almost beautiful. Like the fair damsel in Gram's fairy stories. She felt tempted to descend the staircase in slow, measured steps, gloved hand gliding down the banister.

At the bottom of the staircase, Liam spoke to his steward. He casually glanced up, and his words trailed off midsentence.

The steward, a slender older gentleman with a quick eye, covered for Liam. "But I have caught you right before dinner, sir. I will find you tomorrow to resolve this matter. Have a lovely evening."

Liam absently thanked him as he exited; his eyes were still watching Em descend.

Em felt her cheeks warm. As she reached the bottom step, she paused, breaking the silence. "Tilly assured me this was appropriate for the festival. It seems a bit much."

"Oh no. It's just right." Liam reached out a hand to escort her off the final step. "Emaline Strider of Brookerby, all eyes will be on you tonight."

She gave him a cheeky grin as she took his hand and stepped down. And if she were being honest with herself, she felt a little tingle as their hands connected.

He gestured toward an open door across the entryway with his free hand, a sincere smile on his face. "Shall we?"

"Yes, please." On cue, her stomach rumbled, and for her, the spell was broken. He tucked her hand around his arm and led her toward the open dining room.

~

It was the fanciest meal Em had ever eaten. Crisply clad serving attendants whisked multiple courses to her. Vegetables, fish, venison, soup, plum pudding—all prepared with skill and served with the perfect sauce or seasoning. Serious conversation was completely forgotten as Em exclaimed over each course. The fish had tiny little bones that required concentration to remove. The soup was heavenly and creamy, and just a bit spicy.

Several times throughout the meal, she caught Liam watching her. Gauging her reaction to fine dining, she imagined. Was she such a bumpkin? A small glass of fortified wine was served with the pudding; it was rich and tart, blending perfectly with the sweetness of the dessert.

Letting out a sigh of contentment, Em set down her glass, relaxed after the wondrous meal. Glancing at Lord Hallson, who was sipping his wine with a thoughtful expression, she recalled her question from earlier. Inching her chair away from the large table, she tentatively revived the subject. "Might I reintroduce the question I asked earlier?"

Liam let out a breath and set down his glass. His tone was serious.

"I knew you would ask. The moment I decided to travel with you, I had to decide how much to share and how much to conceal."

This seemed calculated to Em, but then she recalled the book tucked away upstairs. She had secrets too. She nodded for Liam to continue.

"My father indeed raised cattle in the country. We fled Evederell when my brother and I were on the verge of adulthood. We came to Gillamor with very little in our pockets, and only a hope for something better."

"Why did you leave Evederell?" Em interrupted.

Liam studied her for a moment, then let out a sigh as if surrendering. "We lost our warding tree of protection."

Em leaned forward. That made so much sense, she chided herself for not guessing it sooner. "Is that why you wanted to help me? Because you'd already lived through it?"

Liam nodded.

Pieces clicked into place. Of course he'd wanted to help her. It was a traumatic moment from his own life. He knew what she was feeling. Then she noticed he wasn't continuing, and she met his eyes. He hesitated, then picked up his story.

"It was difficult in Gillamor those first few months. I remember many evenings where we went hungry, and my father came home so tired he would fall into bed, fast asleep with his shoes still on. My brother and I also traversed the city, searching for employment, or at least odd jobs in exchange for coins or bread. But the city had been flooded with refugees from the southern kingdom's war, and we could not even beg for our supper. We were also fighting the ill effects of a fallen tree. I think you've probably seen what that looks like."

Em nodded.

"Finally, my father received a bit of luck. He had an old friend who worked for the empress, managing her vast estate, who was looking for additional help. My father met him by chance in the street and was hired on the spot. My brother and I were also offered positions in the empress's service, which we gladly took. There was food on the table, and all was well.

"Ten years passed in this way. My father had been given more responsibility and more trust until he was regularly with Her Majesty, providing her information and counsel. She trusted him implicitly. Everything flourished under him. When an elder statesman died, leaving a vast estate and fortune with no heirs, the empress bestowed the title and estate to my father for his years of service."

Em jumped in. "So Lord Hallson—"

"—was the elder statesman who died. We assumed that family name. It still doesn't really feel quite right, but the name comes with the title."

"Your father must be an incredible man to have inspired such generosity."

"He was." Liam smiled sadly. "He passed a few years ago. And my mother soon after."

Em felt a sudden kinship with Liam. She knew, perhaps in a different way, what it was to be left behind when parents died. She reached across the table to touch his hand.

"I'm so sorry, Liam. About Evederell. About your parents."

Liam shrugged, looking down at her hand. Then he brushed her fingers with his own and spoke wistfully. "More than anything, if I had a wish to make, I would wish for my family back. Like it was before the tree fell. But just having them back would be enough." He glanced up again and met Em's eyes with his. "You can see why your project roused such enthusiasm in me. If I could help you..." He left the words hanging in the air, his eyes searching.

Em flashed a gentle smile. She knew what it was to lose family. She hoped to never find out what it was to lose her home. For her, it felt like nearly the same thing.

"What about your brother? Is he still in Gillamor?"

"My brother is still in service to the empress. I do not see him often, I think he travels a great deal, but he does still officially reside in town. Not in this house."

Em noticed Liam's clenched jaw with these words, and the unconscious tension he now carried in his body. She pried. "Why don't you see him?"

Liam's lips pursed. After a brief silence, he said, "He and I have had many disagreements over the years. About our family. About the trees. About life decisions. The differences feel insurmountable."

Em withdrew her hand under the guise of picking up her spoon once more. But then looked down at her empty pudding bowl and set the spoon back down. She felt as if she had stumbled into a very uncomfortable place.

The silence started to grow between them, and Em cast about for a way to break the tension. Changing the subject, she picked up her glass, downed the remaining wine in one gulp, and stood, saying, "I believe, Lord Hallson, you have promised me a glimpse of the festival?"

Liam let out a surprised laugh, which made Em grin. He stood as well, and circled the table to her side, offering his arm. "My lady?"

She rose and demurely placed her hand on his forearm, and then suddenly sprinted for the door, letting out an unladylike, "Whoop!"

Laughing again, he charged after her toward the hallway and out the engraved front door.

CHAPTER 15

The empress summoned the mage who had designed the trees for a reckoning. The mage, Bronwyn Featherweight, arrived at the Golden Lark Palace in style, astride a braided white stallion, flanked by seven mages of skill and renown. The woman was formidable in her power and in her indignation. Bronwyn knew she would be blamed for the backlash and was prepared to use any means to protect her legacy.

THE STREETS WERE FILLED with colored lights, the aromas of food being cooked over open flames, and voices shouting happily.

Em and Liam did not have to walk far to be in the midst of a colorful carousel of activity. Individuals of all ranks comingled, waltzed, and jigged to the sounds of fiddle and drum. Most had worn their finest attire, and Em spotted more than one dress that looked like the wildly impractical purple gown from Mendel's shop window. Torches lit up the night with flickering warmth. The smell of roasting meat mixed with that of warm spiced wine and candied nuts. Buskers were juggling, singing, and performing simple card tricks up and down the street, and their voices collided with the music and the vendors' shouts in a symphony of rowdy joviality.

Liam and Em drifted among the dancing and selling, not speaking, but occasionally pointing out some marvelous sight to each other. Em was ready to drop all of her coin at the iced cream stand when Liam pulled her over to a street vendor selling knotted dough, baked in oil, and covered with colorful sugar. Buying one, he tore it in two and handed half to Em.

"I can't believe you think I'm hungry after that wonderful meal—" Em took a bite anyway and groaned. It was warm and sugary and melted in her mouth. She had never tasted anything so magical.

"One of my favorites." Liam grinned, trying to brush the sugar off his fingers. "I have more to show you. Come on!" He pulled her hand, and she quickly ate the rest of the pastry while trying to keep up. Her fingers were grainy with sugar, and she had to stop herself from wiping them on her dress. *Tilly would have my head*, she thought.

They arrived in front of a game where the object was to throw small bags full of dried beans through holes in an upright wooden board. The more times you made it in, the more points you got, Liam explained and dropped a halfpenny on the counter for the game operator. The operator handed him five bags to throw.

"I used to be good at this game," Liam said confidently as he threw his first bag. It bounced high and wide.

"Just a practice throw," Em allowed. Liam said nothing and threw the second bag. It got closer but bounced off the edge of one of the holes.

"They're weighted a bit differently," Liam said nonchalantly, picking up the third bag. Em hid a smile. The third bag went through the lowest-point circle, and Em let out a cheer. The next two also scored, and Liam turned away, shrugging. "Not as good as I remember. Do you want to try?"

"Yes!" Em stepped up, dropping one of her coins for the operator.

She was dreadful. Most of her throws bounced uselessly off the board, but her last throw went in the smallest hole for high points. "Yeah!" Em pumped her fist, and the operator handed her a small toy as a prize; it was a tiny baton that could be balanced and twirled between two small sticks. Turning back around, she flashed a smile at Liam and waved her new possession. "What next?"

He stashed her new toy in his pocket and reached out a hand to grasp hers. "You pick," he said, and it was her turn to lead him down the street toward a juggler.

They stood watching the man juggle handkerchiefs, balls, batons, and finally apples, which he took bites out of as he juggled. It was quite impressive, and they cheered and whooped as loud as anyone else.

Em glanced over several times during the performance and found Liam looking at her. He quickly looked forward when he noticed her noticing. She felt the warmth of his arm next to hers, and it drove her to distraction. She tried to imagine a romance with Liam, but every time she tried to picture it, she instead thought of Gram waiting in a jail cell for her return. Of Ilna and her printing press. Of Brookerby burning. And then she felt guilty for enjoying this beautiful night, in a lovely dress, with a handsome man beside her.

The performance ended, and the crowd began drifting away. A young man in a colorful patchwork cloak approached, flourishing his hands dramatically. "Would the beautiful woman like to know her fortune?"

"Ah." Em blushed to be referred to as beautiful, but she remembered her dress and attributed the attention to that. "Yes, thank you. What's my fortune?"

Liam had moved in protectively, but the man smoothly shuffled his cards, not deterred in the slightest. He slid closer to Em, continuing his bit. "The beautiful woman wonders whether she will find love? She has found it in a humble street performer, no? Or perhaps the lady wishes to know how many children she will have?"

Em was not very interested in this line of inquiry. She interrupted. "My friend, I have a different inquiry, if your skill extends beyond the mundane?"

The man's eyes glittered dangerously. "Aha, mademoiselle is no ordinary girl, I see. Ask any question, and I shall provide you an answer."

"We can go," Liam whispered, trying to steer Em away, but she stayed firmly rooted in place.

She cleared her throat and spoke imperiously, "I am on a quest of utmost importance. I would like to know if I will be successful in this endeavor." She heard a forced cough from Liam, but chose to ignore it. It wasn't like she told the busker anything of substance.

The man raised his eyebrows, but bowed obsequiously and then shuffled his cards again. "Select three," he instructed, fanning them out before her. She chose and handed them back.

"The first card"—he revealed it and handed it to her—"is the knave of gardens. Look for rogues and treachery in beautiful places."

"The second card is the charging stallion. It represents quick, decisive action." That card he also handed to her. Em didn't see a connection yet, but she nodded encouragingly. Liam was getting antsy.

"The third card..." The man revealed a card showing a headman's axe, stuck into tree stump. "Oh dear. The executioner. Perhaps this is..." The man's smoothness was gone as he fumbled with the cards and his words. "You will move quickly. You will be betrayed. This card would indicate your quest does not end as you expect. I'm so sorry, belladonna. But it does not always indicate...uh..." He snatched his cards back, bowed shallowly, and all but ran away.

Em's feet were stuck in glue. Her tongue felt dry.

"Em," Liam coaxed, "you can't believe him! It's just luck of the draw." He chuckled cautiously. "But that's literally the worst card you could've drawn."

"But what if it's true? What if, after all this, Brookerby is doomed? Or worse, my fate is death?"

"I wouldn't let that happen."

"You don't control life and death, Liam."

"I don't, but I can be by your side."

"He said someone would betray me...I can't..." She couldn't finish the thought, but knew she had to get away. She turned, but he grabbed her hand and gently pulled her toward him. She scowled. "Liam, stop. I can't..."

He stepped closer, reaching for both her hands, which he held sandwiched in his. "And I couldn't bear it if something happened to you." She felt the weight of his words, his eyes pleading.

Em felt a little dizzy. This close, she could smell pine and lavender. She felt something from him. He wasn't just an ally. A friend. He wanted... She couldn't finish the thought. Alarmed, she met his eyes.

Liam spoke. "I told you I would help you find a tree. I will help. I don't care how many impending death cards turn up. I'm in this."

Em tensed, feeling cornered.

He continued, "You cannot dissuade me, Em, so don't even try."

Em bit her lip and looked away. Speaking quickly, she shifted her jumbled thoughts back to the cards. She tried to explain. "My whole life has been a series of secrets and half-truths from the people I love. They treat me like the child that I once was. But I can fix things. And when I finally am able to fix something big—something important—I learn that I will fail? Miserably? I can't..." She felt helpless.

"You won't fail."

"How do you know? The card—"

"—the card is bullshit. You, Emaline Strider, won't fail, because you are determined to succeed. And you are a fully capable person. After only a few days of knowing you, I'm ready to stake my life on that."

At this declaration, Em lifted her eyes to meet his. She felt the knot in her stomach untie, replaced by a solid warmth in her chest. A thick quiet fell between the two as the world blared around them.

Liam broke the silence with a soft request. "Dance with me?"

She nodded. He dropped one of her hands and stepped back into the flow of people with Em in tow. She let him pull her down the street, toward the other dancing couples.

LIAM TWIRLED EM AGAIN, a flourish to the end of a lively two-step. The other dancers and spectators applauded the fiddle and lute players. Cries went up for an encore, and the musicians obliged, starting up a lilting waltz.

Em caught her breath. "I told you I'm not a dancer."

"I beg to differ." Liam had a light sheen of sweat on his brow.

"You told me you weren't, but you're quite good."

Liam laughed. "I said I didn't dance. Not that I couldn't dance. Let's try this one. It's…slower." Em nodded. Liam placed his hand under her outstretched one, and with a gentle tug, pulled her closer, placing his other hand softly around her waist. She felt the warmth of his hand through the thin fabric of her dress, and a little shiver went through her.

They began to step. Em was a bit uncertain, but Liam knew the dance well, and guided her through it while keeping his own toes safe. Em relaxed into the one-two-three pattern of the movement and looked up.

Liam was watching her.

"What?" Em blurted. Then blushed. She was wearing this beautiful dress. Maybe she should consider some manners to go with it. She backpedaled. "I mean, I—you have been looking at me tonight. Differently."

"I have."

The music carried on and they waltzed in silence, eyes locked. Em didn't know what to say. She expected denial or explanation. He could claim she had something stuck in her teeth, or her hair was out of fashion, or—

"Is that okay? If I look at you?"

"I don't know. I've never had this problem before. Not that it's a problem. I just—" She was babbling. She took a breath, collected her thoughts, and started again. "It was never my goal, back in Brookerby, to be the girl that gentlemen looked at. It seems a bit frivolous. I never dressed that part. And now I'm here. In a dress that I would've never worn. And you're looking at me like that—"

"Like what?"

"You're going to make me say it?"

Liam's eyebrow quirked up mischievously. "Sure. Like what?"

"Like Gleb looked at my friend, broken-nose Millie. He looked at her that way, and now they have four children."

"So…you're saying?"

Em huffed, and briefly lost the dance steps. She caught back up, and then took a deep breath and looked up at him again. "I like you, Liam. But I'm not ready to have four children with you."

Liam laughed heartily. To the point where other dancing couples turned to stare.

Em felt annoyed. "What?"

Liam, still chuckling, managed to squeeze out, "Four kids, great stars, Em. I don't think I'll ever be ready for that."

"So I'm imagining it? The look?"

He was silent for a moment, his smile fading. Finally, he said, "You're not imagining it."

Em felt warm and cold at the same time. This complicated everything. How could she rely on him as an ally when he was—?

Liam interrupted her thoughts. "Maybe my look means something different. Admiration. Respect. Happiness that you are here with me."

Em darted her eyes up to his. His words registered, and Em softened. She responded sincerely, "I'm happy to be here with you."

"That dress *is* pretty good. I might have to give Tilly a raise." Liam smirked.

Em *accidentally* stepped on his toes.

THEY DANCED A FEW MORE DANCES, Em was adding to her blister collection. On the last, a spirited line dance, she heard a voice behind her shout, "Anne? Anne!" Turning toward the voice, she saw a portly man with graying hair approaching her. He saw her face and looked slightly confused, stumbling back a step. "Apologies, miss," he stuttered, "I thought you were someone else."

On a hunch, Em asked, "Anne Strider?"

The man heaved a sigh of relief, "Oh, you know her! Of course, you're the spitting image. Her sister or niece, perhaps?"

A larger woman bumped into Em, who was standing still in the middle of the dance. The woman shot her a dirty look. Em stepped out of the way, leading the man to the edge of the dance floor with urgency. "Sir, please, could you tell me when you last saw her?"

"Oh, lass, couldn't tell you. It's been many months."

"How many?" Em asked sharply.

"Oh, a year or two. No more than five, to be sure. You know, you really look very similar. Are you a relation?"

"Yes, I am. Where was she staying? Did she tell you where she was going?"

The man viewed her suspiciously. "Cousin? Younger sister?"

"Daughter," Em replied tersely.

"Didn't know Anne had a daughter," the man wondered, scratching his chin.

"Apparently, neither does she," Em muttered bitterly.

"Well, no matter. She was staying with the Liverwoods down by the harbor. Excellent people, quality dinner parties. But like I said, it's been some time since she's been in Gillamor. That fellow Farrigan might've been with her. He always seemed to be sniffing around."

My father. Em thought. Aloud, she said, "Can you tell me anything else? What was she doing in town? What did you speak about?"

Liam had observed Em and the man on the edge of the dance and made his way over. "Everything all right, Em?"

"Oh, hello there, Lord Hallson! Do you know this young lady?"

"Good evening, Lord Birmingsquare. Miss Strider and I have mutual business in Gillamor, so I was showing her the festival." Liam's eyes were still on Em, questioning.

Lord Birmingsquare was oblivious. "Ah yes, the festival, such fun, especially for you young people, eh?" He touched his nose knowingly and winked at Liam. Then, he added, "I must be off! Lovely to meet you, Emaline. If you see your mother, say hello for me. Card games aren't the same without her."

He wandered off. Em was frozen, mind running through a million reasons why her mother would be cavorting in Gillamor, instead of dead and buried. None of them made any sense. Shouldn't she be happy? But Anne and Farrigan alive meant something worse. That they had left her behind.

"Em." Liam brushed her sleeve with his fingers. "What did he say?" Em felt numb. "That I look like my mother."

~

THE FESTIVAL HAD LOST its sparkle. Em held herself together remarkably, but Liam feigned exhaustion and suggested they call it a night. Weaving through the boisterous crowd toward Hallson Manor, they heard trumpet sounds up ahead, and a large crowd had gathered around a raised wooden platform.

Em slowed.

"It's an execution, Em," Liam cautioned, tugging at her hand to pull her away.

"That's festive," Em said. She felt sorry for the poor sap who was going to lose their life in the middle of a party.

"They do it every year. Usually it's not a violent criminal, but someone who has displeased the empress. Sometimes it's a magic user."

Em stared, mouth agape, at Liam. "They execute someone who doesn't deserve it?"

Liam tilted his head sadly. "Sometimes the magic users have caused problems in the country. Or it's a traitor or a spy. Sometimes, but not always. Not good, eh?"

"Really not good. Can no one stop it?"

"The empress. But she ordered it, so it's unlikely."

Em was horrified. They passed through the crowd, near the platform, and Em recognized a standard gallows erected in a square with the trapdoor already set for the event. She had seen such a structure in Gram's history books, but Brookerby never had need of one. It was shocking to Em to think this simple wooden contraption could end a life.

"Em, we should go," Liam coaxed, tugging her hand away from the gallows.

Trumpets sounded once more, and the crowd around them parted. Em and Liam backed up also, making way for the procession. The accused was being led along the narrow path through the crowd, surrounded by armed guards in shiny armor bearing the crest of the empress. A crier, a person appointed to read the accused's crimes, paraded ahead, with the trumpeters. An executioner walked behind, dressed in black.

Em's horror turned to surprise, and then back to the most abject terror she had ever felt.

The accused—

—the man who was going to hang—

—was Mendel.

CHAPTER 16

$\mathcal{E}$m had once fallen from a ladder while fixing Ilna's rain gutter. She had been distracted by a small robin's nest in the eaves of the roof and leaned a little too far. The tumble wasn't enough to break anything, but she lay on the ground for nearly a quarter of an hour, unable to breathe, as if her whole body had just been sucker punched.

She felt that way now.

Mendel walked steadily, flanked by two malevolent-looking guards, hands tied in front of him.

Dear, lovely Mendel. Who only wanted an orderly shop. Who had built a fashion empire under everyone's noses. Who would be delighted to see Em in a dress. Who now, in wrinkled and torn clothes, was being led to his death.

Em gasped breath back into her body.

"Em?" Liam was still coaxing her the opposite direction, but she had to move, she had to do something. She could not—

Weaving quickly through the crowd, she pushed through the front row and ducked below the gallows platform.

She glanced around the scaffolding frantically. There was room enough for her to crouch, and she made her way to the trapdoor, observing the mechanism from underneath. Above, Mendel and his guards scaled the steps.

The mechanism was a simple lever that the hangman would pull from above. Blocks holding up the platform were attached to the lever. The lever would yank the blocks suddenly free from the door, which, unencumbered, would swing down on its hinge, dropping the person to their death. How to stop the mechanism? Or was there another way to prevent the door from falling? Or Mendel from falling.

Liam followed her under the scaffolding. "Em, what are you—?"

Em cut him off with a harsh "shh." She could jam the lever, then she just needed a few moments of crowd misdirection and she could cut Mendel loose and run. "Do you have a knife?" Liam shook his head, puzzled.

She frantically turned back to the mechanism. She could either block the door from opening or jam the lever. Barring that, she could place something to stop Mendel from falling completely, but there was too great a chance that anything stacked beneath the door would be dislodged when it swung open. No good.

Liam had lost patience. "Em, you have to tell me what's happening."

"Give me that prize I won." Liam pulled the toy out of his pocket, and Em began to wedge the baton into the crossbeams around the trapdoor hole. Her lace gloves tore, and she yanked them off frantically.

While continuing to wedge the mechanism, she hissed out an explanation. "That man up there, he is one of my dearest friends from home. He's done nothing wrong, and I cannot let him die."

She continued securing the sticks on other corners of the trapdoor, wedged between the platform floor and the door's frame. "When they pull the lever and the door doesn't open, we have a small window of time to grab him and run. If you don't want to help me, you don't have to. But I cannot lose him." Successfully wedged, she gave the baton and sticks a tug, and they held firm.

Liam stood frozen, as if deliberating.

She whirled on him. "Get clear then. Go!" Em spat.

This last spurred Liam to action. Hurt in his eyes, he turned and ducked out from under the scaffold.

Em didn't have the capacity to register Liam leaving. Her only thought was for Mendel as she exited the other side, closest to the stairs.

A man with a rolled-up parchment and a floppy hat declared Mendel's supposed crimes. Something about treason and magic. The executioner placed a sack over his head. Em hated that man and his stupid hat. She hated that executioner.

Her heart pounded like a thunderstorm, and she shifted from foot to foot at the base of the steps, waiting for the right moment.

The executioner moved to the lever. Em felt bile rise and fought to keep it down. Her jam should stop the door. It *would* stop the door. Mendel's life depended on it.

If only there was a distraction, she thought. *A fire maybe.* She felt a small spark at her fingertips, like when she touched her metal tools on a dry day. Suddenly, smoke wafted from the other end of the stage.

The executioner pulled the lever.

"Fire!" a woman in the crowd shouted. The onlookers panicked, running in all directions. The whole left side of the wooden platform was up in flames. The trapdoor hadn't flown open as intended, and the executioner, who was yanking the lever harder, stopped to help with the fire. Mendel's guards and stupid hat guy were trying to stomp out the flames with their feet.

Em saw her opportunity. Leaping up the stairs, she ran to the unguarded Mendel. She ducked behind him, yanked the poorly tied ropes off his wrists, and pulled the sack and noose off. While doing so, she spoke in his ear: "In two seconds I'll have you free, but we need to run—now!"

"Hey, you! Stop her!" shouted floppy-hat man, pointing angrily, but the guards couldn't hear over the chaos. The crowd's attention was on the fire, and avoiding being trampled, leaving the man help-lessly pointing at his disappearing prisoner.

Em yanked Mendel's hand down the stairs. She glanced back, and shock registered on his face.

"Emaline—?"

"Not here!" she shouted, running down a side street with Mendel in tow.

Liam was nowhere to be seen.

THEY RAN until they escaped the crowds and the party lights, and could no longer hear the chaos of the fire. Em slowed in a remote alleyway and sank onto a wooden crate to collect her breath. She had released Mendel's hand early in the run, as he assured her he was quite capable of following her without being dragged. Now, he wheezed and leaned against the wall.

They stared at each other for a few moments in the dim light, unable to form the right question.

Em broke the silence. "You okay?"

Mendel nodded. He looked exhausted and sad to Em.

"The soldiers brought you all the way here from Brookerby? Just to execute you?"

"There was a bit more to their motivations than that. But essentially, yes."

"And Gram, and Ilna?" Em drilled.

"I believe they're safe in Brookerby. Gramalia was released the same day she was brought in. Ilna was never taken. They weren't on the empress's radar like I was."

Em's eyes narrowed. "Does this have anything to do with that paper in your button jar?"

"It's complicated." Mendel dropped his eyes.

"I know that."

Mendel looked at Em, as if deciding something. Finally, he sighed. "The empress keeps track of any known magic users. Myself and Gramalia were on that list."

Em felt her jaw fall slack. "Magic users?"

"It is highly illegal to use our powers, except in great need. It is considered treason to use magic to replant trees of protection. Somehow, Her Majesty discovered my part in the previous replanting. The soldiers arrived in Brookerby to arrest me. The fact that their appearance coincided with the tree falling is mere happenstance."

Em's brain was buzzing with twenty noncoherent thoughts. She managed to squeak out, "Gram is a mage too?"

Mendel nodded. He began rubbing his eyes.

"Another secret," Em said bitterly.

"Emaline," Mendel shushed. His hands moved to his temples. Perhaps soothing a headache.

"So you or Gram could fix the tree. I didn't even need to come here," Em supposed.

Mendel was shaking his head halfway through her sentence. "We tried to use our scant skill last time. We don't have that kind of power."

He slumped onto a crate, looking older than Em remembered him being.

At that moment, a small group of festivalgoers passed the alleyway, colorful lanterns flashing, and were gone again.

And then silence. Em studied Mendel for wounds. He glanced up and a corner of his mouth lifted. "That dress is very beautiful, Emaline. It suits you well. But you really should be wearing lace gloves in public."

Em twisted up inside as she pictured her lace gloves lying under the trapdoor. *He almost died tonight.* Of course he'd still notice what she was wearing. "I thought I'd lost you. I thought I'd have to watch them hang—" Em broke.

And then Mendel was there, arms wrapped around her as she sobbed into his rumpled shirt. The one he was wearing the day he was arrested, with the brown paisley swirls. Between her wails, she recounted how she'd found his message and the tree paper. How soldiers had raided Gram's cottage after his arrest, burning the parchment. How they'd taken Gram. How Em came to Gillamor, looking for a new tree. And she knew about his secret fashion empire. And about her parents, who might not be dead after all.

Mendel said nothing, apart from sympathetic words like "uhm" and "oh, my dear girl." Em finally cried herself out and took a few deep, shuddering breaths. Sitting back, she immediately felt remorse. "Oh, Mendel, your shirt. I'm so sorry. I—" He had a large wet spot where she had cried all over him.

"It was ruined anyway. I'm delighted when my clothes can be useful." She let out a sniffly giggle, face red and puffy from crying. He stood from the wooden crate and held out a hand to pull Em up. "Now, I believe we should probably relocate. I imagine Her Majesty's guards are probably now searching for me, and I'd prefer not to be hanged today, if I can help it."

"Of course!" Em leapt up. "I was staying with a friend, but I'm not sure I should bring you there." Em felt a sharp pang, remembering Liam's indecision at the gallows. "I cannot count on discretion from him or his staff."

"I suppose I could find one of my establishments to seek refuge. Although I have not met any of the employees personally, I have corresponded with them a great deal. Perhaps they would deign to house their founder, who is now a fugitive."

Em thought of the fashion houses, wondering if their service to fashion would override their sense of duty to the empress. Then an idea sparked. She gestured down the alleyway. "I just thought of someone I can trust, I think. Follow me."

"Mendel? Of Drecovia!?" Tilly squealed in delight.

"Shh, keep your voice down," Em said harshly. It did nothing to quell Tilly's glee, but she did drop her volume somewhat.

Em had managed to corner the maid in the empty kitchen of Hallson Manor. Tilly had finished up her evening dish duties and was getting ready to go home for the night.

"But the fashion icon? The master designer? In trouble and needs my help? I would do *anything* for him."

"Great," Em said flatly. "He needs a place to stay for a few days. Tilly, absolutely no one can know, okay? The empire tried to execute him."

"What—?" Tilly's voice wavered with emotion. "Why would the empress want to do that?"

"I don't know," Em lied. "He did nothing wrong. Do you have somewhere he can stay? Somewhere safe?"

"Yes! Ummm"—she pursed her lips in thought—"I know! The flat above mine is empty. The landlord keeps storage there, but doesn't ever go in. I bet he could stay at least a month without anyone ever knowing."

"Would the other tenants hear him?"

"Oh no. It's one of the reasons I chose that place, it's very quiet."

"That sounds perfect. Thank you."

"No, thank *you*! I have wanted to meet Mendel my whole life. Do you think he would be willing to look at my fashion designs? Just to give me a few pointers."

"I think there's a really good possibility."

"When do I get to meet him?"

"Now. He's waiting outside for us."

Tilly yelped and practically dragged Em out the servants' side door into the narrow garden that led to the street. Mendel sat on a bench, looking very regal despite his uncharacteristically messy appearance. Tilly froze.

"My dear tailor, I've found you a safe place to stay," Em said quietly.

"Wonderful, Emaline. Thank you for looking out for me." He rose and crossed to them, smiling softly. "You must be Miss Tilly?"

Tilly nodded frantically, temporarily unable to form words.

"Yes, this is Tilly," Em continued, hoping the girl would find her tongue soon. "She helped me choose Gillamor-appropriate attire and is studying fashion when not working for Lord Hallson. Oddly enough, she's heard of you." The last was spoken with a wry smile. Em was still getting used to the idea of Mendel being known outside of Brookerby.

Tilly nodded, even more frantically, and finally blurted out, "Everyone's heard of you— It's such an honor— I've studied all your designs— If I had money, I'd buy everything you've ever made. You are my hero." And then she blushed and dipped into a deep curtsy to hide her red face.

Mendel extended a hand kindly, and gently took the girl's trembling hand. "My dear Tilly. I'm just a tailor who has had some good luck. But I am delighted to meet you and forever in your debt for your kind help. If it isn't too tiresome, perhaps we can discuss Gillamor fashions? I'm afraid I'm woefully behind the trends this season."

Tilly broke into a smile, and her face glowed like the sun. She led Em and Mendel along side streets toward her flat while chattering away about the latest designs and fads and asking Mendel questions, which he answered just as enthusiastically.

Em fell behind, watching the two become fast friends with relief. Mendel would be safe with Tilly, for now. And maybe soon, he would be able to satisfy some of Em's unanswered questions.

CHAPTER 17

The empress showed the mage all due consideration to a person of her ability. Nevertheless, Bronwyn's pride prevented resolution, and instead triggered a fiery confrontation. Bronwyn felt the failure of the trees as keenly as Her Majesty, yet insisted that the planting tour should continue.

EM CREPT BACK to Hallson Manor after seeing Mendel and Tilly safely home. The streets had quieted in the wee hours of the morning; only a few revelers remained. One man drunkenly sloshed about to a tired fiddle, unwilling to admit the evening had ended. His companion sagged with drink and weariness, moaning to his friend to stop the madness. Em avoided even these partygoers, hyper-aware that she had committed a serious crime this evening by freeing Mendel. At any moment she might be recognized and reported. She would work out what to do about that later. The important thing was that Mendel was safe, and provided she could make it back to Hallson Manor unscathed, she would sleep soundly.

She decided to use the side garden and servants' entrance through the kitchen. It was more discreet and should be abandoned at this hour. Not for the first time, she wondered what Liam would say to her. He promised to stay by her, and at the first test of it, he had failed. Something she could sort out in the morning.

Quietly unlatching the side door, she crept into the kitchen and closed it behind her with a gentle click.

"Em?"

She jumped, suppressing a yelp. Spinning, she saw Liam leaning against the counter, eyes dark.

"Oh, stars, you scared me," Em breathed, pressing a hand to her chest to slow her heartbeat. "I expected you to be fast asleep by now."

He stood like a statue. Unreadable.

"It was not fair of me to ask that of you—" Em began stiffly.

"I made you a promise," he spoke over her. They both stopped.

Em began, "What? You left...?"

"I caused that fire," he said. "Or I would have, at least. I grabbed a torch. But I don't know, it kind of, well, started on its own."

Em remembered the spark on her fingertips. Even now, she felt them tingle at the memory.

Liam exhaled and seemed to sag. "I didn't know where you'd gone."

Em had assumed the worst of him. That he had left her. Betrayal, as the card said. She began to apologize. "I'm so sorry. You're probably furious with me, but I—"

Liam crossed the room in three steps and collected Em in a fierce hug. Shocked, Em's words trailed off. Her heart pounded at the suddenness and the closeness of him.

Not letting go, Liam leaned back to look down at her. "Is he okay?"

Em nodded, heart pounding. "He's somewhere safe."

"Are you hurt?" He stepped back and put a hand on the side of her face, brushing stray hairs back from her face. "Were you crying?"

Em shook her head. "I'm okay. I'm okay." But she felt very much like she could start crying again. "He's one of the dearest people in the world to me. He loves me like I was his own daughter. And I couldn't—"

"I know," Liam said simply. His hand now cupped her face tenderly. "And I couldn't lose you."

Em stared into his eyes, and she felt a tiny jolt travel from her cheek to her throat to her lower back, where his other hand rested. Suddenly, she wasn't thinking of Mendel. She was thinking about Liam's hands on her. His lips on hers— Her breath caught.

And then, just as she thought he was going to lean in, Liam backed away and cleared his throat. She felt a little hum of disappointment in the back of her brain.

"It's late, I'm sorry. I'm glad you are safe," he said more formally.

"The distraction—um, the fire, was brilliant. Thank you."

Liam bobbed his head in acknowledgment.

Em continued, trying to cover her confusion. "I'm hoping no one saw or identified us. But I suppose we'll find out soon enough."

"True. What is the agenda for tomorrow?"

"Keep looking for a new tree. A seed. A clue."

"Ah. In that case, I'd like to come. We can search more speedily with two."

"I'd greatly appreciate your help."

Em inwardly cringed. The conversation was so formal. Had he not just embraced her?

"Well, goodnight, Emaline of Brookerby. I'll see you in the morning." He bowed slightly and left the kitchen quickly.

"Goodnight," Em whispered, bewildered.

THE NEXT MORNING CAME QUICKLY. Em awoke to a little yellow bird chirping happily by her window. "Go away," Em said crabbily, flopping onto her stomach and pulling the pillow over her head. Then someone knocked at the door. Em groaned, "Come in."

It was Tilly, buzzing with happiness, her frizzy black hair floating around her. Em pulled the pillow tighter to block out the maid's chattering on about fashion, and Mendel, and her drawings.

"Oh, Em, come on. It's almost midmorning! Lord Hallson is waiting for you downstairs."

Em sat up, startled. "He's waiting?"

"Yes, Miss Em. He went ahead and had breakfast without you, but he said you had very important business together today. Would you like to wear the mint-green frock with—"

Em leapt from her bed, panicked. She hastily pulled a comb through her tangled hair, which she hadn't fully taken down the night before. Tilly *tsk*ed and pulled a frilly light green dress from the wardrobe. Em shimmied into it, too rushed to put up a fight. It felt wholly inappropriate for a quest, but Liam was waiting. As a small act of rebellion, she pulled her old boots out from under the bed and pulled them on.

"Oh, Miss Em!" Tilly scolded. "Those don't go—"

"No one can see them, so it doesn't matter. The other ones gave me blisters," Em reasoned while wiping the sleep out of her eyes. Glancing into the mirror, she decided she looked tolerable. As a last-ditch effort, she snatched up her knapsack with the book tucked inside. Maybe she could find a clue in its pages today. "Thanks, Tilly," she tossed back as she charged out the door and down the stairs.

Liam waited in the main hall, sitting on a plush scarlet bench near the door. He stood when he saw Em, smiling. "Thought I'd get a jump on you today. You have a habit of slipping out without me."

"Good work, you caught me," she admitted awkwardly. "Is there anything I can grab for breakfast?" Liam produced a pastry with apples, earning Em's grateful smile. "How did you know?"

"I know it's important to feed you at mealtimes," he said with a small smile, handing her the treat.

Em took a bite, inhaling the scent of apples and cinnamon and feeling the flaky pastry break off in her mouth. "Mmmmmm," she hummed happily.

"Okay, ready?" He had reached the door while she chomped away. She nodded, mouth full, and they exited into the heart of Gillamor.

Em and Liam started at one of the larger libraries, one Em hadn't visited the day before. The books were housed in a vast cavernous space, and Em had the feeling that if she got lost among the stacks, no one would find her for days. Buried deep in the shelves was a whole row of books on Gillamor gardens of note, and magical plants. Liam listed the gardens of note on a spare piece of paper; they could plan to visit each in turn. The magical-plants books were fascinating but provided no clues for warding trees of protection.

Throughout the morning, Em sneaked peeks at Liam. He seemed the same as before. But different. Something imperceivable had shifted. He was helping, and she was grateful for his help. But did she feel anything else? She remembered last night, the feeling of his hand on her cheek, on her lower back, and a warmth flooded her core. Had he been about to kiss her? Why had he stopped? She imagined his kiss would have been soft, but firm. Warm. Inviting.

At that moment, Liam closed the cover of a heavy book and grabbed another from the pile, all without glancing her direction. Feeling foolish, she doubled down, burying her eyes in the volume she was meant to be studying. Brookerby needed her.

While Liam was off seeking more reference books, Em pulled *The Standard Book of Anything* out of her bag. Even if he came back, it would blend right in with the other books, she reasoned. She flipped it open to a random page.

Social Niceties of Gillamor Society.

Em groaned. How was an etiquette lesson supposed to help her right now? But she read on, trying very hard not to question the book's odd leadings.

Gillamor high society is eager to expand their social circle but are wary of outsiders unfamiliar with their customs. It is important to observe the customary code of this society to gain admittance to the most extravagant parties.

It is extremely important to accept all invitations that are proffered. The moment an invitation is declined, you will no longer be considered a member of the inner circle. When accepting an invitation, you must bow or curtsy and exclaim, "We would be delighted" in an affected tone. This signals your willingness to be a good guest.

When attending an event, it is customary to bring a gift for the host or hostess. Flowers or a wheel of cheese are appropriate. If you bring flowers, you are technically allowed to collect an equivalent amount of foliage from their garden. (See "Gardens of High Society" for details about prestigious landscaping designs.) Most hosts frown upon their garden being carried away by their guests, so the polite guest will collect clippings subversively.

"Bingo," Em muttered.

"What'd you find?" Liam asked. Em hadn't realized he'd returned and jumped slightly. He stood there, head cocked, with an armful of large reference books.

Scrambling, she quickly flipped to the "Gardens of High Society" article, which showed diagrams for garden layouts, complete with a specified area for rare and unusual plants. She showed him the page. "I found layouts for private gardens, and there is typically a place for rare plants. This says most nobles hire someone to analyze and label their plants too."

"Ah. Good. There are a few private gardens on our list. That will come in handy. Which book was that?"

She silently cursed. She'd hoped to not draw attention to the book, and now he was interested. "Uh, not sure." Trying to play the ruse, she flipped to the cover page. The book had conveniently changed its title for her. "Flora of Gillamor," she supplied.

Liam had already flipped open two reference books and grunted in response. Em let out a breath. Opening another reference with one hand, she carefully slid the book back into her bag with the other. She had no idea why she was still hiding this from Liam, but the book had come to her aid by concealing itself. She turned her eyes to her newly opened book and tried to read.

~

THE CITY GARDENS were on the list for many unusual and magical plants. They happened to be a block away from the library. Em and Liam entered under wrought-iron gates, and the garden greeted them with flowers of many colors and shapes.

Em rushed forward and crouched down to smell the wheel-sized red blooms. They looked nothing like the flowers Gram grew, but Em had the sudden urge to pluck one for Gram. Straightening, she gripped her skirts to keep her hands in check. Any bloom would surely die before she could return to Brookerby anyway.

They strolled down the wide path slowly as they admired the arrangements of the gardeners. Liam stopped at a plant with tiny, white flower specks and long, oval leaves. "This one looks like a plant we had in our garden growing up," he exclaimed, bending down to read the placard. "Warfern. It doesn't say what it does."

Em inspected the tiny blooms. "I've never seen anything like that in Gram's garden."

"You should take a sprig. As a souvenir." Liam broke off one stem, holding it out to Em. Glancing up, her eyes caught his. He beheld her with such steadiness that Em felt a bit weak-kneed. It wasn't a practical gift, but from Liam, it felt special. She accepted it with a smile, and gently tucked the tiny flower into the side pocket of her satchel.

They wandered the gardens the rest of the morning, looking for protective trees, with no luck. Em kept glancing to Liam. Noticing the way a stray hair fell across his forehead. Reading meaning into his ordinary conversation. *This must stop,* Em scolded herself. She turned down another path, keeping at least three arm lengths between them. They found themselves back at the entrance, and Em suggested they try their luck elsewhere.

"First," Liam announced, "it's time for some lunch."

As if on cue, Em's stomach rumbled. She smiled wryly, wondering if she should be embarrassed that Liam had surreptitiously placed her on a strict feeding schedule.

∾

THEY FOUND themselves at a small café opposite the city gardens. They sat at finely worked iron chairs next to a large window that overlooked the park. Liam quickly folded his oversized menu and laid it on the small table they shared. Em continued to study hers. It was full of dishes with ingredients she had never heard of, and she was having a hard time selecting a meal that didn't have something unfamiliar.

"Good afternoon, Lord Hallson! Enjoying the day?"

She lowered her menu a few inches, peering over the top at an attractive woman seated at a nearby table. She had golden hair, arranged in a fussy updo, and sat alone with a saucer of tea. Her violet dress was covered in frills and bows; Em mentally scanned her own dress, which was simple by comparison, and inwardly thanked Tilly for not going too overboard with the design. She recalled, uncharitably, that bows were out of fashion, according to *The Standard Book of Anything.*

Liam chatted back sociably. "Miss Lanesby! Such a pleasure to see you. No, unfortunately, we are on a quest of utmost importance. The gardens and sunshine are merely footnotes in our day."

"Oh! A quest! How exciting! Indeed, I should love a quest."

"I'm sure you would excel at one, Miss Lanesby."

Em's ears followed the conversation as her eyes tried to scan the menu. Was Liam flirting with this woman? She felt like growling, and then checked herself. *He's not yours, Em.*

"Oh, Liam, you always were a tease. You mustn't stand on ceremony. I'm always just Cass to you."

That was it. Em needed to stop this little conversation before Liam ran off with this woman. Em lowered her menu to the table, folding it gingerly. Liam noticed. "Decided?" he asked.

"Everything looks so amazing, I can't pick," she simpered.

"I'll pick for you. You'll love it!" he enthused. "Em, I want you to meet one of my oldest friends. This is Cassandra Lanesby. Cass, this is Miss Emaline Strider, of Brookerby."

"Delighted to make your acquaintance," Cass said sweetly.

"Thank you, it's nice to meet you also," Em said, trying to be friendly.

"I've never been to Brookerby, but I have an aunt who lives in Drecovia. It's so sweet, all the little country villages. So different from here. You must love it."

"I do. It's my first time in Gillamor, and it's almost overwhelmingly large. But I have really enjoyed my time here," Em shared. Cass was listening with a kind smile, which seemed genuine.

"Well, if you have time while you're here, you must take tea with me. I'm delighted to make the acquaintance of anyone whom Liam deems a friend."

"Likewise, Miss Lanesby," Em responded in the affirmative. She mentally kicked herself for having a guarded first impression. Cass was lovely.

"Well, I don't want to interrupt your luncheon—" Cass said quickly, as the waiter arrived at their table.

"Why don't you join us?" Em interjected. Liam's eyes widened a bit, but then he grinned.

"Yes, Cass, please do," he added.

"Really? That would be marvelous, I believe I shall."

The waiter transferred her chair and teacup, and Cass moved to their table. Liam placed their order quietly. Em prayed he ordered something semi-ordinary for her.

"Might I inquire about this quest, Liam. What is the aim?" Cass asked while delicately holding her teacup.

"We must travel to each garden in the city to enjoy its beauty and study some of the more unusual plants the city has to offer," Liam supplied.

Em nodded. "My Gram is quite the gardener. I promised to bring her back something very rare." Both she and Liam had spoken the truth, Em realized. They had just omitted certain details. Em wondered at how easily the half-truths had come to her.

Cass beamed. She was radiant when she smiled, and Em couldn't help a slight pang of jealousy. "I have a suggestion. My family is having a gala tomorrow evening at our home, for Rashorbuj. We have truly magnificent gardens, which you are welcome to explore and take what you'd like, if only you will agree to attend. Please say you will?"

Liam glanced to Em, silently asking the question.

A proffered invitation, Em thought, remembering the article from this morning. Em rose from her seat, attempting a low curtsey. "We would be delighted," she intoned, elongating the vowels.

Liam started, looking uncomfortable. But Cass burst out in laughter. "Oh, Emaline, you've read *Reice's Rules of Polite Society*, how droll! I can tell you are going to be so much fun!" She turned to Liam, "It's satire, Li, you wouldn't understand."

Liam laughed, relieved. Em grinned and blushed. The book had not led her astray. Well, not really. Not yet anyway.

But like herself, and Liam, it had left out some important details.

CHAPTER 18

*B*ronwyn Featherweight left the Golden Lark Palace with rage in her heart. Her finest worldly accomplishment, the warding trees, were being disparaged by this child-empress. And now she had been ordered to stop planting. But she would not. Snapping her fingers, she summoned her entourage of mages. They gathered at the outskirts of Gillamor as they planned their rebellion.

"THERE'S SOMEONE WATCHING THE HOUSE," Liam announced the following morning.

"Where?"

"Standing by the hedge. He's been there all morning."

Em snuck a glance out the front window and saw a thuggish fellow loitering across the street. She cursed. She had expected imperial soldiers would eventually track her down regarding Mendel, but not this quickly. And not this subtly.

"Maybe they don't have enough to arrest me," she mused aloud.

"Maybe they're waiting for you to lead them to Mendel," Liam countered.

This landed. Em was planning to visit Mendel this afternoon. She had already passed him a note via Tilly setting the time and place. But it might be difficult to go without leading her shadow directly to him. She explained this to Liam.

"We have some options." Liam detailed his ideas for escaping the house unseen. One involved impersonating servants, but Em dismissed that; they would likely still be recognized, even in different clothes. Another option was to hide in the refuse barrels that were carted to the dumping grounds outside the city. Em wrinkled her nose, hoping for a third option.

"I've saved the best for last. You can easily make your appointment with Mendel by leaving through the attic."

He guided her to the top of the house, a dusty attic with old furniture and broken floorboards. Liam indicated a small window facing the rear of the house, and a row of overhanging trees.

"So we climb down that tree? And we won't be spotted because it's the back of the house, and the leaves are thick enough?"

"That's the idea, yeah. I've never actually attempted it, but I think it could work."

"I like the attic window," Em assessed, climbing up into the sill of the window and peering out. "I could attach a wire so we could glide down instead. It would be quicker than climbing."

"Glide?" Liam wondered.

"Sure. I did it from Gram's roof once. I need a wire attached tightly at both ends and something to slide with. This is much higher than Gram's cottage, but the principles are the same. We just have to avoid running into tree branches."

"Are you sure you don't want to try refuse barrels? That sounds safer," Liam quipped.

Em rolled her eyes. "Leave it to me. I can make the wire attachments. I could even send out one of your staff to attach the other end to that maple. It's a straight shot. Perfectly safe."

Liam grasped her hand to help her down from the sill. "I'm coming with. I can't let a lady glide alone."

"Let?" Em lifted an eyebrow, even as their hands touching sent warmth flooding through her.

He laughed. "Actually, it sounds fun. I don't want to miss out."

Em leapt down and dropped his hand. "I'm going to find your steward to see if he can wrap the wire around that tree."

She trotted out of the room without a backward glance.

EM'S SLIDING wire worked perfectly. One end was secured just above the attic window, looped through the eaves. The other was wound tightly around the base of a tree many lengths away. Over Liam's protests, she insisted on being the tester. She draped a piece of old leather over the taut wire, tucking her fingers into the grips she had cut on each end. She hoped they would hold. Taking a deep breath, she stepped out the window of the attic and pushed off the roof with her feet. She slid through the tree cover at the back of the house and between two townhomes behind Liam's, ultimately landing on a small patch of grass next to the neighboring street before crashing into the terminal maple.

Proud of herself, she turned back to watch Liam slide with his identical piece of leather. He flew down, much quicker than Em, and dropped to the ground with a muffled "oof" just before he would've smashed into the tree.

She rushed over and offered a hand up. "Sorry, Liam. That went a little faster than I planned on. You okay?"

Liam rolled over and reached for her hand with a grin. "Don't you dare take that wire down. That's the best way to leave the house ever."

Em wheezed in relief and pulled him to his feet. He stood very close to her, her hand in his, eyes bright. She felt herself flush. There was definitely a spark. She liked this man. She liked the feeling of her hand in his, and his eyes on her. Would he kiss her right here? Remembering where they were, Em quickly slipped her hand out of his and refocused. "Step one complete. How do we get to the Plaza Abingdon?"

175

THEY STROLLED from corner to corner, ducking through alleyways. The streets had a steady hum of traffic, but the less attention they drew, the better. Once, they ducked into a recessed wall niche as a squad of soldiers marched by. Trying to stand casually in close quarters, Em could hear Liam's heart thumping in time with her own.

"Almost there." He grinned.

Em nodded imperceptibly, stomach doing loops at his nearness.

They waited for the sound of footsteps to disappear, and then darted to their next shadow, the arch that graced the center of the Plaza Abingdon. It was a massive stone structure declaring Esnania's glorious victory over their southern neighbors. That war was won many centuries ago, and the archway was aged and crumbling. Mendel waited at its base, hat tilted down over his face.

Em hugged Mendel tightly. "You're still safe."

"Indeed. My accommodations are quite pleasant, and thus far, have remained undiscovered." The corners of his eyes crinkled as he smiled. He nodded to Liam, "Do I have the honor of meeting the illustrious Lord Hallson?"

"Just Liam, sir. It's a pleasure." Liam dipped his head in greeting.

"The pleasure is mine, Liam. Although I was a bit perplexed by our surroundings."

Em interjected, "I didn't want to inadvertently reveal your lodgings. I'm being watched."

"Ah. I hope nothing to do with my rescue."

"I needed to talk to you. About the tree."

At this, Mendel's eyes flickered to Liam uncertainly. Liam caught the look. "I'll wait over here while you two talk," he offered, stepping toward a nearby raised pool that sat in the center of the plaza.

Em watched him go.

"He seems lovely," Mendel offered with a smile.

Em smiled back. Then frowned, remembering her questions. "You had years to tell me you were a magic user. Why did you lie?"

He shifted uncomfortably. "Ah. I knew this discussion would happen. I didn't expect it so...directly."

Em held her silence, waiting for him to answer.

"Gramalia and I have the spark, but neither of us are trained. Our magic can be used for small things. To enhance the skill we already possess. But it has never been a life-changing secret that we have been concealing."

"So you used your magic to start a fashion empire," Em said.

"Yes. Well, no. I still worked very hard. But I had a few lucky moments—"

"And Gram? How does she use hers?"

"Gramalia has always loved her stories and references. She created a book that contained wondrous knowledge from an ordinary reference tome, if only you knew how to look. I never quite acquired the knack of reading it, but she became quite good. The book produced knowledge that she had never given it. Through it, she studied the trees extensively, and shared her knowledge with me."

Em clenched her jaw. Gram had made *The Standard Book of Anything*? She nodded for Mendel to go on.

"I was working on methods to recreate the tree parchment, the result of which you found in my button jar, but I didn't quite get it right yet." He held up his hand to stall Em's admission. "Yes, yes, I know it has been destroyed. It wouldn't have worked anyway. Gramalia thought she had found a way to plant the trees without the parchment of runes—without the taint of the curse that came with them. She had a failed attempt about six years ago, and it triggered the illness that took her voice."

Em felt a sudden, burning hatred for *The Standard Book of Anything*. It must have given Gram just enough information to lead her into danger. She began to flip back in her brain through all the advice the book had given her. Never the whole picture. Never exactly what she expected.

"We are hoping, my dear girl, that your gift will lead you to a solution where we have failed."

"Do you know—am I a magic user?" Em asked. She held her breath, watching his face.

Mendel's eyebrows furrowed almost imperceptibly. After a brief silence, he sighed. "Yes. Maybe. We don't know." Mendel paused, and

Em inched nearer under the shadow of the archway. "Gramalia and I have discussed it. We have applied multiple subtle tests over the years that have been inconclusive. Your mother and father had the gift, and it is often passed to children…"

Em nodded tersely, letting out her breath. He couldn't tell her what she was. At least they hadn't been keeping it from her.

She refocused. "The trees. Can you tell me what happened at the last replanting?"

"Aha. Let me needle out my memories. Your parents and I set off on a journey to discover a new tree, as instructed by Gram's book. To my shame, I left the expedition before they reached Gillamor. I had the opportunity of a lifetime to study with a designer in Drecovia, which we passed through. Anne and Farrigan encouraged me to stay, saying they could find the tree on their own." Em recalled Gram's scathing letter about his empire of needle and thread. And Mendel's connection to Drecovia.

Mendel continued, "They returned to Brookerby with a piece of paper. That parchment was prepared by a magic user your parents sought out in Gillamor. And it is the only known way to plant a warding tree. They had learned, on their journey, that if a magic user spoke the words on the parchment whilst dropping the very same paper, and a seed as depicted, they could plant a new tree. Gramalia spoke the words. Anne dropped the sycamore seed. Shortly after, Anne and Farrigan died—perhaps some affliction from traveling."

Em spoke up. "They are alive. At least I've heard—"

Mendel nodded. "I have heard rumors as well. But I have not encountered your parents anywhere in my travels. If they are alive and have not returned, I can only conclude that Anne and Farrigan are much altered. Perhaps their minds were enchanted."

Em bit her lip to keep it from trembling. Believing her parents were addled was a better conclusion than believing they chose not to come back.

Mendel patted her shoulder gently.

Em glanced over. Liam was trying to coax a duck to his side of the pond with clucks and hand gestures. She smiled. "We'll keep looking. I will find a solution, Mendel. I promise."

"I believe you will, dear girl. In the interim, I should return to Gramalia and my friend, Ilna. Even if no town remains, I would like to keep them safe."

Em gave him another quick hug, promising to return to Brookerby quickly, and telling him to be careful. Then, she gestured to Liam that they should go. Mendel slipped away, back toward Tilly's flat.

Liam walked silently alongside Em through the streets, blessedly not prying for details. With Mendel returning to Brookerby empty-handed, she was their only hope now.

CHAPTER 19

An edict was circulated throughout the empire. Protective trees had caused great sorrow and were henceforth forbidden. Trees that were already planted could remain, but no more would be established in Esnania. Anyone violating this edict would be executed. The ruling passed with little fanfare or recognition from the populace.

LIAM MET her at the door that evening, dressed in a formal dark coat and trousers. He looked like one of Mendel's impeccable male mannequins come vividly to life. He perhaps recognized the dress Em wore from the Gray Horse, but he said nothing as he helped her into the ornate Hallson carriage, holding her black lace-gloved hand for balance. Tilly had insisted she wear this beaded gown again. The maid had kindly repaired the dress and sewn on new buttons for the occasion. Em found the gown uncomfortable, not only for how much it revealed, but also for the Gray Horse associations that came with the dress. She hoped it was not the wrong thing to wear, but Tilly had gushed over it. Still, Em fought the urge to tug it up an inch or two.

Em noted Liam's somber expression, and that he appeared to be looking everywhere but at her. His supporting hand didn't remain under hers a moment longer than necessary.

If Em were being honest, she had noticed Liam separating himself from her. His silence this afternoon. The distance when they searched the garden yesterday. It was all so unlike the version of him she had known on the road. Perhaps he regretted their closeness the night of the festival. Maybe he regretted inviting her into his home at all, after she rescued Mendel. Em felt unhappy at this cold turn, yet she chose not to delve deeper into her own feelings. She rationalized that it was best for Brookerby if she remained unencumbered. Then she resisted the urge to tug up this ridiculous beaded gown again.

Em filled the short journey with staccato questions about the Lanesby gardens, which Liam seemed to have some knowledge of. He detailed the order of events for the evening, which included an hour of mingling, followed by dancing. After the first hour of dancing, Em could sneak away to the gardens. Liam would try to meet her there if he could get away quietly. Em nodded, storing each morsel of information. He seemed to know what to expect from the evening and could perfectly describe the layout of the house. Her imagination wandered to those previous nights. In her mind, Liam was smiling and dancing with numerous elegant women, including the lovely Cass. Perhaps he was courting them. Being romantic with them. She shook her head. She was here to save her town, and quickly. It mattered not who Liam had danced with.

Their horses arrived at the Lanesby mansion at dusk. The house, which sat on an outlying hill overlooking the city, was lit up from the inside with artisanal oil lamps that shone through the numerous ground-to-ceiling windows, and from the outside with torches lining the long brick walkway. Other carriages were parked along the way, a few without any horses or even wheels. Em openly stared out the window at these curiosities as they rolled past. She would love to examine them and try to understand the mechanics.

Em shifted nervously on the stiff velvet seat as their conveyance rolled to a stop.

Descending from the carriage, Liam silently offered his arm. Em took it, feeling a slight wariness as they approached the grand entrance glowing in the torchlight. She remembered, belatedly, that they had brought no gift for the host. She hoped, in that regard, that her book was being satirical yet again.

The grand wooden doors were open, revealing a cavernous entry hall, which led down a half stairway directly into a great room with enormous windows on all sides. The room teemed with stylish people, huddled together in conversation, bathed in bright light from the crystal chandeliers that hung throughout the room. Delicious smells wafted through the air, and servants in crisp white uniforms circulated through the room with numerous trays of bite-sized food. There was a general din of chatter and laughter, punctuated by the sounds of glassware clinking.

Em and Liam had paused on the entryway. Em was unclear whether they should wait to be invited in, or if they should simply join the crowd. Her dilemma was short-lived when a slender older woman approached.

"Dear Liam! You've decided to join us—how lovely! And you've brought your business associate as well? Cassandra let me know you would be attending. Miss Emaline Strider? Your dress is stunning, Miss Strider."

Em bobbed her head. "So kind of you to invite me."

"We are delighted, Lady Lanesby," Liam interjected. "It has been far too long."

"Yes, yes, dear. You are always welcome here. Well, come in. Cass is waiting for you somewhere in there, Liam. Be sure to get a dance in, for old times' sake."

Lady Lanesby flitted away, and Liam led Em into the room. Em suddenly felt out of place, holding loosely to Liam's arm as he wound through the crowd. He was approached almost instantly by an older gentleman and lady, whom he knew. They politely greeted Em, but then focused their sole attention on Liam, inquiring after his estate, and asking whether he had heard the latest Gillamor gossip.

Left out, Em curtsied to excuse herself, and ducked through the finely-dressed people, attempting to find a seat. This was a waiting game until they could get into the gardens, she reasoned, absently selecting a small baked pastry from a proffered tray. She found a purple chaise unoccupied near an open window, and she lowered herself to perch on it, biting carefully into the small golden triangle. It was filled with root vegetables and gravy, and the liquid dripped on her gown.

Em swore and began to swipe at the spot, only successfully blending the sauce further into the delicate fabric.

"Perhaps I could be of some assistance?" A woman, about Ilna's age, sat on a matching chair nearby.

Em flushed. "I'm afraid I've ruined it."

"Might've been worth it for the excellent samosas, but I think the dress can be saved." The woman opined. "Come on, then." She motioned, and Em followed her through a glass door that matched the windows, out onto the veranda. "I'm Della Liverwood."

That name. "Are you acquainted with the Liverwoods who reside near the harbor?" Em asked breathlessly.

The woman didn't break stride but chuckled as she moved. "I *am* the Liverwoods who reside by the harbor. This way." She led Em through another door at the end of the long outdoor porch, and they were suddenly inside, headed toward a set of narrow stairs where a servant had just disappeared down.

"I'm Em, by the way. Where are we going?" Em panted, exhausted by Della's pace.

"The pantry. We need something to absorb and lift this stain."

Della strode down the stairs and barged into a tiny room just outside the kitchen lined with wall-to-wall shelves containing various preserved and dry goods. Della made herself at home, muttering to herself and reading labels, finally reaching for a jar filled halfway with white power. "Okay, hold out your dress," she commanded.

Em complied, pulling the fabric taut, away from her body. Della carefully sprinkled the white powder on the stain.

"We'll have to let that sit for a few minutes, then we'll borrow a wet towel from the kitchen. The stain will come right up, promise. I'm a messy eater myself."

"Thank you, Della. Truly."

"Oh, it's nothing, dear. It's a very beautiful dress. And I'd do just about anything for Anne Strider's daughter."

"You know my mother!" Em breathed, astonished.

Della looked puzzled. "Of course, Em. And dear Farrigan too. I'm assuming he's your father, although it's never safe to—that is, to say, she never mentioned you before, so I was a bit surprised to see you sitting there, but you look so much alike, you could be twins."

"I've been told. I haven't seen her since I was very young."

There was an awkward silence, Em fighting emotion, and Della averting her gaze.

"It's been several months—we attended a dinner party together," Della offered tentatively. Em breathed in and out, trying to calm herself, but nodded for Della to continue.

"She was in good spirits that evening and suggested several games of cards. She's been on a lucky streak with cards lately. After conning several of the guests out of their coin, she spent the rest of the evening stolen away in the library of our host, pulling numerous books off the shelf. I found her there, sitting on a pile of books, thumbing through each like she was searching for some bit of information. I offered to help, and she confided in me that she would be leaving town again for some time. She had found something interesting in the northern part of the country and had to make a journey with Farrigan. Oh, not to worry, dear, that's quite normal for her to pick up and travel like that. Be right back."

Della dove out of the room and returned moments later with a damp cloth from the kitchen. "Okay, now I'll just dab, see? Dab, dab, and it's coming right up! Aren't you a lucky girl! Just like your mum. Your dress will be good as new."

"Thank you," Em said simply.

"Anyway, I hope you find her. It really is quite shocking that she had a daughter all this time. There she is crossing the country on adventures, and you not able to see your mother. If I think really hard, maybe I can remember the name of where they went." Della pondered for a bit, and then brightened. "I have no idea. But isn't that the way of it? I'm sure it will come to me." She tossed down the damp cloth on the pantry shelves and declared they should get back to the party.

Back in the grand hall, Della gave Em's hand a quick squeeze. She promised to return if the name of the place came back to her, and then vanished into the crowd. Em sat back on the chaise lounge, feeling overwhelmed by twenty different emotions. Her mom had been spotted mere months ago. It didn't sound like she was addled either. But they were probably long gone to the north by now. She took another long breath and turned toward the open window. A soft breeze wafted in, brushing the curtains and cooling the over-warm room. Perhaps no one would notice if she escaped to the garden now.

At that moment, the musicians began playing a quadrille. The floor began to clear, and couples started to form in the middle. Liam was laughing with Cass, and they moved naturally toward the other couples. Em stiffened. He appeared to have forgotten about her completely. She stood and started to move toward the open double doors to the veranda when a young gentleman appeared in front of her.

"Miss? The younger Lord Kinsler at your service. Will you do me the honor of a dance?" He offered his arm. Em thought he looked pleasant enough. Her eyes darted imperceptibly to Liam; being asked by this gentleman was salve enough for the moment, so she dipped her head in assent, and reached for his arm.

Em's dancing was still very unpracticed, but she managed not to squash Lord Kinsler's toes. He even requested a second dance. Another gentleman approached for a third. Em complied, thanking Lord Kinsler for his excellent dancing. She twirled away, all the while keeping Liam and Cass in the corner of her eye. He said something in her ear as they danced, and she smiled happily. Em felt like her insides were breaking. Fighting her feelings of smallness, she beamed brighter at her new partner. She didn't even remember his name, but at least she wasn't sitting sadly in the corner, she reasoned.

After the fourth dance, another gentleman approached, but Em begged off with minimal attempts at politeness. She felt a strong urge to find that pantry and hide for the rest of the party. Instead, she escaped to the vacant veranda. Em sagged on the railing over-looking the finely manicured garden. In the dim moonlight, she let her face fall, and unbidden, a few tears spilled through her lashes, dropping over the railing into a shrub below. She didn't know if the sudden flood came because of what Della Liverwood had shared, or because she wished she could be the one Liam danced and laughed with.

She felt foolish. She was wearing this ridiculous dress, and she didn't belong here. She wanted Gram more than anything to magically appear and hug her and make her laugh.

Gram. She was here for Gram. And the longer she dallied, the longer Brookerby would be in danger. With another glance back to confirm the terrace was empty, she swiped the moisture from her eyes with the back of her gloved hand and descended the staircase into the vast landscaping below.

THE NIGHT WAS MILD, with a soft breeze rustling through the hedges, as Em wandered into the vast grounds behind the Lanesby mansion. The gardens were some of the finest Em had seen from her garden tour of Gillamor. *The Lanesbys must be employing a whole team of garden-ers,* she speculated. The hedges were expertly trimmed into whimsical figures and shapes that lined the flagstone walkway from the house. Then a series of geometric gardens were laid out in intricate, repeating patterns. Em passed the first section of garden that utilized white flowering bushes, a purple ground moss, and ornamental grasses. The white flowers smelled strongly of sweet honey. Walking to the next area, immaculate conical trees were planted along the walkway. Em caught herself counting her steps between the trees to verify. They were exactly spaced. Marveling, Em noticed they were also all the same height. *How in thunder—*

"Lovely, isn't it?"

Em jumped at the voice, which came from a nearby bench. She knew that voice. Her head swiveled.

"By the way, I recognized the dress first. I would call you a thief, but you seem to be making better use of it than I did."

"Sam Monterey," Em started, horrified, realizing how very far they were from the house. She twisted her head frantically, trying to gauge if they were within screaming distance. She was turning to run when the pleading in his voice made her pause.

"Stop. Please."

"Why?" she demanded, whirling on him, enraged. "You held me against my will. I had to climb a rope out the window. I tried to tell you what I know, but you didn't even believe me."

"I know that now."

"How?"

He had the decency to look abashed. "I had you found and followed."

Em's jaw dropped. "What?" Another wave of anger hit her. The man watching Hallson Manor that morning was probably one of Sam Monterrey's men, not a detective looking for Mendel.

He leapt from the bench and crossed to her. "I had no choice. Your parents are my only clue to what happened to Arrenmore. I found out about the state of Brookerby, how it—well, the same thing that happened to us. The magic was lost. And you're here, looking in every garden in town. You are as desperate to save your town as I am mine. We can work together! What kind of plant are you looking for?"

Crumb. He was a scoundrel, at best. But Monterey's good looks and earnestness gave him an air of sincerity. She wanted to trust him. Then she reminded herself of how their last encounter went and hardened her countenance.

"Mr. Monterey, I'm very sorry about Arrenmore, but it sounds like you know about as much as I do. Now if you'll excuse me—" She turned on her heel.

"I also know about the tailor," he stated calmly.

Em froze, back turned to him, deliberating. "What about him?"

He crossed behind her, placing a hand on her shoulder, lips next to her ear. "You freed a man who was condemned to die." Em repressed a shiver and yanked away, all goodwill for this man instantly evaporated. "I could turn you in. You and the boy with the dog." He sniffed. "Lord Hallson, I should say. I never would've guessed. What will all those fine folks say? Respected lord, fine member of society, is in bed with a criminal." Em twisted around with her fists raised. Sam's eyes narrowed, and his mouth turned up unpleasantly. "But from the looks of things in there, you're not his type. Maybe it's a matter of time before he turns you in himself."

"Or what?" Em said, seething.

"Pardon?"

"You'll either turn me in, or what? I work with you?"

"Or tell me how to find your parents."

"I've had no luck in that endeavor."

"I doubt that. You've had two people approach you about your mother in the past three days."

Em sucked in a breath. He really had been following her. Her mind quickly raced through the conversations she had, wondering what else had been overheard. Thinking quickly of her parents, her anger was momentarily directed toward parts unknown in the north. She took another breath. "What does 'working with you' look like?"

"Any information you discover, you share with me. In full. Including how you discovered it."

Em's mind wrapped around the ramifications. She could not reveal the book, but maybe she could omit that detail.

"Also, if a new tree, or whatever, is found, Arrenmore gets it," Sam added.

Em started. "Absolutely not. I will not condemn my own town. No."

"I can turn you in right now. For treason. You can hang right alongside your beloved magic-wielding tailor."

"I will not be blackmailed into condemning my own town," she seethed.

"Then you have made your choice," he said coldly.

"Fine." Em turned to walk farther into the gardens. He pushed past her, striding toward the house, and was gone.

Em started to tremble. She stood still for many minutes trying to burn the feeling of his hand on her shoulder out of her brain. Her mind flowed like molasses over the conversation, trying to draw conclusions. If his threats were not idle, she might be arrested soon. "The knave of gardens. Treachery in beautiful places," she muttered, remembering her fortune from the festival. She was running out of time.

And then her feet were moving. Taking her away from the grand house and toward the farthest corner of the gardens. Toward the rare plants.

~

RUSHING among the strange flora in the moonlight, Em didn't know what she was looking for. Brookerby's old tree looked normal. Maybe bigger than average. Quick growing. Perhaps that was a clue. But she had no inkling of what might provide protection.

The Lanesbys had kindly provided a small description etched on a wooden post by each plant, consistent with what "Flora of Gillamor" had indicated about private gardens. Em crouched down to read each in turn.

Lippewort. Suitable for curing earaches when blended with a lavender essence.

Holyrod. Essential ingredient in most love potions.

Dregwing. Utilized with hair dyes to create vibrant hair color.

Some were more interesting than others. Em did not pause to consider applications, simply looking for "protection" and moving on if she did not find it. The rare-plants section was a large one, and Em followed the meandering paths, trying to keep track of where she had been.

In the far corner of the garden, there was an open spot. A wooden post with no corresponding plant. Em approached this spot and read the following.

Warding laurel. Provides a shield of goodwill and safety to those within twenty paces.

Em let out an involuntary yip. This must be a related species to the tree, or perhaps the tree grew from the plant. She reasoned that a different plant might have an extended range, or perhaps the size of the laurel determined how far the protection extended.

But there was no sign of it. Em crouched close to the description post, peering at the spot where the plant should've been. Even the dirt appeared undisturbed. Where was the shrubbery? Surely the hostess, Mrs. Lanesby, would know. Em stood, frantically brushing dirt off her dress. She would have to get to the hostess before the party concluded. And she needed to get out of here before Sam Monterey or one of his spies figured out what she was looking at. Jogging back toward the house, she nearly ran over Liam.

"Oof. Sorry," she muttered.

"Em!" Liam's voice was filled with amused merriment. It brought Em's mind screeching back to the evening. Liam's dancing partner. Sam's stinging comments. Liam's merry tone reintroduced another flavor of Em's sour feelings.

Em straightened her shoulders. "I need to find Mrs. Lanesby immediately. I might have found something," she informed Liam woodenly.

"Of course. I'm sorry, Em. I tried to get out here as soon as politely possible."

Em bit the inside of her cheek, willing herself to be happy for him. Cass was lovely. Em didn't need to make rude comments to Liam simply because he seemed quite attached to a beautiful, kind woman. She settled for a statement of fact. "You and Cass seemed to be having fun. I didn't want to interrupt."

"Did you get a dance in?" he asked kindly.

"One or two," she admitted. Inwardly little spikes were growing into her gut. He hadn't even looked for her. She felt instantly ridiculous again. She was wearing this foolish dress, a dress that had made it so easy for Sam Monterey to track her down. She had spent far too much time dressing up, and talking with Liam, and thinking about Liam. To hide her mortification, she turned back toward the house. "I need to move. To find Mrs. Lanesby. Before time runs out." She strode quickly in the direction of the house.

"Time?" Liam puffed, running to catch up to her side. "What are you talking about?"

Em kept walking, and Liam jogged to keep up. "Sam Monterey is here. He was here tonight. He said he had me followed. He knows about Mendel."

"What? He followed you?"

"Either I find him a tree, or he turns me in. His stipulations were untenable, so I refused. Any moment, I expect to be dragged away to prison."

"Em—"

"I shouldn't even be near you anymore. I'm endangering you, your staff, your friends, your family name—"

"Em! Stop!" he commanded.

She stopped walking but did not turn to him. She felt antsy. She had to find that laurel, and she had to leave the estate before Monterey made good on his threats. Standing here talking to Liam would not help her. But still, her feet would not move.

"Em," Liam started, his voice rising. "We're in this together."

"But—"

"No. Would you look at me please?" She turned. "I will not tolerate blackmail from a second-class barkeep like Monterey. We need to find a tree for Brookerby, and I promised to help."

"I do not hold you to that promise. Not in light of, well, everything," Em said flatly, shaking her arms loose.

Liam's eyebrows shot up. "After all the times I saved you?"

Em counted in her head. Up a tree, she would've been fine. The fire—well, who knows how that started anyway. "I could've managed on my own."

"You were up a tree with a sprained ankle! How would you have managed?" His voice was getting louder.

Em's face flushed. "I would've figured it out. That's what I do best."

"Really? I thought what you did best was stubbornly refuse help and drive everyone away from you."

Em felt like he had slapped her. She took a step back, and her traitorous feet were unglued.

Liam's face shifted to regret. "Em—" he started.

Em held up her hand to block his words as she took another backward step. Without another sound, she turned on her heel and continued toward the villa.

Five minutes later, Em saw the lights of the house—and lights from torches that weren't there before. Imperial soldiers descended the back steps of the veranda, Sam Monterey leading them.

He pointed directly at her.

CHAPTER 20

he soldiers stood at the base of the veranda stairs, three of
them, in addition to Monterey. They wore the gilded
peacock crest of the empress on spotless armor. Em slowed her steps
and cursed. Her choices were two: Continue toward them and be
arrested or run, and be arrested in a much less dignified manner. She
continued walking in their direction, not slowing or turning. No need
to cause a scene.

She was close enough now to see their faces, and she let out an
involuntary gasp. Briggs, the soldier from the road, stood shoulder to
shoulder with Captain Marcellus. The man whose squadron had
invaded Brookerby. Captain Marcellus, who had her detained her on
the road. She shuddered. Briggs seemed more human than the
captain, but she had given Briggs the slip after the woman had shown
kindness. Both had their reasons to dislike Em. The third man she did
not know, a short, squat fellow with a distracted look, but he hardly
mattered.

"Halt!" The command came from Briggs in her musky alto voice.
"Emaline Strider of Brookerby, you are under arrest for crimes
against the empire. Possession of banned documents. Possible magic
user. Aid and comfort to a condemned criminal. Resisting arrest."

"I am not resisting," Em said, voice calm but small. The third man flowed into action, moving languidly to restrain her hands behind her back.

"No matter, Miss Strider," the captain grunted. "Sounds like you've been causing mischief from the moment we met in Brookerby. Glad this upstanding citizen had the wherewithal to report you." He gestured at Sam, who stood a few paces away with a predatory gleam in his blue eyes.

Em took a deep breath. If she was going to be arrested, she could at least keep her wits about her. She addressed the scowling captain. "You could at least explain this nonsense about magic. I am not a magic user."

"The tailor was. And there have been enough incidents surrounding you that we're not taking chances. Not with a warding tree on the line."

Em's jaw nearly hit the ground. How did the captain know about the tree?

Liam approached, eyes wide. "Em, what are—" Then he caught sight of the captain. "Marcellus?"

The captain's scowl intensified. "Lord Hallson. I didn't expect you to be mixed up in this."

"Let her go, Marcellus."

"This is baffling, Liam. But, then again, you latch on to any kind of hope. Why would you go chasing this wild goose again?" The captain's brows furrowed.

"Marce," Liam growled warningly.

Em glanced from one man to the other, trying to read the unknown subtext of their conversation.

"After all, you know what these trees do. Or have you forgotten?" Marcellus's words felt tired. Like this argument had been revisited many times. Em's eyes grew wide in understanding. These men knew each other.

"You know I can't just give up. No matter how numb to it you've become. No matter how many punches you throw," Liam spat back.

"You need to stop using these poor tree seekers. It isn't fair to them." Marcellus gestured at Em. "Although she is better looking than the others. Much improved over the last few times I've seen her."

Em felt her jaw drop. There had been others? Had Liam's attentions been an act?

Liam was thrown off by the later part of Marcellus's comment. "What do you mean, 'last few times'?"

"I was sent to Brookerby to contain the mess. She gave me a bit of trouble. And then again, on the road. We had to tie her hands."

Em's head was spinning, so she focused on Liam's face, looking for context or denial.

Liam was gratifyingly incensed by the man. "That was you? That is an outdated rule that should never have been enforced. This whole thing has been a petty vendetta for Brookerby. Release her at once."

"The Brookerby tailor was scheduled to hang for magic use and treason last night. We have reason to believe Em orchestrated the tailor's escape. "

"On what? This guy's word?" Liam gestured toward Monterey derisively. "Let her go, Marcellus."

"No can do, little brother. Empress's orders."

Em felt her mouth fall open. *Brother?* This monster that had invaded her town, arrested her friends, arrested Gram, hit her in the head, held her at gunpoint…was Liam's brother? She felt a moment of horror, followed by shaking anger.

She shook off the relationship, as Liam would have no way of knowing that she had met Marcellus—if you could call their encounters "meeting." But Liam knew more about the trees than what he had shared. An unforgivable concealment, given her days of searching.

Liam was saying something; he looked like he was pleading, encouraging her, but she heard nothing. She stared past him, feeling nothing, as she was led away from the glittering house.

～

EM WAS PACKED AWAY in the back of a covered cart. There was a single bench of roughhewn wood that Em clutched awkwardly with her tied hands while the wagon bumped away from the Lanesby home.

The journey was a silent one, except inside Em's mind. She scanned through her prior interactions with Briggs and Marcellus. She also tried to recall everything Liam had recounted about his brother. Not much, except he worked for the empress, lived in town, and they did not see each other often. All that was true. Liam had not lied. But had Liam been a soldier also? Em tried to imagine him in the band that invaded her town, and she shivered. He did tell her he was formerly employed by the empress; she was foolish to assume that meant anything but soldiering. She had trusted him. She had almost kissed him. And the whole time—

The cart abruptly stopped, and Em's thoughts were suspended, given where the soldiers had taken her: the palace in the center of the city. The Golden Lark Palace. Marcellus and Briggs pulled her down without fanfare, gripping her upper arms and guiding her toward the impossibly ornate building.

There was nowhere to run in the wide gold-and-marble corridors of the palace. She considered breaking free and hiding in one of the many rooms they passed, but Marcellus and Briggs weren't loosening their grips one bit. They traveled through a series of ornately carved doors that were as tall as Gram's cottage and twice as heavy. Em wondered at the master carpenter who had hung the massive doors. Had it been done by magic? How did they open without a sound?

The final door was of age-darkened ivory, carved with realistic birds and plants and highlighted in liquid-gold details. It must have weighed a great deal, for two muscled guards pulled it open, revealing the central garden of the palace.

The air changed. It was moist, but not heavy. The room was well-lit by moonlight. All around were trees, shrubs, and flowering plants, none of which were familiar. Sounds of running water, and lazy cries of unseen tropical birds greeted her ears, instead of the earlier bustle of footsteps and palace business. *Why have they brought me to a garden and not a jail cell?* Em recalled that this place was on her list of gardens. Perhaps she could attempt a search if they allowed her to wander.

Above their heads was a huge dome, presumably the same one visible from all over the city. On the inside, it was painted to look like the night sky. But then Em saw a shooting star, and she studied the dome more closely. The moon was nearly full, same as the moon outside at this moment. *It's enchanted to look like the sky outside,* she thought with awe. The ceiling must have been developed during the Age of Magic.

They led her to a three-tiered, star-shaped fountain in the middle of the garden. The guards stopped and stood at attention, flanking her but releasing her arms. She glanced uneasily at Briggs, who was standing stiffly at her side. The woman was definitely annoyed that Em had given her the slip before.

"I hope I didn't cause too much trouble on the road," she ventured carefully.

Briggs nodded once. Em assumed that was as close to forgiveness as she would get.

Marcellus spoke up. "You did indeed. Several hours were wasted trying to recover you."

Briggs rolled her eyes. No love lost there. Then Briggs spoke, "If I may, Captain, it doesn't seem very hospitable to tie up travelers. It's a wonder more of them don't run away."

Marcellus grunted noncommittally. "Miss Strider, I'm not sure what my brother has communicated to you, but he has not told you the whole story."

Em turned her head and met the captain's eye. The man was, surprisingly, not scowling. He appeared to be analyzing her response. She turned her head back. "I am not opposed to having more information, Captain. But you have not been particularly communicative."

Briggs snorted, and Marcellus shot her a withering look.

Suddenly, the guards stiffened. Em heard a horn blare and the sound of many footsteps approaching.

An older woman, about Gram's age, glided along the path, wearing a filmy, peacock-patterned robe that trailed elegantly behind her. Her silver hair was carefully crafted into an elaborate twist that looked very much like a crown. There was a group of men and women in uniform flanking her, all bearing the crest of the empress. A man declared in a resonant bass, "All hail to Her Imperial Majesty, Regina de Silviana Augusto."

Em's guards knelt in a single movement. Understanding struck her. This was the sovereign herself. Em quickly knelt, although less smoothly, as she was still in an evening gown with her hands tied behind her.

"Marcellus, you continue to serve with distinction." The woman's voice was like warm buttermilk with a hint of spice.

"Thank you, Majesty. I live to serve," Marcellus replied with the standard phrasing.

"What is your name, girl?" This to Em, only slightly less warm.

Still kneeling, Em tried to keep her voice from shaking, "Emaline Strider of Brookerby, Your Majesty."

The woman cupped her chin in a bony, bejeweled hand and studied her face. Em tried to keep the terror out of her eyes.

"She is young, and unskilled, according to my information," the empress pronounced, releasing Em's face. "I don't believe her efforts were an act of rebellion."

One of her attendants, a gray-haired man dressed in black, cleared his throat. "Your Majesty, there is the matter of the tailor."

"Ah. The tailor." She turned back to Em, tapping her lips thoughtfully. "Well, Emaline of Brookerby, I think it's time you and I have a talk." She waved her entourage away. "Leave us."

They trotted out, leaving Em and her original guards. The empress glanced at Marcellus and raised a single eyebrow.

Marcellus protested, "Ma'am, we cannot leave you unprotected."

"From this little girl? You underestimate me, dear boy. I'll be fine. Please wait outside."

Marcellus schooled his face into neutrality, made a deep bow, and trotted out with Briggs and the other man.

"Stand, Emaline. Let's take a walk."

Em struggled to her feet, hands still tied. The empress started down a side path, and Em stepped quickly to join her. Em couldn't help but think that this woman could end her with a single word. She felt terror, mixed with curiosity. Why would the empress speak with her alone?

"I am too old to mince words, Miss Emaline, so I will speak frankly. I hope you will too."

"Yes, Your Majesty."

"Did you orchestrate the release of Mendel of Drecovia?"

"No." It was not quite a lie. Nothing about Mendel's rescue had been "orchestrated."

The empress was silent. Studying her.

"I understand that Brookerby has lost its warding tree."

Em's eyes grew wide, but she nodded. "Yes, we have."

"And I understand you have come to Gillamor in search of a new one."

It was a statement more than a question, and Em did not attempt to deny it. "Yes, Majesty."

"Very well. To your credit, you are honest. That brings us to the point quickly. I must ask you not to replant."

"What?" Em blurted. "Your Majesty, my town. Without a new tree, we are ruined."

The empress stopped walking and narrowed her eyes at Em. "Do you believe you are different from the countless others who have faced the same tragedy? The loss of a town is not what I would wish for my subjects. Nevertheless, I must ask this of you."

"Why?" Em blurted, and then wished she could take it back. Such impertinence was not wise.

The empress made no sign that she had heard. Instead, the woman reached inside a fold of her dress and pulled out a piece of weathered, creased paper. She held it up to Em. "Do you recognize this?"

Em's eyes scanned the page, and recognition dawned. It appeared to be Mendel's notes on the tree. The ones the soldiers had burned in Gram's cottage. She looked up in confusion. "I thought it was destroyed."

The empress quickly folded the parchment and returned it to her pocket. "It is a copy. Definitive proof that a magic user intends to plant a new warding tree. The runes needed for the planting, in your tailor's handwriting. It is a very damning thing for him. The copy that was in your possession—" She paused. "I don't believe you knew what you had."

Em held her face steady. Mendel had told her the parchment wouldn't work. That it wasn't quite right. But perhaps the empress didn't know that. Perhaps she didn't care.

The empress watched Em's face and misunderstood the emotions that flashed there. "Yes, Emaline. You could have done a great deal of damage without ever leaving home. That is, if we had not come to collect the tailor that day. You may do damage still if you have the gift. Which I suspect you do, given your parentage and the company you keep. Therefore, I will have Captain Marcellus share some history with you. And then you will swear an oath promising not to seek out a new tree for your village. Be glad that you are retaining your freedom and your life."

Em was silenced by the last, and by the harsh look on the empress's face. Then, the sovereign strolled to an ornate silver tray and rang the minuscule silver bell that sat upon it. As the bell tinkled, Captain Marcellus appeared again, this time alone. The empress gave him a brief nod, gave Em a dissecting look, and floated away. Em remained rooted to the spot, trying not to give in to the swirl of feelings threatening to engulf her. She had met the sovereign. Lied to her. The empress had commanded her not to do the very thing that would save her home.

Marcellus waited a moment, until the sound of the heavy ivory doors signaled the empress's exit. Then he turned to her, his stern face weary.

"I have shared this history with scores of people searching for a tree. It has become a routine, but your involvement with my brother complicates matters."

"How?" Em asked.

"Because he does not believe what I am about to tell you. The moment you are released, he will endeavor to show you all the ways you can still plant a tree. Ways to circumvent the oath you will take."

Em began to protest, but Marcellus held up his hand to stop her. "Please, let me get this out." He exhaled heavily, and then his gray eyes locked on to her blue ones. "My brother is optimistic. I admire that in him. He is a good man. But he has acted wrongly toward many a tree seeker, including you. And in continuing his search, he is wrong. You must be strong enough to stand against him."

Em's eyebrows knotted together in confusion. This was not the same Marcellus she had previously encountered. He was being open. Brutally so. Em trusted what he was saying, but it did not reflect well on Liam.

"Let me start with the standard script. Then I promise to answer your questions." He gestured toward a stone bench; Em warily sat. "Fifty years ago, Her Imperial Majesty, Regina de Silviana Augusto, was early in her reign. She assumed the throne from her father, Henrich, who had neglected Esnania and allowed all manner of thievery and villainy to run rampant throughout the empire. The wealthy and elite could pay for protection from mages, but the small towns, the working farmers and shopkeepers, had no protection from the degeneracy that ravaged the country.

"Our empress was a young woman with idealistic notions. She devised a solution. Magical trees in each village. Trees that would protect the town from harm and bring prosperity to its people for years to come. Most citizens received this news with joy, and Her Majesty engaged the services of renowned mage, Bronwyn Feather-weight, to perform the magic.

"They planned a tour. A planting every day, and the empress would caravan from town to town with her mage and entourage. But during the tour, strange things happened. Terrible things. A drought, floods, deaths, wars, assassinations, magical ruination. These events were connected to the very hour of planting, and planting caused them. Horrified, the empress called for an end to the tour, and returned to the palace to try and stem the damage.

"She demanded an audience with her mage, asking for a full review of what went wrong. But Bronwyn was a volatile woman who was enraged that she was being blamed for numerous Esnanian disasters. In a tantrum, she fled the palace, and tried to continue the planting tour, despite the empress's orders. The empire caught and executed her. But there were others. Bronwyn's apprentices, who wanted to continue her work.

"A decree was issued. Any magic user who, after learning the truth of the warding trees, attempted to plant a warding tree would be put to death. And so, it has continued to this day."

Em sat for a moment, staring at nothing. Mendel. He had that paper. Had he known the truth? Then, as the silence stretched out, she turned back to Marcellus, who was studying her.

"It doesn't matter to the empress that these towns are ruined when their trees eventually fall?"

"She thinks it is a tragedy, but a necessary one. New towns may spring up from their demise; towns that are not living under the control of magic."

"Not everyone will accept that," Em argued.

"I know it better than most. It wasn't long after the first trees fell, nearly forty years ago, the empress's soldiers discovered tree hunters, like yourself, scouring the country for a new protecting tree. Even non-magic users were a danger. The empress removed the knowledge from libraries, and demanded an oath from any seekers. If they refused the oath, they were executed."

"So that's why you visited Brookerby? To force an oath from us and watch us fall?"

He inclined his head. "That is what you might think. But we were simply there to collect the tailor. We stumbled on some information linking him to the previous tree planting in Brookerby, and he is a known magic user. He was condemned even before the tree fell."

"How did Mendel get to Gillamor? He wasn't with you on the road."

"We sent him back with another squad that we joined in Drecovia. We had business there as well."

Em was still puzzled.

"I am not a magic user, Captain. And I have never seen Mendel or Gram use magic."

"I have found no evidence for you. But you were on a prospective list, based on your lineage. Your tailor was already condemned, but the paper with the tree and runes was damning. We had originally attributed it to Gramalia, as it was found in her home, but Mendel claimed the document. Then we found a second copy in his shop."

"I see," Em whispered. "What about Evederell—your hometown? Do you ever wish you could restore it?"

Marcellus placed his hands on his knees and let out a breath. "I do. I did. I would've done anything to fix my town. I made many mistakes when I was a youth, and most of them are connected to those trees. But there's nothing to be done that wouldn't hurt more people. That's why you should stop. Why Liam should stop. Planting these trees will only cause more destruction."

Straightening suddenly, Marcellus rose from the bench. Taking a few steps away, he pivoted and appeared to be back in an official role. "The charge for escaping on the road is a small one that has been waived. You were ignorant of the trees' history, so no crime has yet been committed regarding them. Finally, you have been accused of freeing the tailor before his execution. We do not have enough evidence, beyond hearsay, to prosecute you for that crime. But I would not be surprised if you were involved. I must let you know, the empire will be watching you. Every moment."

Em trembled. She didn't know if his words were a caution, or a threat.

"Miss Strider, do you have any other questions for me?" The request was surprisingly gentle after his official recitation of her charges.

"How much of this does Liam know?"

Marcellus's eyes softened. "All of it. Except regarding the tailor, and Brookerby."

Em felt like she had been punched.

"Miss Strider?"

"He let me look in all the libraries for information. He gave me hope. Yet he knew."

The captain remained silent.

She met his eyes and spoke the only question she had left. "What is the oath?"

He gestured, leading her back toward the large fountain. As he untied her hands, he spoke the words, slowly and clearly for her. "You must hold one hand in the fountain as you say them," he explained.

"If I do not speak these words—?" Em's voice wavered.

"You will be hanged."

CHAPTER 21

Intentionally violating the law, Bronwyn Featherweight planted a protective tree in the small village of Abingdon. At the planting ceremony, she gave a rousing speech of defiance against her sovereign. She set off magical sky flowers to commemorate the planting.

IT WAS the early hours of the morning when Em was deposited on the stairs in front of Liam's blue door. Marcellus departed after she spoke the oath, and the cart carrying her guard escort sped away from the house without ceremony. Exhausted physically and mentally, she slumped down on the stairs. She felt the weight of the evening.

I swear by the empress of the realm, and by my eternal honor, that I shall not seek to replant a warding tree of protection. Nor shall I search for knowledge of these trees or instruct anyone else to seek them.

The words of the oath were seared in her mind. The chill of the fountain's trickling stream still rested in her palm's memory. Oaths were cautionary tales to small children of Esnania. Eat your greens, or I'll make you swear an oath to eat only greens, or other such nonsense. Every child knew that swearing an oath meant to be bound —painfully and irrevocably—for life. Em never expected to be bound by one.

Em dropped her head into her arms and wept. Her body shook with exhaustion and the mental pain of what she had done, and she bit her lip to keep her crying from waking everyone up. She was a coward. She had folded under the threat of death. She spoke the oath. And Brookerby was doomed. She scrubbed her eyes with the back of her hand, vowing to go in and get rest. Tomorrow, she could figure out how to live with herself.

She stood, a bit unsteadily, and crossed over to the side of the house, hoping the garden door would be open and she wouldn't disturb anyone. In the dark, she fumbled along the pathway, and yelped when a human-sized shadow moved toward her.

"Em, it's just me," Liam soothed, stepping out of a shadow, barely lit by the waning moon.

Em paused, uncertain.

"I was so worried. I went to the jail, but they said you weren't there."

"They took me to the empress."

"Em." It was almost a sigh. Like he had expected this, and dreaded it.

Em was nearly falling asleep where she stood. Too tired to feel angry.

"You look like you need rest. Come inside."

She nodded, blearily, and stumbled along as he held the door for her.

In the kitchen, he lit a candle to guide them through the house in the dark. "Do you..." he began haltingly. "I mean, want to talk about it?"

Em scrunched her eyes closed. "No."

"Okay." He led the way through the kitchens, up through the dining room and the main hall, up the stairs, and down to her room. Em's feet were leaden bricks. Holding open the door for her, he leaned in the room and placed the candle on the table for her, then stood just outside the door. "Would you like me to wake up one of the maids to help you get to bed?" he spoke quietly, gesturing to the little buttons on the back of her gown—the cursed Gray Horse dress.

"Don't wake anyone up, I'll manage." To prove her point, she twisted her arms, trying to reach them herself. Finally, she let her arms flop down uselessly. Tilly would be upset if she ripped it. "I'll just sleep in it," she grunted.

"I promise, I'm not trying to be forward—but can I help you?"

For the first time, she looked him in the eye. He stood in the doorway, concern on his face. She didn't know what she felt anymore. His care was calculated. He had used her. He had lied to her. So what was this? Too tired to fight with herself she nodded, and moved toward him, turning her back.

His fingers fumbled, undoing the first few buttons. He was careful not to brush her skin with his hand and stepped back quickly. "Can you reach from there?"

Em contorted her arms again and found that she could reach the remaining buttons that traveled down her back. She grunted, "Yes."

He nodded. "Sleep as long as you want. Let me know when you'd like to talk. I'll be here."

As she closed the door, she heard him quietly move back down the hall.

～

EM SLEPT WELL into that day. She woke to noises of bustle in the streets below, and full sun streaming in through the window. Groaning, she rolled over and pulled a pillow on top of her head. Then a knock on the door. She ignored it. Someone quietly entered, placed a tray on her bedside table, and tiptoed out.

Em lay there a few moments, willing herself back to sleep. But it was too late. She was awake. Peeking out from under her pillow, she saw the tray containing her lunch. Savory smells wafted toward her, but Em's stomach lurched dangerously when she considered eating.

She closed her eyes, trying to close out the day. And last night. Everything from last night.

"Ugghhh," she groaned, eyes flying open again. She flopped out of bed gracelessly, stumbled toward her bureau, pulled out her old blouse and a plain black skirt, and yanked them on messily. She could at least try to—

Then her mind stopped. Try to what? She couldn't seek the tree anymore, on threat of great pain from her oath. She didn't dare visit Mendel for fear of giving away his location. What else was left to her but return home and try to keep Gram and Ilna safe. From bandits, from mobs, and from themselves. Somehow.

Mendel was a magic user. The empress seemed to think so. Perhaps he could—then a sharp stab of pain interrupted this thought. Instinctively, Em knew the pain was the result of her oath. The oath prevented Em from asking Mendel to pick up where she left off.

The empress suggested that Em had the gift of magic. Em looked at her own hands, strong, slender, with scars and cuts from years of hammering and nailing and lifting and repairing. They were capable. But not magic. She had never seen any indication of anything beyond a job well done. Then she thought of the spark. At the hanging. Of Liam's words about the fire: *it kind of started on its own.* Had she done that?

Not that it mattered. Even if she had some kind of magical gift, Brookerby was still doomed. Standing by the bureau, she removed *The Standard Book of Anything*, weighing it in her fingers. She had lugged this thing from Brookerby, believing it would guide her. But instead, it had given her very small bits of the full picture. It had not given her the full truth, at least, not what the empress and Marcellus had revealed.

Flopping back in bed, she flipped it open, this time to the title page.

The Standard Book of Anything
   A Useful Reference for Finding the Next Step

Em snorted on reading the word "useful" and flipped to the next page. After the total and complete dead end of last night, she needed a next step.

The History of Esnanian Magic. While magic is quite rare in Esnania, it once flourished throughout the region in what is known as the Age of Magic (668– 756 RQ). Before the rise of the empress, it was common for trained magic users to travel throughout the land, conjuring solutions to problems and enchanting objects in villages in exchange for shelter and a meal for the evening. Some unscrupulous mages would cast additional spells that would cause mischief in the town after their departure. These magic users would often travel with storytellers and jugglers, and their enchantments were part of a performance.

Many magical items remain from this era and are still functioning to the present day. These include spoons that stir on their own, a small box that heats up food without fire, a speaking mirror that provides advice on clothing choices, among many others. The items are considered very valuable, if in working condition. Once broken, the item will no longer contain magic.

Mages are not commonly found in Esnania in the present era. They were banned from practicing the art after a series of larger projects, commissioned by the empress, led to tragedy. Many mages were banished or executed by imperial law. Now, the skills and knowledge from the Age of Magic are all but lost.

For other solutions to your local problems, see "Household Fixes You Can Perform Without Magic."

Em bit her lip. The trees. They were the project that ended in tragedy. She wondered if the method of planting was incorrect. *Perhaps...* She felt a sharp pain in her temples and shook her head. No more thought of trees. She took an oath that she could not break. She was useless. Rapidly, she flipped to the article on Household Fixes.

Household Fixes You Can Perform without Magic. Many keepers of house-holds long for the early days where magic solved your problems, and dust dusted itself. This is no longer the case, but homeowners should not despair.

There are many tasks you can perform with a few simple tools and absolutely no magic, although your friends will be so amazed they will accuse you of casting spells.

Em read the cheeky article, a lengthy list of repairs that could be made. Em knew many, but also learned a few tips she was anxious to try. There were no cross-references, and no hints in the article. Just a list of chores. Sitting back, she glanced at her tools, untouched where they had been placed on her arrival in Gillamor. She had always been happy repairing, improving, creating solutions to problems. It was a next step, at least. If nothing else, she could repay Liam's funding of her wardrobe with repairs. And then she could leave this place. Picking up her tools, pulling on her old boots, she began to survey the room for problems, big and small.

THE SERVANTS SEEMED INITIALLY AMUSED by Em's new hobby. She helped the cook stabilize the kitchen table, which had wobbled dreadfully for years, and built a new spice rack for all the seasonings, which could be folded into a cupboard when not in use. She repaired chipped and cracked tiles in the main entryway. She fixed a squeaky step on the back staircase.

At first she received praise and gratitude from the staff—but after several days of flurried repairs, their attitudes changed. Em was perched on a ladder in the garden, repairing the front gate and securing roof tiles, when the steward tried to coax her down with tea and scones. The maids clucked disapprovingly when they passed.

Liam tried several times to discuss the oath and the revival of their search. Em chose these moments to bustle out of the room or pretend she hadn't heard his question.

By day four, the staff began to grumble. Em supposed they feared for their own jobs, but the sooner Em paid her debt, the sooner she could go. She was like a hurricane, sweeping through the house identifying every crack and crumble. She was preparing to inspect the chimneys when she overheard a maid mentioning to Lord Hallson that the young lady might consider taking a break.

Liam strode into the parlor to find the furniture covered in white sheets and Em peering up the chimney while opening and closing the flue. He cleared his throat.

"These haven't been inspected in some time. The flue is not closing properly," Em critiqued without pulling her head out of the cold fireplace.

"Em, do you have a moment?"

"I'm in the middle of something, can it wait?" She had been putting him off with this phrase, eating meals in her room (when she remembered to eat), and leaving abruptly whenever he entered a room.

"No," he said firmly.

At his tone, Em ducked out of the chimney, and turned. There was soot on her jaw, and her hair wildly escaped her simple plait. Liam gaped, and Em knew she must look a mess. He schooled his face back to stern and gestured for her to sit in one of the covered chairs.

She strode to the armchair and perched on the edge, fingers fidgeting in her lap.

Liam crossed to the sofa opposite her and took a seat, studying her for a moment. Finally, he broke the silence. "I thought I could give you some time, but now you're scaring the servants. We need to talk."

Em met his eyes briefly, angrily, before she glanced back at the fireplace. She said nothing.

"Em, please talk to me. About what happened that night."

"I got arrested. They took me to the empress. I told you all this," she said with a hint of surliness.

"That's *all* you told me, Em. I want to talk about what she said. What Marcellus said. I want to know why you've given up."

Em was shaking with anger. "Given up?"

He met her gaze, unflinching. "Yes."

"For one thing, Lord Hallson, I don't believe I owe you any explanation, after all the half-truths and information you've concealed from me," she blurted, narrowing her eyes dangerously.

"About my brother? You're angry that I didn't tell you more about my older brother?"

"No! I don't care about that. Marcellus said you knew the truth about the trees. You knew! And yet, you led me to libraries when you knew I would find nothing. You wasted my time. You let me believe that there was hope."

"There was hope! There is more—"

"Marcellus said you would say that. He said you would try to convince me to keep going."

"Marcellus has given up."

"Whenever a tree is planted, tragedy befalls the town, and tragedy befalls Esnania. How could I continue after that? Surely you weren't planning on forging ahead after knowing that! How much information *did* you conceal from me?"

Liam sat back and took a deep breath. But Em wasn't finished.

"I was dragged before our monarch, after an excruciating evening of watching you and Cass cozied up, I might add, and found out that everything I was searching for was a lie. That our friendship was a lie. That you were using me. I had to make a choice between death and an unbreakable oath."

Liam slowly exhaled.

"I chose the oath, the coward that I am. And now my town is lost." At these words, tears filled Em's eyes, but she continued to glare.

Liam was stone. He let out another breath before leaning forward. "What were the exact words of the oath you took?"

They were imprinted on Em's brain. She repeated them slowly for Liam. He took them in, mouthing the words as he turned them over in his mind.

Em sat, watching him think, not bothering to swipe the tears off her face. After a few minutes, she stood to return to the fireplace, but her energy from the past four days was gone. She sagged against the mantle with her back to the room. She heard him stand and cross to her.

"I was not cozied up with Cass." His voice was gentle next to her.

"It's fine if you were. She's a lovely girl, Liam," Em said robotically.

"She was engaged to Marcellus, until he broke it off last year. She's like a sister to me."

Em's eyes turned to him, dumbfounded.

"There's only one woman I'm interested in cozying up to," he said with a miserable smile. "And she's very angry at me right now. For good reason. I'm sorry." He reached out and gently wiped the soot from her chin with his thumb. Em's brain hummed softly, without her permission. Marcellus's words came back to her. *You must be strong enough to stand against him.* She stiffened her spine. "I need to finish this chimney, and then I will have paid you back for the clothes. Then I can leave."

"Is that what this is about? All the repairs?"

Em met his eyes, and he wilted. Had he thought she would stay? "Maybe I'm just doing what I do best," she said.

Liam winced. No doubt he remembered saying those awful things to her in the Lanesby's gardens. "Leave the chimney and get some rest. You owe me nothing. Except maybe a chance to explain and apologize. Will you allow me that? Tonight?"

Em dipped her head, but still said nothing.

"Thank you. See you at dinner." With this, he strode out. Em sagged against the fireplace, realizing for the first time in days how exhausted she was.

CHAPTER 22

*I*t has been ten days since the breaking. Brookerby residents are encouraged to remain in their homes except in cases of urgent business. You may feel a sense of loss, or anger or hopelessness, without being able to pinpoint the cause. You might feel like lashing out. Like destroying something or someone. This is an effect being felt all over town. Try not to act upon these impulses.

Gendry Houton has offered to knit a sweater for anyone who has need. Too bad her knitting looks like a horse's ass. Nobody wants your sweaters, Gendry.

The whole world is going down in flames. There are wars, and famines, and it's only a matter of time before Brookerby is no more. The empire wants us to fail. Be afraid.

If you hear crying in the Leaflet office, pay it no mind. Also, I would appreciate it if the person who broke my door would confess and pay for a new one. Otherwise, I will start airing everyone's dirty secrets until the culprit comes forward. You have been warned.

Brookerby Leaflet, 8th lunar month, 806 RQ
The Standard Book of Anything

EM HAD TAKEN A SHORT REST, but her calm was shattered after she read a disturbing *Leaflet* edition that appeared in *The Standard Book of Anything.* It was dated two days ago. Ilna was clearly losing her grip. The town must be in shambles. And Em's oath prevented her from doing anything about it.

Fighting despair, Em bathed for the first time in days and donned a square-necked black gown with only a few bits of lace on the sleeves. It seemed appropriately somber.

When Em arrived in the dining room, Liam was waiting for her at the oversized table. The servants had laid out an elaborate dinner for them. Whose side were they on? His, of course.

Liam sat on one of the long sides instead of at his place at the head of the table, and gestured to a chair directly across from him. She met his eyes, barely. He watched her warily. She let out a breath, lowered herself into the chair, and reached for the plate of cheeses.

"I should tell you the rest of the story," Liam said abruptly.

Em lifted her eyes from the plate and locked on his. "The rest—?"

"The first dinner we shared in this room, I told you how my family had come to Gillamor. How I had come to inherit Hallson Manor. I did not share a few things that I believe you are entitled to know."

"More half-truths," Em muttered.

"No more half-truths," Liam insisted. "From here forward, I will tell you everything I have to share. And I hope, in turn, you will trust me enough to do the same."

Em took a bite of cheese, but then pushed the tray away. She was still not hungry.

"I have told everything about leaving Evederell. Except we didn't learn of the trees until later. When Marcellus and I were serving the empress, we discovered warding trees of protection. On occasion, the empress ordered our squadron to the towns with standing trees. We were to seek out any older residents who might be aware of their existence. And any magic users. Her Majesty kept a complete list. Marcellus and I would stay up late, talking about Evederell, and how we might acquire one of the trees for our own. Meanwhile, during the day, we were preventing others from discovering this knowledge. Marcellus even joined Veritas Hamadryads for a short time. I mocked him mercilessly for that."

Em stared at a crumb on the tablecloth.

Liam was still chuckling when he noticed Em's lack of response. He let out his breath in a frustrated whoosh. Abruptly, he stood and offered a hand, "Come with me."

Em stood without taking his hand. He stepped back, awkwardly dropped his arm, and led the way out into the main hall, down a corridor, through a door that led to a narrow, creaking stairway. Em noted the stair creaks. She had missed these in her repair frenzy. At the top of the stairs, there was a small bedroom. Inside, a four-poster bed dominated the room, and a large wooden trunk sat at the foot of it.

Em hovered in the doorway. Liam strode forward, dropped to his knees, and flipped open the trunk. Out of it, he pulled maps, books, and papers, spreading them out on the floor around him. Em stepped closer and surveyed the growing spread of documents. "What is this?"

"Marcellus's research," Liam said, placing another document in an open space on the floor.

Em leaned over and reached for a map of Esnania. Certain towns were marked with a green triangle, including Brookerby. Some towns had a black X through that triangle. Evederell was one of them. "Towns with trees?" she inquired.

Liam nodded. "Marcellus was obsessed. He found a town-by-town record of the original tree-planting tour and made this map. He carefully documented each town we were sent to, including any strange events that occurred around the time of planting, or around the time the trees fell. He was looking for patterns."

Em picked up another paper. It was a list of families who left Evederell after the tree fall, and the favorable luck and misfortunes that had befallen each. Liam's family was listed first, but there appeared to be no pattern to this list. She knelt on the floor to continue studying the papers around her.

"Marcellus discovered the misfortunes tied to the trees' plantings. Deaths. Wars. Strange occurrences. Throughout our service, we also encountered a few combative mages and extremists who didn't care what the plantings did. Those experiences altered him. He had a complete change of heart. Knowledge of the trees and their plantings brought more harm than good. He willingly took the oath that he would not seek to replant in Evederell. I was coerced into that same oath, but I left the service soon after."

Em dropped the paper she was holding. "If you took the oath, how have you continued with your search? The oath carries consequences—"

Liam smiled crookedly. "Aha. The oath holds you to the words you spoke. No more. No less. I vowed that I would not seek to replant in Evederell. And I haven't. But that does not preclude me from trying to replant elsewhere. Apparently, the empress is trying to close those loopholes with additional statements she made you swear to."

Em's head was spinning. "So, when you agreed to help me, you knew that you could never save Evederell?"

"I considered that. But I hoped you could replant for me. If I first helped you."

"And the disasters that accompanied the trees did not dissuade you? I wouldn't consider planting, knowing the outcomes."

"Therein lies the mystery I must solve. Is there a way to replant without those consequences?"

Em took a breath. She glanced at the papers around her. Here was knowledge of the trees, but it wasn't triggering the sharp pain in her head that signaled a violation of her oath. "Liam, I vowed that I would not seek knowledge of the trees—"

"—and you haven't. You did not seek anything. I brought it to you." He finished her thought. "That's why I asked for the exact wording. I believe your oath still allows you to stumble upon knowledge, and work with others who already have knowledge of the trees. As long as you don't go looking."

"But I can't save Brookerby."

"You can't replant in Brookerby. But I could. Once we arrive upon a way to do it safely."

Em fell silent again. Marcellus had warned her about Liam's loopholes. And after everything she knew, she wasn't sure she wanted to take advantage of them.

Liam continued as he sifted through the trunk. "Marcellus was quite angry with me that I quit the empress's service. I wanted to get as far away from him as possible. I believed that our oaths had doomed our town. We fought over it. He broke my nose. That's when I went back to Evederell. Hoping that by sheer force of will, I could remake the town without a new tree." Liam sat back and picked up the map, tracing a route with his finger. "It was deserted. There was no one left to build the town back up. Nevertheless, I tried to open a bakery. Tried, and failed. When I came back, my father's health was declining. Marcellus was engaged to our friend Cass, but his single-minded devotion to eradicating the trees broke them."

"What do you mean?"

"Cass asked him to get reassigned. To stay in town with her. They quarreled. He ended it. She was heartbroken."

"And the others? Marcellus said you had used other tree seekers."

Liam hesitated. "I wouldn't call it that. But yes. I sought out tree seekers and offered my aid. In the hopes that, if they discovered a solution, they would in turn help Evederell."

"And—"

"None of them were successful. Most were arrested. And a few refused to take the oath when they were arrested."

Em stood, feeling nauseated. "Were you not ashamed?"

Liam didn't meet her eye. "I have no excuse. It was wrong of me. But it didn't feel wrong at the time, except that I wasn't forthcoming about what I knew."

"So, I was no different, then," Em summarized. "How many others did you spark up a fake romance with?"

Liam's head jerked up. "What?"

Em drifted back toward the door, ready to leave. "You know, the dancing. The pastries. The hand touching. It was very charming, so you must be quite practiced."

"Em, none of that was an act."

She didn't know if she trusted his words, but they still hit her like a wooden beam. Feeling numb, she crossed to the foot of the bed and sat once more. "Is that all?"

"I stole the Lanesby's bush of protection."

"What?!" Em felt a smile for the first time in days.

"Two years ago. Probably while attending a very similar party to the one we went to. I had some luck replanting, but it wasn't useful. No matter how large it grew, its protection only encompassed a small area."

"I wanted to ask Mrs. Lanesby where it had gone, but I was arrested before I had the chance," Em said.

"She wouldn't have been able to tell you."

"Where did you plant it?"

"The garden."

Em laughed for the first time in days.

"It's out there now. Want to see?" He smiled mischievously.

Em ignored the offer. "Did Marcellus document the disasters in Brookerby?"

"Maybe. These papers are five years ago and older, so it wouldn't have this latest tree fall, but it might have the planting from seventeen years ago." He flipped through the papers as he spoke. "Ah, here we are. Brookerby. Large disaster: merchant fleet overtaken by pirates, causing a nation-wide shortage of imported goods for the next year. Small disaster: two people in the town were believed dead and buried. They appeared outside of town with large memory gaps. Suspected barrier is around the town and residents, which barred them from returning and, Em?"

Em felt like her heart was about to explode. She grabbed the bedpost for support as she gasped for air.

Liam jumped up and ran to her. "Just breathe. Breathe. What is it?"

Em gulped air, and slowly gained control of her body again. Liam stood before her, anxiously. She turned, locking eyes with him. "My parents. They got sick. We had a funeral. I—"

Liam's eyes widened in understanding. "Your parents were the Brookerby disaster."

Em nodded, taking steadying breaths. They had memory gaps. They were alive. They maybe didn't even know she existed. She remembered Gram explaining they were gone. Were there bodies at the funeral? She couldn't remember. But this was good, right? They hadn't left her behind. They had just forgotten.

Em still clutched the bedpost, but her vision had cleared, and she no longer felt like her lungs were imploding. Liam closed the lid of the trunk and sat, assessing her as if for the very first time.

"You've told me everything?" her voice croaked.

Liam nodded, not breaking eye contact.

"Then I need to do the same," she said.

Em started at the beginning, describing what she knew of the first tree falling, and worked her way forward. She included everything she knew about her parents; being raised by Gram; dinners with Ilna, Mendel, and Gram; the tunnels; every encounter with a person who knew her parents; and everything the empress and Marcellus had revealed. She shared about the paper that had been burned, which would enable a second tree to be planted, and that they might require a magic user to plant again. She shared about Mendel's potential magic use, revealed after she rescued him. About Gram's potential magic use. About hers.

Liam listened without interrupting. When Em paused or lost her way, he would ask a simple question, "What happened next?"

She finished her story and let out a long sigh. "I have wanted to tell you all those things, but I didn't know if I could—"

"If you could trust me." Liam finished her sentence with a knowing nod. "One thing I don't understand, Em," Liam asked gently, "Why did you come to Gillamor? Did Gram tell you all this before you left?"

Em stood and gestured toward the door with her head.

"Something else?" Liam asked, puzzled.

"Yes. Something Gram gave me. That she made. Follow me." She strode quickly, leading him out of the small room, down the stairs, and winding through the halls back to her bedchamber. In her doorway, he hovered uncertainly, but she grabbed his wrist, pulling him in and closing the door behind him. Leaving him leaning on the door, she marched to the bed, and pulled *The Standard Book of Anything* from under her pillow.

Liam watched, uncomprehending. "Is there more in the book? Something you can't say?"

"Sit please," she commanded. He did so, slinking to the floor with his back against the door and his legs outstretched. She placed the book carefully in his lap and sat beside him. "Open to a random page."

Liam did, slowly, as if he suspected something to jump out at him. He read out loud, "Major and Minor Nobles of Esnania." Puzzled, he glanced over at Em, who watched with bated breath. "Some kind of reference book?"

"Something like that. But there's more. Read a bit."

Liam turned his eyes back to the page, reading silently for a few minutes. He glanced up, stumped. It was just a boring article to him.

Pursing her lips, Em tried to explain. "Was there anything in the essay that seemed odd? That didn't quite fit? Were there any cross-references to other articles?"

Liam shook his head, baffled. "What are you saying?"

"Maybe it doesn't work for everyone. For me, it gives me clues. It tells me what's next." Em explained how it worked for her. How she saw the *Leaflet*. How she knew to go toward Gillamor.

"Is it different every time you open it?"

She nodded. "It doesn't always tell me what I want to know. But it sometimes tells me what I need, exactly when I need it."

"And it's always right?"

"Yes, but." Em hesitated. "Like us, it sometimes does not reveal the whole truth."

Liam closed the book gently and presented it back to Em. "It sounds like a wondrous object. Maybe only a magic user can wield it."

The statement startled Em. But she nodded tentatively, taking the book and setting it beside her. Leaning back, she felt the carved door on her back. "Now you know everything I know."

Liam leaned back with a small smile. "Freeing, isn't it?"

"Now that you mention it—" She smiled back, feeling a warmth spreading through her. Then she started. "Oh! I also have a magical waterskin. It makes whatever liquid I can think of."

Liam laughed. "You should've led with that, squirrel."

Em grinned at the old nickname. They sat on the floor in companionable silence for a moment or two. Liam's fingers reached out and brushed hers tentatively. Heart pounding, Em placed her hand in his.

"I'm sorry I said you drive everyone away," he murmured. "It's not true. But I needed it to be in that moment."

Em shifted, pulling her knees up—and her hand out of his. "Maybe I do."

"You don't. It's the opposite." He turned toward her, leaning his shoulder on the door. "You have pulled me to you, effortlessly, but I didn't think you wanted that, um, kind of connection between us. So I pretended I didn't see you dancing with all those nitwits. That I didn't see you leave the ballroom. I pretended I didn't want to—" He broke off with a sigh. "I was just tired of pretending. And then you didn't want me around. And my hurt came out in an awful way. I'm so sorry, Em."

He shifted and leaned back against the door. Em sat, stunned. She had read the situation so badly, it almost made her laugh. And the sting of his comment was replaced by a flickering flame deep within her. She didn't want to leave anymore. Not the way she had planned. She wanted—

She reached out and slipped her hand back into his.

CHAPTER 23

The Chronicles of Esnanian Rulers, Age of Pewter
House of Clavonion rose to power at the dawn of the Age of Pewter. They successfully overthrew the House of Garvine to obtain their positions, using trickery and several well-placed spies.

Tranton I was emperor in the years 460 RQ to 484 RQ. He fell in the battle to subdue the northern colonies, which was ultimately successful in expanding and solidifying the empire. He was succeeded by his only daughter.

Manitra the Gentle was empress in the years 485 RQ to 525 RQ. She ruled for nearly forty years of peace and prosperity in Esnania. She succumbed to a brain fever that baffled the royal physicians. Her two sons jointly succeeded her.

Henrich IV was crowned emperor of the northern colonies, and his half brother, Jerrifree, was crowned emperor of the southern states. This all worked harmoniously with the half brothers for nearly five years, until Henrich joined with rebel forces in the south with the aim of usurping his brother and unifying the empire once more. Jerrifree was poisoned during a feast day and died quickly and painfully. (See "Poisons and Antidotes.")

Henrich—

. . .

EM STOPPED READING. This was getting her nowhere. Also, the subject matter was less than savory. She tried not to imagine death in battle, or by poisoning. Even brain fever made her stomach do queasy flip-flops.

Liam and Em were in the parlor. They had returned to Hallson Manor from a fruitless morning of seeking out gardens and plant experts. The book had pointed toward some promising leads, but nothing of value resulted. Now Em thumbed through *The Standard Book of Anything*, hoping for a new clue to chase. Instead, she found Jerrifree and Henrich. Yuck.

She turned to the "Poisons and Antidotes" article, expecting more gruesome details, but hoping the "antidotes" might tell her something useful.

Common Esnanian Poisons and Antidotes

Esnanians have used poisons for centuries, either in weapons—quickening the death of one's enemies—or in horrendous accidents when discovered by an apothecary making medicines. In more recent years, including the Age of Pewter, poisons were used in assassination attempts. The use of fatal substances might be utilized to dispose of unwanted rivals in politics, economics, or romance.

The salacious details of these poisonings can be discovered in the correspondence between historical figures. (See "Correspondence of Important Persons")

Em was getting nothing, but salacious details sounded interesting. She flipped over to the correspondence page, and nearly fell out of her chair. It was a letter. In Gram's handwriting. To Em.

Dearest Em,

If you are reading this, you have a talent for magic. Congratulations, my dear girl! Only a magic user can take advantage of the guidance this volume offers. By now you have discovered what this book can do. And, hopefully, you have discovered its limitations. I learned this the hard way. I was so excited about saving a neighboring town that I took information from the book, used it, and the direct result was the illness that damaged my vocal cords.

All the information in this book is 100 percent correct (at least, that's what I created it to be). But rarely does it provide the full picture, the context. I am writing this letter now because I know, sometime very soon, I will share this book with you for the first time. I am hoping that this letter will reveal itself to you when the appropriate time comes and it will confirm your suspicions about your own abilities, and about this magical item. The book has been marvelously helpful over the years. But it does not take the place of good common sense, and due diligence.

My dear girl, my greatest wish for you is a happy life, doing things that give you purpose. The kind of purpose you find in a well-mended roof. If this book serves as a guide, I will be delighted. But do not spend your life waiting for signs from it.

With All My Love,
Gram

Em read and reread the note. Strong emotions swirled. Deepest affection for Gram mingled with ire at the book. The note confirmed what Mendel had said. Gram lost her voice after following advice in the book. Why did Gram give her this item in the first place if it had caused harm? It was a different kind of poison, this faith in an inanimate object in the face of overwhelming evidence against it. The book had physically damaged Gram, and now she was gifting it to Em? But maybe that was the warning inherent in the letter. Don't rely on it. But also, rely on it?

Growling, Em heaved *The Standard Book of Anything* across the floor. It slid across the hardwoods, through the dust, and came to rest under one of the parlor chairs. She flopped back into Liam's plush high-backed chair in frustration.

Bob raised his head, woken by the thump, ears up and alert. Liam turned from the bookshelf in the corner, one eyebrow raised.

Em huffed and ranted, "The book nearly got Gram killed. I don't think it's helped me much either. Most of my information has come from you, or the empress, or Marcellus. Not the book."

"Maybe you're just underestimating its value? You wouldn't have even come to Gillamor without it." Liam idly fingered the spines of his books. "Maybe you should be consulting it more, not less."

"I don't think this object is my friend."

"It pointed you right to the retired city gardener this morning. I would have never thought to ask the man who was head of unusual plants for the empress for nearly thirty years."

"And did he tell us anything useful? No! Just more riddles. More wild chases."

"I wouldn't say that. He described the trees, and their properties—"

"—which we already knew."

"Right. He explained the effects of the tree on towns, and the disaster side effects—"

"—we also knew that."

"Okay, but he suggested another planting process without the parchments. Enchanting a seed or using a protective herb. Also, that fascinating story about the tree whose branches became roots when planted upside down—"

"The man is nearly ninety. He said a lot of strange and useless things."

Liam crossed the room and took a seat in the parlor chair, retrieving the book from where it had been flung. Bob put his head down and started snoring softly.

Liam focused a frown on Em. "It's something. It's more than we had before. We just need to find a magical procedure or object that endows the seed with the right qualities as they are planted. Or something with the roots."

Em crossed her arms, slinking back farther into the sofa. "We don't know what magical objects do that, or where to find them. It's not like these relics are sold on every street corner. Feels like we're right back where we started. Oh yeah, and now I can't even actively participate." Em remembered standing idly by, like a ninny, while Liam asked the city gardener questions this morning.

Liam flipped open *The Standard Book of Anything*, idly thumbing through the pages. "I think we're going to eventually get a clue that helps us. And I think it will come from in here— oh! I've never made this pastry before...I wonder..."

Em craned her neck and saw the page Liam had opened contained a recipe. She sighed again. "Go ahead. Go try it."

With a grin, Liam cradled the open recipe against him as he jogged toward the kitchen. Em shook her head. She was done looking for clues in the book today. If nothing else, she knew there would be something tasty to eat in a few hours. As long as the book didn't try to secretly poison them. She started to call out, but then stopped. Liam was a smart fellow. He would know if something wasn't right in a recipe.

She glanced over at the fireplace, remembering the stuck flue. Perhaps she just needed a distraction from her not-hunting. Standing, she went to seek out chimney-sweeping brushes from the household staff. Bob continued to sleep.

EM CHANGED into her old trousers and a plain gray blouse, suitable for hiding chimney soot. She was just wrangling her hair back into a basic knot when she glanced out of her bedroom window, and instead of the familiar silhouette of Monterrey's henchman watching the house, she saw a different man loitering on the street below. Em stuck her face against the glass to get a better look. And then she gasped.

Yanking open her bedroom door, she flew down the stairs, ignoring the puzzled stares of the housekeeper, who was dusting the foyer. Her face was nearly a snarl as she charged out the front door toward the man.

"Sam Monterey!" she shouted, fists raised. "You have a lot of nerve."

"I told you I was following you," he said calmly, eyeing her. "I see you've gone back to laborer attire. Pity."

"You had me arrested," she hissed. "Now I can't help either of us, even if I wanted to."

Sam's pale eyes flickered uncertainly. "What does that mean?"

Em took a step closer, placing her fists on her hips. "It means, the empress has asked me to take an oath. Now, I cannot replant a tree in Brookerby. I cannot seek out knowledge. I cannot guide anyone else. I'm utterly useless. Thanks to you."

"Hm. That's very convenient for you. Very convenient. How do I know you're telling me the truth?"

"I have no incentive to lie, Sam. I've been to Arrenmore. It's a manure heap. It needs help more than anywhere."

Sam held up a finger, a warning. "That's my town you are disrespecting."

"I can't help. Ever. So stop following me. And if you ever find my parents, don't try to use me against them. They don't even know I exist."

Sam's eyebrow quirked. "What's that now?"

Em turned impatiently. "Are we done here?"

"Not quite, Em. Turns out, I have found your parents. I didn't expect the little twist you just revealed, but perhaps—"

"Where are they?" Em asked breathlessly.

"Aha, details. We come to the purpose of my visit. If you come with me now, I can take you to them. They are in the city. Only in exchange for the information you have about these magic trees."

"I cannot guide anyone else," Em said stubbornly. "The oath forbids—"

"Yes, yes, you said. But I'm sure we can find some loopholes. Do you want to meet your parents or not?"

"Yes! But I don't trust you. At all."

"You don't need to trust me."

Em huffed. She didn't expect him to agree. "And why is that?"

"It's just a simple trade of information. Something you want, for something I want." Monterey's clear aquamarine eyes seemed to be laughing at her.

"How can I guarantee you'll keep your side of the bargain?"

"I will fulfill my obligation first. You don't have to tell me anything until you've met your parents."

Em considered, glaring at the man who had placed her in multiple bad situations. He stood with hands clasped, waiting. Finally, she sighed. "Give me five minutes."

"Don't bring the boy. Or the dog."

"Why?"

"Just don't. Or the deal is off."

"Fine. Five minutes."

Em rushed back inside and charged up to her bedroom. She grabbed her knapsack with her tools, just in case. The book was still in the kitchen with Liam, but she didn't think it was wise to bring that anyway. She grabbed a piece of paper and scribbled a hasty note to Liam, which she left on her bedside table. She would probably be back before he found it, but she had a sneaking suspicion that any outing involving Sam Monterey could end in disaster. Nevertheless, the prospect of finding her parents was worth the risk. Tripping down the stairs and out the front door, she nodded her assent, and Monterey began to stride down the street, away from the main square. Em hiked up her bag on her shoulder and followed.

CHAPTER 24

*W*hen *the young empress heard of Bronwyn's betrayal, she was irate. When she received news of an earthquake in the north —the cost of the planting—she was incensed. That hour, she sent out her soldiers to track down the defiant mage and drag her back to Gillamor for justice. They were instructed to take her by any means necessary.*

THEY WALKED AWAY from the center of town, Monterey striding quickly, and Em had to jog to keep up. After fifteen minutes, she felt a salty breeze on her face, and the air developed a distinctly fishy smell. The smell grew stronger as they passed seafood restaurants and vendors, and it hung thickly in the air as they approached the harbor.

The area bustled with late-afternoon activity: shoppers rushing home with large damp parcels and crew from the fishing boats straggling into the pubs and taverns after a long workday.

This was the waterfront, home to a series of whitewashed warehouses used for collecting and distributing fish and shipping goods that arrived on merchant vessels.

Em stopped for a moment to catch her breath, staring at the vast field of aqua waves that was the Friendship Sea. It had been named such because it linked Esnania to the ally country of Brildonia. The sea lapped gently against the large wooden pier, which stretched along the length of the shore, with wharfs jutting into the water at irregular intervals for docked boats, large and small. Em had never seen anything like it, and she felt suddenly small. She wondered how the piers were built under water, and how the boats were constructed not to leak, or sink.

Glancing away from the water, Em looked around for Monterey, only to see him disappear around a corner farther down the waterfront.

"Wait!" she yelped, running to catch up. She rounded the corner and nearly ran into the man. Sam had stopped and now stared at a simple wooden door in the side of one of the warehouses. Skidding to a halt in the alleyway, Em threw a skeptical look at the door. "Here?" she asked simply.

Sam nodded.

"Do we knock?"

Sam stepped back and gestured toward the door. Em took a breath, stepped forward, and rapped her knuckles on the wood a few times.

They waited.

Hearing no sound or movement, Em commented sarcastically, "They must be out."

In response came the sound of hurried footsteps, and a latch being undone. The door was pulled open, but only a few inches. "State your business," demanded a stern female voice. Shadow obscured the speaker, and Em was starting to feel uncomfortable with this errand. "I'm Emaline. I'm looking for Anne and Farrigan? I was told they might be here." She sounded calm, but her heart raced.

"What is your business with them?"

"I'd like to see them. Ur, ah, speak to them. I'm their daughter."

The shadow closed the door quickly. Em turned to Sam with a baffled look. He stood a few steps back, face neutral. He held up a finger, a gesture to wait.

A few moments later, a series of clicks sounded, and the door opened again. Again, only a few inches.

"Hello?" Em spoke into the darkness.

The door opened a bit more. A lit lantern held aloft revealed a middle-aged woman the same height as Em: same blue eyes, same nose, same honey-colored hair, except for a few gray strands. The woman stood in the doorway, studying Em carefully, eyes wide as saucers. Em dared not move, but a small noise escaped her lips. "Mom?"

The woman started, white as a ghost. Then she took a step toward Em, and then a step back. Quickly, she fished in her trouser pockets for a pair of wire-rimmed spectacles and put them on. She started moving her head back and forth in sweeping motions, looking intently at Em and Sam.

Em watched the woman, concerned. Perhaps Anne was more addled than she anticipated. She should have prepared for this possibility—

"All clear," Anne announced, removing the spectacles with a flourish. "No concealments or disguises. You are who you appear to be. You look just like me. Maybe a recessive gene? A distant cousin..."

Em stood frozen. Her mother didn't remember her, or she was trying to explain her away. "I'm Emaline. Em. I would've come sooner," she apologized softly, "but I thought you were dead. We had a funeral and everything."

Anne wrinkled her forehead, "In Brookerby?"

Em nodded.

"How old—?"

"I was three."

Her mother nodded, thoughtfully. "We didn't remember anything when we woke up. I suppose it's possible..."

Em fought tears. This was painful in a way she never anticipated.

Sam pushed in. "I hate to interrupt this reunion, but can we come in?"

Anne eyed him and spoke to Em, "We should get out of the alleyway."

Em nodded, stepping back and hastily blinking to keep the tears away.

"Who's your friend? Your husband? Boyfriend?" Anne gestured toward Monterey.

Em nearly choked. "Neither. This is Sam. He found you. He led me here."

"Very well. Come in both of you." She ushered them quickly inside, closing and locking the door behind them.

In the dim light, Em could make out very little of the warehouse interior. It felt cavernous yet the air was thick with dust—and something else she couldn't quite identify. She could make out Anne's shadow moving along the wall, next to what looked like numerous rows of tables and shelves. Glancing around, her eyes started to adjust to the dim light.

"Is Farrigan—?"

"He's out, but should be back soon," Anne said. "He's hunting today."

"Hunting? In the city?" Em questioned.

"A different kind of hunting," Anne tossed back a quick smile. "Here we are!" she sang, flipping a switch, and the warehouse corner they approached lit up with expensive electric lights. It was haphazardly decorated with mismatched couches on a threadbare rug. Books were spread on the small sofa table, and scattered throughout the space in various crates. A map of Esnania was nailed to the wall with colored sewing pins marking seemingly random locations.

"Home sweet home," she said fondly. "For now, at least. Sit down, please." She quickly cleared the books on the table and set them in the nearest crate. Em glanced at the titles of the nearest books: "Ancient Artifacts of the River Region"; "Renowned Mages of the Pewter Age"; "Herbal Remedies." The titles reminded her of the random articles from The Standard Book of Anything.

Monterey wandered over to the map, studying the pins.

Em dropped her bag beside the sofa, sank into the lumpy seat, and began, "Do you remember anything from before?"

"It's so strange. We both remember our childhoods. We remember meeting, falling in love, getting married. But then it's a blur until we woke up in that field. We've since calculated almost a five-year gap in our memories."

"That must've been disconcerting." Em tried to remain cordial, but she was dying on the inside. Her mother was so cold. So matter-of-fact. It was not the warm reunion Em had imagined.

"Indeed! At first, we were obsessed with piecing the details together, but without the ability to reenter Brookerby, our information was quite limited. So we moved on."

There was uncomfortable silence. Em pulled out the only memory she had. "I was very young. I remember you both had arrived home after a long journey. And then you got sick. Very sick. There was a funeral. Then Gram took me home. Gram raised me. As far as I know, the whole town believed you had died."

"How interesting. Gramalia? I remember her. Very kind woman. Excellent cook."

"You must've grown closer in those lost five years," Em suggested. "She knows you and Fath—Farrigan better than most folks in town did."

"Curious. How I wish I could fill in that memory gap!" Anne exclaimed.

Another silence. Em had most of her questions answered, except one. "What prevented you from coming back?"

"Some kind of magical barrier. We were unable to see the town, and if we walked in the direction of it, we would suddenly find ourselves turned around, walking the other direction. We tried to send messages inside through travelers, but they would forget us once they passed the barrier, and any written communication would disintegrate. After months of trying, we chose an alternative course. Studying magic and magical items themselves. We hoped someday we could return with the right artifact that would break the barrier and solve the mystery of our memories. That initial study has bloomed into, well, a lucrative enterprise." She gestured with her hand to the shelves that filled the warehouse around them.

Em cast her eyes on the shelves in wonder. There had to be thousands of items. Maybe hundreds of thousands. "These are all magic?" she breathed. If that was true, they were sitting next to the richest collection of items in Esnania. Maybe the whole world

"We believe so, yes." Anne watched Sam suspiciously.

"Do you remember the warding tree of protection?" Em asked, then suddenly felt a sharp razor slice of pain in her skull. She was seeking out information related to the tree, and her oath was punishing her. She cried out, cradling her head in her hands.

Anne leapt up, alarmed. "Is she all right?" she asked Sam.

"Apparently, the empress required her to take an unbreakable oath about the warding trees," Sam said lazily, not taking his eyes off the map. "What was your business in Arrenmore?"

Anne didn't take her eyes off Em, and answered distractedly, "Magical items. The pins on the map mark our findings. Emaline, what can I do? Are you all right?"

Em moaned, clutching her head and willing the stabbing pain away. She had learned her lesson. No tree questions. Ever.

Anne disappeared into a walled-off room, returning with a glass of water. Sam started to survey the shelves nearest them. Em's torment finally started to dissipate, and she sat back, panting and exhausted. "I'm so sorry. I shouldn't have asked that."

Anne handed her the water and changed the subject. "Did you know, Emaline was my grandmother's name?"

"Really?" Em asked, pleased. She never knew the origin of her name.

"She was a magic user. One of the finest. And so clever. I remember my mother telling me stories, and she was like a heroic legend to me. I imagine we named you in honor of her."

Em felt a sense of pride swelling within her. "Although you don't remember naming me, I still thank you. It's a good name."

Anne smiled warmly at Em. "I don't suppose you've inherited the gift?"

Em tilted her head. She wasn't ready to share her suspicions. Especially not with Sam Monterey in earshot. "I'm not sure. Do you have it?"

"Yes and no. I have the spark, but I have never been formally trained. Or if I have, it was in those five years of lost memory. I've picked up a few tricks, and sometimes, I can do surprising things…"

Sam spoke from between the shelves. His voice echoed around the warehouse. "Are these all stolen?"

Anne's demeanor turned chilly. "Sir, although I have invited you in because I trust this young woman, I did not give you unlimited access."

"Mr. Monterey, please," Em pleaded.

"It's interesting that you find the intrusion unappealing. I was about to comment that you had done the very same to my home." Sam's voice bounced around the room, and it was difficult to pinpoint his location in the stacks of shelves.

"Sam!" Em scolded.

Anne glanced back to Em anxiously. "What is happening here?"

"He owns a large resort in Arrenmore. He thinks you and Farrigan did something to magically ruin his town."

"That's putting it succinctly, Em. Well done." Monterey's sarcastic reply echoed off the rafters.

"Do you trust this man?" Anne asked quietly.

"He was my only way to find you. But no. I don't trust him. And I have good reason not to," Em whispered apologetically.

Anne cursed quietly. Em saw her reach inside her boot and retrieve a small blade.

Suddenly, a large crash sounded from deep within the warehouse. It grated and screeched, like metal on metal.

Anne sprang into action. Crouching against the wall, she inched along it, toward the noise, wielding her knife.

Em leapt up from the sofa, watching her mother with wide eyes. Anne gestured for Em to stay down and disappeared out of sight.

Em decided to keep Sam talking.

"Mr. Monterey, perhaps you can have a civil discussion with my mother and father? Instead of pilfering from their warehouse?"

"Em, Em," Sam's voice came, dripping with pity. "There is no shame in stealing from thieves. You should know that by now. Although I can see now that you are exactly what you appear to be."

"And what do I appear to be?" Em asked angrily. Another crashing sound. He must've been pushing things off the shelves.

"A stupid girl. Clueless. Honest. I had given you a little more credit for cleverness than you actually possessed. Still, you have led me to the right place, so I suppose you've been useful after all."

Em was speechless. Irate. But his words also sliced through her. What he said was true. She was a clueless, trusting girl for following Sam Monterey directly into danger. Again. She gritted her teeth in frustration.

And then she heard multiple footsteps from the direction of the door. Panicking, Em reached around the sofa into her bag and retrieved a pry bar. Standing and taking a few practice swings, she turned toward the rows of shelves. Instead, she heard a whooshing noise behind her, felt something smash into her head, and she crumpled to the ground, losing consciousness.

CHAPTER 25

Bronwyn Featherweight retired with her entourage through the Sun Corridor and into the foothills of the Antillei Mountains. It was there she established her own palace, the Silver Nightingale, in opposition to the empress's residence, the Golden Lark. The palace was crafted almost entirely from magic, and the entrance was a labyrinth that only a mage could navigate.

EM AWOKE in the dim warehouse with a splitting headache. She sat in the sea of shelves, unable to see the electric glow of light from the small living area. *Did the lights get turned off? How large is this warehouse?* The only sounds came from birds roosting in the rafters. Raising her hand to her head, she discovered her hands were tied in front of her with rope. Her head didn't seem to be bleeding, but she had a lump the size of a potato. She felt a little woozy.

"Hello?" she ventured. Her voice echoed slightly in the large room, but she received no other response.

Her back leaned on the corner of a shelving unit, and the metal dug uncomfortably into her spine. Shifting to stand, she discovered her feet were also securely bound with rope, and she fell back against the shelf with a painful thump.

"Ow," she moaned. She felt like crying. Going off with Monterey had been stupid. She was lucky his cronies didn't just kill her. Worse, Em had just found her mother and immediately lost her again. Maybe forever, if Monterey's sense of revenge overwhelmed his humanity. She needed to get out of here. Find them.

Glancing back at the shelf just behind her, she saw various odds and ends. A wooden box. A silver oval locket. A green parasol. A butter dish. Nothing that would cut rope.

Em glanced at the ceiling, where various skylights were propped open. The sky was dark, but the full moon cast a silvery glow that allowed her some light in the dimness. If the moon was out, she had been here for at least half a day. Liam had surely found her note. Maybe. Not that he knew where to look for her. *Stupid Em. Stupid.*

Liam's face flashed into her head. The look in his eyes when he said he didn't want anything to happen to her. That he was with her. It made her stomach flutter. If she didn't get back to Hallson Manor, he would surely come to find her. Maybe.

Pulling herself to a standing position, she instantly became dizzy. Her head still throbbed. Feeling frantic, she searched the shelves around her for anything sharp to free her hands and feet. Her mother had suggested the items in this hodgepodge of junk were magic. Maybe something would be useful.

She opened a small wooden box with mother-of-pearl inlay. Inside was a velvety cushion. A small tinkling tune began to play, and Em started to get drowsy. Her eyelids drooped and her brain felt fuzzy. She kept her wits long enough to slam the lid shut with her hands, and suddenly she was alert again.

"Careful, Em," she commented. *Magical items are rarely safe.*

Feet together, she hopped along the shelves, finally spying a small hatchet with a wooden handle.

She sat on its long handle to hold it steady, and then, twisting her wrists at an awkward angle, she dragged the rope across the edge. It took a lot of pulling back and forth, and Em nicked her hand more than a few times, drawing blood. But finally, one strand of rope broke, and she was able to loosen the rest enough to wiggle out.

Holding the head of the hatchet with her hands, she repeated the sawing process on her bound ankles. The tool hummed under her touch, and she hoped it wouldn't release a hex that would turn her into wood. Finally cutting her ankles free, she stood once again, which made her momentarily lightheaded. She swayed dangerously, gripping the side of the metal shelving to steady herself. Then she took a survey of her surroundings.

The shelves near her were still intact, but beyond those, she saw a row of toppled shelves, the items they used to hold broken and scattered along the cement floor of the warehouse. She saw more than a few slivers of broken glass, and what looked like dried blood. She wondered how the rest of the confrontation played out. From the state of her surroundings, she guessed not well. But had Sam or Anne prevailed? She assumed Sam. Her mother wouldn't have left her alone and injured. *Would she?*

She remembered the sound of footsteps. Sam had backup. Maybe he had even brought his cronies to the warehouse when he led her there. Em felt a stab of guilt. She had gotten him inside. This was her fault.

Carrying the hatchet, Em moved in a random direction, hoping to find an exit. As she tiptoed through destroyed shelves, she listened for voices. Silence bounced back to her.

She reached a wall. Turning left, she traced the perimeter of the warehouse, finally stopping at a metal door. The handle wouldn't turn, but there didn't appear to be a lock. She gave the handle a yank, but the door didn't budge. Inspecting the latch, she didn't see anything out of the ordinary, yet the door would not move. Using the hatchet, she tried to pry it open, but it didn't seem to even make a dent.

It was clear that this door was tightly sealed shut.

Continuing along the perimeter, she came across a second door in the wall, sealed in the same way. On this door, Em tried removing the hinges by hammering them out with the hammer from her bag. They didn't budge. Next, she tried unscrewing the handle with her screwdriver, but the screw kept spinning without ever coming loose. Using the hatchet again, Em began hacking at the middle of the door to create a hole. Nothing worked. Her head throbbed like crazy.

Turning the corner, she discovered the small living area they'd sat in hours before, and the walled-off room behind it. It was dim, lit by the moon, and empty. Em stumbled to it, feeling faint, and flicked the switch that turned on the electric lights. Squinting into the sudden brightness, she set the small axe into her bag alongside her tools and plopped to the floor in a heap.

Em reached her fingers up to her head and found the large lump where she'd been hit. She felt nauseated, and the wooziness was getting worse. Sleepiness crept over her, and somewhere in the corner of her mind, she knew that was probably bad. Maybe if she slept, she would feel less nauseous. Then she noticed something tucked in the side pocket of her bag.

"Warfern," she said, woozily. The little sprig didn't appear wilted, even after spending nearly a week in her knapsack. She remembered the look on Liam's face when he gave it to her. It had reminded him of his home. Evederell. Hands shaking, she held it up to her face, breathing in the blossoms. They smelled like fresh cherries mixed with dew-covered grasses. She tucked the small flower back into her bag.

And then suddenly, she felt a little better. Her headache and nausea were gone. Maybe she had just needed to sit down for a bit. Even the knot on her scalp didn't feel as terrible as she first imagined it.

Standing was much easier when she wasn't dizzy. Em wandered into the walled-off room. It was a simple living space. There was a small cast-iron stove with a stovepipe that stretched impossibly to the ceiling, an unvarnished wooden table with two chairs, and in the corner, a bed with no frame, just a lumpy mattress and a blanket. No decorations hung on the walls. Papers and notebooks were spread on the table, and Em reached for a piece of parchment. It was a list of cities in Esnania and surrounding countries. Each place had one or several items listed next to it, along with a person's name.

She was unsurprised to find under "Arrenmore" the words "large, polished stone" and "Monterey." It must be what they had taken. All of the items listed seemed ordinary: music box from Cadnin, Harrison; shoulder bag from Yellowbrook, Jerichon. The list went on and on. Brookerby was not on the list, but Em mentally added, "Book from Brookerby, Lichebee, Gramalia"—for surely this was a list of magical items.

Dropping the list, Em picked up another paper. This detailed one item, a gray sewing thread that was stronger than metal. It described the object and included a sketch, listed the lore of the thread and its known locations throughout history, and someone had written a list at the bottom of possible new uses. These included:

Building and repairing structures
Tension bridge
Restraining enemies
Woven armor
Heist?

The last, with a question mark, made Em drop the parchment. It fluttered back to the table. What exactly was happening here? Were her parents criminals, and were they collecting all these items for their own personal gain? The first few items on the list pointed to some larger societal good, but perhaps Sam was in the right: he had only stolen back what was rightfully his. She also found herself listing her own potential uses for the exact same thread. Was she any better?

Picking up another piece of paper, she saw the words "Woodland Staff." The sketch depicted a carved wooden staff. As Em read the notes below the sketch, she felt a spark of excitement. The staff could be planted in the ground, grown into a large tree, and imbued with magical properties. Smiling, Em had a single thought: *I can replant Brookerby's warding tree.*

Then her skull exploded in pain.

~

EM DIDN'T KNOW how long she writhed on the ground, fighting against the conditions of her unbreakable oath. It felt like a thousand knives were slowly cutting off parts of her body. She finally resurfaced as the pain ebbed, gasping for air, tears leaking out of the corners of her eyes. She was exhausted and parts of her still trembled uncontrollably. She had no idea what time it was. She had to get out of there.

Using the table, she pulled herself to standing, and immediately averted her eyes from the table of papers. She knew that she should have no further thoughts about the woodland staff. She could not think about it, share its existence, or seek it out in this giant warehouse. If she did, the unbreakable oath's punishment would continue.

Turning quickly, Em shouldered her bag and left the room. She had one more wall to search—the one with the door through which she had entered this foul place so many hours before. Surely that door would open.

Minutes later, Em struggled against this third door, becoming more and more frantic as her brain registered its immovability. She pulled until her arms were ready to fall off. And then she started pounding, scratching, punching, over and over, until her fingernails broke and her knuckles started to bleed. Letting out a guttural yell, she punched the door once more, and then collapsed against it in resignation, forehead leaning against the immobile surface, utterly drained.

Sliding to the ground, Em gave up. What was the point, after all? She was a simple, foolish girl from a destroyed town. She was weak. She could do nothing helpful. She recalled Sam Monterey's words: honest and stupid.

She couldn't even leave this room, much less save the town. What had Gram been thinking? Then she remembered that Gram didn't send her. Gram had already been arrested, and Em had claimed the mission on her own. Nobody sent her. She was nothing. She was no one.

A dull, leaden weight settled in her stomach. She huddled at the base of the door for what seemed like hours, feeling wooden, the cold of the concrete floor seeping into her bones.

Once again, someone would have to rescue her. Look after her.

Tell her how foolish she had been.

Tell her to be careful.

Once again, she would sit here and cry until someone heard and let her out. Her jaw hardened at this. *No,* her mind pushed back. *No crying.* But this whole situation—the oath, the tree hunt, Sam Monterey, her parents, this deathtrap of a warehouse—was beyond repair.

WHEN SHE WAS fourteen years old, Em had agreed to repair the old smokehouse behind the butcher shop. It was dilapidated and dangerous, and Alfred had stopped using it until it could be made safe. Em had been fixing small things for some time and had no doubt she could also help with the repairs on the small shed.

Em arrived at the smokehouse early one morning with a hammer, nails, and some fresh lumber. Inspecting the site, she identified the rotting boards, and began to pull them up and replace them. It was grueling work, but Em worked diligently through the day and made good progress. By the time she left that evening, there was a pile of rotting boards behind the building and the smokehouse was a patchwork of new and old. Wiping away the grime and sweat, Em praised herself for her cleverness and strutted home, proud as a peacock.

The next morning, she arrived to find her previous day of work in shambles. Half of the new boards had fallen, and the old wood supports had split from the weight of the new. The patched floor creaked and shook, threatening to give under her weight.

Young Em had stood outside the shed, demoralized. She would have to dismantle her hard work from the day before and start completely over. She might have to tear down the whole building and somehow build a new one. Irritated, Em ripped off a few boards, and then stomped home. Gram met her at the door.

"How is Al's smokehouse?"

"Ruined. I ruined it. He'll have to pay someone else to fix it," Em huffed, dropping her bag of tools.

"What do you mean?" Gram asked.

"The whole building needs to be torn down and rebuilt. It's beyond repair." Em dropped into a chair and began to massage her temples, feeling a headache come on.

"So what are you doing here? Sounds like you have a lot to do."

"Didn't you hear? The whole building needs to be rebuilt. I can't do that."

Gram, sat beside her, eyeing Em critically. "Really? You can't?"

"I've never done it before."

"You can learn."

"What if I mess it up?"

"Then you'll try again until you get it right. You said you would do something, now you have to figure out how to keep your word." Gram's eyes were steely as she spoke those words. Em knew better than to argue further. She sullenly stood, grabbed her bag, and trudged out the door once more.

In the weeks following, Em learned more about structures than she ever thought possible. She took careful notes of design as she dismantled the shed. She read every book she could find on building construction and talked to several builders in town to receive pointers.

Many weeks later, she finished a brand-new smokehouse, complete with a fireplace and vent. Alfred was ecstatic. Em had never worked so hard or been so proud of anything else she had done to that point.

Em softened at the memory. She was so certain of her limitations, yet Gram always pushed her outside of them. It was one of the last lessons she remembered Gram giving her before she lost her voice. It took on extra importance because of that fact. *If Gram were here,* she thought, *she would think I was brainless for giving up in a room full of magical objects.* She snorted at the thought.

Gram never held her back. Neither did Ilna. Or Mendel. They gave her a chance to learn and grow. She didn't need to earn their respect. She had it. She needed to earn her own esteem.

Em didn't know how to help Brookerby. She didn't know how to get out of this warehouse. But she had to figure out how to keep her word. Her mother might be in danger. Her town needed saving, somehow. There was no time to sit here and wait for someone to bail her out.

She felt something humming inside herself. The will to try. Taking a deep breath, she stood and strode back into the endless shelves of wondrous items.

Time to do some shopping.

CHAPTER 26

*E*m approached a shelf and chose an item at random, a golden teardrop brooch surrounded by tiny pearls. She turned it over in her hands, looking for some kind of clue to its unseen properties. The golden convex surface gleamed innocently. Em pinned it onto her blouse and waited a few moments. Perhaps her skin would tingle, or her hair would stand on end, she hoped, waiting for some kind of indication of magic. Nothing happened, and Em finally unpinned the brooch and placed it back on the shelf.

This might be difficult, she realized. It was not always obvious what magic an item held. She decided to devise tests. Remembering the out-of-place clues in *The Standard Book of Anything*, she would visually inspect each item, looking for something out of place. Then she would use it as intended to see if anything unusual happened. Remembering the high-strength sewing thread she'd read about, she would test for strength, also. It wasn't much, but Em felt her shoulders shift down as tension leaked away. She would find something to help her get out of here.

Approaching another random shelf, she selected an umbrella. It appeared ordinary, with a hooked wooden handle and a dark blue canopy. Inspecting every inch, she found nothing unusual in its form.

Applying her second test—use—she opened the umbrella. Instantly, she was pushed back a few steps as a huge pocket of air rushed up and away from the convex side of the fabric. The air banged into the high ceiling, blowing out one of the skylights, and birds roosting in the rafters flitted out of the way in terror.

"Whoa." That was something.

She closed the umbrella, pointed the end at one of the shelves, and quickly opened it. The air whooshed away from her with such force her ears rang. The air pocket blew over the shelf, and the one behind it. Items crashed to the ground, and Em carefully closed the umbrella again.

"That might come in handy," she spoke aloud, crooking the handle around her arm.

Walking to another random shelf, she picked up a lantern. Inspecting it for abnormalities, she found nothing except a slight charring around the base of the half-burned candle.

I need to light it, she thought, setting the lantern back down and plunging her hand into her satchel for matches. Her fingers groped blindly, pushing tools out of the way, and she finally found a few loose matches sitting at the bottom of the bag. She grabbed one and, dropping her bag and retrieving the lantern, took a nervous breath, struck a match, and lit the candle.

It flickered for a brief moment, and then a bright flash engulfed everything. Em blinked, but all she saw was brightness. She blinked again, still feeling the lantern in her hand and her bag at her feet, but was unable to see them. It was the opposite of pitch-black, yet somehow the same. The brightness did not cease, and Em began counting. She reached twenty-three and then realized that perhaps the blindness would continue forever. Panic seized her. Then it occurred to her that she should try to blow the candle out. Raising the lantern to what felt like the right height, she blew blindly. And then the brightness was gone. Em blinked a few times, eyes adjusting to the moonlit dimness once more. The smoke from the extinguished candle wafted lazily upward.

Em quickly set the lantern back on the shelf and backed away.

Then, before she could talk herself out of it, she grabbed it quickly, and shoved it in her bag.

Turning around, she spotted a spool of gray thread. "Strong thread!" she yelped. She snatched it quickly and cast about for something to test it on. She noticed a ball on a lower shelf consisting of several bands of iron bent in a circle and welded together to form a spherical shape. She struggled to lift it, and was only just able to drag it off the shelf and onto the floor.

She looped the thread through the ball's iron bands and pulled the end of the thread over the metal shelf stack. Standing on the other side with spool in hand, she backed up, pulling the ball a few inches off the ground. Her muscles strained painfully, and her fingers struggled to hold onto the spool. The top shelf bent in from the weight, but the thread held firm. Convinced, Em lowered the metal ball, unwound the thread, and tossed the spool in her bag.

Glancing up at the open skylights, high above her, Em wondered if she could use the thread to climb out of the warehouse. And then lower herself down from the roof. But how would she secure the thread from the ceiling? She filed away the thought as a plan B and kept searching.

Picking up a bag, she examined it inside and out. It looked very similar to her own knapsack, but perhaps a bit nicer, and it had a single cross-body strap. Nothing unusual. She took the gusting umbrella out of her knapsack and placed it in the bag. It disappeared completely. She did the same with the lantern, and the bag didn't grow any bulkier or heavier. Baffled, Em reached her hand in and was able to retrieve both items quickly, but there also seemed to be ample room for any items she wished. She dropped her tools, the waterskin, the thread, the warfern, and finally her own knapsack into this new tote. The cloth retained its original shape. Shouldering the pack, Em was pleased to find it lightweight.

No longer concerned with storage restrictions, Em ran back to retrieve the hatchet from the living quarters. Then, she began to test more items. She found a small gold ring, decorated with etchings of feathers. She couldn't discern its purpose, but she thought it was pretty, and slipped it on her finger. Nothing happened. She tried on a decorated mask that concealed the top half of her face in lace and gemstones, and discovered that she could see through the wall of the warehouse to the alley outside. It wouldn't help her escape, but it seemed useful nonetheless. The mask went in her magical satchel, which she slung across her shoulders.

Glancing to the shelf on her right, she spotted a small map. It was hand drawn and contained Esnania and a partial map of a few neighboring countries, including Brildonia to the south and the Tribal Prutians to the north. Em spotted the tiny dot representing Brookerby. Picking up the map in one hand, she traced the road she had taken to Gillamor with her finger. She stopped at the place where Liam's cabin was (she guessed) and tapped it thoughtfully. How had—

And then suddenly the world spun around her. Long circular streaks of color whirled in her vision. She heard faint noises, as if she were passing conversations and people very quickly. And then, in a moment, the streaks and noise were gone, and she stood in a clearing at the edge of a forest, bathed in moonlight, gazing up the hill at a shed that looked remarkably like Liam's cabin.

The map was still in her hand.

~

IT WAS INDEED Liam's cabin. The map must have brought her there when she touched the spot. But she had touched other points on the map. Maybe a double tap?

Nevertheless, Em was relieved to be out of the warehouse and somewhere familiar. She entered the hut and lit a normal lantern Liam kept by the cot.

Em couldn't push back the surge of emotion that came from being back in this place. When Liam was a stranger, and Bob had trapped her in a tree. He had invited her home, wrapped her ankle, and fed her. She felt her stomach start to rumble.

"Ah. My old friend. When will you be satisfied?" Em scolded. She opened Liam's cupboards, searching for any nonperishable food, as her stomach continued their conversation. Finding nothing, she apologized to her gut and sat down. Em pulled out her waterskin and debated the most filling liquid she could think of. She was grateful the magic bag was on her shoulder, or the waterskin (and all the other magical items) would've been left back at the warehouse.

She decided upon a thick mushroom soup, one of Gram's specialties. The waterskin was unable to produce mushrooms, but the soup was thick and warm and creamy, and it seemed to satisfy her appetite.

Hunger assuaged, Em gently dropped the waterskin back in her marvelous new satchel and studied the magic map.

Her next move would be to find Monterey and his thugs and rescue her mother. She supposed they were still hiding in Gillamor, but there was a chance they had returned to Arrenmore, if Sam had found the polished stone that had been stolen from him. Em wished she knew what the stone did. Her parent's notes had been frustratingly vague.

Holding the map, Em thought of Liam. She didn't know the time, but she guessed it was close to dawn from the cautious bird whistling outside. She'd left a note yesterday afternoon. He had to be panicked and searching for her. He was probably angry she had gone without him. She pictured his face lighting up at the pastry recipe in *The Standard Book of Anything*. She wondered if he had successfully made the recipe, or if the book had left out crucial information, like it sometimes did. She thought about the way he embraced her, the night Mendel was almost executed. How he had almost set that fire to help her. Had put himself in danger. His hand in hers as she showed him *The Standard Book of Anything*.

She needed to go back. She moved her finger to Gillamor to tap the gilded icon of the capital city. And then she paused.

No.

There wasn't any time to waste. If all went well, she could rescue Anne and be back in Gillamor before the sun came up. And then she could transport back to Hallson Manor, collect *The Standard Book of Anything*, and say her final goodbyes. She needed to get home. It had been too long already. She'd found no solution, but she needed to get home to Gram. With these new objects, and maybe with her parents' help, she could still save Brookerby without a new tree. Liam didn't make sense in that plan. For him, it was a tree or nothing.

She recalled her fortune from the Rashorbuj festival. The second card was a charging stallion, she reminded herself. "Quick, decisive action," she murmured.

Glancing around once more at the cabin, her heart twisted painfully as she whispered, "Goodbye, Liam."

She blew out the normal lantern, set it down, and double-tapped Arrenmore on the map.

CHAPTER 27

The empress's soldiers arrived at the Antillei Mountain foothills and stared in dismay at the fortress they were expected to penetrate. Their orders were to bring Bronwyn Featherweight back in chains. With a lengthy siege beginning, they despaired of ever completing their orders.

THE WORLD SWIRLED in bands of flashing color once again. The sensation was less jarring this time because she expected it, but it still felt like she was balancing in the very center of a spinning disk, like the happy-go-around she had built for the kids of Brookerby.

The spinning stopped abruptly, and Em stood in the main entryway of the Gray Horse. The sky was beginning to lighten, and the silence of the inn was charged with anticipation, like a concert hall before the beginning of a performance. She glanced around for a place to hide and ducked behind one of the numerous chairs dotting the spacious lobby. Her back was to THE PARLOR bar, which was empty, yet she still felt exposed. She darted over to the overstuffed sofa by the barroom's external wall. Pulling the couch out from the wall, she inched in behind it. From here, she could stay hidden until she worked out a plan. She peaked over the top of the sofa, scanning the room. It was still quiet and empty.

Perhaps Monterey wouldn't come here after all. If he and her mother had left directly from the warehouse, they could have traveled to Arrenmore by now. But maybe they stayed in Gillamor. Em wondered how long she should wait before using the map to spin back to Hallson Manor.

Em reached into her bag and pulled out the ornate mask that let her see through solid walls. Peering around, she discovered the limits of the mask. She could only see through one set of walls. Gazing behind her, through THE PARLOR walls, gave no great insight. Looking ahead and about the lobby, she concluded that nobody seemed to be in the Grand Dining Hall or the changing rooms of the spa. Glancing up, she could only see what was directly above her, which was the high ceiling, and the pearly pink sky beyond. She would have to climb the stairs and peer into each room to determine if Monterey and his cronies were in the Gray Horse. Or proceed back to the steam room or the kitchens. A risky venture.

Keeping the mask on, Em edged along the wall, stopping each time she found cover. At a large potted plant by the curving staircase, she ducked down, listening and surveying the hall. Had the Gray Horse been left totally unattended?

She stood up by the base of the staircase. Feeling exposed, she ran up the stairs as quickly as she could, trying to step lightly on the creaking wood. At the top, she crouched behind a tufted bench and looked through the walls of each nearby room. No one slept in the neatly made beds, and Em began to feel a little foolish that she had rushed here without a plan.

She was making her way along the hallway when the front door banged open, and a flurry of noise entered the Gray Horse. Em caught the sound of many feet across the lobby, and Sam Monterey's voice giving swift orders. Footsteps thumped on the stairs. Frantic, Em cast about and saw a broom closet through the wall opposite her. She dove for it, yanked open the door, and pulled it closed behind her.

It was a small cabinet that smelled like vinegar and dust. Em had to hold her nose to keep from sneezing, but she otherwise felt secure in the tiny space. She hoped Monterey's thugs wouldn't get the sudden urge to mop a floor. Still wearing her mask, she watched through the closet's wall as two men in gray tromped down the hallway and entered a room two doors down. Looking below her feet through the floor, she saw only the changing room for the spa.

She continued to slowly spin, surveying the world beyond the closet. She craned her neck, looking for signs of her mother, or perhaps some indication that Monterey had taken back the object that had been stolen. Her parents' paperwork said it was a polished rock. Perhaps it provided prosperity for a town if it was physically present. Or maybe it magnetically pulled travelers to the resort.

It was at this moment, feather duster brushing her shoulder, that Em spotted Sam Monterey at the top of the stairs with a black marbled stone in his hand. His aqua eyes gleamed. "Gray Horse is back in business!" he announced loudly to the air.

Em held her breath, willing her heart to thump more quietly, as he strode past. He pulled open a door at the far end of the hallway, addressing whoever was in the room, "Now, about this stone—"

The stone. Em's frenzied brain went spinning. Whoever was in that back room was either an expert on the artifact, or maybe... *My mother!* Em hoped she was right, but she needed to verify before blasting her way in there. She counted the doors. Four doors down on the right. She could use the strong thread—no! The lantern. Get eyes on Anne, then light the lantern and pull her out of there while everyone was blinded.

Idly, Em wondered if these rooms were ever used for hotel guests or if Monterey just had a rotating schedule of kidnappings.

At that moment, the main door slammed open, smacking the wall, the sound reverberating through the hall. "Monterey, where is she?" a clear, strong voice called. Em's every muscle tensed. A short bark of a dog rang through the high-ceilinged lobby.

Liam and Bob. *Crumb.*

Sam paused midsentence. Pulling the fourth door on the right closed with an "Excuse me," he started toward the staircase once more.

Em's heart sank as she stood in her broom closet. Liam must've found her note, grown tired waiting for her, and started searching. He had traveled all the way to Arrenmore to find her. And now, his appearance would complicate her plans significantly. She strained her ears as Monterey greeted his latest guest.

"Welcome to the Gray Horse, Lord Hallson. We are so honored to host you. Your dog is welcome to wait outside, but perhaps you'd like a mug of spiced ale after your journey?"

"I'd like you to release Em, you giant swine bucket."

"Em? Is she lost? You two aren't fighting, are you?" Sam's voice held a gleeful twinge barely disguised as concern.

Liam's voice snarled, "She went off with you yesterday, and she's missing. What did you do?" The last four words were staccato bursts of rage.

"Calm yourself, sir. You cannot come in here and disturb my guests in this manner."

If Em weren't so anxious, she would've snort-laughed. What guests?

"If you hurt her—"

"Perhaps a cooling off period before we discuss." Em heard fingers snap and then the scuffling of multiple feet.

An extended period of grunts and thuds assaulted Em's ears, interspersed with growls and barks from Bob. She heard a smacking sound and a loud thump as a large body hit the floor. One of Monterey's goons? A scuffle. A punch. A second body hit the ground. A yelp from Bob. *Oh stars.* She imagined Liam fighting several Gray Horse thugs as she sat there, useless. Horrified. Finally, Em heard a pistol being cocked. *No!* The scuffling stopped.

"Lord Hallson, may we offer you accommodations until you find your friend?" Monterey's voice was solicitous, but Em heard the underlying mockery.

"If you have hurt a hair on her head, Monterey, you will pay." Liam's voice grew louder, and they finally came into Em's view. Three large gray-uniformed attendants were hauling him up the stairs. She assumed Monterey had a pistol trained on Liam's back. Liam had cuts on his face, and one arm hung at an unnatural angle, but with the gun on him, he was no longer fighting back. It took all her willpower not to step out of the closet and help. She stuffed a fist into her mouth to stifle a whimper when one of the attendants wrenched Liam's arm, causing him to yelp in pain. The man shoved him toward the second door on the left. A sickening thud echoed down the hall as another guard clubbed Liam over the head, and Liam went limp. Em's breath came in gasps. Her hand was on the door handle, ready to run to Liam the moment Monterey's bruisers were out of sight. She felt a tingling in her fingers. A spark. But could she magically unlock a door? Heal a broken bone?

More feet on the stairs kept her pinned in the closet. The tingling in her fingers grew more insistent. Monterey crested the top step, holding Liam's pack between two fingers as if it were dirty underclothes. He summoned two gray-clad cronies, stifling a yawn. "Perhaps we pick this up at a more reasonable hour? I'll be in my office. Find that dog." The burly men tromped back down the stairs and disappeared from Em's view.

Em turned her eyes upward, trying to take calming breaths. Bob had escaped, at least. Through the ceiling, she saw the glow of the sunrise and wondered why she didn't feel weary. She had been running on pure adrenaline for many hours. But one look down the hallway toward the room that housed both her mother and an unconscious Liam, and she knew she had to keep going. Her body still surged with the spark, and she had to try something.

When Monterey's door at the end of the hall closed and all was quiet, Em slipped out of her closet. She wore her mask, although it was disorienting to walk down a hallway when she could see through the solid surfaces all around her. She checked the second door on the left. Liam was unconscious on the floor, but appeared to be breathing. His arm lay at a funny angle. Em felt a fist squeeze her heart. She would save him.

Trying the handle gently, Em found the door locked. She focused on the lock mechanism, the pins and tumbler, and tried to focus the spark from her fingers into those pins. Nothing happened except a slight dissipation of the tingling in her hands. Em whispered a string of foul words. She would come back.

She continued peering in rooms, finding most empty. At the end of the hallway, fourth door on the right, she found Anne. Her arms and legs were tied tightly to the chair she sat in, and her head was lolled back, eyes closed. Em tried not to let her thoughts run. Was Anne sleeping? Drugged? Dead? Her breath caught. She needed to keep moving.

Glancing through the nearby office door with the mask, she spied on Sam Monterey. He sat at a large mahogany desk in the growing morning light that streamed in from large windows behind him, through diamond-shaped panes of glass separated by diagonal muntins. The office was lined with large bookshelves, sparsely populated. Sam's attention was fixed on the pages of a book that sat on his desktop. Liam's pack sat on the floor nearby.

He looked almost normal, sitting at his desk reading. Like an honest businessman, studiously balancing his books. Em supposed he probably was, most of the time. When he wasn't blackmailing, drugging, and kidnapping. Her empathy waned. He held two people she cared about behind locked doors, and whatever she did next, she needed to remember that.

She glanced quickly into her bag. Nothing could unlock a door. She could probably use her umbrella to blow it open, but the noise would alert Monterey and prevent her from rescuing both Anne and Liam. On top of that, both were unconscious. She would have to try and wake them after the door was open. She concluded the best plan of action was stealth. She needed to find the goon with the keys.

Em felt dizzy from seeing through walls, so she removed the mask, dropping it into her bag. She tiptoed back down the stairs, checking around every corner as she went. The henchmen had disappeared. They had gone back to the spa, or the kitchen, or outside to chase Bob. Kitchen employees were the most likely to have keys, she decided. Em quickly crossed the lobby into the Grand

Dining Hall. It still appeared faded and run-down in the morning sun, so whatever the polished stone did, it hadn't worked any miracles yet.

She was halfway to the kitchen when suddenly a large muscled hand tugged her pant leg toward the nearest table. Em nearly jumped out of her skin.

"Hey!" she hissed. "Let go!" She kicked the hand and prepared to run.

"Anne!" A deep voice came softly from under the rounded table.

Em stopped fighting, but crouched down, lifting the corner of the tablecloth.

A burly man huddled under the table, contorted comically. He had dark salt-and-pepper hair, a beard and mustache, and warm brown eyes. He was smiling, but his smile fell when he saw Em, and his eyes widened in confusion.

"I beg your pardon, miss. I thought you were someone else," he said apologetically. "You look just like my wife. Well, just like her twenty years ago, actually."

Em felt immediate warmth toward this man. She smiled softly. "I met Anne yesterday. We noticed the resemblance. You must be Farrigan."

He nodded. "Pleasure to meet you. Of course, I assume you're a friend, and not one of her captors."

Em ducked under the table, and pulled the tablecloth back down behind her. "That's accurate, sir. Anne is locked in a room upstairs. A friend of mine is up there also. I'm looking for the keys now."

"May I ask what happened?"

"You took a magical item from the wrong guy," Em said bluntly.

Farrigan's brown eyes locked on Em's blue ones. "It's not the first time we've made such a mistake. Who did you say you were?"

"Emaline, from Brookerby. Call me Em."

Farrigan was silent for a moment, eyeing Em thoughtfully. Finally, he gave another nod. "Now, tell me how we're going to get keys."

Em explained, "Sam Monterey's henchmen disappeared into the kitchens. I was going to, uh, follow them. And somehow get the keys."

"Do you have any weapons or tools at your disposal?" Farrigan inquired.

"I have my toolkit," Em said, rattling off the list of her tools. "And a few things from your warehouse."

Farrigan raised a thick black eyebrow. Em held up her hands quickly. "I was trapped in there. I was trying to figure out how to get out, and I started testing things."

Farrigan surprised Em by grinning. "We established a system of magical locks that recognize only Anne and me. Anyone else is unable to get in or out. I'm delighted to know they are functioning as intended."

Em shot him a dirty look. "They're functioning all right. I thought I was going to die in there."

"Just for security purposes. How were you able to escape?"

"There was this map—" Em pulled the map out of her bag to show him. He bobbed his head. "First time I used that, I ended up in Fridera, covered in snow." He chuckled. Then he looked at her appraisingly. "The ability to properly use that item requires some skill in magic. Are you trained in the magical arts?"

Em shook her head, feeling a little overwhelmed. "Not trained. I didn't even know that was gift of mine until a few days ago."

"You have the gift, I'm quite sure of it. I would be delighted to train you in some basic spells. After we rescue my dear wife, of course."

Suddenly, Em heard footsteps, and shushed him. They sat with bated breath, waiting for the steps to cross through the dining hall and exit into the kitchen. They both exhaled quietly.

"I hesitate to ask, but what else did you take from our storehouse?" he probed.

She pulled everything out, one by one, and lined them up. Reviewing the items, his hands brushed the bag and he smiled. "Ah. You have taken the bag of holding. It could've carried away the entire collection. We're lucky you didn't clean us out."

"It wasn't my intention," Em apologized. "I was just trying to find something that would help me leave. I'm happy to return everything as soon my friend and Anne are rescued. What does this do, by the way?" Em held up the hatchet she had used in the warehouse.

"That chops wood, obviously."

Em rolled her eyes. "No really, what's the magic part?"

"Not sure. We haven't used it yet."

"I tried it on your metal warehouse door. It did nothing." Em grumped. "Oh! Also this," Em took off her tiny golden ring and placed it beside the other items. "I've been wearing it for a few hours. I don't know what it does."

Farrigan picked up the ring, squinting at the feather etchings. Finally, he handed it back to Em. "We couldn't determine that either. Have you noticed any ill effects on your person? Any strange happenings? Are you slowly turning into a goose?"

Em shrugged.

"Hmm. It remains a mystery, then. You can keep it on for now."

Em slipped the ring back on while Farrigan surveyed the other items. "I don't recognize this." He pointed to the waterskin.

"That's mine," Em let out.

Farrigan picked up the vessel. "It feels quite powerful. What does it do?"

"You can feel the magic?"

"Yes. A little zip of energy rushing through it. Can you not?"

Em reached over, placed her hand on the waterskin, and focused her attention. Now that she thought about it, there was something different about it. Like water rushing just below the surface. Like the tingle she felt when she repaired things. Was that what magic felt like? "I can," she revealed.

Farrigan wiggled the waterskin. "So?"

"It can make any liquid you can think of. And it's always full."

"That sounds promising." Farrigan studied the waterskin for a moment, opened the cap, and took a drink. Then he sighed contentedly.

"What did you try?"

"None of your business, young lady. But a very rare distilled spirit. Just for scientific purposes, of course." He winked. Then he recapped the waterskin and reviewed the other items once more. "This I don't recognize either." He indicated the tiny flower, warfern.

Em thought back to the Public Garden in Gillamor. How Liam had presented her with the tiny white-blossomed sprig. She felt herself blush. "That's nothing. Just a souvenir from Gillamor." She put the flower back in the side pocket.

Farrigan was busy studying the items. "I don't think we have the right things for an attack. But it is possible we can use the items before us to get the keys all the same." Suddenly, Farrigan smirked. "We might have to devise an elaborate scheme, Em. Are you up for that?"

At this, Em broke into a grin.

CHAPTER 28

*T*wo scouts were sent to discover alternate entrances into the Silver Nightingale fortress. The scouts discovered a small tunnel that led to the castle—but first, the perilous maze. Only one scout survived, the youngest of the Glaumhausers, and he was able to enter the castle unbeknownst to Bronwyn and her compatriots.

FARRIGAN FINISHED EXPLAINING his plan in elaborate detail, and Em sat back silently.

"You've said nothing," he prodded. "I believe our best chance of success is following this course of action. Do you agree?"

"Hm," Em vocalized.

"Yes?" he asked.

Em tried to phrase it delicately. "There are a few...uh...wrinkles to work out."

"Elaborate, please."

"How will we rig up our diversion in broad daylight without getting caught?"

"We must act quickly. Next?"

"How will we know who has the keys when they all rush into the room after we create the diversion?"

"We listen for the gentleman that jingles," he said with a self-satisfied grin. "What other concerns do you have?"

"Okay, say we create the diversion, grab the keys, blind the thugs, and blast our way out of the dining room. What then? We still have to get upstairs, get two people—probably unconscious—free, and then escape."

Farrigan shrugged.

Em was incredulous. "So, we're doing this, huh?"

"Unless we can devise another plan."

Em bit the inside of her lip, thinking. "We could go through that kitchen door. Search them one by one and tie them up."

"Not feasible. That would take quite some time. And in the meantime, our discarded victims would be discovered."

"If our goal is smash and grab, we're going to alert everyone anyway. Do we really need keys? Maybe we could pick the lock or blow down the door?"

"I'm not as skilled as Anne with lock-picking. But..." He tugged at his beard absently. "I don't recall how strong that umbrella is. We should perform a brief experiment on another door, perhaps?"

Em glanced over at the kitchen door. "That one. Let me know if anyone is coming, okay?"

Farrigan nodded and slipped on the mask. Em snatched the umbrella and ducked out from under the tablecloth into the dining room. She quickly crept toward the kitchen door, umbrella hoisted like a lance. When she was several paces away, she glanced back at the table, and saw Farrigan's arm sticking out of the white linen with his thumb up. Turning back to the solid door, she took a breath, and shoved open the parasol's dome.

A rush of air issued forth. The kitchen door banged open, and the hinges ripped from the door frame, leaving a ragged hole where the door had been.

Certain someone had heard, Em rushed back to the safety of the table.

"That will do," said Farrigan, emerging quickly and tossing Em's bag to her. "Let's attempt the same feat upstairs." He was still wearing the glittering mask, which looked downright silly with his large beard and hulking frame.

Laughing, Em slipped her bag over her shoulders, still clutching the umbrella. They both charged toward the main staircase.

In the doorway between the Grand Dining Room and lobby, Em skidded to a halt, nearly bumping into Farrigan, who had stopped. Peering around him, she saw their path blocked by several large gray-clad attendants who did not look pleased. They stood with arms crossed and identical foreboding scowls. Em squeaked.

Farrigan uttered a soft curse.

"Didn't see these?" Em asked.

"Unfortunately not. These gentlemen blend in with the furniture."

Em rolled her eyes. Hoisting the umbrella and stepping around Farrigan, she let out a few quick blasts with it. It successfully blew back two of the men and toppled some furniture in the lobby. The men—still standing—lurched toward them. Farrigan found himself grappling with one particularly mean-looking henchman. Em could barely open and close the umbrella quick enough to keep the whole group of brutes at bay, and she couldn't do anything about Farrigan's battle.

Scanning the lobby, she saw an open path toward the stairs on the left clear of furniture and spa attendants. She could find the way, but could Farrigan?

"Farrigan!"

"Kinda"—he grunted—"busy, Em."

"I'm lighting the lantern!"

"Do it," he yelped, taking a hit on the jaw.

After one final blast, which sent several gray-clad men tumbling, Em reached into her bag, released the umbrella, and yanked out the lantern. With her other hand, she rooted around for one of the few loose matches. The blessed bag brought it right to her fingers.

She only had a few seconds before two of the men would reach her. Quickly, she struck the match on the side of the lantern and held it to the half-burned candle.

The men were three steps away. Two. One—

The room went white.

Em leapt to the side and heard two burly gentlemen crash into the wall behind her. Moving carefully, holding the lantern aloft, she took her remembered path to the staircase. There were grunts and curses from the gray-clad men as they stumbled about in the blinding light, trying to find their way. She dared not call out to Farrigan and give away her position, so she hoped he could find his way as well. Only once did she collide with a small ottoman, which must have shifted during the fight. Finally, her foot bumped into the bottom stair. She started to climb.

"Em," came a soft command. Farrigan was next to her. She paused on the second stair.

"You made it," she wheezed.

"The lantern works when it's in view. Once we leave the room with it, they can see again."

"So should we leave it here at the base of the steps?"

"Yeah. I think we should. We can collect it on our way back out." Em heard Farrigan start to move up the stairs. Setting the lantern on the bottom step, she turned and followed. In the lobby, the gray men stumbled over furniture, calling out insults to one another.

As soon as their line of sight to the lobby disappeared, Em could see again. She blinked, emerging into the upstairs hallway. Farrigan used the mask to glance through the walls, inspecting each closed door. Stopping at Liam's room, he called back, "This room appears to contain your young man."

Em colored slightly at the casual insinuation, but she confirmed, "Yes, that's Liam."

"He appears damaged," Farrigan observed grimly.

Em was at the top of the stairs looking back down into the lobby, which was a wall of impenetrable white. Farrigan's words registered with a flutter of worry in her gut. But, she huffed out a quick breath, thinking about the stairs. Nothing would keep the guards from coming up once they found the stairs. She needed to buy more time. Turning, Em tossed the closed umbrella to Farrigan. "Get him out. I'm going to shore up our defenses."

Reaching in her bag, she pulled out the waterskin of many liquids. Fixing her mind on the image of an oil she used for lubricating machinery, she lifted the flagon and started pouring horizontally along the top step. Oil slid out of the waterskin and flowed down the staircase, coating everything in a slippery sheen. She left a narrow strip on the right side bare so they could make it back down with Anne and Liam.

Meanwhile, there was a whoosh-bang behind her as Farrigan umbrellaed open the door to Liam's room. The impact ripped the doorframe from the wall and flung it across the room. Liam sat leaning against one of the velvety gray chairs, awake but badly bruised and dazed. When Farrigan poked his head in, Liam woozily pulled himself to standing, his left arm held gingerly to his chest. "Wrong room?" he asked.

Farrigan paused in the doorway. Liam pointed to his own face with his right hand, indicating Farrigan's mask. "It's a little early in the day for a masked ball."

Farrigan began to chuckle. Leaning his head back into the hall he said, "Em, your gentleman doesn't seem to want rescuing."

Em's face appeared in the door. Liam gasped "Em!"

"You look terrible," Em responded, heart unclenching slightly at the sight of him awake. She rushed over. "Are you sure you don't need rescuing?"

"I came to rescue you," he winced. "I found your note, and when you didn't come home, I tracked down Monterey." His face contorted. "Monterey has the book. I'm sorry."

Em felt a surge of frustration. They would have to steal back the book from Monterey before they could leave. But that frustration was quickly replaced with remorse. If she had gone back for Liam, or not gone off with Monterey in the first place, they wouldn't be here. "I shouldn't have left you behind," she said. "I'm sorry." And she meant it too.

In response, his good arm slipped around her waist, pulling her closer to him. She felt heat in the gesture. She tried to maintain her composure by studying his left arm. "Is it broken?"

He shook his head. "I think the shoulder is dislocated."

"I could…" she began. She didn't really know how to fix a dislocation.

"I'll just hold it steady until we can pop it back in," he said, cradling his arm against his chest.

She held up a hand to touch his face. "Does that hurt?" She indicated a cut and a purpling bruise on his cheek, brushing it with her fingers.

"To be honest, I hurt all over, but I can take inventory later."

They stood there, her hand on his cheek and his arm around her waist. And Em forgot for a brief second where they were.

"Excuse me," Farrigan interjected, still in the doorway. "If you lovebirds are finished with the examination, we need to find my wife."

Em's face turned crimson, and she started to protest. But Farrigan had already gone back to the hallway, uninterested. Em broke away before meeting Liam's eyes.

He raised his eyebrows and grinned. "He's delightful. Where'd you pick him up?"

Em blinked, "Farrigan? He was hiding under the tables downstairs, also on a rescue mission."

"His wife?"

"Yeah. My mother."

Liam's mouth dropped open. "Em—"

"I know. Also, that guy is my father, but I haven't gotten around to telling him yet."

"Wow." Liam searched her face. "When will you…?"

"I don't know. We can all catch up later. We need to get out of here first." She caught his hand and pulled him toward the hallway.

Farrigan was already aiming the umbrella at the door containing Anne. The subsequent whoosh-boom blew the door off its hinges, and it went cartwheeling across the room, smashing out the windowpane and landing in a large tree nearby. Anne was still tied to a chair, but now fully awake and unimpressed with her husband's entrance. He dropped the umbrella, tore off the mask, and ran to his wife. Em and Liam peered in the doorway.

"The umbrella, Fare? Seems like overkill."

Farrigan grinned impishly. "The device packs a wallop. Had I planned this rescue effort, I would've selected the letter opener. More precise."

She beamed back. "Thank you, darling. I'll admit, I've come to expect it, but it's still nice every time you show up."

He was crouched next to her, expertly untying the restraining knots when Em and Liam sidled into the room.

"Emaline! You've made it out. Bravo!" Anne's eyes shone with pride.

"Out?" Liam asked.

"I found the traveling map." Em shrugged. "I figured I'd come rescue you, but Farrigan beat me to it."

"Shouldn't you just call him Dad?" Anne teased, helping undo the last of the ropes.

Farrigan's head jerked up, a question on his face.

"We hadn't gotten to that yet," Em admitted, warily watching Farrigan.

Confusion flickered in Farrigan's eyes. "Explain?" he asked softly of Anne.

"Remember when we woke up, outside Brookerby?" He nodded jerkily. "Emaline was in town. She was three. She thought we were dead."

"Oh, stars," he breathed, horror filling his face. He focused on Em. "I had surmised you were related. Your appearance is strikingly similar to Anne's. But this..." His eyes watered. "I'm so sorry."

Em nodded, unable to speak. Her heart felt so full, yet so broken at the same time. Anne put her hand on Farrigan's shoulder. Liam squeezed Em's hand gently, his left arm still cradled against his chest.

"Touching." A smooth deep voice came from behind them.

Em turned her head to see the smirk and aquamarine eyes of Sam Monterey. He leaned casually in what remained of the doorway, dangling the umbrella idly from one hand, the smooth, polished stone in the other.

"As much as I've enjoyed this sweet little reunion, you four are trespassing."

"Sam—" Em started forward, but Monterey dropped the stone in his pocket and raised the umbrella, prepared to strike.

"No sudden movements or you get blown out the large hole where my window used to be. I'm displeased that you felt the need to damage my property, but I'll add that to your final bill."

"Sam. Please. They stole your rock. You kidnapped Anne and injured Liam. Let's call it a truce," Em chided.

"A truce?" Sam growled. "My hotel fell into disrepair. My town crumbled around me. Because of them. I hardly think our actions offset."

"We didn't know the rock was the only thing propping up the town, or we would've left it alone," Anne said. "Actually, quite extraordinary, that," she pondered.

"Yes," sneered Monterey. "You've certainly made use of it for years. Funding your little operation with gambling wins and lucky breaks. Because the stone belongs to me, everything you've acquired through it is rightfully mine. Including that warehouse of wonders you've stolen."

"Gambling wins?" Em asked.

Anne looked abashed. "We needed money, so we would join games of chance when the stone was in our pocket."

"I heard from someone in Gillamor that you always win at cards." Em eyed her parents critically. "The stone brings luck?"

"Turns out, luck can make the difference between success and failure for the Gray Horse," Liam muttered.

"Exactly, boy," Sam sneered. "And considering the years of languishing, I feel entitled to a significant amount of recompense. So now we discuss." Monterey waved the point of the umbrella toward Em and Liam and gestured for them to back up. Liam placed his good arm in from of Em, shielding her. Anne and Farrigan had not moved. Sam continued.

"I will be taking any items of value on your person. I will send my men to clean out your warehouse. To make sure this happens, I will be keeping the four of you under lock and key until the job is complete."

"Impossible, sir. You will be unable to breach the locks," Farrigan began.

"A detail that I'm sure we can work through. Once the collection is transported here, you will instruct me on the use of each object, leaving nothing out. If all goes to plan, I won't kill you."

"What!?" Em yelped.

Sam ignored the outburst. "I will also be retaining the wondrous book Lord Hallson brought. My people were fooled by it when Em first arrived, but it might be as valuable as anything else in the collection."

Em gasped. She assumed Sam would find the same archaic reference book that others found when reading *The Standard Book of Anything*. The fact that he could read it made him something else entirely. It made him a magic user. Her brain cycled through the ramifications of Sam Monterey as a mage, and none of them were good.

"What book?" Anne questioned.

"The book isn't part of the deal." Em stood angrily.

"You have no choice, Em. One way or another, you will all pay for what your parents did. Perhaps I should send you in search of a new warding tree for Arrenmore. We could use the extra protection." Em's head began to throb dangerously. The warning signs of her oath. She could not find him a tree even if she wanted to. But she could see him trying to plant one.

And then something snapped in her. She was tired of being double-crossed by this man. Being threatened, and drugged, and kidnapped, and left for dead. And bigger than it all, she couldn't let him ever find out the potential he held within him. It would mean disaster for Arrenmore, and maybe the whole empire.

"No," Em breathed. She pushed off the bed frame and leapt at Monterey, hands spread wide, reaching for the umbrella. His eyes widened and he took a step back. Then, narrowing them, he held up the umbrella and pushed it open.

Em felt herself blown backward at an incredible speed, out the hole where the window used to be. Her eyes locked onto Monterey's, where she saw a flash of aquamarine panic that quickly hardened into resolve as she fell out of view.

The image of the headsman card from her fortune flashed through her vision as she plummeted toward the ground.

CHAPTER 29

*E*m felt time slow down. Her brain spun frantically. She was airborne, and out the window. They were on the second story. A high second story. She might survive the fall. She might only break every bone in her body. Or, the force from the umbrella might prove deadly when she smashed into some unmovable object, like the ground. As she flew into open space, she saw the horrified looks of her mother and her father. The devastation in Liam's eyes. And then she blasted over a treetop, her feet skimming the leaves as her body began to arc downward, and their faces were lost from view.

She closed her eyes, took a breath, and braced for pain. And waited. And waited. Her mechanical instincts kicked in. *Shouldn't I be falling faster than this?* she wondered. Opening her eyes, she glanced around. The Gray Horse was still visible, but she'd been blasted a vast distance horizontally, beyond the main shops of Arrenmore, and was finally falling into an untended field, encircled by trees. "Falling" was not the right description. She was floating. Her blouse and skirt gently flapped as she drifted gauzily to the ground.

This is strange. Maybe I'm already dead. Or unconscious, she thought. *Perhaps I'm doomed to live my last moments in slow motion.* She held her hands in front of her face, looking for signs of wispy incorporeality.

Instead, her eye caught the ring on her finger. The tiny golden ring with etchings that looked like a feather.

Em's eyes locked on the tiny band as she sailed to the ground, landing gently on her feet. She was vaguely aware of a yellowing field of spiky grass around her. Her breathing came in gasps, and her mouth felt like a potato sack. She bent over, trying to catch her breath.

Sam Monterey had just tried to kill her. She didn't think he was capable. The enormity of what had just happened did nothing to restore breath in her body. She would be dead if not for...she glanced again at the ring on her finger. Maybe she was dead. She felt herself starting to hyperventilate. Grabbing her sides, she forced her breathing to slow. Once she felt in control, she turned back to the ring. Pulling it off her finger, she studied it carefully. It looked like a simple band, apart from the etchings. There were no instructions or magical glimmers about it. Not that she expected to see any. Had this thing saved her life? She had to know.

She eyed a stump at the edge of the field; dropping the ring in her pocket, she jogged toward the small platform. She clambered onto the stump and then jumped off, trying to get high in the air. Falling at a rapid pace, she landed with an "oof" and a crunch on the dry ground.

Taking the ring out of her pocket, Em jammed it back on her finger. She climbed and jumped again. This time, she floated gently to the ground, like how a feather might fall.

She glanced once more at the ring.

It had saved her life. She would wager money on that one. Glancing toward the broken window, she came back to herself. Sam had tried to kill her. And he was still up there with three people she cared about. She felt her heart pound. The ring had saved her. Now she needed to save everyone else.

She heard a bark. "Bob!" she bawled as the dog appeared out of the trees, sprinted across the field, and leapt around her. She knelt, petting the dog. "You need to stay here, sweet boy. I don't want anything to happen to you too." He licked her cheek happily. Standing, she held out her hand to Bob. "Stay." Bob whimpered but sat, watching her sadly. "Stay," she said again as she turned away.

She started sprinting back toward the Gray Horse while mentally taking stock. She lost the lantern to the lobby, the umbrella to Sam, and the mask to Farrigan. It was probably safe to assume Sam had gotten the mask also. She didn't have the book or the lucky stone. But she had her bag on her shoulder. She had the thread, the ring, the waterskin, the hatchet, the map, her tools, and her brain. Surely she could devise a rescue plan and vanquish Monterey, even if luck and magic were on his side.

WHEN EM ARRIVED BACK at the Gray Horse, the lobby was deserted. What she could see of it anyway. All was quiet, and the wall of bright light from the lantern hit her almost immediately after she came in the door. She trudged into the wall of light, feeling her way toward the stairs. Bumping into the bottom step, she carefully felt for the lantern, collected it, and blew it out.

Glancing up the still-oiled staircase, Em assumed her people were being held in the rooms up there, but she marched toward the spa instead. No point in rescuing them before she dealt with Monterey. She would have to work quickly, before he decided to blow someone else out the window. Someone she cared about.

The smell of eucalyptus hit her at the arched entry to the main steam room, the Atrium. She recalled her only other visit to this place and frowned. She would be calling the shots this time.

She entered the foggy room, and the moist air instantly made her sweat and completely obstructed her view. *The lantern wouldn't be able to do a better job than this*, she thought. She circled the perimeter, inspecting the system of pipes and hot water that supplied the room with steam. There was a reservoir in the far corner where water was heated to boiling, and the steam was distributed throughout the room via the pipe system. Em studied this system, a plan hatching in her brain.

Next, looking up, she tried to pinpoint the height of the ceiling skylight. The room looked to be taller than average, but it was hard to gauge with steam obstructing her vision. She marched blindly into the middle of the room until she stumbled across a bench. The wood was strong and sturdy, despite years of sitting in heat and moisture. She would have to disassemble it, and a few others besides. Pulling out her tools, she plopped down on the floor and began quickly taking apart the bench.

Monterey was smart. And with the stone, he was lucky. So her first task, apart from removing the threat of Sam's henchmen, should be to lure him into the steam room and relieve him of the stone. Then the rest of the plan could be triggered. Breathing deeply in the fresh, green-scented air, Em began to devise an elaborate scheme.

A SHORT WHILE LATER, Em exited the steam room boldly, without her bag. She marched down the wide hallway to the lobby and turned her head up the stairs.

"Monterey!" she bellowed. "Monterey!"

Gray-clad attendants began to poke their heads out of the rooms upstairs and the various archways on the first floor. They made no move toward her, waiting for orders. Em ignored them and continued to shout. "Murderous sewage! Show yourself!"

A door at the end of the hallway opened, and Monterey stepped out, umbrella still in hand.

"Em!" A shout came from behind a closed door, which sounded like Liam. At least he knew she was alive.

"Monterey!" she yelled once more, trying to sound menacing. "Release my friends and the things you have taken. Or prepare to fight."

Monterey calmly walked to the end of the hallway and towered over the stairs. As he glanced down, she saw a glimmer of uncertainty in his face. He assumed she was dead, she realized angrily. His face smoothed, and he snapped his fingers.

Gray-clad goons leapt into action, coming at her from the stairs and the front rooms. Em sprinted toward the back of the hotel, seeking refuge in the steam room once more. She heard a few bodies tumble down the stairs, probably slipping on the oil. The ones still on their feet followed her en masse, disappearing into the wispy fog after her.

Em made her way around the perimeter of the room to the reservoir where steam was made from boiling water. Grabbing the waterskin stashed nearby, she mentally brewed a tea of summer junoberry, a plant Gram grew in her garden. On rare occasions, Gram drank a tea with a small pinch of the herb when she couldn't sleep. It was powerful stuff. Em significantly increased the potency in her mind, and then poured the contents of the jug into the reservoir.

The steam instantly took on a woody scent. Em quickly tucked a pre-set spa towel around her mouth and nose to avoid breathing in the sleepy mixture. Within minutes, she began to hear thumps as the henchmen, one by one, succumbed to the herb and fell sleepily to the ground.

Laying a large spa towel alongside the first downed, snoozing man, she rolled him onto it and dragged him along the slick tile to a nearby spot along the wall. Extracting her towel, she went in search of the others. These men were large and muscled, and it took a lot of pulling and grunting, but she was able to drag them all to the same area. But, if her counting was right, she was still missing a few.

Walking in a random direction, Em kept searching. In the far corner of the room, a hand shot out and grabbed her ankle. She felt pain shoot up her leg. The hand gripped tight, pulling her right leg backward and twisting. Glancing back, she saw the outline of a large man on the ground, grimacing as he continued to try and pull her down.

He must have a high tolerance for junoberry, she thought frantically, trying to pull her foot free. In a frenzy, she searched for something in front of her to grab hold of as the twisting pain in her ankle continued to grow. She tried to twist her leg the opposite direction to wrench it from his grip, but that only succeeded in doubling the pain she felt.

She let a yelp escape her, but then bit the towel wrapped around her mouth to keep silent. If any more goons were still conscious, she didn't want to draw the whole horde to her location. He continued to tug her toward him, and Em hopped on her other leg, trying to put up some resistance. At the moment she decided to fall to the ground for more leverage, she felt his grip slacken. *Finally.* She saw his eyes sleepily close, and her leg was her own again.

Moving awkwardly, she rolled him into the back corner and tied him to a large bench. The job was now going to take twice as long because this guy had hurt her ankle. Again. She felt like kicking him but figured that would be childishly vengeful, given his current state. Tying him up, Em willed away the shooting pain in her ankle, and crossed the room once more.

After a frustrating hunt, she finally rounded up all the other gray men. It had not been fun stumbling about in the steam, trying to drag the dead-weighted men with her good leg leading. She finally gave up trying to drag them all to one place and ended up tying them to the nearest wall piping with the strong thread.

Em returned to the first group of men, rolled them carelessly against the wall, and restrained their hands. Finally, she looped the strong thread around the pipes that squiggled behind them. They should sleep for hours, but even if they woke, they wouldn't be able to break their bonds. She hoped. She hadn't figured out a way to break the thread, so it zigzagged all over the room. She needed to take care not to trip on it. But maybe a trip wire was a helpful feature for phase two.

Hobbling out of the steam room, Em untied the towel from her face. She felt a bit woozy from the sleep gas, but phase one had gone *almost* to plan.

Taking a few deep breaths of unsullied air, she examined her ankle. The same one that Liam had so carefully tended to less than a week ago, and here it was, purple and bruised once again. She was able to walk, although painfully. Sighing with frustration, she retied the towel around her nose and mouth and ducked into the room once more to prepare. The steam should be returning to normal soon, and then she could commence with phase two.

~

EM EMERGED from the steam room again, sans her breathing towel. The Gray Horse was eerily quiet, and Em felt the tiny hairs on her arm stand on end. Monterey should have come looking for her by now. Where was he? He had surely noticed she hadn't been hauled back to him by his cronies. Perhaps he was planning his next move as she planned hers.

And then another thought occurred to her. How lucky was that stone? Was it even possible for her to best him when he had that thing in his pocket? Somehow, she had to redirect his luck until she had taken the stone. Make him think he was winning.

Then she heard a scream. A woman's scream. Her mom's scream. Her pondering abruptly ended, and her heart rate spiked. She lopsidedly sprinted for the second floor.

Em avoided the oil spills by clutching the banister, but her ankle wasn't doing her any favors. The screams coming from down the hallway were torturous, and Em felt frantic. The screaming stopped as Em reached the top of the stairs, and the silence was almost worse. *What is Sam doing to them?*

She narrowed their location to somewhere at the end of the hall. Limping halfway down the corridor, she considered shouting to gain Monterey's attention, but then she spotted the door at the end of the hall. His office. She could recapture *The Standard Book of Anything* and the stone, if indeed he left them there.

Tiptoeing past the end-of-hall rooms, she heard low murmuring and some quiet whimpers. Her heart twisted. She needed to hurry.

Trying the door handle on the office, she found it unlocked and pushed it softly open. The room appeared empty. Papers littered the large mahogany desk in the middle of the room. Light from a single lamp with a green glass shade intermingled with the sunlight that streamed through the large windows along the back wall of his office. It gave Em the feeling of being in an ancient forest, silent and almost reverent. But she felt no awe at this moment. She started moving papers around the desk, searching for the book. Finding nothing, she turned to the bookshelves, pulling books off haphazardly, looking for the familiar worn cover. It was nowhere. She grunted in frustration. And then a polite cough sounded behind her.

Whirling, she saw Monterey standing next to his desk, surveying the mess. His pale eyes finally landed on her. Amused.

"Searching for something, are we?"

Em hissed out the breath she had been holding. This was not how she planned phase two.

Monterey picked up a paper from his desk, idly scanning its contents. "What have you done with my employees, Em? There seem to be less of them running around."

"Perhaps you should fight your own battles," Em fired back acidly.

"I tried, dear Em, but you simply won't die, and it's very frustrating."

Em clenched her fists. He deserved everything coming his way. But she had to give him an ultimatum. Before phase two. "Tell you what, Sam. Give me the book and the other items. Let me take my parents and Liam. You keep the stone. The Gray Horse will thrive, and you'll never have to see me again."

Monterey took a step closer. "Mm. A tempting offer to be sure. A few days ago, I would've gladly taken that deal."

Em's eyebrows shot up. "What changed?"

"I'm not about to let a warehouse of wonders out of my grasp," he said simply. "Also, your parents deserve to pay for what they've done to me."

"Yes, I heard," Em spat. "I wouldn't have thought you capable of torture."

Monterey's face twitched. "No more than what they deserve. That book is invaluable, by the way. It gave me some very helpful tips. For example, I learned the most interesting things about magical oaths."

Em started. The book had shown him that? Why hadn't it told her?

"What did you learn?" she asked casually.

"Well, the mechanics of the oaths, for one. I believe I can start requiring them of my staff and guests, if I can track down an object or mage to administer the oaths. But what was most interesting were the consequences. The simply jaw-wrenching pain that comes from even the slightest violation."

Em tried to keep her face neutral, but inside she was trembling. She felt her back pressed up against the bookshelf.

"You said you were under oath," he said solemnly, with a wicked gleam in his eye. "The empress imposed one upon you. You cannot search for the trees anymore."

Em said nothing. Monterey was closing in on her, but her feet were rooted to the ornate gray carpet.

"Think how your friends and family in Brookerby will suffer terribly from your failure. Is there not any way around it?" he asked cruelly.

Unbidden, Em's mind began prodding the oath for loopholes. And then a searing pain, like an awl into her brain, made her cry out as she doubled over.

"Too easy," Monterey remarked. "You—a thorn in my side—become completely helpless after mere suggestion. Delightful."

Em took quick, shallow breaths, trying to beat the pain. In a few moments, it subsided, and she shook with exhaustion, attempting to stand up straight.

"Shall we try again?" Monterey taunted. "Or shall I tell you how to beat the oath? The book was quite detailed."

Em began to hope, against reason. Perhaps the book had a solution to— And then the pain came again, a flamelike searing behind her eyeballs that wrought tears and yelps from Em.

Monterey laughed cruelly as Em held the bookcase, struggling to recover. "So you *are* interested in a cure. Interesting."

"Damn you, Monterey," Em wheezed.

"Now, now," he soothed. "I can probably find a place for you in the Gray Horse kitchens. Although you would also make a lovely spa attendant."

Em growled, fighting the agony she felt.

Monterey continued to muse. "I could probably make use of your repair skills. Or I could use you to punish your parents. Or I could make you dance for my amusement. Where to begin?"

Em slowly reached behind her for the biggest book she could find on the shelf. In a flash, she flung it at his head and charged quickly past him and out of the room.

She heard a grunt from Monterey as the book contacted with his forehead. Moving as quickly as she could on her ankle, she jogged down the hall. She skidded down the stairs, heading back toward the steam room. She heard Monterey's footsteps close behind.

Leaping down the last three steps, Em nearly wiped out. All the oil she had poured on the stairs had started to pool at the bottom. Clutching the banister, she felt her ankle twinge on the slippery surface. And then Em felt a wind tunnel erupt right above her head. She ducked and swiveled back. Monterey stood at the top of the stairs with the umbrella pushed open. Cursing, she whipped around the corner, using her hand on the railing endcap as a pivot, skidding in an arc on the oil that coated the floor.

All she needed to do was make it safely to the steam room. She heard Sam's shoes clatter on the foyer tile. He must've jumped over the slick puddle.

Then she heard a bark from behind her in the lobby. *Bob! I told him to stay*, she panicked. Then she heard a bark, a growl, a human body hit the ground, and another umbrella blast. An animal yelp. Monterey's footsteps had stopped. Inching back to the lobby, she saw Monterey in a heap by an armchair, and Bob's limp body by the front doorway. "No!" she wailed. Monterey clattered to his feet and pointed the umbrella at Em once more. Lifting her knees higher and ignoring the sharp pain in her ankle, she put on a burst of speed and arrived at the steam as the second air burst from the umbrella weapon hit her. He was at the far end of the hallway, so it was not a concentrated blast, which might have knocked her to the ground, or into some painful solid object. It did, however, blow her forward a few feet, and it dispersed the steam in her immediate area. Ducking down and crossing to the side wall near the entrance, she watched the tendrils of fog creep back into place. The umbrella would not provide more than a few seconds of visibility. Good. Phase two had begun.

Sam stood on the threshold of the steam room, as if uncertain. "Hiding is cowardice, Em. I've already won."

Em stayed quiet, not giving away her position. He just needed to walk a few feet into the room. Just a few steps.

She heard a blast come from the umbrella once again, and out of the corner of her eye she saw a tunnel of clear air that was quickly being folded back into the steam.

Monterey took another two steps forward. Em held her breath.

"You know, you don't have to plant the tree yourself, you could just pass knowledge to someone else," he baited.

Em tried very hard to think of nothing. Then the idea sank in. She could share the woodland staff with Gram—and immediately she felt a thousand needles being jabbed deeply into her skin. Inadvertently, she let out a cry of pain. The agony made her drop to the ground right as an umbrella blast cleared the air where she had been standing. She began to crawl away, trying to ignore the sharp pain everywhere. He just needed to take another step, and all would—

"What's this?" Sam had stopped and was bending down. "A trip wire? Sneaky, Em. But I'm not as dumb, or as unlucky, as I look."

Em silently cursed. The initial part of phase two would not work. He would have luck on his side for the rest of this encounter. She carefully stood and tiptoed toward a large staircase made from the wooden benches, floated across the room, and hung from the huge skylight with the magically strong thread. She was rather proud of the haphazard stairs, built in a hurry but appearing quite sturdy.

Em began to climb her creation. Carefully, as there were no banisters. She counted the steps as she went: One, two, three, four...

Another blast, now from below. The open-air tunnel revealed the lower steps of the staircase to Monterey.

Em heard "What the—" from Sam as he discovered the structure.

"Em," he called, irritated, "what have you done with my benches?"

"The Gray Horse was in need of a new staircase," Em taunted. "The other one is covered in oil."

The steam thickened as Em continued to climb her creation.

Condensation beaded on the wood, and Em carefully placed her feet. Twelve, thirteen, fourteen... She was dripping with sweat.

The structure shuddered as Monterey climbed behind her.

"Where do you think this ends, Em?" he demanded, stopping around step eight. "Eventually you'll reach the top of that thing, and then what? Some kind of ill-conceived booby-trap? To what end?"

"I'm hoping I'll never have to see you again," Em responded, still climbing. Twenty-one, twenty-two, twenty-three... Monterey was close behind.

"What will you do after you end me? Go home to your destroyed town? You have no power unless the book shows you what it showed me. How to break the oath. That's what you need. Without it, you're useless."

Em stopped on stair twenty-seven. She considered Brookerby. She remembered what Liam told her about Evederell. How it was never the same. How it couldn't be fixed. Not without a new tree. Monterey was right. She needed to break the oath.

And then it felt like someone was sawing her head in two. She dropped on step twenty-seven, cradling her head and wailing, shielded momentarily from anything but the throbbing pain that had erupted. A moment, a lifetime, passed. And then she became aware of where she was. Step twenty-seven. Steam room. Gray Horse. Sam Monterey standing over her on step twenty-six. Umbrella in one hand, her golden ring in the other. He had taken it off her while she was writhing.

Em groaned, pulling herself to a sitting position.

"Ah-ah," Monterey gestured with the umbrella. "No sudden movements. I'm assuming this is how you were able to survive getting blown out the window." He held up the tiny gold band with feather etching, inspecting it. "Feathers? A bit on the nose." Smirking, he jammed it onto his pinky finger.

Em felt a growing sense of horror. She stood, wobbly, not taking her eyes off him. And then she backed up a step. Two steps. Only briefly did she put pressure on the left side of step twenty-eight. And she stopped. Then she backed up another step. She was nearing the ceiling. If he didn't follow...

Monterey followed. Step twenty-seven. Step twenty-eight.

A crack sounded; twenty-eight was not secure. By design. On the right side. Monterey's foot flew off as the board gave way beneath him. His arms flailed as he fell in slow motion. The umbrella flew out of his hand and disappeared into the steam. His hands caught step twenty-nine, and he growled up at Em as he tried to hoist himself up. Em peered at him from step thirty.

"Your plan was to make me fall? Brutal, Em. But I have your ring. I can just float to the ground. You, on the other hand—"

One of Sam's hands released step twenty-nine and groped recklessly for her leg. He was going to pull her down with him! Em felt his fingers brush her shin and started wishing very hard that she had made step twenty-nine unstable as well. And her fingers began to tingle. And then she felt something spark within her.

And then suddenly, the step twenty-nine board beneath his hand tore off, as if it were made of bread. Em watched Sam's eyes go wide, his arms flailing wildly as he sailed slowly into a waiting net of thread, inexpertly woven and suspended below the staircase. The net tightened with his weight, entangling his legs as his body continued to drift forward.

Em leapt back down the steps, hardly noticing her ankle. Monterey now hung entirely upside down, struggling with the net. She heard a clunk as the polished stone, the lucky stone, fell out of his pocket and hit the damp tiled floor.

She ran to the wall near the steam reservoir and quickly retrieved an item from her pack where it had been stowed and tucked it in her pocket. Then she traced her steps back to where Monterey dangled helplessly, uttering a string of foul-mouthed curses and trying to reach up to free his legs.

She approached him in the fog, and he grew quiet, watching her apprehensively, slowly twisting as he hung there.

She spoke. "Sam Monterey, you have kidnapped me, drugged me, stalked me, betrayed me, blackmailed me, tortured me, and tried to murder me. Do you deny these things?"

Sam squeezed his eyes shut. "If you're going to kill me, just do it."

"Do you deny that you have done those things?" she insisted.

"No. I do not deny it."

Em studied Monterey, searching for any hint of remorse. She saw only apprehension.

"And I have done nothing except cower, and run, and react," Em continued, feeling shame and strength somehow woven together inside her. "I'm done reacting, Sam. I'm acting to protect all of us. You will not hurt my family, my friends, my town, or me ever again."

Scooping up the lucky stone, she dropped it into her pocket and retrieved the one wondrous item that would help resolve this. He began struggling anew with his trap, trying to escape what terrible fate Em had in store for him. Quickly, she snatched his hand, pulled off the gold ring, and grabbed his pointer finger. Flattening out the map below him, she moved his hand to the farthest left corner and tapped his finger twice. At that moment, Sam Monterey disappeared, leaving a broken staircase and an empty net dangling above Em.

CHAPTER 30

he young Glaumhauser crept through the Silver Nightingale, searching for signs of the rogue mage, never conceiving what he might do if he found her. He encountered a room—empty save for three ewers on three pillars. He passed through into a second room—empty save for three beautiful pastries on three small tables. He passed through into a third room with three bejeweled crowns on cushions. Passing by these rooms, he found the mage alone in her chambers.

SURROUNDED BY STEAM, Em felt herself sag in exhaustion. She was ready to lie down on this very spot and sleep for two years.

Glancing up, she saw the thread-net dangling loosely below her staircase. The structure looked benign now, as if it were part of some half-baked spa treatment. Her head throbbed slightly, and her body felt pinched from ears to ankles. Remnants of torture inflicted by her oath.

Her sore ankle was still throbbing.

Monterey was gone. For how long, Em did not know. It would take him months to travel back from Fridera, a frozen, desolate country about as far from Esnania as you could go. Em hoped never to see Sam Monterey again, but he was not dead. So there was always a chance.

The Gray Horse employees were still tied to the pipes along the wall, sleeping peacefully. Em heard a gentle snore from one. She would free them, eventually.

Limping back out of the steam room, bag slung over her shoulder and umbrella crooked on her arm, Em made her way to the second floor once more. In the lobby, she looked to where Bob lay. He was gone. She assumed he had gotten up and walked away. She hoped he had gotten up. She stepped over the pool of oil and ascended the grand staircase.

Using the umbrella, she blew open each closed door one by one. She discovered Liam first.

He was holding a large dresser drawer like a battering ram, trying to break a hole in the window. At the noise, he spun, holding the drawer defensively in front of him. She peered in the door hole she had created, and his eyes widened in shock. They were red, and he looked like he could use a week of sleep. Dropping the wooden drawer, he took a step toward her and stopped.

"Are you—" he started.

"Dead? Nearly." She took a step toward him.

"He blew you out the window. I thought—I mean, we thought—" Liam stepped closer, eyes taking her in.

"I know. I survived that one. And all the things after, turns out."

"Monterey?" he asked.

"Taking an extended vacation. He won't be back in Esnania for months." Em set down her bag. "Before anything else happens, I need to let you know that I couldn't bear it if anything happened to you. Ever. I shouldn't have left—"

Liam closed the distance between them, and then softly, his lips were against hers. Shocked, she let out a squeak. He pulled back, looking abashed. "I'm sorry, I—"

She threw her arms around his neck and connected her lips with his. It felt like home. Soft and warm and exciting, and something else she couldn't place. She felt one of his arms tighten around her, and a tingle started at the base of her spine.

A moment much later, they broke off, and Em leaned back. Eyes connecting, they both grinned wildly. He kissed her again, and she kissed him back. She moved her hands down to his shoulders, and he jerked. Em pulled back.

Eyeing his shoulder, Em quipped, "Perhaps we should relocate your shoulder before we continue? Also, would you like to meet my parents?" Liam let out a shaky "ha."

"Incidentally, where are they?"

"I think in one of the other rooms." Liam suddenly became somber. "I heard screams. Hopefully, Monterey didn't do any serious damage."

Em tensed, suddenly frightened about what they might find. "Let me get the other doors open." Picking up the umbrella, they went once more into the hallway, continuing down the row of doors.

Three doors blown off their hinges, and three empty rooms greeted them. Em lowered the umbrella, flexing her forearm to work out some stiffness. Her ankle still throbbed. Suddenly her brow wrinkled in disgust.

"What?" Liam responded to the face she made

"Maybe they can just tell me where they are," she chided herself. "Brilliant, Em."

"Aren't we still worried about the Gray Horse staff?" Liam countered.

"Nope. They're sleeping peacefully. All the henchmen anyway," Em responded absently. Liam's eyebrows shot up.

"Anne? Farrigan?" Em shouted into the hallway.

She heard a faint scuffling from two doors down and darted toward the noise.

"Mom? Dad?"

"Emaline?" came the response from behind the door.

"Stand back!" she commanded, raising the umbrella once more. She waited until the sound of rustling feet in the closed room abated, then blasted open the room.

The door bounced across the floor, propelled into the opposite wall, and dislodged some plaster. As the dust cleared, Em spoke, "Mom, are you okay?"

"Em!" Two figures straightened from a crouch behind the bed and clumsily hurled themselves toward the doorway. Em met them halfway, flinging her arms wide around her parents.

"Em, we saw you get blown out the window," Farrigan chided. "Although we are delighted to see you unharmed."

"I figured out what that gold ring does. It makes you fall like a feather."

Anne started laughing. "If I didn't know better, I'd say *you* had the lucky stone, Em."

Em stepped back from the hug and studied her parents for any overt injuries. "Did he hurt you?" she inquired.

Anne's face twisted. "Yes. But physically we are functional. Do we need to go quickly?"

Em shook her head. "Monterey's gone. I sent him to Fridera."

Farrigan grinned. "Ah, yes. The old send-your-enemies-to-a-frozen-wasteland trick. Very clever indeed."

"We just wish you'd been with us all along," Anne commented quietly, sitting on the edge of the bed, looking morose.

"Oh, Anne, you mustn't be glum, darling." Farrigan patted his wife's hand, sitting next to her. "It was a misfortune, but it was not of our doing. Emaline knows that. And look how splendidly she turned out, despite it all!" They both turned their eyes on Em and smiled.

Em let out a breath. And then another. Her childhood flashed before her. Learning to read from Gram. Doing her first repair job for Mendel. Cooking. Climbing onto roofs. All within the safety of the tree that had protected their town. Because of her parents.

She took another breath, and then carefully crouched in front of her mom, taking her free hand. "I'm heartbroken that you two weren't there when I was growing up. But I also had an amazing, happy childhood. Our town was beautiful, safe, and neighborly. And that was because of you." She looked at them in turn. "Both of you. You brought the tree to Brookerby. It's almost like you were there all along."

A tear slipped down Anne's cheek, and she wordlessly squeezed Em's hand. Farrigan nodded gratefully at Em, who smiled back.

Liam cleared his throat, and the three swiveled to face him.

"Ah, this may not be the greatest time, but I wanted to introduce myself. Liam of Evederell. Lord Hallson of Gillamor." He made a small, serious bow, which Anne and Farrigan accepted with benevolent nods. Em stifled a laugh at the formality.

"Lord Hallson, we are pleased to make your acquaintance," Anne responded kindly.

"Liam and I met on the road to Gillamor. He's been helping me find a new tree for Brookerby," Em explained. When she felt a slight pinch from the last statement, she quickly clarified, "Before the oath, that is."

"And what are your intentions with our daughter, Lord Hallson?" Farrigan interrogated, with a twinkle in his eye.

"Oookay. Glad we've all met," Em jumped in briskly, flushing. "We should probably free all the attendants in the steam room. And find Bob. And determine what to do with the Gray Horse. Also, I still need to find my book."

"We'll help," Liam said. "I need Farrigan to pop my shoulder back in its socket first."

"Yes. Okay," Em conceded. "Be careful, Farrigan. I'm going to track down *The Standard Book of Anything*."

Giving a mock bow, she hobbled out of the room. Voices began to murmur inside the room she had left, too quiet for her to make out words. Her brain felt foggy, but she knew she had to secure the book before anything else happened.

She inched toward Monterey's office once more. Maybe the book could explain something that was itching at the back of her brain—the breaking of step twenty-nine.

～

AFTER A THOROUGH SEARCH of Monterey's office, she found the financial statements from the Gray Horse, indicating severe debt and a nearly empty facility for several years. Em nearly sympathized before remembering how awfully Sam had responded to that adversity.

She found some sentimental items. A note from his father. A book of poetry gifted to him by a former lover, with a racy inscription inside the cover. Em quickly hid the latter in a drawer, blushing furiously at the private words.

Through his possessions, Em could gather a picture of the man she had just banished to a frozen wasteland. He was not so different from her after all. Doing his best to save his town. Perhaps if they ever met again, they both would be a bit wiser. Or—conversely—he would discover his own magical abilities and try to kill her all over again. Time would tell.

She finally discovered *The Standard Book of Anything*. It was hidden between two reference volumes on a low shelf, looking ancient and ordinary. Relief coursed through her. She had not lost Gram's one-of-a-kind magic reference book after all. With it secured, she realized that her worry was the only thing keeping her on her feet. And now, with the book found, she needed to sit.

Pulling up Monterey's dark wooden chair, she sat, flipped open the book, and began to read.

Famous Operatic Performances of the Hidomet Empire
    Of all the performances throughout time, there were none more famous than those during the twelfth century centering around the Hidomet Empire. The extravagant garishness of the Hidomet performance spaces, paired with the exaggerated styles of singing and movement, combined to create larger-than-life theatrical experiences for the viewer. Oh, that we could go back in time to view the—

Exhausted, Em felt her eyelids droop and her patience for the book wane. She scanned ahead, looking for a cross-reference in the story. She saw one referencing "Spas," and quickly flipped to the corresponding page. She saw the following headline.

Cleaning Tips for a Pristine Spa Experience

She read a bit about the appropriate cleaning solutions to wipe down steam room walls, and how often this must be done. The importance of sanitizing massage tables. The herbs that would provide a pleasing scent throughout the spa area. Nothing out of the ordinary. She woke with a jerk. Had she just dozed off for a few seconds?

Perhaps the book was suggesting she leave Monterey's establishment in good condition when she left? She didn't care right now. Em closed the book once more and slid it into her bag. Heavy with sleep, she crossed her arms on the desk, put her head down, and lost consciousness.

JOLTING AWAKE, Em was immediately disoriented. Had it been a few seconds? Or weeks? The room was dark, and faint moonlight came through the large windows behind her. What time was it? Her arm was numb, and she gently shook it, feeling the unpleasant buzzing sensation creep up to her shoulder.

She glanced around and remembered the events of the day. Or was it yesterday? Monterey's banishment. And then she started. The Gray Horse employees were still tied up in the steam room. Panicking, she leapt up quickly, grabbed her bag, which was still at her side, and made for the large, polished door. Why had nobody woken her?

Pulling the office door open, Em found a deserted hallway. The floor was scattered with crumbling plaster from multiple doors being blown open by the umbrella, and faint sounds of laughter and cutlery drifted up from the dining hall below. Who was down there? What day was it?

Stepping carefully on the stairs, she noticed the oil spills had been wiped clean. The entryway sparkled with polish, and the broken chandeliers glittered with light. Voices came from the Grand Dining Hall, and Em crept in cautiously.

Sitting at tables all around the room were Gray Horse employees in a variety of gray uniforms, casually chatting and eating and drinking. In the middle of the room sat Anne, Farrigan, and Liam. Between them was a large loaf of bread, multiple cheese samplings, and half-drunk glasses of wine. Bob sat next to Liam's chair, enthusiastically gnawing on a large bone. Em felt disoriented. Were they safe? Had the attendants let bygones be bygones? Where had they gotten the food?

The nearest table of gray attendants fell silent, eyes on Em. And then came a cascade of halted conversation as the room noticed her standing in the large archway.

"Emaline!" Farrigan jubilantly called across the silent room. "Join us!"

Uncertain, Em shuffled quickly to their table, trying not to make eye contact with the silent employees. She was walking into a hornet's nest. And all the hornets were scowling at her.

"It's all right everyone. She's with us," Anne soothed the crowd. They slowly returned to their conversations, and the din in the room returned to a dull roar.

Reaching the empty chair at their table, Em sunk into it quickly. "Why did no one wake me?" she demanded.

"We thought it better to let you sleep. After all, you had been up for two days, hadn't you?" Anne said gently.

Em hesitated, and then acknowledged the statement with a bob of her head.

"We found some of the employees crouched in the kitchen, terrified," Liam explained, sipping at his wine glass. "After we explained the whole thing, they seemed to understand. Seemed a little bit relieved that Monterey was gone, to be honest. Since we found them, they've been helping us get the place back into working condition."

Farrigan jumped in. "We also discovered the fellows tied up in the steam room. How in the world did you manage that?"

Em briefly explained about the junoberry, diffused through steam.

Farrigan laughed delightedly. "You are so clever! I'll have to commit that maneuver to memory. They all seemed a bit groggy but also quickly surrendered. One or two were aggressive at first, but we got it all sorted out in the end."

"What do you mean, aggressive?" Em asked warily.

Farrigan let out a hearty laugh, "They took a swing at me. Were itchin' for a fight. But once I told 'em how it was, well—" He gestured over at a table in the corner. Two big fellows sat there, one holding a cut of raw meat against his eye but happily drinking a glass of wine. The other had a cut lip and was animatedly telling a story, wildly gesticulating with his wine glass. Em's jaw dropped.

Liam added, "It seems most of the employees just want to clean up and keep operating the Gray Horse. They've worked out a system of management and will share the profits. They were tired of the additional work from Monterey's extracurriculars. If Monterey returns, they'll allow him back as the manager only if he adheres to their new structure."

Em's head was swimming. "So, they're okay with us being here?"

Anne nodded.

"And the Gray Horse will continue?"

"Yes, to both. We did promise them some free repair work in exchange for food and lodging," Liam confessed. "After all, the upstairs is pretty beaten up. Luckily, we know a skilled repairman. Er, woman."

Em was speechless. Realizing they were all waiting for her to respond, she nodded once more. "Of course. I can help repair the damage."

Farrigan patted Em on the back congenially.

Anne poured Em a glass of wine, and Farrigan quickly jumped back into the middle of a story he had been telling about his accidental trip to Fridera via the magical map, with Liam asking incredulous questions and Anne offering clarifying details. Farrigan laughed with delight as he related the tale. Em half listened, watching with a growing sense of happiness mixed with a kind of homesickness for Gram and Mendel and Brookerby.

∽

As EVENING SLIPPED INTO NIGHT, the Gray Horse grew quieter. Em found herself alone in THE PARLOR with Anne as the last of the gray-clad employees wandered away to their own homes. They sat at a cozy corner booth. The wood seats creaked with age, and Em leaned back into the threadbare gray cushions, cradling a pint of spiced ale.

Anne stared down at her ale in deep concentration. "I should've known," she said flatly.

"Should've known what?" Em asked, taking a sip.

"We should've waited outside Brookerby. Found another way in. Sent a verbal message with a traveler. Anything besides just packing up and leaving."

Em tried not to choke. She gently set her cup down and studied Anne. The older copy of herself was rubbing a water spot on her glass, face drawn and eyes hazy.

"I mean. I knew something wasn't right. I knew it. But Farrigan"—she let out a sigh—"he is so practical. He wanted to move on. Start over. I had no reason not to, except for a gnawing feeling in my gut that something wasn't right."

Em glanced down at her own cup. The ale shimmered like bronze in the candlelight and swirled lazily. Her tipsy mother was trying to apologize yet again, and Em was starting to feel guilty for existing. She wondered if it was something Monterey had said. Anne had been like this since she'd endured whatever brand of torture he'd administered. Maybe it was psychological. "You had no way of knowing," she soothed. "Even if you had stayed, you wouldn't remember me."

"I know," Anne lamented, dropping her head from exhaustion and wine. "It's all so logical. But it doesn't fix the giant hole in my heart where you should've been."

Em nodded, allowing a loaded moment of silence between them. Finally, she replied, "I had a great childhood. I was loved."

"I'm so glad." Anne's voice wavered as she took a swig of her wine. There were tears forming in her eyes, and Em stared fixedly at a large knothole in the table to try and keep her own at bay.

Another thought occurred to her. "Did you have any other children?"

Anne dabbed at the corners of her eyes with her fingertips. "We tried. It just never happened. Probably for the best. We were never in one place long enough to put down roots."

"How does Farrigan feel about it?"

"Oh, your father is a very forward-looking person. He doesn't dwell on the troubles and regrets of the past. What's done is done." Anne's eyes grew misty again.

Em jumped in quickly. "Gram is a lot like that too. When she taught me to cook, she didn't harp on the twenty pots of stew I burned and over-seasoned. She'd just toss it out and hand me an empty pot to start again." Em laughed at the memory.

"Gram taught me to bake bread," Anne volunteered. "My mother wasn't much of a cook, and there was this young man I wanted to impress with a sourdough loaf."

"My father?"

Anne grinned conspiratorially. "I think she threw out nearly thirty loaves before I got it right. She was such a patient woman. Funny too."

"There were a lot of things I messed up when I was younger. Gram would just ask, 'What did you learn?'" Em said laughingly. "She really put up with a lot."

"She did well." Anne smiled.

Em nodded. "I miss her. I need to get back to Brookerby. Especially since the tree is gone. They need me."

Anne pressed her lips together and looked toward the entrance. "When will you go?"

"Soon. I need to fix all the umbrella damage. And put the benches back together in the steam room." Em took a big swig of her mead.

Another silence bloomed between them. Em's thoughts shifted to home. Gram, Mendel, Ilna—all the people who had cared for her and their world, which was likely continuing to break apart at this very moment. She dreaded arriving. What if it was worse than she imagined? What if everyone was gone?

"What if we come with you?"

The simple question hadn't occurred to Em. And a thousand objections came to mind. *You still can't enter Brookerby. Where would you stay? What would you do? Wouldn't that be too painful?* But she only voiced one: "What would Farrigan think?"

"Farrigan feels the pain of leaving you. In his own way, of course," Anne answered the last. "He thinks you are an amazing young woman, you know."

"That's kind of him," Em said.

"You are. I know you don't need parents anymore," Anne began tentatively.

"But I always need friends who have my back," Em offered quickly, smiling at her mother. An identical smile beamed back at her. Em continued, "But I don't think you should come to Brookerby. I don't know what to expect when I get back there. And you still might not be able to enter."

Anne smiled sadly. "I thought you'd say that. You're right of course." A beat. "What if we met back here, say—in three months' time?"

Em nodded. "I'd like that." Then, raising her glass to clink with her mother's, she said simply, "To friendship."

"Friendship," Anne repeated, tapping her glass to Em's.

CHAPTER 31

There is no record of what negotiations or swift action were taken in Bronwyn's private chambers. But hours after he entered the Silver Nightingale Palace, the young Glaumhauser emerged from the keep with the mage walking docilely behind. Thus, she was captured with no fanfare and little bloodshed and carted under heavy guard back to Gillamor.

THE NEXT DAY was a sprint of repairs. Em was able to acquire lumber from local merchants, who had considerably warmed to her presence since the disappearance of Sam Monterey. One by one, she patched up the plaster walls and framed up new doorways. It was energizing work, and Em found herself fixing things she hadn't broken, like jammed windows and drafty corners.

Liam spent most of the day in the kitchen, teaching the cooks the latest pastry trends from Gillamor. Every few hours, he would come visit her on the second floor with a new baked creation for her to taste and for a few prolonged kisses. Em enjoyed the affection and the pastries but was tongue-tied when it came to the subject of Brookerby's tree. She expected a blowup. He'd had his heart set on replanting for so long. How would he feel if she let him down? They would need to discuss it before Em brought him home. If Em brought him home.

Farrigan had been using the map to travel back and forth to Gillamor, setting the warehouse to rights and retrieving various magical objects that could aid in repairs. He encouraged Em to take the lucky stone to Brookerby. He also allowed her to take her collection of other items to help her town, provided she promised to return them.

As the sun set that day, Em had to admit completion. The Gray Horse was habitable. The employees were mostly friendly, and she felt confident they were going to run a highly respected establishment, lucky stone or no. Nevertheless, the stone belonged with them. She would return it once she had revisited Brookerby.

She fingered her pocket, where the lucky stone lay, and knew she needed to get home.

EARLY THE FOLLOWING MORNING, Em and Liam met in the foyer. Bob padded at their feet, not quite awake yet. The sky was awash in pinks, lavenders, and oranges, and Em fought back a yawn. Anne and Farrigan had encouraged them to use the map to travel quickly to Brookerby, so Em clutched the parchment, ready to make the jump.

Her parents had risen early to send them off.

"Three months, yes?" Anne confirmed, giving Em a quick embrace. Em nodded. "Three months."

Farrigan stepped forward and squeezed Em's shoulder affectionately. "My offer stands. Anytime you wish to join us, you are welcome. We have many more discoveries to make, and skills to acquire."

"Maybe someday. But for now, I'm needed at home."

"I respect that. I hope your repair abilities can fix what ails Brookerby."

"I hope so too," Em said.

Farrigan patted Bob on the head and stepped back to take Anne's hand in his. He made eye contact with Liam and tapped the side of his nose. Liam did the same back, mouth quirking into a smile.

"Watch out for our girl," Anne called to him.

"Watch out for Em?" Liam asked in mock surprise. "I don't think she needs it. If I'm lucky, she'll watch out for me."

Em rolled her eyes, then waved goodbye. They both placed a hand on Bob. Liam held the map in front of them, and Em decisively tapped a spot on the map. Suddenly streaks of color from the Gray Horse flew around them as they traveled back the way they had come.

Oomf. Their feet connected with a meadow, and their hands flew apart as they struggled to stay upright. Bob immediately dropped down to roll in the grass.

Looking around, Em recognized the sunny field. Liam's shack sat among the wildflowers.

Liam stated the obvious. "This isn't Brookerby."

"I know. I thought you might want to stop off at your cabin and get supplies," she explained. "Also, it will give us a chance to plan our approach."

He acknowledged her with a grin.

The sun was peeking over the horizon as they hiked up to his snug little cabin. He unlatched the door and held it open for Em to enter first.

It was just as she had left it several days before in her frenzied jump from the Gillamor warehouse. The place was spartan, but Em felt strangely cozy here.

Liam began rummaging through the cabinets and boxes, pulling out clothing and other supplies. Em leaned against the doorframe, studying him. She remembered the last time they were here; Liam was a handsome, kind stranger. Now, she had shared so much with him he felt like family. But also, she liked the way his lips felt on hers. And she wondered—

He stopped his rummaging and turned his eyes to her. "What?" he asked, puzzled.

"Nothing." Em flushed. Could he hear her thoughts? Her eyes

darted around the room, searching for anything else to look at but him.

But he was on his feet, crossing the room in two steps, putting his hands on her waist and his lips on hers.

Instant electricity. She responded, fingers in his hair, kissing him back with abandon. His hands slid down to her hips, and she felt a surge of excitement run through her. She leaned into him and found her back against the closed door and her body pressed against his.

Em broke off the kiss, heart pounding.

He hovered over her, looking at her with tenderness, and something a little wilder.

"Liam, this is not what we came here for," she said softly. His name was like a musical note in her mouth. She put her hands on his chest, nudging him back a step.

"Isn't it?" he asked with a wicked grin. Brushing a wisp of hair out of her face, he kissed her again, capturing her lips with his. The kiss was slow and sensual. Em closed her eyes and gave into the feeling of everything spiraling away.

When he broke free, he locked eyes with her again. Em reached her hand to his stubbled jaw. "Stars," she murmured.

"I know," he said happily. Not moving. Kissing her briefly, he said, "Em, I love you. We can fix the whole world together, one tree at a time."

"Liam," Em groaned, feeling a warning ping in her brain. "About that. We need to discuss." Em twisted away.

Liam's eyebrows knit together as he watched her move.

Em locked eyes with him, feeling like a cold wind had just swept through, "I love you too. But, we can't replant. And we need to talk about what alternatives we have. I meant to discuss this sooner."

"Uh huh." His tone was several degrees colder than it had been moments ago.

"We can try to repair the tree through magical means. But a replanting is impossible."

"But there are loopholes—"

"I don't care. After what happened to my parents, I can't do that to anyone else."

"You can't fix this. Not without a tree."

"I can fix anything," Em declared.

Liam's frown deepened. "Your parents still think planting is the right move. Despite everything they went through."

"What?"

"Your parents. I asked them. They thought we should still try." Liam's voice almost sounded like a pout.

Em bit down on her cheek, drawing the metallic taste of blood in her mouth. "You asked Anne and Farrigan? Is that what all that nose tapping was about back there?"

Liam nodded, confused.

"They have no right to make that call." Em's face flushed, and her voice grew louder with each word. "I grew up without them. They haven't lived in Brookerby for decades. They've barely known me for a week! What right do they have to determine anything?"

"They were affected," Liam said, seeming a bit cowed.

"Affected?" Em fought for calm. "I was affected. I grew up without parents. Because of these damn trees. We don't replant. And if you can't respect that, you are not coming to Brookerby." Em stalked out of the hut, slamming the door behind her.

EM WAITED OUTSIDE, hoping Liam would respect her decision. She replayed their conversation over and over in her mind, trying to discern where it had gone wrong. He had said sweet, lovely things to her. And then he assumed his agenda was still a go.

Then the assumption that Anne and Farrigan could just slide into the decision-making—after a nearly twenty-year absence—was triggering. Their opinion? They had no right to even give one. She liked them a great deal, but they were practically strangers to her. Liam should've known better.

But he loved her.

She shook her head. *Probably not now,* she thought bitterly.

The sun was rising higher in the sky, and she set her focus on Brookerby and steeled herself for what she might find. She fingered the lucky stone in her pocket and sent up a silent, fervent wish that it would work.

Liam exited the cabin and latched the door quietly. Crossing to Em, he wordlessly passed over her bag. She took it with murmured "thanks," which he didn't acknowledge. Instead, he hiked his own bag and waited. Like they were strangers, waiting for a public carriage. Em cringed.

"Liam—"

"It's fine." He brushed her off.

She set down her bag and took his hand, pressing it to her lips. "Liam. I love you. You are warm, and funny, and an amazing baker—"

He turned his head to her, scoffing, but also softening a bit. "Thanks."

She continued, "I'm scared, Liam. I've never been so afraid in my life. I don't know what we're going to find in Brookerby. It could be disastrous. And I really need you by my side when we get there. But if you want to replant..."

He nodded, not meeting her eyes. "I'm with you."

"No matter what?"

He finally met her gaze. "Yes. No matter what."

"Okay, then. Should we leave Bob? We can come back for him later today. Once we know what we're walking into." The dog was chasing a cricket on the side of the hut, oblivious.

Liam whistled, and Bob came running. "He's more help than he looks," Liam said. That settled the matter.

Em nodded her assent. Reaching into her bag, she pulled out the map once more. Liam grabbed her hand, Bob leaned against her leg, and Liam double-tapped Brookerby on the map.

Once again, the world around them began to swirl, creating a vortex of streaks of color. The sensation was becoming more familiar, and Em caught herself counting the expected number of seconds until they were deposited in Brookerby. The uneven cobblestones came up to meet their feet, and the swirling abruptly stopped. Em absorbed the shock of the ground, bending her knees and feeling her not-quite-healed ankle twinge in protest. Liam nearly took a tumble. Em held his hand firmly as he regained his balance. When he was stable, he let go and they looked around. Bob whined.

They had been dropped in the center of town, not far from the felled tree of protection. The streets were dry and dusty, but dark storm clouds bubbled overhead, threatening a downpour. A gusty wind blew rubbish in swirling mini-cyclones through the streets.

"It's worse than I thought," Em breathed.

Half of the storefronts were boarded up, and many more had fallen into disrepair. The cobbler's shop had an ugly word painted on the window in whitewash, and the bright green door was off its hinges. Alfred's butcher shop still had a broken front window, with glass shards sprinkled on the ground around it. Had no one cleaned up from the riot? Rotting meat hung in the butcher's display, surrounded by overeager flies. Em cringed. She had personally seen to the upkeep of many of those shops. Was it the fallen tree? Or her absence that had driven them to such a state?

She felt unbearably sad, each new mess like a wound. Turning to Liam, who surveyed the abandoned street with a critical eye, she asked, "Is this like Evederell?"

"Close," he muttered.

Em did not like to hear that. According to him, Evederell was beyond repair.

Glancing at each storefront, Em tried to decide what to do first. "Where do you think everyone is?" she asked.

Liam shrugged. Em started to trot down the row of shops.

Liam ran to catch up. "Where are we going?"

"I need to find Ilna. At the *Brookerby Leaflet*." Em wanted to make sure her friend was okay. That she hadn't given up. Maybe she had rallied and would know what to do.

They crossed to the *Leaflet* print shop, which sat quietly on the corner of a row of shops. The wind had kicked up and now tore around them, yanking Em's skirt about and freeing her hair from its messy knot. Approaching the shop, Em had flashbacks to the awful day the tree fell and she had been pulled into Ilna's shop by Mendel. Nothing was normal that day. Or any time after.

There was a large hole chopped in the yellow door of the shop. The windows were boarded up.

She knocked. "Ilna?"

No response came.

"Ilna? It's me. It's Em." She peered through the hole in the door, trying to spot movement inside.

"I don't think anyone's there, Em." Liam's voice was strained with worry.

"Someone has to be somewhere," Em said ferociously. "A whole town of people doesn't just disappear."

"Who else would be around?" Liam probed.

"Mendel was supposed to be back by now. Marshall Denget might still be here. You go find the tailor shop—that way—and I'll find the marshall." Em took off up the street to the marshall's customary seat outside the jail cell. Her ankle was bothering her again, but she tried to not show it. Liam jogged the opposite direction with Bob slinking behind, tail between his legs. The dog also seemed to feel the wrongness here.

Em skidded to a stop outside the holding cell. Denget was not there. And neither was the cushioned stool he usually perched upon.

"Hello? Marshall?" Em forced out.

"Em?" But it was not the marshall's voice who responded. Someone familiar, yet the voice sounded weak and strained and came from inside the jail. "Ilna!" Em cried out. "Are you okay? Who put you in there?"

"I did."

Another familiar voice. Em whirled away from the jail door. Marcellus stood there alone, casually. Stern of face, scar across his cheek.

"We meet again, Miss Strider."

CHAPTER 32

*E*m felt her heart sink. "Captain Marcellus, what are you doing here?"

"I could ask you the same question, Miss Strider. I thought we had come to an understanding back in Gillamor. And yet I find you here. Planning to replant the tree."

"I am not replanting," Em snarled, pushing away the stab of pain in her head. "But look around you—I couldn't leave my town like this. And I can't leave my friend locked up. I'm letting her out."

"I imagine if you try, I will stop you. I'm the one who put her in there," Marcellus leveled.

"Why? What did she do?"

"I arrived yesterday to find a *Leaflet* full of inciting comments and babbling. I thought it prudent to protect her from herself."

Em recalled the *Leaflet* she had read a few days ago. Maybe Marcellus had a point. Then a low cry came from Ilna inside the jail cell. Em felt like a fist had grabbed her heart and started squeezing. "You can't just lock people up for doing something foolish," Em tried to reason.

"I can. I did. I have locked up a few other key citizens. There have been fewer violent incidents than yesterday, so I believe my tactics are working," Marcellus bragged.

At that moment, Liam came trotting up the street. Without Mendel. "Marce." Liam winced, seeing his brother. "What are you doing here? Haven't you done enough?"

Marcellus strode over and gave him a searching look. "Well, little brother, I'm not surprised to see you. You seem to be fixated on Brookerby." He nodded toward Em. "I, however, came to protect the town."

"I don't think you did." Liam's eyes narrowed suspiciously. "What are you really doing here?"

Marcellus turned back to Em. "Miss Strider, when you left several days ago, I warned you that my brother would try to convince you that there was hope. That there were loopholes. But his entreaties were wishful thinking. You understood this. And yet, here you are again. With him. Trying to fix what cannot be repaired. Care to explain?"

Em let out a sigh. "If there is a way, without replanting—" she added quickly.

Marcellus's eyebrows climbed to his hairline. "Perhaps I did not impress upon you the futility of your situation. Miss Strider, I tried for years. Every method I could try. Magic users. Magical items. Nothing worked to fix Evederell, I concluded, not because I wished it, but because I had tried thousands of alternatives. I beg of you— believe me. Go restart your life somewhere else. Take my stubborn brother with you if you wish."

"I can't," Em pleaded. "But how are you any better? You are so wrapped up in these trees—preventing them, I mean—that you can't settle down with the woman you love."

Marcellus shot her a withering look. "That is absolutely none of your business."

"He didn't try *everything*," Liam muttered to Em, hand on her shoulder.

"What?" Em turned.

"Shut up, you," Marcellus growled. "You were there with me. You should know better."

"I am going to do everything I can to help Em put this town back together, and nothing you say can prevent that," Liam taunted.

"What if I stop you?"

"Try it."

"I'm not afraid to break your nose again," Marcellus threatened.

The brothers squared off. At that moment, lightning split the sky, followed almost immediately by the growling of thunder. Marcellus's calm exterior was gone. He seethed. Liam's hands were curled into fists as he planted his feet.

"Em," Ilna called faintly. "Gram's in here too."

Em hissed. Gram too? She called quietly, "I'll get you out. I promise."

Experimentally, Em placed her hand on the jail doorknob, but didn't take her eyes off the brothers. She had worked on this lock before. She knew it well. The old pins were worn and rusty. If only she could visualize the tumbler turning, perhaps she could... She felt the small spark in her fingertips...if only she could direct the energy in her hands to the right place. A raindrop hit her nose. Liam feinted, and then Marcellus took a swing at Liam's head with his fists; Em's concentration was broken.

"Stop!" Em shouted, annoyed. "You are not going to slug it out here in the middle of a rainstorm."

Marcellus had regained his outward calm. "I will need to lock you two up as well."

"Not likely," Em muttered. Liam tossed her a wink, then took a swing that connected with Marcellus's stomach. Marcellus doubled over in pain, muttering curses. Taking advantage of the opening, Em darted away toward the footbridge. Toward the gaping hole in the sky where the sycamore used to be.

Em tromped toward the footbridge and came to a stop in front of the broken-off warding tree of protection. The tree itself lay in the brush where it had fallen; the stump had not been flattened, and a jagged side of the tree reached toward the darkening sky. No one had bothered to repair the guardrail on the footbridge, and the whole area had a neglected appearance.

Em thrust her hand in her pocket, pulling up the lucky stone. She hastily balanced it on the stump. She wasn't sure what would happen, but maybe luck would help as she tried each item.

She pulled the mask out of her bag. The wind flapped at the feathers and fabric; Em struggled to hold it up. Maybe she could see the innards of the tree. But all she saw was the field behind the stump and the creek bed beyond.

The feathered ring would do her no good. Nor would the lantern.

She could try to graft the tree back together with the strong thread. Em considered this for a moment and realized it could work, but it might not actually return the tree to normal. Nevertheless, she crossed to the downed trunk and started to loop the thread around the bulk of it. Raindrops speckled her hands as she worked. Having done this, she realized there was no way to drag or straighten the trunk without at least two dozen people to help. She might have to return to that idea if nothing else worked. She returned the spool of thread and considered the stump again. The lucky stone had tumbled from its perch and now lay in the damp grass.

Em picked up the stone and dropped it into her pocket. Perhaps she needed to be holding the lucky stone for it to have an effect anyway. She had no idea whether it could affect the luck of another magic object. Did other objects *have* luck?

Em rummaged in her bag. The map wouldn't help. *The Standard Book of Anything* would just tell her about coins in fourth-century Esnania, or some other such nonsense.

She retrieved the waterskin and thought about a tree super-growth serum. Then she emptied its contents on the stump. Two fat raindrops hit Em's cheek. She stood, waiting.

The viscous serum flowed down the jagged side of the trunk and slid off to the ground.

Em was frantic. Marcellus would be here soon to arrest her, and this wasn't working. The serum wouldn't stay on long enough to take effect if the stump wasn't level. She returned the waterskin to her bag and reached for the last untried item, the hatchet. She would just level off the tree, and then maybe the growth serum would stay long enough to work.

She squared up and swung the hatchet at the broken-off point of the stump. The axe made quick work. It cleanly knocked the jagged piece off after a few strokes, leaving a little flat plateau on the edge of the stump. It would be enough.

Em relaxed, lowering her arms.

But the hatchet tensed in her hands. Of its own volition, it twitched forward for another strike, leaving a large indentation in the trunk.

Em yelped, trying to drop the object, but it seemed to have been glued to her fingers.

"Stop!" she commanded. The hatchet paid no attention. It swung again, carving out a wedge from the wood.

Em tried to gather the spark of magic within her mind. The one that had helped her defeat Sam Monterey. The one that had helped her free Mendel at the gallows.

The axe took another chunk out of the stump.

The spark was nowhere within her. Raindrops bounced from the axe head, taunting her efforts to stop it.

Speaking every variation of a command that Em could muster, she tried to pry her hands from the tool. The hatchet was merciless. It methodically swung, destroying the remaining stump. One chink at a time. With herculean effort, she pried her pinky finger loose.

Em was whimpering now. "Please! Stop. Don't do this. Please." The remaining tree was being shredded before her very eyes. And she was the one holding the swinging axe.

She freed her ring finger, but the axe continued to swing.

In her desperation, Em remembered the card from her fortune.

The headsman. An axe in a tree stump.

The card that had warned her. That predicted the fated action playing out in this very moment.

Your journey will not end as you intended.

Em realized her mistake. She was not the repairer of her world, as she had hoped and worked for.

She was the destroyer.

The rain was falling in earnest when Captain Marcellus arrived with a surly look and a swollen left eye. He found Em on her knees in the middle of the clearing, sobbing into one hand. She was surrounded by a pile of wet wood chips. The other hand was attached to a small, self-swinging axe that was rhythmically striking a decimated tree stump.

CHAPTER 33

The mage, Bronwyn Featherweight, did not speak or try to escape, and she was transported back to the Golden Lark Palace. The trial was speedy, and the mage was put to death by hanging. The man who had captured her, the youngest Glaumhauser, disappeared before the empress could express her favor and bestow riches upon him. The matter of the rogue mage and the protective trees was cataloged in the annuls of history, along with many other early deeds of Empress Regina de Silviana Augusto.

THE RAIN HAD NOT SLOWED. Ilna shuddered and shifted uneasily on the sparse wooden bench with each crack of thunder. Liam sat next to her, holding a handkerchief to his bleeding lip. Gram perched on the edge of the bench and studied them both with a chilly, appraising look.

There were others in the large holding cell. More than it had ever held before. Alfred the butcher was there, gazing listlessly out the barred window. Earl McBean leaned against the back wall, clenching and unclenching his hands. The new bookseller, Cornelius, sat (almost comatose) on a stool near Earl. Gendry Houton was there, without her knitting needles, but her hands were moving like she was still knitting. There were others. The school-teacher, Fern. The cobbler. Miranda. Several farmers who lived just outside the town. Even Marshall Denget had gotten himself impounded in his own cell, somehow. It was quite crowded, but no one spoke.

Gram hugged her when she arrived. Ilna squeezed her hand. Liam had tried to talk, but Em felt too numb to answer his questions. So, he had let her be. Em hadn't moved from her spot in the corner for several hours. The cold stone floor of the holding cell offered little warmth after she was soaked by the autumn storm. Her hand hurt from gripping the axe, then trying not to grip the axe. And the silence of several hours bloomed into a weight that felt oppressive.

Ilna finally broke it. "I'm glad you're back, Em." Her voice sounded small and childlike. *Still not herself,* Em thought callously.

Gram reached across Liam to pat Ilna's knee.

Ilna tried again. "I put out several *Leaflets* since you left. Maybe you'd like to read them?"

At this, Em's head jerked up, eyes connecting with Ilna. Did she truly not remember the awful things she had printed? *It's only a matter of time before Brookerby is no more.* Obviously not. But those things were burned in Em's mind forever. Em waved a dismissive hand. "It doesn't matter anymore."

Ilna flinched.

Gram patted Ilna again, then set her jaw. She turned a steely-eyed glare on Liam. Liam got the hint. He got up from the bench and wove his way through the lethargic bodies in the holding cell to Em's corner. "Can I sit?"

Em shrugged.

He slid to the floor beside her and spoke softly. "I'm sorry about Marcellus. He means well."

Em did not acknowledge that.

"We can get out of here and try again. There's loads of things we haven't tried. Maybe something in the warehouse—"

"Stop," Em commanded, louder than she meant. Everyone's head swiveled toward her. She decided she didn't care. "It's done, okay? It's beyond repair. I am the destroyer, and I've ruined any chance we had. I messed it up."

"What are you talking about?"

"The hatchet. Once it starts it won't stop. By now, it has hacked everything that remained of the sycamore to tiny wooden bits. The trunk. Maybe even the roots. Okay? It's done. Brookerby is dead. And it's my fault." At this, Em dared to lift her eyes—and met Gram's. Gram's expression of steely determination had not changed.

"Em—" Liam tried.

"No." Em's voice came out as a flat roar. "Don't you listen? Any of you? I've screwed it up. I've failed. You should've sent someone better when the fate of our town was at stake. Because now, we don't have a home anymore."

Silence. The townsfolk in the cell shuffled uncomfortably.

A thin voice called, "Are our homes gone?"

Em's eyes sought out the speaker. It was the owner of the mercantile, Miranda, a stern woman who had only accepted one repair from Em ever.

"I think they're still there." Alfred turned from the window. "Maybe a little worse for the wear while Em's been gone."

"Then we still have a place to live, so long as Em is here," Miranda concluded simply. Then the cell was silent once more.

Em leaned back against the stone. They didn't understand. She glanced over at Liam again. "I'm sorry," she said softly. "I've led you here. You put such hope in me. You'll have to find another tree seeker and start all over again."

Liam clasped both of her hands with his. Her fingers were ice, and she trembled slightly with the cold. He noticed and began to rub her hands to warm them.

"We need to talk about that," he murmured. "You seem to be under the delusion that I'm still using you for some kind of tree solution. I'm not. I haven't been since a few days after we met. You know that, right?"

Em shrugged noncommittally. She didn't know that.

"Em, please hear this. I am not following you in the remote hope that you'll replant. I'm sticking this out because you are the most capable, inventive, lovely, infuriating person I've ever met."

Em met his eyes. There wasn't a hint of teasing. "You were so adamant this morning," she bit back.

"I was having a hard time letting go of the original plan. But I realized that if anyone can repair a destroyed town, it's you. I'm not betting on trees anymore. I'm betting on you."

Em felt Liam's warmth flow through her, from her fingertips, up her arms, and into her core. Then suddenly her face flushed. She glanced up to see Gram listening, not with a steely gaze but a quirked mouth and a twinkle in her eye. Em gave her a wince. She felt suddenly guilty for how she had spoken moments ago.

"Em fixed my staircase last year," the cobbler volunteered suddenly, out of the somber group of townspeople. "Rickety, wobbly thing it was. I had to stop storing my shoes up there for fear I'd fall and break my neck. And then comes this young lady with a bag full of tools. Wouldn't take no for an answer." The other cellmates chuckled softly. "I would've turned her away, but she had that look in her eye. And darn if she didn't fix the thing. Better than new. Would trust her to repair anything." Em flushed at the memory. She recalled all the research she had done on how to properly construct a staircase and wanted to try the knowledge out. It could've gone very badly.

"My sink had been leaking, leaving an awful mess everywhere," Alfred volunteered. "Em fixed that in ten minutes."

"The desks in the schoolhouse have never been sturdier," Fern chimed in. "Although it was impossible to convince Emaline to take a break until the job was done. She sat there tinkering and cursing for a whole day." Several others laughed appreciatively.

Earl spoke up. "Miss Strider came to my farm a few months ago. She had heard I was hard up for harvest help and offered her assistance. I scoffed, but she was worth five hired hands with the steam-powered conveyor she built to process the grain. Couldn't have done it without her." Em felt a swell of pride. That one had been a huge challenge.

Cornelius added, "When I arrived in town, I was told that she had cleared out my building, fixed the floorboards, and repaired the roof. It would've taken me months to get the bookstore going without her. I haven't thanked her yet." He met Em's eyes and nodded gratefully. She bobbed her head back, embarrassed at the attention. Ilna let out a tiny smile and met Em's eye.

The stories kept going. Not all of them were flattering to Em. She had made a mess of more than one job. Some of them had the towns-people rolling with laughter. But most of the tales ended with a fix, and with gratitude. And with Em feeling bolstered in a way she hadn't in, well, ever. She could've opened her fix-it shop long ago.

A change had come over the cell, almost in time with the weather. As the rain slowed to a trickle, and then a drip, the townspeople came back to life. The stories of Em gave way to funny stories about each other. If she ignored the locks keeping them in, it felt almost like a gathering at the mercantile. Finally, Em stood to stretch, pulling Liam up next to her.

"Does anyone own a hound dog?" Alfred wondered from his perch by the window. A faint bark sounded from outside.

"Bob!" Liam cheered. He rushed to the window, crowding out Alfred.

There was a general din in the cell as everyone pressed toward the window to see the dog. Bob was dragging a dirty bag along behind him, which he dropped in the excitement of finding his master and so many other new friends. But Liam coaxed him to pick up the sack once more and push it up toward the window. Bob's tail wagged, thoroughly enjoying this new game.

Liam reached an arm through the bars and pulled up what turned out to be Em's satchel. It was coated in soggy mud. Liam handed it gingerly to Em, then he reached back out to pat Bob's head. "Thanks, buddy. Try to stay dry, okay?"

Em heard panting and then a massive splattering of water from the dog shaking out all the rain from his fur. Liam laughed. Alfred and Earl reached out through the bars to pet the dog also, cooing to Bob in high-pitched voices. Em stifled a laugh, then carefully opened her filthy bag.

Most of the items were still relatively dry. *The Standard Book of Anything* was at the top of the pile, looking innocuous. She pulled out the book and crossed to Gram. "This is yours. I'm not sure it helped, but I don't know if you meant it to."

Gram took the book gently, set it to her side on the bench, stood, and pulled Em into a bone-crushing hug. Em hugged her back with abandon, eyes welling up. This was her family. Her Gram. How she had missed her.

Gram turned her gaze to Liam, arms crossed. She raised an eyebrow, waiting for the introduction. Em nearly laughed. She had often imagined how Gram would react to her bringing home a man, and this was exactly what she had pictured. "This is Lord Hallson of Gillamor. Liam, this is Gram."

Liam made a formal bow. "Em has spoken of you warmly and often. I am honored to meet you."

Gram took a step or two closer, inspecting Liam like she would a livestock purchase. She peeked in Liam's ears, and Em had to stifle a giggle.

Liam shifted uncomfortably.

Finally, Gram made a flippant gesture with her hand, and then turned back to Em.

"Did I pass?" Liam mock whispered.

"She hasn't made up her mind yet," Em said seriously. "She'll let you know."

Em looked back at Gram, whose mouth was set in a decidedly neutral expression, but Em caught a twinkle in her eye. She liked him just fine.

Then Gram retrieved *The Standard Book of Anything*, plopped down, and flipped open the tome.

Meanwhile, Ilna was speaking, and Em overheard, "—to prioritize the repairs?"

Em hung back. Despite the kindly stories, she couldn't help but feel that she'd still made a mess of everything. She listened to them plan repairs and develop humane ways to intervene if their neighbors were having a case of the "sads" or "mobbies." To Em, this was far too cutesy a descriptor for arson and vandalism. The plan seemed reasonable, but so many of the folks in the cell were starting to fall silent after the bout of storytelling, looking pale and lost again. They couldn't carry on without a magical intervention.

Em turned back to her muddy bag. Reaching in, she retrieved the items one by one and laid them out. The lucky stone. The waterskin. The ring. The mask. Ilna noticed Em's items and asked her to explain. Em pointed to them one by one.

"A lucky stone. This was helping the town of Arrenmore prosper, even though they never had a tree. We will probably need to return it eventually, but it might jump-start Brookerby's revitalization."

"Interesting," Ilna remarked.

"Mendel's waterskin. Can make any kind of liquid you can think of. A featherfall ring. Stopped me from plummeting to my death. Maybe if we're working on roofs, this can be worn along with a safety rope?"

Em continued to fish in her bag. She put her tools on the table, dumping the bag. The warfern fluttered out and settled on the floor. She was sure there was something else in there she had forgotten.

"What's this?" Ilna held up the wilted warfern gently.

Em shot a glance at Liam, "Oh, a flower from the public garden. Warfern." Liam winked at her.

Gram started coughing in the corner. Em dashed to her, trying to pat her back. "You okay, Gram? Can I get you some water?"

Gram caught her breath and gestured at a page in *The Standard Book of Anything*. Em leaned over Gram's shoulder and read.

Warfern Properties

    A naturally occurring magic herb grown in only a few locations in Esnania. This tiny flowering plant is extremely useful for healing wounds and curing maladies. It is so named for its use in sixth-century FQ battle, where it would bring back soldiers to health, even if they were on the brink of death. The plant is hardy and could last weeks after being harvested.

    The plant is considered part of the school of healing magic, a rare practice where energy is expended once by the magic user or the plant itself for an act of repair. Best swallowed for internal injuries.

Em's jaw dropped. Gram looked up at her with a quizzical look.

"What? What did it say?" Liam asked.

Em brain flashed quickly back to the night in the warehouse, where she felt so nauseated…until she smelled the blossoms. How had she not realized? But she needed to test it. She dropped to the floor, pulled off her old boots, and peeled away her sock. Her ankle was still swollen from her fight at the Gray Horse.

"Warfern, please?" Em reached out a hand.

Hesitant, Ilna presented her with the tiny sprig.

She plucked a petal and placed it on her twisted ankle. Nearly instant relief in the form of an icy flowing feeling spread across her lower leg. She gasped at the coolness and the vanished pain. She performed some experimental ankle stretches. Rotating her foot, she discovered complete range of motion, and no stiffness. Something that had not been true since before its first injury on the road.

"It heals," she stammered. Pulling her sock and boot back on her restored ankle, she had a truly crazy idea. "Hand me the waterskin!"

"Em?" Liam questioned.

Em stood, still clutching the warfern like it was a lifeline. If she could knock out grown men by just thinking about junoberry, surely she could heal with the same flask and a thought. Liam held out the small pouch. Em reached for it and thought very hard about a tea brewed with warfern. Sniffing the spout, she detected a hint of cherry and dew-covered grass. Thrusting the vessel at Gram, she commanded, "Think of warfern tea, and then drink."

Gram's eyes sparked in excitement. She took the waterskin, paused for only a moment, and then sipped. The others watched, holding their collective breaths. Finally, Em broke the hush. "Do you feel anything, Gram?"

Gram looked up. She opened her mouth hopefully, and painfully croaked out a "no."

Em felt stormy. She turned away, kicking her bag in frustration.

Why would it not work? That book was worse than useless. If the warfern could bring soldiers back from the brink of death, surely it should be able to heal Gram's throat...

Ilna murmured, "Try dropping a petal into the brew."

That might work. Or it might..."Swallowing this plant feels dangerous," Em cautioned. "Gram tried a method from this book before and ended up losing her voice. How do we know it won't hurt her again?"

"We don't," Liam said simply, looking at Gram.

Gram stood, walked over, and held out the waterskin solemnly. By now, the townsfolk watched with rapt attention.

Em protested, "Gram, I got your letter. You said the book was a guide. That it shouldn't take the place of common sense. What if this is a trick?"

Gram shook her head, pushing the waterskin close to Em.

"Okay. Gram. Okay. We'll try it." Em's hopes lifted again. She plucked another tiny petal from the sprig and placed it into the mouth of the waterskin Gram was still holding.

Gram swirled the brew and took a sip. And then another. Em watched her eyebrows rise and her eyes slowly widen.

"Gram?" Em ventured. "How do you feel?"

"A little better, Em," Gram spoke while taking another sip. "It tastes like hot musty grass, but it feels cool on my throat." That was the first full sentence Gram had spoken in six years. Her voice was clear and brassy.

The emotions of the past twelve hours whirlwinded through her and then smoothed into a joy so profound Em thought she might burst with the sensation. She let out a whoop and grabbed Gram in a giant embrace, spinning her around. "It worked! It really worked," Em sang.

The people of Brookerby were in an uproar. Some cheered. A slow clap turned into scattered applause. The cobbler did a jig. Ilna's eyes shone with tears, and she held her hands to her heart. There were calls from the back, "I'll take whatever she's drinking!" The waterskin quickly got passed around the room.

"I have been feeling a little down lately," Earl admitted before taking a sip.

"Down?" Alfred teased before taking a sip, "You mobbed my shop, you crazy sonofabitch." Then after passing along the waterskin, they both chuckled and slapped each other on the back.

Ilna took a drink, and Em watched some of the no-nonsense humor trickle back into her face. "Oh, goodness," she gasped. "I feel as if a fog has lifted!"

The bookseller drank, and patchy color returned to his face.

The owner of the mercantile sipped the brew and grimaced. But then a faint smile crossed her lips—the first Em had ever observed from the woman.

One by one, each person took a sip of the warfern tea. As they did, the healing of a tiny little plant overwhelmed the magic of the felled tree. Em watched each of her neighbors, her friends, return to their authentic selves. Her eyes brimmed with tears. She hadn't succeeded, not really. But she had done enough—provided the tools at least—to save the town. And that's all that mattered. Brookerby would endure.

Outside, the rain stopped, and a small beam of sunshine shone through the gray.

CHAPTER 34

The holding cell maintained a party atmosphere for several hours. Gram was the liveliest of the bunch, making up for six years of not being able to speak. She shared some of her observations over the years—the time she caught Marshall Denget picking his nose in public, the time Ilna had intentionally inserted a dirty word in the *Leaflet* to see if anyone would notice, the day the cobbler accidentally left a sausage in the old schoolmaster's shoe. Her brassy laugh was infectious, and Em felt like Brookerby was becoming what it should be. Without enchantment.

Captain Marcellus reappeared as dusk started to fall. In tow was Mendel, whom he unceremoniously deposited into the cell. Everyone quieted, and many pairs of eyes were trained on Marcellus. But instead of speaking, the captain motioned to Em, who followed him out of the cell. She felt her neighbors' eyes boring into her back as she left the room, and she wished she could soothe them. Don't worry. She would fix this.

After he relocked the door and they had moved out of earshot of the window, he turned on Em with a bewildered look. "What's gotten into them? Is it mania? Another riot in waiting?"

Em pumped her hands, attempting to calm him. "Nothing like that. Captain, I think you can let them out."

He ignored the last and raked his hands through his hair. "I tried to stop the axe at the tree, but it wouldn't cease until the last bit was mangled. The tree is gone. I'm so sorry." As an afterthought, he said, "The tailor tried to help me stop the thing."

Em raised her eyebrows. Assistance and apologies were the last things she expected from Marcellus. "It's okay, Captain."

He took a breath, straightened up, and suddenly looked more official. "The other thing I need to verify is if your oath is still intact."

Em did not expect this. "What do you mean?"

"Just say something about replanting. Anything."

Em winced, waiting for the thought to trigger an onslaught of pain. But it didn't come. "There are always options for replanting," she ventured, waiting for the knives inside her head. That feeling didn't come. "Let's replant!" she said boldly. Nothing. Her puzzled gaze met his swollen one.

"I thought so," he muttered, letting out a brief curse. "When you destroyed the tree—an irreversible action, nearly the opposite of what the oath was preventing—you confounded the bindings. In those cases, the oath usually dissipates."

Em was speechless. And giddy. Her oath was gone. She was free. And it could never be used against her again. Her mind flashed to Monterrey, the look of glee in his eyes as he prodded the bounds of her oath over and over... She hoped he was very cold and miserable, wherever he was.

"That's how I got rid of mine," Marcellus volunteered, his words snapping Em back to the present. "But I have no intention of replanting, so I failed to mention it to Her Imperial Majesty. You, on the other hand—"

"But I don't want to replant anymore either!" Em protested.

They were standing in the middle of the street. Marcellus looked around at the desolate town, the trash blowing in the wind, and then back to Em. He was baffled. "Miss Strider, you were inconsolable a few hours ago. Your tree is completely gone. What has changed?"

"I have my town back. We can fix"—Em gestured around them—"all of this. But the tree did something to my friends and neighbors that required significant magical healing. All respect to the empress's gift, but with our tree gone, we are free. I don't ever want anything to hold that kind of power over us again."

Marcellus studied Em, weighing her words. Finally, he nodded. "The empress doesn't have to know about your erased oath."

"Thank you, Captain."

"Don't make me regret it, Miss Strider."

Em nodded. He gestured her back toward the holding cell. Surprised, Em followed him back. "Are you keeping us all locked up?" she blurted.

He didn't break his stride. "I'll let everyone go. But I plan to remain for the next week for observation. I want to make sure the change is permanent."

He stopped suddenly and turned. "You mentioned healing. May I ask what you used?"

"We brewed a tea with warfern. Everyone took a sip. They feel much better, I think."

"I haven't heard of warfern."

"It's a healing herb we found in the Gillamor Public Gardens," Em admitted.

Marcellus's eyes crinkled in amusement, then he winced. His eye was still quite swollen. "I never thought to look there. Well done, Miss Strider."

"It was Liam who picked it. He said it looked like a plant from your family's garden in Evederell," Em admitted. "I kept it more for, uh, because he gave it to me. I didn't know how powerful it was until today."

Marcellus let out a small "hah." Em tilted her head. It was the first sound resembling a laugh she had ever heard from the captain.

"Now I'll have to forgive him for blackening my eye. That little bastard."

∾

MARCELLUS WAS true to his word. He released everyone, even Mendel, with a warning that he would be checking in on them for the next week. Any mischief would be followed by a swift impoundment. The residents of Brookerby were in good humor that evening, which seemed to carry through to the next few days.

Em regaled her friends with stories from her quest, including her discovery of Anne and Farrigan Strider, alive and well. Many of her neighbors remembered the couple and were delighted to learn they were still alive.

More than a few times, they caught Marcellus listening curiously at the door, especially during her telling of the battle at the Gray Horse. Finally, Em invited him to pull up a chair.

Turns out, Marcellus had an endless repertoire of funny stories from his years in the imperial army that kept the whole group in stitches. Even Liam seemed delighted to have his brother around and in good spirits. With this acceptance, Marcellus lightened up. On his visits to each neighbor over the next week, he never came empty-handed, bringing a loaf of bread, or a bouquet of wildflowers, or a bottle of mead. He was treated as a local hero, to his great embarrassment.

GRAM WAS SETTING up for storytime when Em left the cottage one morning. It had been over a week since Em returned, and life had settled into a new rhythm.

"What are you reading today?" she asked as Gram spread out pillows and rugs on the floor around the hearth.

"I was thinking *Knights of the Dragonwraith*," Gram said with a grin. "It's longer, but we can do it in installments. The kids'll love it!"

"Isn't that too scary?"

"It will be, the way I read it," Gram cackled. Then she switched to her evil-dragon voice, low and gritty, "What mortal dares to steal my gold?"

Em laughed. "I had nightmares for days when you did that voice."

Gram patted her on the shoulder. "How else are they going to get the full effect? Also, I might gender swap some of the knights. It's silly that they're all boys."

Gram was in her element telling stories and lending books to the children. They had never been so entertained, but it also kept them out of danger during the town-wide repairs.

"By the way, Liam dropped by half an hour ago, but you were still sleeping. Something about a pastry shop."

"Ah, I know exactly where he went. Thanks, Gram." Liam had been eyeing an empty storefront for a new bakery. Em hoped it meant he was staying.

Em pushed out the cottage door and shouted a quick farewell. A mother was dropping off the first two children as Em marched down the garden path.

"Good morning, Mrs. Cassini. Good morning, Xander. Violet."

"Good morning, Miss Strider!" The kids went inside, and the woman lowered her voice to a whisper, "What does she have in store for them today? I hope she doesn't keep filling their heads with adventure and magic."

Em shrugged noncommittally. "Gram read those stories to me when I was a kid. I turned out just fine."

This didn't seem to comfort the woman.

Em waved and started toward the center of town. Gram was going to catch an earful from a few parents after today's reading, but it didn't really bother her. She would listen politely and then point out that their children didn't have to attend morning stories. The parents would get a panicked look and quickly backtrack their statements.

EM CROSSED the footbridge and eyed the flattened stump where the sycamore had stood. She wondered if the happy-go-around might fit there. They could plant a normal tree nearby. Maybe a playground, or a bench by the creek.

At that moment, Mendel spun into existence at the edge of the clearing. He was carrying the travelers' map.

Em waved. "Good trip? How's business?"

"Oh, Booming, Emaline, just booming. Tilly is very talented! Her designs are already in production and selling spectacularly in Gillamor."

"I'm so glad to hear it! Is she part of the fabric empire now?"

"I'm not sure what you mean, my dear, but I have hired her on as my apprentice."

Em recalled Tilly squealing and tongue-tied when she first met Mendel. Now, she was getting to pursue her dreams, with him guiding her. Em was so proud.

Mendel handed the traveling map back to Em. "Thank you. It was very convenient."

"You're welcome to use it anytime. Did you go to Arrenmore?" Em asked. She had suggested it before he left yesterday, hoping to send a familiar face to Anne and Farrigan.

He nodded, less buoyant. "It was a delight to see them after all these years. However, the conversation was not an easy one."

Em met his gaze. "Did you tell them I'm fine? That I'm grown, and can look after myself?"

"Actually, yes. That didn't seem to surprise them. After all, they have met you. I shared stories of your upbringing. I also impressed upon them how we all looked out for you. How much you've done for the town. How your abilities saved..." He trailed off as Em wiped the corner of her eyes with her sleeve. His eyebrow raised. "You really should be carrying a handkerchief, dear."

Em laughed. "Thank you for looking out for me. One more question, and then I need to get to work. Has there been any word from Sam Monterey?"

"From the information I gathered, there has been no sign of him. It may be impolite to say, but it doesn't seem a great loss."

"Not at all," Em agreed. She thanked Mendel for the update and promised to come by the shop tomorrow to catalog his repair needs. He strolled down the street, and she cut across to the butcher shop.

~

A SMALL CROWD HAD GATHERED. They were carefully sweeping up the glass and removing any remaining rotten meat. Alfred was scrubbing down the counters inside. Em offered a few pointers to two of the farmers who were framing up a new window. She shared her master checklist with Earl and outlined the repairs for the day. She was going to check on the *Leaflet* office and then meet them all later at the mercantile to replace the ruined floorboards. After she gained agreement from the other volunteers, she called out a few encouragements and moved on.

Em walked down the street to the *Leaflet* storefront. The door still had a large hole in the lower third. It would need to be replaced. Inside, papers and metal letter blocks littered the floor. The press sat silent.

Em heard tiny feet behind her. She turned to see a small boy in her shadow. "Hello, Grady."

Grady shuffled his feet. "Do you need help, Miss Strider?"

"Shouldn't you be at morning stories with the other kids? Gram is doing some really fun voices today."

Grady shrugged. "I wanna help. 'Cause I broke the tree."

That felt like an arrow in Em's heart. She bent down to meet the boy's eyes. "Grady, that was not your fault. You know that, right?"

He shrugged again. "I wanted a treehouse, but everyone got angry and sad and broke everything."

Em didn't even consider that Grady might blame himself. She felt a deep pain for the little boy and wondered what the last few weeks had been for him. She sat and patted the chair next to her. "Come sit."

He shuffled over and slouched into the chair.

"I want to tell you two things. First, you are a good kid and would never intentionally hurt anyone. Am I right?" Grady nodded solemnly. "Great. Second, the tree was already broken. And it would've been hit by lightning whether you hammered that nail in or not. None of that was your fault. Do you believe me?"

He met her eyes and nodded. Em hoped all this would make him feel better, but he still looked gloomy. Em considered, and she suddenly realized what he really wanted. "I'll make you a deal. Once we get all the big repairs done, I can help you and your younger brother make a treehouse. Would that be okay?"

Grady's eyes grew wide, and then he nodded enthusiastically. "That would be the best! But, can I still help clean up?"

Em glanced around the room. "Huh, it is kind of a mess in here. Could you pick up all these metal letters and put them in that tray, in order? I'll pick up all the other stuff on the floor."

The little boy hopped off the chair and set to his task. Em stood and started collecting and sorting papers. She had a "to burn" stack that included any of the *Leaflets* Ilna had printed in the last month. She glanced again at Grady, who was lying on his stomach quietly singing his ABC's as he alphabetized the letters scattered around him. She was going to build him the best treehouse that had ever been.

AFTER TEN DAYS, with no disasters or relapses in town behavior, Marcellus announced he was returning to Gillamor. He would report on Brookerby's success to the empress herself (excluding, of course, any damaging details like the erased oath), and he promised to recommend a pardon for Mendel.

"Do you think he will?" Em asked Liam as they strolled across the footbridge one evening. She had learned to appreciate Marcellus's many good qualities, but she was not quite sure she fully trusted him yet.

Liam nodded. "Marce wouldn't lie. He'll smooth everything out with the empress. He may even make it possible for us to help other towns."

"Is that what we should do?" Em wondered aloud. "Go save the other towns? It might be dangerous."

Bob loped along beside them, sniffing a random spot every three steps.

"That hasn't stopped you before," Liam pointed out.

Em paused at the spot where the sycamore trunk used to be. She bent down and picked up a wood chip. Just looking at it, she relived the worst day of her life. "I didn't intend to chop it down," she mused. "And yet, that turned out to be the best possible thing." She dropped the wood chip into her bag alongside her tools. "I've been thinking about the unbreakable oaths. I want to try and remove yours. And maybe others too."

"Em, if you get caught—"

"I know. But it's cruel. And the oath was very easy for Monterey to use against me. I don't think anyone should have to suffer like that. I don't want you to suffer like that. We can save the towns, but I think we should do both."

Liam was quiet for a moment. Em knew he was thinking about his bakery. And his plans for a simple life in Brookerby, with her. A life she was actively destroying. Em softened. "It will only be for a few months. We don't need to fix the whole empire."

Liam relented. "We can try. But if the empress finds out, I don't think Marcellus can smooth that over."

Em crossed to him and wrapped her arms around his neck. "After that, we can come back here, and I'll be your pastry taste-tester."

"The job is yours, squirrel," he declared. Then he tilted his head down and caught her lips in his. It was a tantalizing promise, and for one tiny moment, Em allowed herself to be swept up in his dreams.

ACKNOWLEDGMENTS

Writing a book is solitary. Publishing a book requires a crowd. I am extremely grateful for the Brookerby-sized village of people who helped me get this story out into the world.

To my beta readers:

- Kathy Bailes: I sent you the first draft before the ink was dry. It was very rough, and you didn't pull any punches. But you gave me just enough encouragement to keep going.
- Jan Street: You gave me great feedback, including some very concrete areas for improvement. You also told me it didn't suck, for which I was grateful.
- Alex Huckaba: So many things. Great feedback. Enthusiasm. Long conversations where you let me bounce ideas off you. Without you, the "Home Alone" sequence would not exist.
- Jessica Sitzmann: From you, I first learned I have a problem with "to be" verbs. (Like Hamlet.) I adored your detailed notes in a color-coded spreadsheet!
- John Creager: Wonderful, detailed feedback. You helped me to think deeply about some of the world-building that led to a pretty big change in the ending.
- Laura Petermann: I have no idea how many versions of the manuscript I sent you. But you are the writer I looked to most during this process. You encouraged me many times. Listened to me work out plot problems. Pushed me to do

better. Also, you are the longest-suffering of my beta readers, as you listened to my half-cooked idea about a magical encyclopedia back in 2019. Who knew it would get this far?!

- Jay Rome: It's a scary thing for a husband to read his wife's book manuscript for the first time. You're required to like it. (But I think you actually did?) I'm glad it didn't turn out like "Funny Farm," because I'm not sure I would've been able to burn the manuscript. Thanks for being a supportive partner through all of this, and for encouraging me to publish.

To my wonderful editor, Shawna Hampton: Thank you thank you thank you. You made my story sing! You offered developmental insights that significantly improved my ending, and you made me a better writer with some well-placed critique. Your line edits were sensible, thorough, and greatly improved the readability of my story. Throughout the editing process, your encouragement gave me just enough of an ego boost to think that I could sell this story.

To my cover designer, Michael Perry: You were a joy to work with. Thank you for being a part of this project, and for developing an image that captures the central issue of the story in such a stunning way. You are a pro, and a true collaborator.

To those who provided self-publishing advice, Lisa Lala and Kathy Altaras: Thank you for your insights and generosity.

To my reader: Thank you for giving this book a chance. There are so many books and so little time; I appreciate you choosing mine.

ABOUT THE AUTHOR

Andrea H Rome lives in Overland Park, KS with her husband Jay, and her two cats, Marty and Jacob. When not writing, Andrea enjoys geocaching, escape rooms, and acquiring craft projects faster than she can complete them. On weekdays, she works as a credentialed actuary. *The Standard Book of Anything* is Andrea's first novel.

Find out more about Andrea's upcoming projects and join her email list at AndreaHRome.com.

Made in the USA
Monee, IL
08 February 2025

11777709R00204